IN

There was a n... that Trager could not drag his gaze from hers. Even though he knew he was taking advantage of her vulnerability, he could not resist pressing his lips to hers. He'd wanted the golden-haired vixen too long.

As they kissed, Serena could feel Trager's heart pounding, matching her own racing pulse. And then his seeking hand began to caress her soft, yearning flesh, igniting a fire that seared her very soul. He traced a path of kisses along the column of her neck, and Serena gasped at the arousing sensations he evoked.

"Rena . . ." Her name floated from his lips in a pained plea as his caress wandered across her abdomen, leaving her skin tingling in its wake. She clung to him in wild abandon, aching to appease the breathless need that engulfed her. Brazenly, she reached out to run her hand over the length of his lean, muscled back, smiling as she heard his quick intake of breath. It pleased her to realize that her touch had so affected him.

"I warned you I was no gentleman," Trager rasped as he caught her hand in his and brought it to his lips. "I want you, Rena."

Serena could no more deny her desire for him than she could command the earth to stop spinning. This was a night to be plucked from reality, to be held as a delicious memory of a forbidden time. And in that dark, exquisite moment that knew no logic or doubt, she yielded to the passions that tore at her heart. . . .

HISTORICAL ROMANCE AT ITS BEST!
by Carol Finch

MIDNIGHT FIRES (1487, $3.75)
Danielle should have been terrified when the handsome
American captain who rescued her told her they were now
in the midst of war. Instead, all she could think of was how
his tight breeches clung to his thighs, and the way his eyes
dwelled on her full red lips!

PASSION'S VIXEN (1402, $3.75)
Mesmerized by his sensuous smile, Melissa melted in the
powerful arms of her captor—the awesome woodsman,
Jack. Having teased him with her charms, she'd leave him
in the morning and pray he wouldn't betray her love . . .

RAPTURE'S DREAM (1037, $3.50)
By day Gabrielle is the insufferable waif who tests Dane
Hampton's patience; by night she is the phantom lover who
brings him to the heights of ecstasy!

ENDLESS PASSION (1155, $3.50)
Brianna was a sensuous temptress who longed for the fires
of everlasting love. But Seth Donovan's heart was as cold as
ice . . . until her lips burned his with the flames of desire!

DAWN'S DESIRE (1340, $3.50)
Kathryn never dreamed that the tall handsome stranger was
wise to her trickery and would steal her innocence—and her
heart. And when he captured her lips in one long, luscious
kiss, he knew he'd make her his forever . . . in the light of
DAWN'S DESIRE.

Ecstasy's Embrace
Carol Finch

ZEBRA BOOKS
KENSINGTON PUBLISHING CORP.

ZEBRA BOOKS

are published by

Kensington Publishing Corp.
475 Park Avenue South
New York, NY 10016

First printing: June 1985

Printed in the United States of America

To my children, Christie, Jill, and Kurt, who held their "when," "where," "why," and "how come" questions an extra moment while I jotted down a thought on a paper before it escaped me forever. For that and so much more, I love you. . . .

And to Ralph and Chris Feddersen. Your assistance is greatly appreciated. With much love. . . .

The Rebel and the Rose

Keen-eyed and intent on battle
The noble soldier goes,
But he glimpsed a crimson petal
And stumbled upon a rose.

Distracted from the cannon fire
And blinded from his foes,
The rebel pauses to admire
A thorny, windswept rose.

Then down upon a bended knee
Out, he reaches to expose
A blossom so splendrous and free.
Beauty rare, possessed the rose.

Its fragrance rapt the early morn
But, to complicate his woes,
He pricked his heart upon its thorn
Then cursed the treacherous rose.

Though the fires of hell are burning
And the warring wind still blows,
His fascination keeps turning,
Yearning ever for the rose.

When the raging storm is over
And the peaceful water flows,
Then returns the rebel rover
In search of the windswept rose.

Upon abandoned battle hill
He smiles as he takes repose.
His wand'ring heart could never still
The desire to touch the rose.

Then, hand clasped 'round the thorn anew
He finds pleasure burns and grows.
This rebel heart so tried and true
Bends to lift and love the rose.

Part I

Chapter One

August 30, 1776

Serena Warren opened the parlor window and inhaled a breath of fresh air as a breeze flowed into the elaborately decorated room. Her emerald-green eyes skimmed the countryside and a hint of a frown knitted her brow, as she thought of the turmoil that had brought upheaval to her life. The colonies were up in arms, and the British sympathizers, her father included, were annoyed by the Revolutionists' cries for independence. Serena had overheard several of her father's conferences with other British officials and had listened to their complaints that the colonists demanded too much from the Crown. Her father, Mitchell Warren, was loyal to his native England and to the roots of his heritage. The Crown had granted him his occupation as magistrate in the prospering colonies, overseeing the governmental process and its colonial subjects. But the revolutionists were demanding representation, a voice in the government.

She had mixed feelings about the controversies that were tearing the countryside apart. All Serena wanted was the pleasant existence she had known before the Rebels had declared independence earlier that summer, before General Howe had driven George Washington from New York and sent the Patriots retreating to Harlem. Although Mitchell was confident that the colonies would soon realize that they were no match for England's military strength, Serena could not share his opinion. The Patriots were a fearless breed, and they were incensed that the Crown expected them to foot the bill for protecting and managing the long arms of the British Empire. Since the American colonies were prospering, the Crown had continued to raise taxes. Nay, Serena mused thoughtfully. The Patriots would not subject themselves to British rule unless they were brought to their knees and forcefully held under the gun.

"Serena?" Her father's quiet voice filtered into her silent reverie and she glanced back over her shoulder to grace him with a smile. "Is young Brandon Scott coming to call on you this evening?" he inquired as he strolled up beside her.

"Aye." Her reply lacked enthusiasm, causing Mitchell to arch a curious brow.

"Then you have not made your decision," he presumed, a faint smile bordering his lips. Mitchell

12

adjusted his spectacles to study Serena for a long, thoughtful moment. "And just how long do you intend to leave Scott dangling, my dear?"

Her shoulder lifted and then dropped in an unconcerned shrug as her gaze glided back to the window. "I am in no hurry to make a commitment."

Her father bit back a chuckle as he rearranged the silver-blond curl that the breeze had lifted from her shoulder. "Young Scott is a patient man, but you cannot put him off indefinitely. And you are almost twenty-one years old," he reminded her. "Most women your age who remain unmarried are considered spinsters. I think you should give Brandon your answer soon, my dear."

Her delicate brow arched, a taunting smile on her lips. "You are ashamed of the gossip that flies around about this old maid and you want me to marry Brandon as quickly as possible," she speculated, knowing full well that he did, since he had harped on the subject once or twice.

"I would insist if I didn't know you so well, Serena," Mitchell replied, returning her mischievous grin. "But you have a contrary nature." His pale green eyes twinkled as he gazed at his bewitching daughter. "Your tendency is to defy me. I would have met with no resistance if I had refused to allow Lieutenant Scott in my house. You would have sought him out and eloped with him just to spite me."

Reluctantly, she had to admit that he was right. She was a mite rebellious, a credit to the colonies that had a hand in her upbringing. Serena had a tendency to set her feet, refusing to be uprooted, when someone made demands on her. Although Brandon Scott was charming and attractive, she was not to be rushed. But Brandon had become more insistent since the colonial uprising, certain that he would be expected to take his place in the British regiment.

"It would greatly please me for you and Brandon to make your announcement at the party we will be giving next month," her father encouraged her, again interrupting her musings. "Olivia has been anxious to see to your wedding arrangements."

His remark drew his daughter's disgruntled frown. Olivia's only interest was to shuffle her stepdaughter out from underfoot. It still amazed Serena that her father had married a woman twenty years his junior, and especially a woman with Olivia's disposition. Serena had made a gallant effort to be civil to the woman, but the task was difficult. Her stepmother was a devious wench, charming her father out of his boots and then glaring at Serena when his head was in the clouds. Mitchell seemed blind to her faults, but Serena had made a mental list of them, categorizing them in alphabetical order.

"I'm sure she is," Serena replied after a long hesitation, attempting to keep the resentment from seeping into her voice. "By the way, where is Olivia?" It was the perfect opportunity to divert Mitchell's attention from the previous subject.

"She has gone riding."

"And you didn't offer to join her?" Her eyes circled

back to the window, wondering why her father refused to see what was going on behind his back.

Olivia supposedly spent a great deal of time by herself. Once, when Serena had dared to voice her suspicions about Olivia's activities, she had spurred her father's fury. Serena could not remember her father's ever completely losing his temper with her before, but in that instance he had come apart at the seams, and it had taken her a week to restitch his good disposition. He had ordered her to hold her tongue and never to spread such vicious gossip about her stepmother, threatening severe punishment. Serena had finally realized that her father was so hopelessly in love with Olivia that he would never listen to reason.

Mitchell released a sigh as he stuffed his hands in his pockets and ambled over to stare at the portrait of Olivia that hung above the fireplace. "I did offer to ride along with her, but she preferred to go alone this afternoon."

And it was little wonder, Serena mused bitterly. Whoever heard of a woman's inviting her husband to a tryst? "I think a ride is an excellent idea. Perhaps it will be cooler on the back of a horse. This summer heat is depressing. Would you like to join me?"

Mitchell gave his graying head a negative shake. "If you go alone, perhaps you can come to your decision about Brandon. I will summon one of the stable boys to follow along behind you."

As he spun on his heels to fetch a servant, Serena clutched his arm to detain him. "I prefer to ride without a chaperone."

15

A concerned frown etched his brow. "I don't think it wise, my dear. In these troubled times, there is no telling who might be lurking about."

A mocking smile hovered on her lips as she swept gracefully across the room. "I'm as capable of taking care of myself as Olivia, perhaps even more so," she defended herself, keeping her tone light, careful not to ignite her father's temper. He was a patient and reasonably tolerant man until he reached the end of his fuse. Serena had seen him explode once or twice, but she also knew just how far she could press him without kindling his ire. "No need to fret over me."

A faint smile caught one corner of his mouth. He was aware of his daughter's tactics. "I was not questioning your ability, Serena. I was only concerned about your welfare." Mitchell suddenly remembered that he had intended to discuss something else before he had been sidetracked. "While you are riding, I have something else for you to consider. We have lost our schoolmaster. It seems he has decided to take arms against us and join the Patriots." His mouth narrowed into a hard line. "No doubt, the knave has been filling our children's heads with propaganda against the Crown. I would appreciate it if you would take the position until I can find someone who is willing to permanently assume the duty."

Perhaps she did need something to occupy her time, she thought as she paused to glance back at her father. There was little else to do of late except ponder the problems her father faced and her decision about Brandon Scott. "I would be happy to take the job," she assured her father.

A pleased smile spread across his lips. "And you are probably more qualified to teach than your predecessor. I was not particularly fond of Cortney. He will be of more service to the Crown by joining the Revolutionists, the clumsy oaf," he smirked.

As Serena turned away she bit back a grin. Her father could not see the colonists' side of any issue and labeled every Whig a bungling fop. Serena, on the other hand, was straddling the fence. Her loyalty was with her father, but she could sympathize with the Revolutionists, to a degree. They had built a prospering country and it went against their grain to have the Crown issuing laws and taxes from across a wide ocean. Who wouldn't complain when the British were taxing everything that moved or made a profit?

But she often found it necessary to swallow her opinions out of respect for her father. She dared not argue the issues with Mitchell, who was such a staunch supporter of the Crown. And yet, Serena was American-born, though educated in England at her father's insistence, and she was heir to that stubborn pride that plagued the colonists. After her six-year stay in England, she knew which way of life she preferred. The British were a little too stuffy to suit her. Once her schoolmates learned that she had been imported from the colonies, they had turned up their noses, tolerating her, but never really accepting her.

Serena tossed aside her wandering thoughts as she hurried up the stairs and closed the bedroom door. At the moment there was another matter that demanded her attention—Olivia. Serena was itching to know where her stepmother had gone. She could not help but wonder if her father had married Olivia out of mere loneliness. While Serena was in England, living with her grandmother, Mitchell had suffered a meager existence. Serena had begged him not to send her away, but Mitchell had insisted that she receive a proper education and that she have a woman of the house to see to her upbringing. Her grandmother had showered her with love, but Serena had felt that her father needed her after enduring the loss of his wife. Obviously, he had turned to Olivia for companionship, a woman who was conscious of status, a social climber who hungered for the wealth Mitchell Warren could offer.

Serena had returned home, bewildered by the dramatic changes that had taken place after Olivia had come to rule the roost. Olivia had redecorated the entire house, except for Serena's room. At least her father had put his foot down with her once, Serena mused. The rest of the rooms were barely recognizable. Olivia had eradicated every memory of Diana Warren, removing every keepsake that Diana had cherished. She had even hauled Diana's portrait to the attic to collect dust and had hired an artist to paint her own portrait, one that practically covered the entire wall. It always galled Serena to walk into the parlor to see Olivia's mock-innocent smile plastered above the hearth.

Muttering to herself, Serena rummaged through

her wardrobe closet to find a riding habit. A spiteful thought tapped at her mind, and she grinned as she wheeled around to fetch the shirt and breeches that were stashed in her dresser. How she would love to catch Olivia with her lover. The deceitful wench might recognize Serena in a familiar riding habit, but she would not expect to see her stepdaughter garbed in beggar's clothes.

After she had tucked the hem of her chemise into her breeches, Serena shrugged on the shirt and then wound her blond hair up on top of her head. When she had pulled the brown cap down around her ears, she glanced at her reflection in the mirror and chortled at the image that grinned back at her. If her British schoolmates could have seen her at this moment they would have claimed that heathen blood spurted through her veins. None of the proper ladies of the court would have been caught dead in such garb, she thought to herself.

Knowing that her father would disapprove of her attire, Serena poked her head around the door to insure that no one was about and then locked it. Painstakingly, she ran her fingertips over the panel beside the fireplace in her room and opened the hidden passageway that wound down rock steps to an underground tunnel that led away from the house. Serena had discovered the passage as a child and had kept it her secret. She had seldom used it, but under the circumstances, she decided, it fit her mission—spying on Olivia.

Serena grabbed a candle and then closed the

sliding panel behind her, cautiously making her way down the steps. The musty smell filled her senses, reminding her of the times as a child when she had imagined all sorts of creatures waiting to leap out at her from the swaying shadows. But now she knew that she was alone, her childhood fears dissolving as the candlelight ushered her through the darkness with only the sound of her own footsteps penetrating the silence. Serena had always wondered about the family who had previously owned the mansion. Had they built the escape route in case of fire, or had one of the family members been involved in some devious activity? Perhaps they had been a clan of pirates who sneaked ashore to hide their loot and then made off into the night to terrorize the New York coast. It had been rumored that the woman who had sold her parents the mansion was a witch. As a child, Serena had pictured the wrinkled old dowager fleeing from her home to stalk the darkness, waiting for her sons to return. Passersby had claimed to see a cloaked silhouette standing on the hill, staring up at the waning moon.

Serena had allowed her imagination to run wild with her as a child, listening to the stories of the Widow Gravitt. Later, she had learned that the widow was an outspoken woman, a bit cantankerous at times, one who seemed to invite gossip but paid it no attention. Superstitious fools, she scoffed as her foot found the last step and she turned toward the tunnel that would take her to the hill below the house. The Widow Gravitt was no more of a witch than she was!

People certainly had a bad habit of labeling others whose views did not coincide with their. Just because the widow had an opinion and was not afraid to voice it did not make her an outcast. It had even been rumored that she had kindled the cause of freedom six long years ago, complaining the Crown held too tight a rein on its colonial subjects. Perhaps she had sold the house and taken up residence in a community that was not as pro-British as this village near New Rochelle was, Serena mused as she came to the end of the tunnel.

Again Serena discarded her straying thoughts. She wedged between the boulder and the underbrush that camouflaged the entrance to the tunnel. Her eyes scanned the countryside as she made her way along the cliff to the back of the stables. Serena watched her father step into the coach and rumble down the path and then she trotted to the pasture gate, squinting in the bright sunlight to see if Sandpiper was grazing with the herd. When she spotted the buckskin stallion with the black mane and tail, she whistled softly. The steed raised his head and pricked his ears. When Serena whistled again he trotted toward her, his head tilted proudly, his dark eyes on her. A smile brimmed her lips as the steed paused to paw the ground and eye her suspiciously.

"'Tis me," she coaxed softly. "'Tis not the time for you to be contrary. We are on an important mission."

The buckskin stepped forward when he caught Serena's scent and recognized her raspy voice.

After Serena eased open the gate she climbed up on

21

the stone post and slid onto his back, chiding herself for not having taken time to get a rope or bridle. But then, she couldn't risk being seen in her outrageous attire. The stable boys might relay the story to Mitchell, and he would cross-examine her. Serena would not enjoy lying to her father. It was best that he knew nothing of her afternoon excursion.

When she nudged the steed he walked along the path until she pressed him to a gallop, grasping his mane to rein him. A satisfied smile pursed her lips as Sandpiper thundered across the meadow and she leaned close to his muscular neck. There was a strange sense of freedom when she went stealing off, dressed like a ragamuffin, galloping on her stallion. It was as if the worrisome problems that encompassed her were carried away in the wind that whipped past her face. If she had not been in search of Olivia and her lover, the outing would have been perfect.

Her delicate brow hardened into a frown at the thought and she tugged on Sandpiper's mane, veering north along the trail that meandered along the shore. Her gaze swept her surroundings, as she tried to decide where she would rendezvous if she were Olivia. There were many secret places that would provide romantic settings for a tryst, but which one Olivia would choose to meet her lover was not easy to guess.

After an hour's searching Serena had had no luck, and she resigned herself to the fact that Olivia was more clever than she had given her credit for. Or perhaps Olivia was not meeting anyone that afternoon. Serena shrugged away that possibility in a split second. Olivia was cheating on Mitchell. She knew it, but she could not prove her suspicions. The next time Olivia went riding Serena would not allow her an hour's head start. One had to stay on one's toes to catch a rat, since the varmint seemed to be quick of foot.

The sound of the waves slapping against the rocks of Long Island Sound drew her attention and she could not resist the temptation. She urged Sandpiper to the quiet cove where she often came to be alone with her thoughts. After she slid from Sandpiper's back she discarded her boots to wade along the sandy shore. The cool water felt so refreshing that she was tempted to submerge completely. Hastily, she shed her clothes, and, wearing only her chemise, she swam out into the peaceful cove.

Now this was heaven, Serena mused as she dived beneath the surface and drifted with the current. Serena emerged to catch a breath and then took to the depths like a fish that had been too long out of water. When she finally surfaced, she wiped the water from her eyes to get her bearings, amazed that she had strayed so far from shore.

She glanced up to see that the sun had begun its descent, but she was not ready to return home. Hot summer days were designed for swimming, and she could not bring herself to move back to shore. Serena eased onto her back, floating on the water's surface as if she were drifting among the clouds, completely content to spend the afternoon with the sun shining down on her face, the cool water reviving her. A satisfied smile hovered on her lips and she closed her eyes, letting her thoughts wander at will. This was her own private haven, the one place where she could think and dream, unhindered, alone with the sounds of nature. It *was* heaven, she decided as she released a sigh, and it was in her own back yard.

Chapter Two

Trager Grayson's tanned face split in a wide smile as he reined his steed to a halt on the cliff overlooking the cove. The scene below him was like a vision from a fairy tale. A young woman with hair the color of the sun cut gracefully through the water. The dancing droplets sparkled on her golden skin. As the clear water molded itself to her shapely figure, Trager felt the quick rise of desire flooding his veins. He edged his horse along the slope and then dismounted, his silver-gray eyes anchored on the bewitching mermaid who was swimming circles in the middle of the cove. Her happy smile seemed as bright as the sun itself. Her hair was pulled back to reveal the exquisite features of her face and the trim column of her neck. She was the picture of raw, natural beauty, he mused as his footsteps led him closer. Mesmerized, Trager parked himself on a fallen log, half hidden by the brush that surrounded the sandy shore.

He watched in silence as the mermaid glided toward the shore, his aroused thoughts making his imagination thunder away with itself. Her skin begged for his touch, her moist lips parting to accept his kiss. Had he died and gone to heaven, or was this some fantastic dream? Trager pinched himself to insure that he was awake and then swallowed his breath as the sea goddess found solid footing and arose from the water. His eyes faltered on the wet cloth that clung to her full breasts and the trimness of her waist. It took a great deal of effort to raise his gaze to her face, but he was not disappointed in what he saw. Even at closer inspection she was perfection. Damn, but she looked delicious, he mused as his hungry gaze ran the full length of her, his gray eyes not missing even the smallest detail of her bewitching form.

Serena sank back in the water and tilted her head, combing her fingers through her hair, rearranging the tangled mass. A contented sigh escaped her lips as she made her way toward the bank. Her enjoyable interlude had to come to an end. She had to return to the house before her father arrived. He would be displeased if he discovered that she had been traipsing about the countryside dressed in breeches.

Her startled gasp pierced the peaceful silence of late afternoon when she spotted the movement in the brush. Serena covered herself and retreated into the water, watching in dismay as the virile form of a man appeared on the shore. Her gaze flowed from the top of his raven head to the toes of his boots, unwillingly admiring the intruder. The linen shirt he wore gaped to reveal the dark furring on his chest, and his brown breeches fit him so snugly that Serena's attention was drawn to his muscled thighs. When she dragged her eyes from his sturdy frame and focused them on his face she found herself captured in his veiled gaze. Long, thick lashes surrounded his smoky gray eyes, and she could feel the intensity of them. Serena shivered beneath his bold regard, her face coloring a deeper shade of red as he quietly measured and assessed her.

She was bewildered to find herself comparing this strikingly handsome stranger to Brandon Scott. And then she silently chided herself when she realized that her keen observation of him left Brandon sorely lacking in every physical attribute. There was something magnetic about the man, a certain strength revealed in the hard lines of his face and the depths of his eyes. No doubt he was the type of rake she had heard discussed when women gathered to gossip, the kind who could sweep a woman off her feet if she wasn't paying close attention.

Clamping a tight grip on her unraveled composure, she raised a courageous chin, determined not to fall beneath his spell, rejecting her feeling of interest in him. "You were spying on me," she accused, a condemning frown stamped on her face.

Trager graced her with a roguish grin that touched every feature on his bronzed face as he strolled to the water's edge. "When a man finds a mermaid beneath his nose, he cannot help but gawk," he defended himself, his husky voice wandering over her like an exploring caress.

Serena felt herself coloring another seven shades of red as his eyes traveled over her once again. "Turn your head so that I may fetch my clothes," she ordered briskly.

His grin broadened devilishly, stretching from ear to ear. "Nay, I'd rather not, my dear. I might miss something," he teased.

She crossed her arms over her breasts and tilted a defiant chin. "Then I shall remain where I am until I shrivel up," she pouted.

Trager chuckled lightly and then sent her another long, measured glance. "It would be a pity to allow such a lovely nymph to waste away." He gestured to the left and then focused his attention on Serena. "I hope you have no aversion to snakes, my dear, for it seems your blinding beauty has aroused the entire den."

His calmly spoken remark brought Serena's frightened shriek when she glanced over her shoulder to see three black serpents skimming the water, winding their way toward her. Serena thrashed through the water, feeling she was moving in slow motion, her heart nearly beating her to death, infuriated that the stranger had allowed her to flirt so long with danger. Although she grasped his outstretched hand for assistance, she hastily flung it away when her feet were on solid ground.

"You would have let them attack me," she spouted angrily, her green eyes blazing like a forest fire. "You, sir, are no gentleman!"

Her insult bounced off both layers of his thick

skin, leaving no mark, for Trager's thoughts were wandering as his eyes traveled over her thinly clad body, drinking in the tempting sight of her heaving bosom and trim thighs. Her wet chemise left little to the imagination and Trager was painfully aware that what lay beneath the clinging fabric was far more exquisite than anything within his wide realm of experience.

Although Trager was not a man to boast of his prowess with women, he found his mind racing through his mental repertoire of dazzling beauties to find that all of them were running a distant second to the somewhat bedraggled and dripping—but no less appetizing—wench who stood silently smoldering before him, drying herself from inside out with the aid of her rising temper.

Serena waited an impatient moment for the dashing stranger to lift his eyes to her face and then flashed him a reproachful glare. "Have you nothing to say for yourself?" she snapped, so annoyed with him that she forgot her modesty.

Trager made a low, mocking bow, letting his gaze stray where it would. "Forgive me, my lady. Rarely have I been referred to as a gentleman, 'tis true," he admitted, as another satanic smile caught one side of his mouth, curving it upward. "And I would not have allowed those snakes to sink their fangs into this tempting morsel, even if I found it necessary to wade in to rescue you myself."

Serena presented him with a cold shoulder that dripped icicles and stalked past him to retrieve her garb, throwing her comment over her shoulder. "I doubt that you would have considered ruining your finely polished boots," she smirked in an intimidating tone.

His eyes flowed over her shapely backside as another appreciative smile traced his lips. "To aid a damsel in distress?" A low chuckle erupted from his massive chest. "My dear, I would have thrown myself to the snakes for their feast before I would have allowed them to harm one sun-kissed strand of hair upon your head," he boasted with bravado, drawing her skeptical frown.

Serena braved a glance as she clutched her clothes as a meager covering to shield her from his hawkish gaze. "'Tis a noble boast for a man who does not claim to be a gentleman," she mocked dryly as she turned to face him.

She swallowed hard as his long shadow fell across her and then she took a retreating step as he reached out to replace a golden tendril that had fallen over her shoulder. Serena nearly quaked as his manly fragrance floated about her senses, entangling her thoughts. Why was she trembling? She had the sinking feeling that the reaction was not a chill caused by her long stay in the water. The man had a devastating effect on her, and she was not proud of what she was experiencing. It was not like her to wilt beneath a man's charming smile. Serena had seen her share of them and had managed to keep her heart intact, defending herself with aloof glances that warned her admirers that she was not easily taken in by charismatic gazes.

Serena took a second retreating step as he grasped her free hand to bring it to his lips. A wild tingle flew down her spine as his silver-gray eyes penetrated hers. She wormed her hand from his and hugged her clothes to her chest.

"There is no need for you to portray the chivalrous knight," she rebuked, acquainting him with her look of disdain.

"What's your name, nymph?" he questioned huskily, his gaze roaming over her without the leer she had noticed earlier.

Serena had swallowed her tongue and it took a moment for her to find it after the way he was staring at her. It was as if he had reached out to caress her without ever touching her. The man had strange powers, Serena thought miserably, and she did not appreciate the way her heart kept doing back somersaults each time he studied her with eyes that could undress and seduce her.

"Serena," she murmured, her gaze falling to the sand beneath her bare feet.

And then his raven head came toward hers, his face only inches away, his gray eyes flickering with a desire that sent Serena's heart catapulting to her throat and then tumbling back to its normal resting place to hammer against her ribs. His lips slanted across hers as his hand glided around her throat to tilt her face to his kiss. And what a kiss it was, Serena thought wildly. There was the type that Brandon bestowed on her, the gentlemanly kind. And then there was an entirely different kind. The stranger's kiss began as a careful inquiry, his lips wandering warmly over hers, testing her reaction. Serena found herself drawn full length against him as he fitted his hard, muscled thighs against hers, his kiss deepening. The feel of his hands on her waist left a smoldering imprint on her skin, burning a path to her very core. She was hot and cold and trembling as his tongue parted her lips to search the hidden recesses of her mouth. His experienced embrace carried enough heat to scorch the moon, and Serena felt herself melting in the circle of his arms, amazed at her reckless abandon. She should have been spouting in protest, but she was as an inquisitive child, seeking to discover the unknown.

The world darkened about her. A myriad of thoughts whipped through her mind and then skitted away before she could grasp them. Serena fought to catch a breath to sustain her, but he had taken it away, only to give it back in a most arousing way.

When she finally found the will to drag her lips away from his kiss, her lashes fluttered up to view the silver sparkle in his eyes. She gulped over the lump that had collected in her throat, pried his hands from her hips, and unsteadily backed away from his embrace, confused and quivering, bewildered by his effect on her.

It was not like her to fall into a man's arms. She had kept most of them at a safe distance, flirting and taunting them occasionally, but never had she been so devastated by a man's kiss and the feel of his body molded so possessively to hers.

With shaking hands she shrugged her shirt over her shoulders and then stepped into her breeches, averting her eyes from his probing gaze, feeling the intense heat of his bold appraisal. When she stood up straight to fasten her shirt, his hands took up the chore, his knuckles brushing lightly against the curve of her breasts. Another exotic tremor skitted across her skin and Serena felt herself coming unwound like a ball of twine on a downhill roll. She had to get a grip on herself. Sweet merciful heavens! She was behaving like a love-smitten schoolgirl who had just discovered the difference between men and women.

The smile that hovered on his lips was slightly mocking. "Is this your usual attire, Serena?" His voice held a hint of laughter as his gaze flickered over her baggy breeches and shirt.

His taunt brought her to her senses and she raised a proud chin. "And if it was the best I could afford?" she challenged.

Trager's shoulder lifted in a careless shrug, a rakish grin hanging on one side of his sensuous mouth. "I have never been one to judge a book by its cover. 'Tis what lies beneath this fabric that interests me," he assured her huskily as his lean fingers traced the opening of her shirt, dipping into the valley between her breasts.

"What are you doing on this land?" she questioned as she removed his wandering hand, hoping to change the direction of their conversation, seeking a safer subject.

"Meeting a friend," he replied as his head came toward hers, his warm breath caressing her flushed cheek.

Serena dodged his intended kiss when his remark filtered into the corner of her mind to intermingle with another thought. Perhaps this was the man Olivia had met that afternoon. He looked to be slightly older than her thirty-year-old stepmother and was just her type, Serena thought resentfully. She presented her back to the attractive stranger, her eyes circling the cove in search of her steed. When she spotted him, she whistled to bring him to attention. Her second command brought him trotting toward her, his black mane flying about him, his nostrils flaring to catch the scent of the stranger who hovered so close to his mistress.

Sandpiper pranced a tight circle and threw his head, bringing a low chortle from Trager. "This is your mount?" he questioned dubiously. The stallion seemed too much horse for this mere wisp of a woman who was barefoot and dressed in breeches. "Where's his saddle?"

Her chin tilted a notch higher. "I don't need a saddle to manage him," she assured the stranger and then frowned. She had neglected to ask his name.

It was as if he had read her mind. "Trager Grayson," he murmured as he lifted her hand to press a light kiss to her wrist and then glanced skeptically at the wild-eyed buckskin. "You do not require a bridle either?" His inquiry had a doubtful ring to it.

"I am quite capable of managing this horse," she insisted, wishing she could look down her nose at him, but he was much too tall for that. Trager Grayson towered at least a foot over her five-feet-two inch frame, and his nearness was as suffocating as the windless August afternoon from which she had escaped by swimming in the cove.

His hand slid around her waist, and before she could stop him his lips melted against hers, strangling her protest, stripping her breath from her lungs. Her emotions were having a tug-of-war, stretching her out of proportion. She was attracted to this bold stranger like a moth to a flame, knowing she could be burned if she didn't put a safe distance between them. And yet she detested Trager Grayson, her stepmother's lover. How could she be responding to his scalding kiss, swaying toward the rock-hard wall of his chest to keep her balance? This was madness, she told herself, but her body was paying no attention. She was embracing the very man who had met Olivia somewhere in the shelter of the woods. Had she lost all her pride?

His gray eyes lingered on the delicate features of her face, memorizing the gentle curve of her lips that had melted like rose petals beneath his kiss. The clean, fresh scent of her had wrapped itself around his senses, and Trager found himself intrigued by this improperly garbed wench who possessed such a bewitching figure and flawless complexion. Impulsively, he reached out to trail his index finger over her creamy cheek, caught and captured by the reflection in her emerald-green eyes.

"Meet me here tomorrow, Serena," he requested hoarsely, his gaze locking with hers.

Serena tilted her head to study him from a new angle, fascinated by the chiseled lines of his face that could soften in his mellow mood. Why should she, she asked herself. Because he aroused her and because she could prevent Olivia from seeing more of him. It was her duty to intervene, for her father's sake. She nodded slightly, assuring him that she would return.

A pleased smile surfaced on his lips. "Until then, Serena."

His lips played temptingly on hers for a long moment before he swept her into his arms and deposited her on the stallion's back.

Serena stared down at him, grappling with the arousing sensations his kisses evoked, well aware of what had attracted Olivia to him. She knew that by agreeing to meet him the following day she was flirting with trouble, but she was obligated to do what she could to keep Olivia faithful to her father. He desired to have his love returned, and Olivia had betrayed him, trifling with his affection. Somehow Serena would put a stop to it. And to her surprise she realized that she was anticipating the next afternoon.

As she pressed her knees to Sandpiper's flanks he trotted up the slope and aimed himself toward the stables. His hooves pounded the ground as Serena leaned close, urging him to a breakneck speed.

Trager watched in awe as Serena moved in perfect rhythm with the buckskin stallion. A faint smile grazed his lips as she disappeared into the woods. A mysterious creature, he mused, as he glanced down to see that Cinderella had left her boots in her haste to escape him before the stroke of dusk. And then the vision of Serena came swimming back to him and he felt his temperature rise a quick ten degrees, wondering if he should take to the water to ease the fever of desire. Again her face formed above him. Her features were perfection. Her eyes sparkled with a lively glint and her body . . . his thoughts stumbled, remembering how the water had hugged the tempting curves and swells of her figure.

He shook his head, shattering the image that kindled his passion. Enough of this, he told himself determinedly. He had important business in New Rochelle and there was a war going on, after all. He had no time to dawdle over some simple maid he had discovered in the cove. Why the hell had he requested that she return? He had a commitment to someone else and it had been foremost in his mind until he had stumbled onto this tantalizing mermaid.

Trager let his breath out in a rush, scooped up Serena's forgotten boots, and hastened to his mount, followed by an exquisite memory that kept tugging at his thoughts. He swung into the saddle and glanced at the cove, rolling his eyes in annoyance when Serena's image drifted toward him. Such nonsense, he muttered as he gouged the steed in the flanks and reined him west. The world was full of beautiful women. He would not return to see this nymph. She was far too distracting.

Serena rode as if the devil himself were hot on her heels. She breathed a sigh of relief as Sandpiper came to a halt at the pasture fence. As she slid from his back she fondly patted the laboring steed and then opened the gate to allow him to return to the mares.

As she made her way along the slope, she grimaced in pain as her bare foot hit upon a sharp rock. Damn, she had forgotten her boots! Carefully, she edged toward the opening in the side of the hill and then moved through the dark cavern that wove its way toward the house, seeking the sanctity of her own room.

She glanced out the window to see the pale shades of dusk settling over the trees that lined the house and then panicked when she remembered that Brandon would soon be arriving for dinner. Serena called to Molly to fetch water for her bath and then sank down in the tub, only to have a pair of smoky-gray eyes materialize in her mind's eye. She glanced away, but they came at her again. Her lips trembled, remembering the feel of his mouth on hers, the possessive way he had held her in his strong arms. Had Olivia experienced the same overwhelming sensations? Damn her! She had no right to taste Trager Grayson's kisses. Olivia was a married woman, wed to a warm, compassionate man who deserved better than to have his wife gallivanting off with that handsome stranger. Well, Trager would have no time to spend with Olivia, Serena vowed to herself. She would keep him occupied. Revenge? Serena frowned thoughtfully. That was not her only motive, and she would be lying to herself if she said it. Aye, she was attracted to Trager Grayson, but she knew nothing about him. And Brandon had asked for her hand in marriage. She would keep Trager occupied and amuse herself for a time, but eventually she would have to marry Brandon. It was what her father wanted—and in time she would come to love Brandon, she told herself. The darkly handsome stranger had no place in her world, nor she in his. They would enjoy each other's company and then they would go their separate ways, leaving Olivia to turn her attention back to Mitchell where it belonged in the first place. Damn that promiscuous woman! Why couldn't Mitchell see through her charade? Olivia only wanted what his money could buy.

Chapter Three

Serena stepped into her pink silk gown and impatiently waited for Molly to fasten the stays.

"You look mighty pretty this evenin'," Molly complimented her, her dark eyes skimming over Serena's reflection in the mirror. "Looks like you got a bit of a sunburn."

Serena nodded slightly. "I went swimming in the cove this afternoon," she explained as she smoothed the silk over her waist and then began arranging her hair.

"By yourself?" Molly cast her a curious glance. "I'm surprised yore papa allowed you to go alone."

"I don't need an audience when I'm swimming in the altogether," Serena chortled, a mischievous smile on her lips. She hadn't needed an audience, but she had most certainly had one.

"Nay, I s'pose not," Molly agreed and then returned her wry smile. "Are you gonna marry Lieutenant Scott?"

Serena eyed her dubiously. "What brought that on?"

41

Molly's shoulder lifted in a shrug as she wandered over to collect the discarded bath towel and then glanced back at Serena. "I heard yore pa tellin' Olivia that he hoped you would make the announcement at the party she is givin' in September."

"I have not yet decided." Serena gave her appearance a final inspection and then bit back a smile. Would Brandon have approved of the way she had dressed that afternoon? Certainly not! He would have been appalled that she had shown her face when she looked so outrageous. "There are several points upon which we differ."

Molly grinned at her. "If I was you, I would snatch him up before someone else does. I think he's extremely handsome."

Serena raised a perfectly arched brow, noting the lovestruck gaze in her maid's eyes. "Then perhaps you should be the one marrying him."

"He doesn't even know I exist," Molly murmured as she walked toward the door and silently took her leave.

Serena almost wished that she carried the kind of torch for Brandon that Molly apparently did. But there were conflicts between Serena and Brandon. He expected her to portray the lady at all times, and Serena possessed a rebellious streak. She was her own person and she did not appreciate anyone's forcing opinions on her. Brandon had a bad habit of subtly suggesting how she should behave and Serena was stubborn enough to resist, often becoming contrary, just to spite him. A frown knitted her brow. She wondered what Trager expected of his women. Apparently, he was not particular about whether or not they were married. He was probably a womanizer, seeking only pleasure. Her mind stopped short. There was no time to delve into that subject. Brandon was due at any moment.

Her father's voice filtered into her room, informing her that Brandon had indeed arrived. Mustering a smile, Serena opened the door and descended the stairs. Brandon positioned himself at the bottom of the steps, leaning on the balustrade while his admiring gaze flowed possessively over her, assuring her that he approved of the image that gracefully floated down to him.

"Serena . . ." The word escaped his lips in an appreciative sigh. "You are bewitching."

She blessed him with a dazzling smile. "Thank you, Brandon."

Her gaze strayed to Olivia, who had emerged from the parlor. Begrudgingly, Serena had to admit that her stepmother was a stunning woman. The ivory gown she wore fit her shapely figure, accenting her assets. The cream-colored lace that adorned the bodice of her dress hugged the fullness of her bosom. Serena knew what Trager saw in Olivia—a woman with a great deal to offer. Olivia was extremely attractive, with her dark hair and hazel eyes. And she prided herself on her unblemished beauty. Her smile could conceal what she was thinking, and occasionally Serena found herself wishing she could disguise her true feelings as well as Olivia could. She was a mistress of deception. Serena made herself a mental note to develop that talent. There were times when it was important to display a smile and camouflage one's inner emotions.

During the small talk at dinner, Serena found herself thinking of the handsome stranger who had taken outrageous privileges with her. Brandon, being the gentleman he was, had only kissed her twice in the six months they had been an item on the gossip vine. But Trager, who freely admitted to being a rogue, had immediately acquainted her with the difference between a warming embrace and a flaming kiss. A rash of goose pimples skitted across her skin, remembering the feel of his muscled arms about her, the experienced way he'd held her against the hard wall of his chest.

"Serena, are you feeling all right this evening?" Brandon inquired, a concerned frown etching his brow. He took her hand and laid it over his arm as he drew her from her chair and strolled into the hall. "You've been terribly quiet."

"I've had a great deal on my mind," she explained lamely, sending him an absent smile.

"Such as . . ." he prodded, arching a dark brow.

"My temporary career," she offered. In truth, it was the first time the thought had crossed her mind since her father had mentioned it. "Papa has hired me as the schoolmistress until a permanent replacement can be found. It seems Cortney has abandoned us to join the Rebel cause."

Brandon sucked in his breath. "You can't be

serious. I do not want my fiancée taking that position. I shall have to discuss the matter with Mitchell."

Serena was quick to take offense. It galled her that Brandon considered teaching a less than distinguished profession, and it burned her to the quick that he would go over her head to her father. The matter was none of his business, and she had *not* consented to become his fiancée. He was taking too much for granted—her, in particular.

"I couldn't be more serious," she assured him, her tone carrying a note of irritation. "It will be a challenging position and I am anticipating it."

Brandon displayed a patronizing smile that caused the hair on the back of her neck to stiffen like that of an angered cat. "Well, we'll see about that, my dear."

Serena wormed her hand from his grasp and stared him straight in the eye. Brandon might as well find out here and now that she had a mind of her own and that she was about to give him a piece of it. "I am quite capable of making my own decisions and I do not need you or anyone else telling me what I can and cannot do," she insisted, her voice rising testily.

"You are certainly in a fit of temper tonight," he observed, noting the rebellious sparkle in her eyes. "Is something else bothering you, sweetheart?"

When he reached for her hand, Serena sidestepped and presented her back to him, staring up at the sea of stars that spread before her. "I think you expect too much of me, Brandon," she blurted out, deciding that the time had come to be honest with him. "You may as well know that I am prone to be a bit impulsive and that I do not spend time dwelling on what others might think if I pursue a childish whim."

His soft chortle filled the quiet night as his arm slid around her waist. It amazed her that her interest in Brandon had drooped several notches since her meeting with Trager Grayson. His touch left her unaffected and slightly disappointed.

"I am aware of your stubborn nature, love," he rasped, his breath warm against her neck. "And I have witnessed your fiery temper, but I'm sure that in time you will learn to control those traits. I still find you a most fascinating creature."

His praise soothed her ruffled feathers and she peered up into his dark eyes. "Then kiss me," she commanded, as she looped her arms around his neck.

Brandon did a double take. "Ladies do not offer such blatant invitations," he gently rebuked.

Serena rolled her eyes heavenward, summoning more patience. He was too proper and predictable. She wanted to be swept off her feet. She wanted to hear music ringing in her ears. "Are you refusing?" she challenged, a mocking smile coming to her lips.

"Nay, 'tis just that . . ."

Serena had come to the end of her short-fused temper. "Kiss me, Brandon."

Heaving a resigning sigh, he bent toward her, his lips brushing lightly over hers, and she waited for his embrace to kindle a fire in her blood. And then she waited another anxious moment as his kiss deepened. Nothing. She dragged her lips away from his and stared at him for a long, thoughtful moment, measuring him and reassessing her opinion of him.

"Again," she demanded, hoping he could put more enthusiasm into it. He was behaving as if her request was a dutiful chore.

When his arms tightened about her, his breathing becoming uneven, Serena melted against him, hoping that he would drop his gentlemanly armor, allowing his desire for her to seep from beneath that controlled exterior. But there was something awkward in his kiss. There was no magic spark, no smoldering fire, only a rough, devouring embrace. If this was his best effort, Serena could imagine what a marriage to Brandon held in store for her. It set her to wondering if he was one of those men who put his wife on a pedestal and sought out a mistress to satisfy his "animal" desires, depending on his wife to supply him with children and nothing more.

"Don't overly tempt me," Brandon breathed as he set her from him. "You have not yet consented to become my wife."

And Serena wondered if she ever would. She knew her father readily approved of Lieutenant Scott. But as much as Serena wanted to please Mitchell she had the uneasy feeling that she could not be content with Brandon. Never would she turn to another man the way Olivia had done. Nay, Serena thought determinedly. She would marry for love the first time and insure that the marriage would be a happy one.

Brandon laid his hand on the small of her back and aimed her toward the house. "'Tis getting late, Serena. I better be going." As he drew her onto the porch he bent to press a courteous kiss to her fore-head. "I would like your answer soon, love. There is talk that I will be sent out with the British troops as a scout. I don't know when I will receive my formal orders, but it will probably be within a month."

"Soon, Brandon," she murmured as she backed away and disappeared inside the house.

As Serena started up the steps Olivia glanced down at her from the landing. "Did you give him your answer?" she questioned point blank.

"Nay, I have not made my decision."

A stilted silence fell like an invisible partition between them and they stared at each other for a long moment.

Finally, Olivia spoke slowly and deliberately. "I am anticipating helping you with all the arrangements." A faint hint of a smile slid across her pink lips. "In these troubled times it would be nice to have something to look forward to."

Serena lifted the front of her skirt and moved up the stairs, the swish of her petticoats cutting through the strained silence. She paused before Olivia to return the pretentious smile. "*If* and *when* I decide to marry Brandon, I will let you know. I do not intend to be pressured into a wedding just so I will be shuffled out from under foot."

Olivia's hazel eyes narrowed on her, her pleasantness evaporating. "And what is that supposed to mean?"

Serena's brow tilted mockingly. "I think you understand my meaning, Olivia. Papa may be blind, but I am not, and I will not leave this house until I am certain that your sole intent is to keep *only* my father happy. That is what marriage is all about, isn't it?"

Olivia gasped indignantly as the well-aimed barb penetrated her calm facade. "You little snip, you have no right to accuse . . ."

"Serena." Her father's voice wafted its way up to them, bringing quick death to their conversation. "Olivia and I are going down to New York tomorrow for a meeting with the government officials. Would you like to travel with us?"

Serena forced a smile. "Nay, Papa. I think you and Olivia deserve some time alone together. Perhaps the two of you can mix business with pleasure." Her gaze anchored on Olivia. "I'm sure Olivia would enjoy an outing with only *you* as company for a change."

Smugly, Serena ascended the last flight of winding stairs, thinking how Olivia had flinched at her sweetly spoken remark. She was allowing her step-mother a choice. Olivia could give Mitchell her full attention or she could leave him. But the question was, could Olivia forfeit the way of life to which she had grown accustomed if her lovers could not provide for her as well as Mitchell could? Serena made a mental note to do some prying into Trager Grayson's affairs the following day. If Grayson could afford Olivia's extravagant tastes then he was welcome to her. It would take time for her father to recover from the loss, but Serena would be there to console him.

A strange loss tapped at her consciousness. After

her confrontation with Brandon, Serena realized that the handsome stranger had stirred her blood far more than Brandon ever could. Determinedly, she discarded the thought. Her foremost concern was her father and his happiness. Even if she was attracted to Trager, she could not allow her fascination to stand in the way of her obligation.

Chapter Four

A wry smile pursed Serena's lips as she formulated her plans. She intended to learn as much as she could about Trager Grayson and as quickly as possible. What kind of man was he, an irresponsible rake, a wealthy business man? Was he married, seeking his pleasure with Olivia because she had a roving eye? Would his mild interest in Serena evaporate if he learned that she was merely a servant?

The rap at the door interrupted her pensive musing and Serena glanced up as Molly walked into the room wearing a bemused frown.

"I brought you the old clothes that you requested, but . . ."

"Thank you." Serena cut her off as she took the garments and laid them on the foot of her bed. "A friend of mine asked me if we could spare a uniform. She has had a difficult time of it since she lost her husband in the battle of Long Island," she explained hurriedly. "Anna Morgan has decided to take a job as a servant to support herself and her boys." Before

Molly could cross-examine her, Serena displayed a cheerful smile. "Are you ready to leave?"

Molly nodded and then opened her mouth to fire a question, but Serena hurried on. "Before you go to the school to collect the books for me, have Sandpiper saddled and bring him around to the back," she instructed. "I plan to take these clothes and some other supplies to Anna this afternoon."

When Molly exited Serena stood at the window, watching her maid stroll down the hill to the stables. After several minutes, one of the stable boys tethered Sandpiper at the back door and Serena began stripping from her dress to don the gray gown and apron.

A mischievous smile turned her lips up as she peered into the mirror to see her reflection. Serena tugged at the muslin gown, dismayed that she and Molly were not closer to the same size. The scooped neck revealed more bosom that she had anticipated, and Serena didn't recall Molly's looking so voluptuous in the garb. Well, it would have to do, she decided as she twisted her long blond hair up on her head.

As she stepped outside the heavy air settled about her. It was a muggy day, probably to end with a storm. Serena assured herself that she would be safe at home before the thunder rumbled and then scanned the grounds, satisfied that no one had seen her. A tingle of anticipation skitted across her skin as she urged Sandpiper across the meadow toward her destination, watching the puffy clouds pile high in the sky.

Serena drew the buckskin to a halt, her eyes skimming the area, searching for the raven-haired stranger who had promised to meet her. When she focused her attention on the cove she saw him skipping rocks across the water, his mount tethered in the brush. Serena swung from the saddle and quietly made her way up behind Trager. A wicked smile grazed her lips as she knelt down in the bushes to watch him. Her eyes flowed over his finely tuned physique, noting the expensive clothes he wore. They were tailored to fit the broad expanse of his chest and his narrow hips. The sleeves of his cream-colored shirt were rolled up to reveal the corded muscles of his arms and the darkness of his skin. Her attention was drawn to his brown breeches and then to the freshly polished boots that reached to his knees. Although she searched for some flaw, some criticism that would encourage her to throw him to Olivia, Serena came up with nothing. Trager Grayson was like a Greek god, the model of masculinity. And his eyes . . . Serena stumbled on the thought of the mysterious glow she had seen in them. They were like liquid silver, reflecting the heat of the sun. He seemed keenly aware of all that transpired about him, like a sleek panther that picked up the scent of danger or of an intruder.

And just as that thought crossed her mind, Trager turned toward her, singling her out of the brush that camouflaged her presence.

"How long do you intend to spy on me, Serena?" he said casually, a wry smile draped on one side of his mouth.

Trager had asked himself a hundred times why he should return this afternoon and he had come up with a hundred different answers, all of them lame excuses. But as Serena stood up in front of him, he knew what had drawn him back to the cove. Her unmatched beauty was her calling card, and he could not resist the temptation of watching the lively sparkle in her emerald eyes, witnessing her smiles, taking her in his arms.

Her jaw sagging, she rose to her full stature. "How did you know I was here?"

He strode toward her and then came to an abrupt halt while he inspected her servant's garb, noting the enticing swell of her breasts that came dangerously close to spilling free with each breath she took. "I have developed a sixth sense," he said, addressing her with a smile that could melt a woman's heart if she wasn't guarding it closely.

If Serena hadn't known that this darkly handsome stranger was Olivia's lover, she would have wilted like a rose in summer. Arming herself with an air of indifference, she accepted his outstretched hand and allowed him to draw her from her hiding place. Serena found herself captured in his strong arms, his lips playing gently on hers. Although she had intended to remain unaffected, her heart was drumming in double time upon her ribs. Why did Trager have such an arousing touch, she wondered as she braced her hands on his chest, her palm brushing over the open neck of his shirt. Brandon's embrace could not hold a candle to this man's. Had Olivia felt this same wild attraction each time he gazed down at her with those captivating silver eyes and each time he brought their bodies in close contact?

Trager raised his head, his gaze flowing over her flushed face, focusing on her trembling, kiss-swollen lips. "I wondered if you would come," he whispered, his voice heavy with desire. His finger traced the enticing bodice of her gown, tracking a path of fire across her quivering flesh.

It was nearly her undoing. Serena was painfully aware that she was standing too close to the flame and took a retreating step, putting a safer distance between them. No man had dared to take such liberties with her, but Trager was behaving as if they had known each other forever.

"And so it was with me," she confessed, as they wandered along the shore. "Where are you from, Trager? What are you doing on Warren land?"

His chuckle drew her curious gaze. He was studying her carefully. "You are a most inquisitive imp. Is that the reason you came back today, to discover my deep, dark secrets?"

Serena smiled in spite of herself. The man was far too clever to be trapped and Serena realized that she was playing out of her league. "You have piqued my curiosity," she admitted. "I want to know what lies beneath that attractive exterior."

Trager caught his breath when she gazed up at him. There was a special touch of sunshine in her smile, a radiant innocence that intrigued him.

Although he had pressing matters to attend to, he found himself drawn to this honey-haired vixen whose kisses tantalized him, leaving him hungering for more.

"Have I now?" His dark brow arched as he tilted his head to observe her from another angle.

"What profession do you pursue, sir?" Serena shot the question at him and then waited an impatient moment. When he did not respond, her eyes narrowed on him. "Have you something to hide?"

"Only my craving to ravish you," he teased as his smile cut deep crows' feet around his alert gray eyes.

Her chin tilted proudly. "I did not come here to be seduced," she informed him, her tone firm and insistent.

"So I have guessed," he smiled.

Serena impatiently stomped her foot, her green eyes flashing in irritation. "Will you tell me nothing about yourself? You are the most frustrating man I have ever met."

"And I suppose you have a vast repertoire to draw upon," he mocked dryly.

"I am not entirely innocent of men," she snapped, annoyed that he was insinuating that he was the first man who had ever kissed her.

He laughed out loud as he swaggered toward her and then curled his index finger beneath her chin, staring deeply into her emerald eyes. "Nor are you experienced with them, either," he speculated.

Serena slapped his hand away. "You are evading the point," she persisted. When he made no offer to enlighten her about his profession, Serena heaved a frustrated sigh and started up the cliff. "Good day, sir. I can see that it has been a waste of my time to return."

His hand snaked out to detain her. "For one of your kisses I will answer any and all of your questions, my dear," he promised, a wry smile hanging on one corner of his mouth as he drew her back beside him.

Now she was getting somewhere, she thought smugly. A kiss was a small price to pay to learn the dark secrets of Trager Grayson.

Serena nodded her consent. "Agreed. Now tell me everything about yourself and do not leave out even the smallest detail," she instructed.

"First the kiss. If it is intoxicating enough, perhaps it will completely free my tongue," he baited.

The challenge was given and quickly accepted. Displaying a saucy smile, Serena looped her arms over his broad shoulders and raised parted lips to his. Using the techniques she had learned from him and calling upon her own imagination, she pressed full length against him. But, too late, she realized she was the recipient of a kiss that carried enough heat to melt the moon. His arms fastened about her, molding them together, letting her feel his desire for her. When his tongue traced her lips and then sought the hidden recesses of her mouth, Serena gasped for breath, but it was too late. She felt like a drowning victim going down for the third time. It was as if an entire butterfly collection had been set free in her stomach. Her pulse was running away with itself as his caresses wandered possessively over her, seeking to know her as no man had. When his hand dipped beneath the bodice of her gown, she felt a strange need awakened, one that she had never realized existed.

Trager drew her down beside him, his heated gaze flowing over her like smoldering lava as he pulled the cap from her head to allow the mass of gold to tumble over her shoulders. He tunneled his fingers through the sun-kissed tendrils that framed her exquisite face, memorizing her perfect features, entranced by the glow he saw in her eyes.

"Damn, but you're a tempting vixen," he murmured before his lips slanted across hers, losing himself to the sweet scent of her, the drugging taste of her kisses. His knee slid between her thighs, pinning her beneath him, making him ache with a need that was slowly driving him mad.

The spark of passion that leaped between them had Serena swallowing air. Nothing had gone according to plan, and she felt herself losing control. Mustering her faltering will power, she twisted away, afraid to meet his unwavering gaze, afraid her resistance would fail her when she needed it most. What the devil had gotten into her? Never had she reacted to a man as wildly as she had when Trager molded his hard body to hers, making every inch of flesh that came in close contact with his sizzle and smolder.

"Let me up!" she demanded, her voice quivering slightly.

Heaving a resigning sigh, Trager noted the determined sparkle in her emerald eyes and then sank down beside her to stare off across the quiet cove. "You are very distracting, Serena. If I didn't possess a shred of decency I would have considered ravishing you, even while you protested."

A shred of decency? If he had *any* at all he wouldn't have attempted to tumble her in the grass in the first place, she mused as she brushed the dirt from her gown. And where was her common sense, she wondered as she watched Trager roll to his feet and stroll toward his horse. The last thing she needed was to become involved with Olivia's lover. Damn, her swim in the cove the previous day must have allowed water to rust the cogs of her brain!

After Trager had retrieved the package that was tied behind his saddle, he ambled back to her and offered her the gift.

Her brows knitted into a frown. "What is this?" she queried.

His shoulder lifted in a leisurely shrug. "A small token of my affection. When I saw it I knew it was made for you. I could not resist purchasing it." Trager drew her to her feet and leveled her a solemn gaze. "I want you to come with me, Rena," he requested as he traced the sensuous curve of her lips.

"Where?" Her frown settled deeper in her fine features.

"To my room in New Rochelle."

"For the night?" she gasped, wide-eyed.

A rakish smile tugged at one corner of his mouth, his gaze holding a glint of amusement. "For the night, the afternoon, and the morning. I will adorn you with gowns that accent your beauty." He directed her attention to her servant's garb. "And you will not be forced to serve anyone but me. And when I must leave, I will find a better position for you."

The nerve of that man! Did he think she was a common trollop who spread herself beneath a man who offered her gifts? Angry red made fast work of staining her cheeks and the sound of flesh meeting flesh cracked the silence. Serena glared at him, watching the imprint of her hand swelling up on the side of his jaw. If looks could kill Trager would have dropped dead twice, but, being no average man, he countered with a blinding smile that deflected the heat of her gaze.

"You voiced no complaint while I was touching you," he reminded her glibly. "I naturally assumed from your response that you were as anxious as I was to ease this hunger for passion."

Her eyes were spewing fire as she drew herself up in front of him, her furious gaze pinning him to the tree. "I would never submit to your bungling caresses," she gritted out, giving the lie without batting an eye.

"Bungling?" He chortled at her insult. "I beg to differ with you, Serena. I have yet to hear a woman criticize my techniques."

"You pompous ass! Do you think for one minute that I would consent to become your whore?" Serena sniffed distastefully at the thought. "I would prefer to sleep with Satan himself before I climbed into your bed." Her voice rose to a fervent pitch until she was shouting in his face, sending the birds to their wings from the overhanging branches.

As she wheeled and stalked away, Trager scooped up her discarded package and followed at her heels. "You forgot this."

"I want nothing to remind me of you," she threw over her shoulder, along with another agitated glower.

As she stepped into the stirrup and settled herself on her steed, Trager tied the package behind her saddle. "Keep it, Serena, you earned it."

Thunder rumbled in the distance, and Serena wasn't certain if it was nature's warning she had heard or the explosion of her fiery temper. His mocking smile hit an exposed nerve, and she knew if she didn't put a greater distance between them she was going to yield to the temptation of trampling him beneath Sandpiper's powerful hooves. Serena cursed under her breath, wondering why she had been polite enough to keep her insulting epithets to herself. Trager Grayson certainly did not deserve the courtesy. She gouged the stallion in the ribs and he lunged into a gallop, leaving Trager in a cloud of dust. How dare he suggest that she would become his mistress. That miserable blackguard! Olivia was welcome to him. Serena swore if she never laid eyes on

Trager Grayson again it would be too soon.

She leaned against the steed's neck, urging him to his swiftest pace, determined to eradicate all thoughts of the brash stranger from her mind. She squeezed her eyes shut, but those taunting silver orbs appeared before her, stoking the fires of her temper. Damn him to hell and back!

Behind her she heard Trager's urgent voice, but his warning came too late. The low-hanging branch struck her in the shoulder, toppling her from her perch. Serena shrieked as the pain shot down her arm and the ground rushed at her with unbelievable speed, forcing the wind out of her.

With a thud she landed and then bounced in the dirt, groaning in misery. And then the darkness circled like a looming vulture and Serena slumped, yielding to the silence that blocked out her own cry of pain.

Chapter Five

The quiet murmuring of voices filtered into Serena's clouded thoughts as she roused and then winced as a stabbing pain streaked across her shoulder and ribs. The sensation was nauseating, and she rolled her head, moaning softly as tears welled up in the back of her eyes. The hushed voices from the adjoining room evaporated as a crack of thunder sought to split the world in two, shaking the cot where she lay. Serena curled herself into a tight ball as a fearful tremor flew down her spine. Howling storms had always petrified her. Since her childhood experience of being lost during a storm she had never outgrown the fear of twisting winds and jagged bolts of lightning. As long as she lived she would never forget that incident, and she had always taken particular care to be safely tucked away when a threatening storm approached.

The second deafening rumble of thunder sent a shriek bursting from her lips and Serena clutched the sides of the cot, ignoring the white-hot pain that blazed across her ribs.

Another murmur of voices reached her ears, and then in an instant a dim shaft of light sprayed across the small room. Someone was beside her, smoothing her tangled hair from her perspiring brow.

"Serena, are you all right?" Trager's soothing voice wove its way through her tormented thoughts, but Serena could not control her trembling. When she made no reply, Trager brushed his lips across her forehead. "Can you hear me?"

The walls of the shack creaked as another crack of thunder ripped across the heavens. Her long lashes swung up, her eyes wide with fear as she clutched at him.

"Don't leave me," she pleaded.

The rain pounded against the shanty like impatient, drumming fingers, and the wind whistled and whipped through the cracks in the walls. Serena chided herself for cowering against Trager, but she could not seem to get a grip on herself. Her senses were groggy, and she felt so alone and deserted, just as she had been when she was a child seeking refuge beneath the trees while bolts of lightning and drowning rain had her crawling like a beast of the wild, searching for safety. As the storm unleased its fury, she huddled against Trager as if he could somehow shelter her from her fears and make the frightening world go away.

Trager frowned in concern when he saw the terror in her eyes. "What is wrong, Rena?" he questioned softly.

"The storm." She buried her head against his shoulder, her body quivering like the tree branches that waved in the wind. "Don't leave me, Trager. Please don't leave me alone," she whimpered against the soft fabric on his chest.

A pair of comforting arms encircled her as Trager stretched out on the cot. "You are safe with me," he assured her as he nuzzled his chin against the top of her head. "Sleep now. I'll be beside you until the storm passes."

Sleep? How could she sleep when the torturing memory would grant her no peace? Her head rolled against his shoulder to peer into his face. The dim candlelight from the partially opened door cast shadows on his angular features, and she tried desperately to concentrate on the man whose sleek body was pressed tightly to hers, anything to keep her from dwelling on the storm that raged outside the flimsy walls of the shack.

There was a need in her eyes, a need so intense that Trager could not drag his gaze from hers. Although Serena was mischievous and hot-tempered, she had an Achilles heel—a fear of storms. Even though he knew he was taking advantage of her vulnerability, he could not resist pressing his lips to hers. The temptation was far too great, and he had already admitted to himself that this golden-haired vixen had stirred a passion in him.

As their lips touched, lightning flashed through the window and Serena clutched at him, digging her nails into the taut muscles of his back, ignoring the pain, losing herself to the sight and feel of him. As his kiss deepened, stealing her breath from her lungs, she could feel his heart pounding against her breasts, matching her own racing pulse. And then his seeking hand cupped the full mound, teasing its peak, starting a fire that blocked out the howling wind.

Serena could not find her voice to protest his fondling nor the will to do so. She needed the comforting feel of his arms. He drew the gown from her body and then traced a path of kisses along the column of her neck to the swells of her breasts. Serena gasped at the arousing sensations his caresses evoked, and her body, as if it possessed a mind of its own, arched toward him. A moan of surrender escaped her lips as his tongue circled the peak of her breast and his hand fanned across her quivering abdomen to discover every inch of her flesh.

"Rena . . ." Her name floated from his lips in a pained plea as his caress wandered across her inner thigh, leaving her skin tingling beneath his searching hand. A burning ache replaced the haunting thoughts and Serena was only aware of the tantalizing feel of his skillful caresses on her flesh.

His hand retracted its flaming path, leaving in its wake a sweet surrender. His lips opened on hers, seeking the depths of her mouth as his hand made yet another deliberate descent to her thighs, his knowing fingers finding her womanly softness.

Serena gasped as a wild fire blazed through her veins. She clung to him in wild abandon, aching to appease the breathless need that engulfed her. The exquisite, tormenting pleasure mounted as he continued his bold fondling, taking her even higher. The sensations were maddening, and Serena was certain that she would die with her want of him. Brazenly, she reached out to run her hand over the dark furring on his chest and then down his abdomen, marveling at the potential strength that lay in repose.

She heard his quick intake of breath as her exploring caress trailed over his hip. It pleased her to realize that her touch had an arousing affect on him, as if she had given him back some small amount of the pleasure he had brought her.

"I warned you that I was no gentleman," he rasped as he caught her hand in his and brought it to his lips. "I want you, Rena." His voice quivered with passion as his gaze flooded over her, the smoldering silver of his eyes reflecting his desire.

"But I know nothing of you." Serena fumbled for an excuse. She had turned to him for consolation, but now his words tapped at her conscience. This was madness, she told herself. Trager had no deep feelings for her. He only sought to appease an animal need, and it would have made little difference whom he held in his arms.

A faint smile came to his lips as he smoothed away her frown. "A man and a woman need not know each other's darkest secrets to share an intimate moment." He eyed her speculatively as his smile broadened. "There is a strange attraction between us, whether you want to admit it or not."

His hand glided over her hips, as if proof of his words. Her skin trembled beneath his touch, assuring her that there was magic in his skillful caresses. And then his mouth swooped down on hers. His kiss was like a multivolt of electricity from a bolt of lightning, sizzling its way to her very core. Serena could have told Ben Franklin a thing or two about the power of his newly discovered electricity and its devastating effect. The intensity of it shocked every inch of her body and she could not release its source.

Trager's free hand slid behind her neck, tilting her head back to his ravishing kiss. Her feeble protest never reached her lips. He was proving his power over her, and all her defenses evaporated as his now-familiar caresses set her nerves on end.

Serena could no more deny her desire for him than she could command the world to stop spinning. It was a night to be plucked from reality, to be held as a forbidden memory of a time that should never have existed. And in that dark, exquisite moment that knew no logic, she yielded to the emotions that tore at her sanity.

Her hand traveled over the finely tuned muscles of his back, weaving intricate patterns that excited and aroused him to the limit of his patience. Trager buried his head in the valley between her breasts, drew a shuddering breath, and then lifted himself above her, knowing that he could never be content until he had made her his possession.

His gaze locked with hers and he knew he couldn't turn away. From the moment he had first laid eyes on this bewitching vixen, he had known he had to have her. She was like an immortal goddess who tempted and taunted mortal man with her innocence. He had become obsessed with this fantasy, one that found her in his arms, taking him to heaven on wings of indescribable pleasure.

As his hips slid between her thighs she braced her hands on his chest, feeling the furious beat of his heart. Her attempt to hold him at bay brought a new experience in pain searing across her ribs and she gasped, unable to bite back her cry of anguish.

Trager froze and then, seeing the pain flashing in her eyes, rolled beside her. "What is it, Rena?" he questioned in concern.

A tear trickled down her cheek and she realized how close she had come to losing her virginity to her stepmother's lover. The throbbing ache went deeper than the injury she had sustained from falling from her horse. It was the stabbing torment of conscience, provoked by her maddening need for him and her belief that there could never be anything between them but physical attraction.

Serena shook her head, her golden hair tumbling wildly about her, afraid to speak, afraid she could not trust her own thoughts, since they were swimming about her in chaotic disarray.

"Are you hurt?" he persisted as he lightly inspected the shoulder she protected.

Serena nodded affirmatively and bit her trembling lips as his hand pressed against her ribs.

"Dammit, why didn't you tell me? I could

69

have. . . ." His voice trailed off as he muttered under his breath, grabbed his breeches, and then reached for her petticoats.

Hastily, he ripped the cloth for a makeshift bandage that would hold her arm firmly against her ribs. Serena was amazed by his gentleness as he lifted her to draw the bandage behind her back. When he had secured her arm, he slid beneath the quilt and cradled her in his arms.

A feeling of contentment settled over her as she nestled against his shoulder, her eyes fluttering shut to relive a dream that had come dangerously close to becoming reality.

"Go to sleep," he whispered against her cheek, his voice holding a hint of frustration. "And count your lucky stars."

A smile hovered on her lips. "You *are* a gentleman, Trager," she assured him softly. "You could have taken advantage of me, but you didn't."

A low chuckle erupted from his chest. "Don't shower me with compliments, vixen," he warned. "The night is far from over, and with you in my arms I'm having one hell of a time controlling my lust."

But Serena fell asleep like a trusting child, unconcerned with his threat. There was more to Trager Grayson than his rakish smiles and devouring kisses. He had a heart, she mused drowsily. It may have been packed in ice, but for that one moment he had displayed more than his selfish desire to force himself upon her. On second thought, Olivia didn't deserve the man. He was too good for her. And then Serena yielded to him in her dreams and fell into an exhausted sleep, feeling his lips playing softly on hers and the gentle magic of his caresses on her flesh.

As the dawn's first light splintered the darkness, Serena raised heavily lidded eyes and then smiled to herself as she glanced over to see Trager's bronzed face soft in repose. Intrigued, she reached out to rearrange the tousled raven hair that lay across his forehead. His long, thick lashes brushed lightly against his high cheekbones, and Serena impulsively followed the path of crow's feet that sprayed from the side of his face. Her gaze skitted down to watch the methodic rise and fall of his broad chest, and she marveled at his masculinity. There was not one flaw on his body, not one weakness to criticize. His muscles bulged on his arms as he moved slightly, and Serena wondered if he could crush her bones if he had a mind to do so. He was the essence of virility, capable of great feats that required strength, and of surprising gentleness, when the mood suited him.

Serena blushed, remembering the feel of his hard body pressed so intimately to hers. A warm tingle followed in the wake of that memory, bringing another wave of color to her cheeks.

While she was admiring him, his lashes fluttered up, his gray eyes burning into her, warming her another quick ten degrees. Trager propped himself up on his elbow, the faintest hint of a smile pursing his lips as his hand made a leisurely caress of her bare shoulder.

"How are you feeling this morning?" he inquired, his voice still lazy with sleep.

"Much better," she assured him and then realized that she had been baited. His exploring hand wandered beneath the quilt to brush across the full swell of her breast. "And I am in full command of my senses," she added, as she removed his hand and placed it on the outside of the cover, flinging him a disapproving frown.

Trager did not seem surprised that he had met with resistance. Indeed, he had expected as much. The previous night he had discovered that there was a passionate woman lurking just beneath the surface. But Serena was equipped with a heavy coat of armor.

"'Tis a shame," he sighed as he swung his long legs over the edge of the cot and then unfolded himself to tower over Serena. "You have just foiled what might have been a very enchanting moment, one which you might later regret casting aside."

His taunt flew in one ear and out the other for Serena was mesmerized by the mere sight of him. She could not disguise the admiration in her eyes as her gaze strayed across the broad expanse of his chest and then trailed slowly downward. He was all male, every virile inch of him, she mused. When she realized that Trager knew where her eyes had fallen, embarrassed red worked its way up her neck and she glanced away, staring at the bare wall as if something there had suddenly drawn her attention.

"Feminine curiosity?" he inquired, arching a mocking brow. "Could it be that you are having second thoughts about ousting me from your bed?"

"Certainly not!" she protested, her voice registering indignation.

Trager scooped up her discarded dress and eased her into a sitting position, despite her resistance. "Hold still," he snapped. "You cannot dress yourself and I am merely offering assistance. Surely you can accept at least *one* of my services without complaint."

Reluctantly, she allowed him to draw the gown over her head while she held the quilt over her bosom, taking particular care not to expose herself to his leering gaze. And then she frowned at the dangling sleeve of her gown. It was most fortunate that her father would not be home when she returned. The lie she would have been forced to give him would have burned the ears off a priest. As it was, she had only to face Molly. Another thought came from the corner of her mind, and she glanced back at Trager as he fastened the stays of her gown.

"Whose voices did I hear last night?"

Trager paused from his chore. "Voices?" His expression was masked behind a carefully blank stare as he took up the task of fastening the rest of her stays.

Serena would have accused him of consorting with Olivia if she hadn't known that her stepmother was in New York with her father. "And don't tell me I was dreaming," she added, tossing him a challenging glance.

"But I'm afraid you were," he said simply. "There was no one here, Rena."

She frowned, grappling with the thought. Could she have been mistaken? She had been groggy and she had been dreaming of that night long ago when she had weathered a storm in the woods, but . . .

"We better be going," Trager informed her as he assisted her to her feet. "I have an appointment in New Rochelle later this morning." His hand traced the fine line of her jaw as he stared into her green eyes. "Although I would be content to spend the day here with you, I cannot overlook my obligations indefinitely."

"Obligations?" Serena pounced on the opportunity of discovering what profession allowed him to indulge his expensive taste in clothes.

Trager quickly saw through her scheme and flashed her a sly smile. "You never give up, do you?"

"And you are tight-lipped when it comes to telling anyone what makes you tick," she countered saucily.

"We're a matched pair, Serena," he remarked as he carefully measured her with his gaze. "Determined and stubborn."

Her good shoulder lifted in a casual shrug. "I inherited those traits. Did you come by yours naturally or were they acquired?"

Trager looped a supporting arm around her and urged her into the main room of the shack. "Both are inborn instincts, which I have sharpened with training," he commented. "Now come along. If we tarry much longer you might make me forget that I am a man of purpose."

A strange emptiness encompassed her as they faced the early morning sun. After sleeping in his arms, Serena wondered if she would miss the feel of his solid flesh molded to hers. What the devil was wrong with her? That thought should never have entered her mind. There was nothing between them, nothing at all.

"A penny for your thoughts," Trager encouraged, arching a dark brow when he noticed her pensive expression.

Serena offered him a smile as he led her to the lean-to where her stallion waited. "'Tis nothing worth putting into words," she replied with a shrug, careful not to include her tender shoulder in the gesture.

"Everything that runs through your mind interests me." He flashed her a devilish grin. "But I must confess, 'tis not your mind that arouses me most." His silver-gray eyes dipped to her scooped-neck bodice and he sighed forlornly. "But the lady does not choose to return my affection."

"Affection?" Her delicate brow raised acutely and then returned to its normal arch. "The word for which you search is *lust*," she corrected.

His mouth quirked as he lifted her in his arms and then settled her in the saddle. "Pardon the slip of tongue. Since you seem to have such a low opinion of me I doubt that it would serve any useful purpose to argue the point."

He was not about to be baited, Serena mused as she took up the reins. Trager was quick-witted and clever. He was no man's fool, or woman's either, she guessed. Whatever his connection or involvement with Olivia, Serena was certain that Trager was in full command. He was not the type of man a woman could wrap around her finger. It would have been an uncomfortable fit, even for Olivia.

As Trager swung into the saddle to follow after her, Serena glanced back at him. "You need not accompany me. I can manage on my own." Her attention settled on the meadow that glistened with raindrops. "Will I see you again?" She amazed herself by braving the question and dared not glance back at Trager for fear she would see the mockery in his eyes.

He leaned over to cup her chin and then slanted his lips across hers, savoring the honeyed sweetness of her kiss. Sandpiper objected to the close contact with the gelding and sidestepped, breaking up their embrace long before Serena would have had it end.

"You could come with me," he murmured huskily.

Her gaze dropped. "Nay, I cannot accept your terms."

"And if it was marriage I proposed, would you have consented?"

Her chin tilted to a proud angle. "I have had my share of proposals and, as of yet, I have not seen the advantage of any of them. Why would I be interested in wedding a man who is as mysterious as the shadows of the night?"

Trager braced his hands on the saddle horn as a wide grin stretched from ear to ear. "Because part of your fascination with me is that I have not thrown myself at your feet," he insisted.

Serena was quick to take offense. "I do not seek a slave. I only search for a man who recognizes me as his equal, not an object for his occasional pleasure."

He leaned close, his warm breath sending a rash of goose pimples sailing across her skin. "My craving for you would be as regular as the chiming of a clock," he assured her as he attempted to place a kiss to her lips.

Sandpiper chomped on his bit and pranced away. And for that Serena was thankful. At least one of them showed good sense. An air of indifference floated about her as she nudged her steed. "I am indebted to you for coming to my aid. Good day."

Trager had leaned so far out from his horse that he came dangerously close to falling facedown on the ground when Serena and her contrary steed eluded him. He pulled back into the saddle and watched as she trotted across the pasture.

When she had put a safe distance between them she glanced back at Trager, but his gaze held her captive. And then he bowed from atop his horse, blowing her a farewell kiss. When he galloped away without looking back, a rueful smile grazed her lips. How could she forget the feel of his full lips on hers, the manly fragrance that had infiltrated her senses, and that devilish glint in his eyes when he graced her with one of his smiles? Serena chided herself for dwelling on the rogue. She would put him out of her mind and that would be the end of it. Besides, she knew nothing more about him than she had in the beginning.

Her eyes strayed over her shoulder. But Trager was gone and she was left to suppress the memory of a night that she continued to harbor like a sweet dream. Forget him! She would never see him again. He was a vagabond, a restless wind that came and went so quickly that she would be soon forgotten. And yet, the emotions that he had evoked from her crept in from the shadows of her heart and she wondered if she fancied herself in love with the man.

Serena rolled her eyes in disgust. She was behaving like a love-smitten schoolgirl. Enough of this! She kicked Sandpiper, sending him off at a reckless gait, one she was quick to regret. His movement jarred her sore arm and she grimaced at the pain that shot across her ribs. The wound would not quickly heal, nor would this gash in her heart, she mused. Trager had burrowed his way into her thoughts, and it would take time to rout him.

Chapter Six

The air was still heavy with the dampness of the previous day's thunderstorm when Serena eased into the carriage and set out for Anna Morgan's cottage northeast of her father's estate. Much to her relief, Molly had been out on an errand when she had returned that morning dressed in maid's clothes. Serena's explanation to her later had been reasonably believable. She had told Molly that she had fallen from her horse on the muddy path and had walked back to Anna's for the night. Molly had been curious about the reason for the second journey to Anna's cottage, but Serena had explained that she had discovered that Anna was in need of a great many other supplies when she chanced to spend the night in her home.

Serena sighed heavily and carefully moved her injured arm, grimacing each time the carriage jolted her in her seat. The pain continued to remind her of her experiences the previous day and of Trager. She felt herself becoming attached to him, and that was the last thing she needed. Shaking off the thought of Trager, she smiled as Anna and her two young boys waved to her. The sight of the young widow and her small children had Serena chiding herself for worrying over her petty problems. Anna had her hands full trying to provide for her family and enduring the loss of her husband, while Serena was stewing over a man who had no place in her life.

"What happened to you?" Anna inquired as she retrieved the packages Serena offered to her.

Serena shrugged leisurely, collected another armload, and stepped from the carriage to flash her sable-haired friend a smile. "I wasn't watching where I was going."

Anna frowned curiously at the box Serena held under her arm. "What is all this? I only recall asking if you could spare a maid's uniform,"

"I found a few things I thought you might need," Serena remarked as she stepped over a mudhole and aimed herself toward the house to deposit the supplies before Anna could protest. She was too proud to accept charity, and Serena did not intend for Anna to think of it as such. It was a gesture of friendship between two people who had known each other forever. "Papa was given these gifts by some British officers, and you know how touchy he is about accepting bribes." Serena walked onto the porch and then glanced back at Anna's skeptical expression. "He didn't want anyone to get the wrong impression, so he asked me to get rid of them. He often carries his honesty a bit far, but I couldn't persuade him to keep the gifts. If you refuse them, I will have to tote them elsewhere, and I do not relish the thought of bouncing across the countryside with my arm in a sling."

Anna was wise to her scheme, but she had swallowed her pride when she had been unable to set nourishing meals in front of her growing children. The time had come for Anna to face the stark realization that she was having financial problems.

"You're very kind," she murmured as she opened the box to find ham, beef, cheese, and other mouth-watering tidbits.

Serena grinned as four eager little hands rummaged through the box for the candy she had strategically placed in it. "You'll have to thank Papa. I'm only the delivery girl." Before Anna could reply, Serena took one partiaular package from her and opened it, holding the exquisite gown up in front of Anna. "And this is for you to wear to the ball Papa is giving in the middle of September."

A surprised gasp burst from Anna's lips, her jaw swinging from its hinges. "I cannot accept this. It must have cost you a fortune."

"Nonsense." Serena was not about to take no for an answer. "You will take it and wear it," she demanded. "Blue is your color and you will look stunning in it. If I hadn't thought it was perfect for you I wouldn't have brought it along." Before Anna could voice another protest, Serena opened the other packages she had brought, intending that Anna accept every item that she desperately needed. To her relief, Anna smiled gratefully and made no effort to return the supplies.

When the boys had gone outside to play, Serena sank down in a chair and accepted the cup of tea Anna offered to her, noting the young widow had replenished the empty cannister of tea that sat on the cabinet.

"Now tell me about your accident," Anna insisted as she clasped her hands around the steaming cup of tea.

"I toppled from Sandpiper's back," Serena said simply.

Anna's motherly expression brought Serena's muffled chortle.

"Are you still riding that high-strung stud?" Anna asked. "I would have thought Mitchell would have found you a gentle mare. Sandpiper is too much horse for you. 'Tis a wonder you didn't break your neck."

"It wasn't his fault," Serena hastily defended her horse. "I was the one who didn't see the low-hanging branch."

"I suppose Prince Charming was behind you and you were straining your neck to keep an eye on him," Anna smirked caustically.

Serena's dark lashes swept down as she stared into her cup. If only Anna knew how close she had come to stating the truth. The long pause drew Anna's curious regard.

"Just what *had* captured your attention, Rena?" she queried.

"A man," Serena admitted with a sheepish smile.

Anna's drawn face split in a wide grin. "So it *was* Prince Charming," she speculated. Easing back in her chair, she stared across the room. "Let me guess. He was tall, dark, and handsome, and you fell hopelessly in love with him."

"Nay, I fell *helplessly* from my horse," Serena corrected with a giggle. "'Twas the devil who was at my heels and I was trying to run for my life."

"And did you escape with your soul intact?" Anna inquired, feigning seriousness. It was good to talk with Serena again. There had been so few pleasant moments for her of late.

"Nay." Serena leaned forward to stare into Anna's blue eyes, her own expression somber. "I was forced to sell my soul to Satan for these offerings I have brought to you. What was left of my conscience bade me to distribute these supplies, hoping you could create some good from this evil and my misfortune. Now you know the dark truth." Serena popped to her feet and displayed a mischievous smile. "And with my mission accomplished, I must return home before the devil catches up with me again."

"Serena?" Anna's voice was pensively quiet.

Serena paused at the door to glance back at Anna, who sat with her head bowed. "Aye?"

"Thank you. I am forever indebted to you," she murmured.

"And if there is anything else you need, do not hesitate to ask," Serena instructed, her smile mellowing. "That is what friends are for. We have known

83

each other a long time, Anna. If I needed help I would come to you, knowing I wouldn't be turned away."

Anna muffled a sniff and forced a wan smile. "You're an angel, Serena, and I do not believe that nonsense about devils being hot on your heels, for you would surely take to your wings to elude them."

"Would that I could, but as you can see . . ." Serena gestured toward her sling. "I have practically broken one of my so-called wings," she replied, then she swept out the door to climb into her buggy, knowing she could never escape the thought of Trager Grayson. He was the devil who was on her mind, and she was having a most difficult time getting rid of him.

Serena braced herself for the encounter with Olivia and her father when they walked into the study to see her sitting amid the books Molly had retrieved from the district school. Although the bruises on her shoulder and ribs had begun to fade after four days, it still pained her to move her arm and she kept it in a sling, as the doctor had ordered.

Even though Serena had had plenty of time to formulate her story and had tried it out on Molly, she was apprehensive about explaining to her father. It was no white lie, but rather a whopper, one which could blow up in her face if Mitchell confronted Anna. Serena could only hope that the incident would be forgotten by the time the party date had come upon them.

"Sweet merciful heavens! What happened to you?" Mitchell gasped as he rushed over to his daughter.

"I met with an accident," she said simply and accepted his kiss.

"I can see that!" he sniffed, his tone carrying a note of sarcasm.

Serena swallowed her nervousness, forced a casual smile, and then began her explanation. "I was taking some supplies to Anna Morgan, and before I could return home I was caught in the storm." She ducked her head and absently thumbed through the book that lay before her, avoiding her father's probing gaze. "I panicked and tried to rush home before the heavens opened up."

Mitchell nodded thoughtfully, knowing how frightened his daughter was of thunderstorms.

"The road was slick and Sandpiper faltered. I fell from his back and had to return to Anna's for the night." She heaved a sigh and braved a glance at Mitchell, wondering if he had swallowed the tale hook, line, and sinker. His sympathetic expression bolstered her confidence and she continued. "My goodwill journey proved to be disastrous." Serena peered at the useless arm that was draped around her midsection. "But at least Anna and the boys will not go hungry."

"It must be difficult for you to move about under the circumstances." Mitchell's gaze traveled over the pile of books that were scattered on his desk. "And I must assume that you have taken the opening at the school, despite your handicap."

"It keeps me occupied." Serena flashed him a cheerful smile and then discreetly glanced at Olivia, who didn't seem the least bit concerned that her step-daughter had met with catastrophe. Not that she expected sympathy from Olivia, Serena mused bitterly. Olivia was far too self-centered to give another's misfortune a second thought. "How was your stay in New York? Did you meet with difficulty on your journey?"

When Olivia made no attempt to respond to the question, Mitchell answered her. "None to speak of." He sighed wearily. "The British troops have secured the city, and Washington has retreated to Harlem Heights. We met with no trouble along the way. The retreating Patriots seem to be keeping to the woods to avoid being spotted. I don't think it will be long before they lay down their muskets and admit defeat."

His voice registered confidence, but Serena was paying little attention. Her thoughts had strayed to Trager, picturing him holding Olivia in his arms the same way he had held her that dark night. Although the voice of reason bade her forget him, Serena kept seeing those dancing silver eyes, remembering the exquisite feel of his sensuous lips on hers. The jealous green monster kept attacking her, causing her to wonder if Olivia had responded to him as easily as she had.

"Serena?" Mitchell frowned thoughtfully at the faraway look in his daughter's eyes.

Her head jerked up and she smiled apologetically. "I'm sorry, Papa. What did you say?"

"I asked if you were enjoying your teaching position," he repeated, eyeing her curiously.

"Aye, very much," she assured him and then glanced around her father's shoulders to see Olivia retreating, much to her relief. The woman always made her uneasy, but now more than ever, because of her association with Trager. "Were you and Olivia able to spend some time together after your meetings?"

Mitchell sank down in the chair across from the desk and nodded affirmatively. "We were treated like royalty. One of the officers, Colonel John Powell, offered to escort Olivia around the city while I attended my conferences, but we were entertained during the evenings. We had the unpleasant experience of watching part of the city go up in flames," he remarked, a resentful frown furrowing his brow. "Arsonists have been at work there. The Whigs, no doubt." His expression softened. "I think you should have come along with us. You would have appreciated a change of scenery. There has been little for you to do of late."

Her good shoulder lifted in a reckless shrug. "I'm not complaining."

"Has Brandon been to see you?" Mitchell cut to the heart of the matter, anxious to know if Serena had come to a decision.

"He's coming tomorrow." She grinned wryly. "And nay, I have not accepted his proposal . . . as

87

of yet."

He heaved another heavy sigh and unfolded himself from the chair. "I think I will call it a night. It's been a long day."

Serena raised her face as Mitchell leaned over to press a kiss to her forehead and then she listened to his fading footsteps. She chided herself for wondering if her father had any idea how dangerous it was to send Olivia out on another man's arm. Would Trager have been jealous if he knew that his lover had been keeping company with a distinguished British officer? Serena frowned at the direction of her meandering thoughts. Lately, it seemed all roads led back to Trager. Damn, why couldn't she put him out of her mind?

She found her feet had taken her to the window to stare out at the darkness, and she began to wonder if Trager was holding another woman in his arms at that very moment, or if he was patiently waiting for Olivia to return to him. This was preposterous! Serena rolled her eyes and then turned back to her books, determined to concentrate on the business at hand. And she did so, quite successfully, until she sank down in bed and the loneliness encompassed her.

This has got to stop! Serena told herself as she tried to settle herself in a more comfortable position. Perhaps she should seriously consider Brandon's proposal, devote her time to planning the wedding instead of dwelling on thoughts of a man who had no place in her life. With that idea in her mind, Serena fell asleep, imagining herself as Brandon's wife. She had to make her decision and learn to live with it. Surely she could come to love Brandon Scott. He wasn't a bad sort, after all. He was just a bit dominating, but Serena could break him down, perhaps even wrap him around her little finger, if she was inclined to do so.

Brandon swung from his saddle and then hastened over to assist Serena from her horse as he arched a quizzical brow. "Is there some particular reason why you wanted to ride to this point? What is so special about it?"

Her spirits sank at his question. The cove was spectacularly romantic at night, and Brandon had to be blind as a bat not to notice. She had brought him to the cove to erase the memory of Trager, to implant a new picture in her mind's eye. "This has always been one of my favorite places," she explained as her gaze swept the peaceful setting, and she listened to the water roll against the sand and then recede.

When Brandon's hand slid around her waist to urge her along the path, she accepted it without complaint, searching for a reaction that just wasn't there. In time she could learn to be content with Brandon, she told herself. After all, happiness was only a frame of mind. Serena had always prided herself on the fact that she could make the best of almost any situation. So what if she hadn't heard bells or the sound of soft music in the distance? There was more to life than pealing bells and violins playing romantic melodies.

She eyed him curiously. She had always wondered, although she had not dared to voice her suspicions, if Brandon had joined the Loyalists because their reinforcement had come mostly from England. Few Tory colonists had been ordered to take up arms. But now the Redcoats were enlisting the aid of men who knew the area and, unfortunately, Brandon had traveled through New York and Pennsylvania on business trips and knew the country like the back of his hand. Serena doubted that he was quick to boast that fact. Most likely, someone had volunteered him, she thought to herself. When he turned to stare out over the water, Serena bit back a smile, certain she could see the faintest hint of a yellow streak down the middle of his back, one that was only recognizable in dim moonlight.

"I want your answer, Serena," he demanded. "I have been a patient man, but the time has come for you to make your decision."

His condescending tone rankled her pride. It always annoyed her that Brandon talked down to her. Then he would do an about-face, putting her on a pedestal to admire her from afar. Serena wanted to be treated as an equal, the way Trager . . . her thoughts came to an abrupt halt. There would be no more comparisons, she promised herself. Trager was gone and Brandon was offering the proposal, but love had not blinded her to his faults. And yet, she could not name a man who was without them. Even her father, as dear as he was to her, had his faults, the worst of them being his acute blindness to Olivia's infidelity.

"I would like to make the announcement next week at the ball Mitchell is giving. We can be married the following week and have a few days to ourselves before I have to leave," Brandon plotted out, as if he had already wrapped the matter into a tight knot.

Serena sighed heavily. She had been procrastinating, but the time of reckoning had come. "Very well, Brandon. We will make the announcement next week," she agreed, her tone lacking enthusiasm.

Brandon pivoted, his face splitting into a broad smile that stretched from ear to ear. "I have waited an eternity to hear that answer." Instead of scooping her up in his arms, he bowed before her and then placed a light kiss to her wrist. "You won't be sorry, Serena. I will make you happy. Whatever you want is yours for the asking."

What she wanted was an ardent kiss, one that spoke of his deep affection for her, and she was not about to ask for it. Before she could protest, Brandon shuffled her along the path, lifted her onto Sandpiper's back, and then stepped into his own stirrup. Trying to mask her disappointment, Serena studied him for a long moment.

"Brandon, do you love me?" she questioned him point blank.

His head swiveled around, a dumbfounded look on his face. "I have asked you to marry me, Serena." His tone held a hint of indignation. "I respect you above all others, and I cannot name another woman whom I would want to claim as my wife. It goes without saying that you have my utmost love."

As they rode back to the manor, Serena was pensively quiet. Brandon's confession made her uneasy. He seemed sincere in his gentlemanly sort of way, but he lacked enthusiasm. Serena pulled her stallion to a halt, but Sandpiper threw his head, objecting to the fact that Brandon's nag had taken the lead.

Brandon glanced back in time to see the steed rear, displaying his contrary nature. A dark frown furrowed his brows as he watched Serena bring the stud under control. "And when we are wed I intend to find you a mare with a gentle nature. That stallion is too much horse for a woman."

Serena's tempered patience snapped, her green eyes flaring with sparks. "I raised Sandpiper from a colt, and I will continue to ride him until the time comes to put him out to pasture. I will not have you or anyone else telling me that I cannot ride him." Her voice rose testily and Serena found it necessary to clamp her jaw shut before her tongue completely outdistanced her brain.

He graced her with an indulgent smile that had Serena grumbling under her breath. How she detested his patronizing.

"But, Serena," he coaxed. "I am only concerned about your welfare." He attempted to smooth her ruffled feathers. "That devil stallion could turn on you without warning. I have heard the stable boys say that he is the most contrary piece of horseflesh they have ever tended."

Serena leaned down to pat Sandpiper's muscled neck and he quieted beneath her soft words. "He doesn't happen to like men, 'tis all," she defended him as her eyes anchored on Brandon. "Since you have already informed me that you are leaving early this evening, I should like to ride a little longer."

"But your arm is still in a sling and I don't think it wise. . . ." Brandon pointed out, but he was interrupted by Serena's distasteful sniff.

"I can assure you that I have nothing to fear from Sandpiper. Goodnight, Brandon." Serena reined her steed to the east and gave Sandpiper his head, thrilling to the thundering of his hooves, while Brandon sat with his jaw gaping, certain Serena would topple from her perch and injure her other arm, or even worse—her stubborn neck.

She was as high-strung as her stallion, Brandon decided. But in time he would bend her to his will. Once they were married, he would be able to tame her. With that confident thought in his mind, Brandon touched his boot heels to the bay gelding's flanks. A smile of anticipation touched his lips as he aimed himself toward New Rochelle, envisioning what lay ahead of him for the next few hours. He had the world in the palm of his hand.

When Brandon galloped away, Serena reined back toward the house. Once and for all she intended to see if her suspicions were correct. After tethering Sandpiper in the bushes, she went around to the front of the house to inform her father that she would be spending the rest of the evening in her room. With

CAROL FINCH

that accomplished, she went upstairs to change into
her breeches, pin her hair beneath her cap, and add a
layer of padding to camouflage her feminine curves.
Serena made her way back to her waiting stallion by
way of the secret passage, intent on learning how
Brandon spent his evenings after leaving her at an
early hour, as was his custom.

Serena frowned in annoyance when she spotted
Brandon's horse tethered in front of one of New
Rochelle's infamous brothels. Her curiosity got the
best of her. Before she realized it, her footsteps had
taken her to the window on the south side of the
establishment, amid the cover of bushes. Serena
gasped indignantly when she spied Brandon with a
young wench on his arm and a wide grin on his lips.
That two-timing scoundrel, she muttered under her
breath as he escorted the dark-haired doxie up the
stairs, knowing damned well that his intent was not a
friendly game of cards. So he planned to take a wife
from a notable family and keep a mistress. Damn his
hide. If Serena could have gotten her hands on him
she would have clawed out his eyes and then fed him
to a pack of wolves. Men! Not one of them was to be
trusted, she mused cynically.

Her eyes circled the parlor and came to rest on the
handsome face of Trager Grayson and she launched
into another round of epithets. He was no better than
Brandon. The cad! There he was, chatting with an
older wench, the madam of the house. Serena had

94

seen Ellen Linstrohm on several occasions and had
heard the gossip that buzzed when the woman ventured out in daylight.

When Trager's gaze strayed in her direction,
Serena ducked her head beneath the window sill and
then waited an anxious moment. Cautiously, she
raised her head, but Trager and Ellen had disappeared. A frown knitted her brow as she glanced
about the room. Perhaps he had taken the woman in
tow, as eager to seek his pleasure as Brandon had
been. Why was she experiencing this overwhelming
sense of betrayal, one far worse than the realization
that her would-be fiance consorted with prostitutes?
She had no claim on Trager Grayson, and she had
known from the beginning that he was a womanizer, satisfying his lust whenever and wherever it met
his whim.

Suddenly, a calloused hand clamped over her
mouth and she was hauled into the alley, kicking and
fighting her captor. Her pained shriek pierced the
night air when her tender arm was twisted behind her
back and held in a vise-like grip that brought agonizing tears to the corners of her eyes.

Her scuffling knocked the cap from her head and
an array of silky blond curls tumbled over her shoulders. Her captor froze and his voice registered
surprise as he wheeled Serena around to face him.

"What the devil are you doing here?" Trager's gaze
flickered over her lumpy figure, amusement glistening in his silver eyes.

"I could ask you the same thing," she countered as

she readjusted her cap, which sat cockeyed on her head. When Trager attempted to draw her back into his arms, she kicked him soundly in the shin and stalked away, smoldering like a volcano that was searching for the perfect location to explode. "Goodbye, Mr. Grayson."

Trager quickly closed the distance between them and grabbed her good arm to detain her. "Would you mind explaining why you were here spying on me?"

"I was *not* spying," she snapped, her tone as harsh as the winter wind.

His mouth quirked as one dark brow arched acutely. "Then what do you prefer to call it, Serena? Window peeking? Do you dress in these ragamuffin clothes to become a peeping Tom after dark, wondering what you are missing by holding men at arms' length?"

Serena fumbled for an answer, drawing Trager's mocking chortle. "I am not some pervert," she flared, her chin tilting to a proud angle.

"Then admit it, my dear. You were spying on me, but for what cause?"

He was studying her in a very strange manner, one of mistrust, as if she were some sort of criminal. She sighed defeatedly. "Alright, 'tis true. I was spying," she muttered. "Now, if you will excuse me, I must be going."

Trager was not about to let her saunter away without interrogating her. "Just a moment, Serena. I demand to know why you sought me out."

The egotistical rogue, she mused as she flung him

a sour glance. Did he think she had nothing better to do than to keep tabs on his activities? "I have fallen madly in love with you and I knew my poor heart would break if I could not at least catch a glimpse of you," she cooed in a honey-coated tone that dripped with sarcasm. "Now that I have seen you, I am content to run along home and dream of your magnetic smile." Serena spun on her heels and stalked toward her steed. Let the ruttish boor think she was enamored with him. What did she care? Damn him. Damn them all!

"I'll escort you home," he offered as he fell into step behind her, not swallowing a bit of her caustic admission.

"That won't be necessary." Serena glanced back over her shoulder, a mocking smile pasted on her lips. "I managed to arrive here by my own devices and I can return home in the same manner. Besides, I can see that you had made plans for the evening. Don't keep the wench waiting. For a price, she might find someone else to replace you."

Trager laughed out loud. "You should only believe half of what you see, Serena," he advised, a wry smile brimming his lips.

She wheeled to face him, her chin tilting a notch higher. "'Tis obvious that a casual conversation was not what you had in mind for the evening," she smirked.

"Do I detect a hint of jealousy?" he inquired as he raised a heavy brow, his smile broadening into a wickedly annoying grin.

"Certainly not!" she objected indignantly. "I don't give a tinker's damn what you do or with whom!"

Trager edged a step closer, despite the fact that Serena's fuming glare threatened to reduce him to a pile of ashes. "You haven't forgotten our night together, have you?" His voice was low and seductive, reminding her of what it had been like between them. When his hand cupped her chin, his thumb trailing along her jaw, it was nearly her undoing. The sensation was like a shock wave that rippled its way to her very core. "It was like a dream, but I awoke before it ended. I would have shown you much more than compassion that night."

His face was dangerously close to hers, his warm breath caressing her cheek. Serena felt the need to conduct an experiment with Trager, the same one she had attempted with Brandon. She had to know if she could live with a man like Brandon whose gentlemanly kisses stirred no fire within her.

"Kiss me," she requested as she peered up into his silver-gray eyes. "Kiss me as if you were madly in love with me, the kind of kiss a man would bestow on the woman he might have chosen for his wife."

It was an odd request, but Trager could not resist the invitation. A rakish smile parted his lips, displaying even white teeth. "With pleasure," he murmured as he took her in his arms, reminding himself that her ribs and shoulder were still tender. But it was difficult. Touching this spirited wench did strange things to his body, and his mind had little control over the matter.

His lips descended on hers, savoring the sweetness of her response, drinking in the honeyed taste of her kiss. Involuntarily, his arms pressed her to the hard warmth of him, molding their bodies together to kindle a fire that was slowly but surely gnawing away at Serena's composure. Why did this arrogant stranger have to be the one who aroused her to such dizzying heights? And why couldn't Brandon be half the man Trager was? It was no use. She could never marry Brandon, knowing he frequented brothels. He would probably continue to do so even after they were wed. Another disturbing thought struck her as she dragged her lips away from Trager's. Could other men instill this fiery desire in her? Was it because Trager was the only man who had dared to kiss or caress her as no one else had? What was this overwhelming craving that his kisses evoked? Was this passionate side of her exposed only when Trager took her in his arms, or could other men spur such a response?

"Was that the type of embrace you anticipated?" he queried, his voice ragged with mounting passion.

Serena forced a shallow smile. "Aye." A curious frown plowed her brow as she took a retreating step. "Do you kiss all of your women with such zealousness?"

Trager sputtered on his breath. "My, but you are an inquisitive little imp." It disturbed him that he had given her more than he had taken from her. His past experiences had found him hungry to appease his desires, and he had given little thought to the woman in his arms. But then he had heard no complaints, and certainly none of his women were brazen enough to pry into his other intimate encounters. Other women accepted what he offered for the moment and were content with it. But Serena was searching for some meaning to it all. "First you demand to know about my personal life, and now you brazenly inquire into my love life. You are a very brash young woman." His expression held a hint of skepticism as his gaze flickered down her padded torso. She felt like a woman when he held her close, but in no way did her present outward appearance resemble the feminine sex. Serena was a walking contradiction who continued to pique his curiosity.

"And as usual, you have tactfully avoided answering my question," she reminded him.

The chiseled lines of his face hardened as he leveled his gaze at her. "I am a private man, Serena," he told her quietly. "I prefer to keep it that way."

"So you are saying that no one really knows Trager Grayson," she speculated as she studied him thoughtfully.

Trager slid his arm around her waist and aimed her toward her stallion. "Would you like to become my confidant, sharing my darkest secrets?" he teased, his smile assuring her that she didn't have a snowball's chance in hell of discovering what made Trager Grayson tick.

"Aye, I would," she admitted honestly.

He stopped short and eyed her warily. "Why?"

His penetrating gaze puzzled her. Suddenly he

seemed so serious, more so than he had ever been. "I find you a mysterious sort, 'tis all," she said lamely.

Trager continued to watch her like a hawk, his gray eyes roaming over her expression, missing nothing. And then after a long, silent moment he flashed her a roguish grin. "Would you like to come to my room and get to know me better?"

Serena wormed her arm from his hand and grabbed her steed's rein. "Nay, I think not. I'm sure the ladies in the brothel could accommodate you better than I."

His snicker annoyed her, as did his remark. "I have no doubt of that. A man of my experience and cravings has no time to train a virgin."

The look she gave him would have mortally wounded the average man, but it bounced off his thick skin, leaving no mark. "And I have no desire to submit to you, receiving nothing in return when those trollops are well paid for their favors," she shot back.

Trager extracted a coin from his vest pocket and waved it in front of her, his taunting smile adding fuel to her fiery temper. "Forgive me, Serena. I had not intended to insult you by not offering to pay for your *limited* services."

"Ohhh!" Serena was seeing red as she stepped into her stirrup and felt a steady column of steam rising from her collar. "You are the most despicable man I have ever met!" When she had settled herself in her saddle she acquainted him with her look of total disgust. "If you were the last man on earth and I the last woman, I would die a virgin, even if it meant putting an end to our species."

When Serena tried to ride away, Trager grabbed Sandpiper's reins, nearly toppling her from her perch. "And I have just recently discovered that my incomplete dream of our night together was a *nightmare*," he spouted in an intimidating tone, annoyed that the chit had cut him to the quick with her razor-sharp tongue. Women came eagerly to him, and often uninvited, but Serena behaved as if he were the scum of the earth, unfit to warm her bed. "My condolences to the man who dares to take you as his wife. He will most surely find it necessary to cut out your tongue if he is to endure a tolerable existence with you as his lifelong partner."

"And I hope your future wife, if indeed there is one, is not so particular that she cannot be content to share her bed with a man who has spent more time on his back than on his feet!" she parried, her words slicing his pride like a scalpel.

Trager ripped her from her saddle so quickly that it made her head spin and then turned her over his knee. His hand found its intended mark—her buttocks. "If your father had thrashed you when you were younger, perhaps I would not be forced to tend to the task," he growled, taking pleasure in hearing her pained shriek. "You are much too big for your breeches, ones that you shouldn't be wearing in the first place!"

Mortified, Serena tore away from him and grabbed her stinging backside, her gaze firing penetrating daggers at him. "How dare you! I'll have you know I'm . . ." Serena bit back her words. She would be damned if she let him know that she was the daughter of a distinguished magistrate. When the time was right, she would have her revenge on him, she vowed. Until then, she would bide her time, waiting for the moment when she would see him strung up on the gallows for molesting her.

"You are an insolent little chit who files her tongue every night to keep it lethally sharp," he finished for her, insultingly.

Her mind raced through several epithets, but she couldn't seem to sum up the contempt she felt for him without spouting an oration. When she did not retaliate immediately, he chuckled, a victorious grin cutting through his craggy features.

"I never thought to see you speechless, my dear, but I must say it becomes you." Trager took a step closer and winked down into her angry red face. "Now shall we dispense with the insults?" His voice was softer now, dissolving her irritation. "We can continue to belittle each other for the rest of the night, but the fact remains that you and I could experience a very fulfilling relationship, if you would give us half the chance."

Her gaze fell to study the toes of her boots. Perhaps she was a bit touchy and overdefensive, fighting the magnetic attraction she felt for him.

"Now come along," he coaxed. "I'll escort you home."

"I can manage satisfactorily on my own." There

was no defiance in her tone, only a note of confidence that assured him that she could take care of herself.

"I realize that, my dear. But I will rest easier knowing that you are safely tucked away for the night."

Her lashes fluttered up and she graced him with a sly smile. "You don't think that a woman can manage without a man, do you?"

"Perhaps others cannot." His grin settled in the shadowed lines of his face. "But not you, Serena. I have the sneaking suspicion that you could emerge from a foul situation smelling like a rose."

His comment pleased her. At least here was a man who accepted her for whom and what she was, unlike Brandon who invalidated her independence. A frown gathered on her brow as another thought crossed her mind. Would Trager expect more of her if he knew that she was more than the serving maid she had led him to believe? Would he be appalled by her behavior if he knew that she was an aristocrat whose name carried a great deal of influence in the community? And what would be his reaction if he knew that Olivia was her stepmother?

As they rode away from the dim lights of New Rochelle, Serena was pensively quiet, grappling with the questions and the comparisons she had made between Brandon and Trager. She could never marry Brandon, she realized. They would make each other miserable. He expected too much from her, and she did not love him enough to change.

"Serena?" Trager slid her a sidelong glance. "What is your last name? You never told me."

She flashed him a mischievous smile. "I will be only too happy to tell you *after* you have revealed all the well-kept secrets about yourself," she propositioned.

Trager chuckled and settled himself more comfortably in his saddle. "I am thirty-three, unmarried, and I have an unquenchable craving for feisty wenches."

She pulled a face at his evasive reply. "You are infuriating."

"One of my many faults," he conceded with a dry smile.

"At least you admit that you have them." Serena glanced up and then reined her steed to a halt. "Thank you for accompanying me. My home is just over the hill." In truth she still had a two-mile ride ahead of her.

Before she could move away, Trager leaned over to sweep her from her horse, planting her on his lap. There was a hungry impatience in his kiss, one that left Serena trembling beneath his amorous assault. It was a long, breathless moment before Trager raised his head to trace the delicate lines of her face. And then he set her back in the saddle, leaving her gulping for air.

"It will be a waste of what might have been a splendrous night, Rena," he sighed heavily. "'Tis a pity. . . ."

Trager tipped his hat and then reined his steed back the way he had come, whistling a light tune that

105

floated back to Serena as she sat watching his silhouette disappear into the shadows. Finally, she shook her head to shatter the spell and turned Sandpiper from the beaten path to return to the manor by way of the tunnel.

It was a long, fretful night for Serena. Trager kept creeping into her thoughts, tormenting her with that rakish smile of his. Why hadn't he asked to see her again? Had he only used a line on her that had been murmured to a score of other women? Damn, why was she thinking of him at all? Enough of this, Serena told herself. She didn't want to see him again. He stirred emotions that she had no desire to face.

Chapter Seven

The heat of summer had melted into the calm days of fall, and Serena sighed contentedly as she rode toward the small village north of New Rochelle to the district school. It was her favorite time of the year, a time when peaceful breezes dusted across the countryside, allowing her to appreciate the grand beauty of nature.

Stirred from her serene thoughts, she frowned slightly as she glanced up to see the tall, lean young man whom she guessed to be about her own age who ambled along the edge of the road.

"Good morning, miss," he greeted her with a polite smile as Serena's horse-drawn carriage drew up beside him.

Serena returned his smile as her eyes flickered over his homespun clothes. Her gaze settled on the pack on his back and then strayed to the books he carried under his arm. Her curious frown settled deeper in her exquisite features.

"Would you, by chance, be a teacher?" she

107

inquired as she reined the mare to a halt. Perhaps the position had been filled at the school and her father had neglected to inform her. But that should have come as no surprise, she decided. Mitchell had been so busy with official business that he practically met himself coming and going.

Nathan Hale glanced down at his books and then nodded slightly. "Aye, that I am, ma'am," he assured her.

"I find it a bit unsettling that I am the last to know," she mused aloud, disappointed that she was about to be ousted from her post. Damn, now what was she to do with her idle time?

Nathan's brows furrowed bemusedly as he stared into Serena's bewitching face, listening to her inaudible mumbling. "Ma'am?"

"'Tis nothing," she insisted with a shrug and then scooted over on the seat to make room for her replacement. "Climb in. What is your name, sir?"

"Nathan Hale, but I . . ."

Serena was annoyed and impatient. "Get in or we will be late," she persisted as she patted the empty space beside her. When Nathan hesitated Serena eyed him sternly and gestured to the seat. "I don't bite, Mr. Hale, and I have no intention of abducting you. Now will you please hurry."

Nathan grinned sheepishly. The young woman probably thought it strange that he should be wary of her. When he settled himself beside her he took the opportunity to study her from a new angle while she popped the horse and squirmed on the seat. She was like an angel, her skin so soft and creamy, her hair the essence of sunlight, her eyes so clear and green.

"Where was your last teaching position?" Serena queried, striving for a casual tone that masked her disappointment. It injured her pride to realize that she was about to be cast aside like a worn-out shoe without the slightest warning. And yet, why was she taking it so hard? She knew she was only filling in until another schoolmaster could be interviewed and hired.

Her question slowly filtered through Nathan's pleasant thoughts and he studied Serena, trying not to notice how devastatingly attractive she was. "I have been teaching in my hometown, a Dutch community in Connecticut," he explained as he pulled his books and papers onto his lap and readjusted the hiked hem of his dusty brown breeches. "But I think you must have me confused with someone else, Miss . . ." He paused like a typical teacher giving a fill-in-the-blank question, waiting for her to supply her name.

"Serena Warren," she replied, her brows coming together over her vibrant green eyes. "Are you trying to tell me that you are not the new schoolmaster who has come to fill the opening at the district school?"

Nathan chuckled lightly. "Why no, ma'am, I *am* looking for a position, but I have not yet found one."

While she sighed in relief she sized young Nathan Hale up and down, liking what she saw. Although his clothes were tattered, he had an intelligent look in his eyes and a pleasant smile. His Dutch accent was intriguing, and suddenly Serena felt like a pouting child. Obviously, the man could use the job and its salary; whereas she had no concern whether she was paid for her efforts.

"Perhaps you might be interested in replacing me. I have been filling in after our former schoolmaster left to join the Patriot forces, leaving the community and its children high and dry."

Nathan frowned thoughtfully as he eased back in the seat. "I was hoping to acquire a position closer to New York City, but I suppose it wouldn't hurt to look over this school of yours." He cast Serena a discreet glance. "You say the schoolmaster ran off to join the Patriots? I would imagine the Loyalists in the area were glad to be rid of him if he was filling the students with revolutionary ideas," he surmised.

Serena chortled, an easy smile on her lips. "You are very astute, Mr. Hale. The villagers were appalled when they learned that the man they had trusted with their children's education had revolutionary tendencies and they had not even realized it."

"Nathan," he corrected softly. "Please call me Nathan."

"Very well, Nathan." Serena nodded agreeably, taking an instant liking to the gentleman who sat perched beside her in her carriage. "The Tories were shocked to discover a Whig right under their noses, and they were outraged that Cortney had been in charge of their children these past few years. They have become cautious of late."

"And you share their indignation and mortification?'' he inquired.

Her shoulder lifted in a casual shrug, thankful that the pain had subsided and the left side of her body could handle the gesture. "My loyalties are divided, I'm afraid," she admitted honestly and then eyed him warily. "Does that offend you?"

It was Nathan's turn to lift a careless shoulder. "Nay, Serena . . . may I call you Serena?" When she nodded affirmatively, he was momentarily lost to the dazzling sight of her smile and the fascinating way her honey-gold hair captured the sunbeams. "But it seems that one must be careful not to voice his opinion these days," he continued. "The colonists are wearing their feelings on their shirtsleeves and one can never be certain who will take offense to some offhanded remark. It becomes difficult to tell friend from foe during revolutionary upheaval."

"So it seems. . . ." Her lashes swept up to peer into his alert eyes. His voice was smooth and appealing and he had a skillful way with words that would probably hold the children spellbound. Aye, he would make an excellent replacement, Serena decided. "And what of you?"

"I also find my loyalties split," Nathan informed her, his emotions masked behind a faint smile. "But during my travels I have seen several reasons why the Patriots have been demanding their rights. They came from the mother country for their freedom, and the Crown still intends to keep a tight rein on them, using their prosperity to pay the bills of a widespread empire, refusing the colonists a voice in government." Nathan smiled guiltily then, feeling a strange trust in this fascinating young woman who enjoyed talking politics. "And I must admit that I never appreciated having others tell me what I can and cannot do, either."

"Nor I," Serena chimed in. "I hope our independent natures don't get us in trouble."

It was easy to talk with Nathan, as if their profession and opinions had given them the common ground to share their innermost thoughts. Nathan questioned her about her home and the surrounding area, and Serena freely offered the information, hoping he would consent to take the position. She was honest with him, explaining what would be expected of him if he accepted the job. There was something warm and vibrant about the young man that made her return his smiles with open ease.

When they arrived at the school, Serena introduced Nathan to the children, and then he wandered off to inspect the area on his own while she tended to the day's lessons.

The following few days he helped to occupy Serena's thoughts. Nathan would appear in the late afternoon to chat with her before she drove home and occasionally he would ride part of the way with her when they became engrossed in conversation and the hour became late. Oftentimes they sat beneath the shade tree in the schoolyard, while Nathan sketched his maps and Serena told him of her day's experiences with the children. The bond of friendship between them strengthened, and she anticipated seeing Nathan's warm smile when the school day ended. He helped to erase the memory of Trager Grayson, one that continued to weigh heavily on her mind.

Serena lifted glistening green eyes and an impish grin as Nathan ambled over and sank down beside her. "I had almost given up on you today," she remarked saucily. "Has some wench caught your eye? What do you do all day while I am trapped in school?"

Nathan chortled as he propped himself against the tree. "Nay, Serena, there is only one other woman to match Alice's beauty." His gaze circled to her for a second and then settled on some distant point. "Some man will be fortunate to have you as his wife, and I have *not* been visiting with another woman," he assured her. "I have been learning the countryside and appreciating its grand beauty."

Serena had previously asked Nathan if he was married and was given a full account of his angelic stepsister—who had captured his heart. Knowing his strong, unwavering attachment to Alice, she scoffed at his teasing flattery.

"My father has begun to refer to me as an old spinster. There is no need for you to attempt to dazzle me with praise," she rebuked, her tone carrying no condemnation, only a threat of a taunt.

"You a spinster?" Nathan laughed incredulously as his gaze drank in every bewitching curve and swell

113

she possessed. "I would imagine that men have stampeded to your door." He studied her thoughtfully for a moment. "But I think you are wise enough to be particular. It will be difficult for you to select a man who can match your wit and intelligence," he speculated, knowing that if his heart was not tied so tightly to Alice he would be one of those eager swains who hungered for her attention.

A slight blush crept to her cheeks when Nathan stared at her with such open affection. "Most men are leery of my independent nature and stubbornness." She laughed softly. "I have been accused of being outrageously outspoken once or twice." It only took an instant to recall the barbed comment Trager had made about her taking the time to file her sharp tongue daily. If Nathan had overheard her conversations with Trager, he might wish to retract his words of praise, she thought to herself. Perhaps it was that Trager brought out the worst in her, the darker side of her passion and the fiery side of her temperament. "I am quick to anger, I fear."

"And justly so, I would imagine," he predicted, wondering if the man in her life whom she refused to mention had spurred that remark. He reached out to brush a lean finger over her flawless cheek and then veered slightly off course from their previous conversation. "Independence is a noble thing, Serena," he said philosophically. "To speak your mind is cleansing to the soul. You should not be ashamed of what you believe or afraid to allow your lips to form those thoughts into words. It is those who are afflicted with ignorance who should bite their tongues and guard their actions.''

"I am not ashamed of what I believe,'' she admitted. "'Tis just that most gentlemen are taken aback when a woman voices her opinion, as if she had no mind of her own, as if being of the female persuasion encouraged ignorance. When I was studying in England I was furious to learn that a gentleman of court expected his female companion to be an empty-headed doll who possessed reasonable beauty and very little wit. And there are many men in these colonies who share those outrageous opinions. Thankfully, you are not one of them.'' She smiled as his hand fell away from her face and he lightly squeezed her arm.

Nathan nodded thoughtfully. "You are a rare breed, Serena. Perhaps you should have joined forces with the Patriots. There are those among them who possess many of your strong qualities and who would admire your intelligence, rather than condemning it.''

"Perhaps I should have.'' Serena sighed as she stretched out her legs in front of her and tugged at the wrinkles of her skirt. "But I seem to be caught in the middle . . . a misfit of sorts, unsuited for the normal man who has ideals that conflict with mine.''

Nathan unstrapped his bag and drew out his papers, absently sketching a map and making notes to himself in Latin while he talked. "Still, I envy the man who steals your heart. He has a great deal to gain by making you his wife.''

"But if this man must bear my father's stamp of approval, I fear the marriage will be a shambles. Papa's social circle of friends and possible bachelors share a good many of the opinions of the British aristocracy, opinions that I detest." Her delicate brows knitted into a frown as she peered around Nathan's shoulders to see him hard at work on his drawings. "What are you sketching, Nathan?" she queried curiously.

He smiled lazily. "'Tis a map of Gaul . . . or as closely as I can recall from the history book I had to leave behind. I find it necessary to jot down maps and a few notes since I do not have a library to refer to when I find a position."

"Have you made your decision about taking this position?" she pressed. "I don't think you require any reference books. You seem to have stored a world of knowledge in your head."

"I only hope I have the opportunity to use it," Nathan mused aloud, knowing that Serena didn't have the vaguest notion that his remark had an entirely different meaning from the one he implied.

His comment slid by in the manner he had hoped. "If you would accept this district school you would have every opportunity to utilize your acquired knowledge. And if you consent to become schoolmaster here, I'm certain that my father will offer you a room at our home."

"All of this will happen with *your* recommendation?" His brow raised slightly, but he continued to concentrate on his map as he passed the light gibe.

116

"But of course." Serena did not take offense. "Although most men do not respect my opinion, my father does occasionally. And in this case he realizes that I am in a better position to judge whether or not you would make a competent instructor for tomorrow's leaders. Now, will you take the job, Nathan?"

"You are very persistent, Serena," he smiled.

"Another notable characteristic of a revolutionist, I suppose." A wry smile pursed her lips as she studied the angled features of Nathan's young face.

Nathan chuckled as he tucked his map away. "Naturally. You realize, of course, that these radical ideals of yours could get you into serious trouble with the good citizens of this community. They would be in an uproar if they learned that the daughter of their respected magistrate was as unacceptable as this Cortney fellow you have replaced."

There was a devilish gleam in her emerald eyes as she met Nathan's teasing grin. "Mayhap I should run off and join up with the Whigs," she suggested. "That would set the gossip buzzing."

His gaze anchored on her, amusement dancing in his own eyes. "And I would be one step behind you, but I fear Alice might frown on my traveling alone with you. She might not understand that it is our common cause that keeps us together."

Serena's expression sobered. "Would you really consider taking up arms against the Crown?" she questioned point blank. They had only discussed the possibility in jest, but Serena wondered if Nathan could be persuaded to take a firm stand, or if he intended to continue to straddle the fence as she would be forced to do.

"Do you think the Whigs have just cause to air their grievances?" he countered, avoiding a verbal commitment.

She nodded affirmatively, knowing her true opinion was safe with Nathan. He would never cause her harm. "The Patriots have every reason to complain about the state of things," she confirmed, and then lowered her voice, as if to give him the rest in strictest confidence. "And if these trees have ears, you and I might be carted away and tried for treason."

"That we would," he whispered as he leaned close. Nathan unfolded himself and rose to his full stature. "Enough of this blasphemous talk." He flashed her a winsome smile as he drew her to her feet. "You better get home before your father becomes concerned. We have stayed to chat longer than usual today."

As Nathan lifted her into the buggy, Serena's eyes narrowed, seeing a hint of sadness that touched the edge of his smile. "Is something wrong, Nathan?"

"Wrong?" His features melted beneath her concerned regard. "What could possibly be wrong when I have been keeping company with the most attractive woman in all of New York State? Except that she is leaving me alone again for another long, lonely night," he added with a teasing grin.

Serena's lip jutted out in an exaggerated pout. "You speak of Alice as the light and love of your life and then you do a complete about-face and flatter me with praise." Feigning annoyance, she tossed him a condemning frown. "I am left to wonder if Alice is as gullible as you seem to think I am."

Nathan stepped back and swept the cap from his head as he bowed before her. "Forgive me for boasting of your unequaled beauty, Miss Warren. No offense intended. If my heart were not committed, I can assure you that I would pursue your affection most zealously."

A warm smile blossomed on her face as she picked up the reins. "You have such an eloquent way with words, Mr. Hale," she complimented him. "I envy Alice. She possesses the key to your soul, but 'tis *my* consolation that I have gained your friendship."

"Truly," he murmured to himself as he watched Serena, her blond hair flying about her, thundering off down the path as if she had a runaway horse attached to her buggy. A fond smile grazed his lips as he walked back to retrieve his books. He then turned toward the west, thinking of the duties that awaited him that evening for the good of his cause.

Chapter Eight

A thoughtful frown creased Serena's brow as she stood in front of the mirror studying the exquisite gown Trager had given her. Her first impulse had been to toss it out, but when she opened the package she could not resist the elegant green silk dress. It was apparent that he had spent a fortune on the gift, and at the time she had begrudgingly admitted that the rogue had excellent taste.

And she had an ulterior motive for selecting the gown for this evening's ball. Olivia had taken it upon herself to purchase Serena's dress for the affair, since Serena's days were devoted to her job. The garment Olivia had selected made Serena look like a child, with its high collar and loose-fitting waist. The prim smile that had settled on Olivia's creamy white features when she insisted that Serena model the gown for her and Mitchell made Serena itch to claw that smug expression right off the woman's

121

face. Damn, but Olivia had a knack of infuriating her, slowly but surely chiseling away at Serena's barely manageable temper.

Serena was anxious to see the stunned expression on her stepmother's face when she descended the steps dressed in the provocative gown that Trager had purchased for her. A spiteful smile pursed her lips as she waited for Molly to finish fastening the stays.

"Olivia is shore gonna be surprised," Molly remarked as she stepped back to scrutinize the elegant gown and the shapely young woman in it. "You're gonna outshine her in this."

Serena grasped the hairbrush and rearranged her blond hair, meeting Molly's gaze in the looking glass. "My intention is not to steal attention away from Olivia, only to spite her for toting home that horrible garment she thought to dress me in as if I were her twelve-year-old daughter."

Molly retrieved the diamond choke necklace from the jewelry box and laid it around Serena's neck. "Forgive my bluntness, Rena, but I've had this uneasy feeling that Olivia has been trying to annoy you since you returned from England."

Serena chortled and nodded slightly as she smoothed the rich silk fabric over hips. "Aye, I have been under the same impression."

Mitchell extended his hand and offered a cordial smile to Colonel Powell, who stepped into the vestibule followed by several other distinguished-looking gentlemen. "So good of you to come, Colonel." He glanced back over his shoulder at Olivia. "And you remember my wife."

John Powell clicked his heels, took Olivia's hand, and placed a light kiss to her wrist. "'Tis impossible to forget such beauty." After a long moment, he dragged his appreciative gaze off Olivia's low-necked gown and, remembering where he was, displayed a polite smile. "And may I present my aide, Lawrence Hill, and a friend of the Crown, Trager Grayson."

Mitchell nodded a greeting to each of them and then frowned curiously at the strikingly handsome Grayson, who was dressed in black velvet. "I presume that you are not in our army, since you are not in uniform. Are you . . ." His voice trailed off as Trager's head swiveled toward the stairs.

Serena descended the staircase, wearing a blinding smile that held a sparkle of mischievousness. Mitchell's jaw sagged as his eyes flowed over his daughter. Never had he noticed such a strong resemblance between Serena and her mother until that moment. It was in the way she carried herself, the ladylike poise, the way her silver-blond hair curled about her face, and the breathtaking way her eyes glowed, he mused, stung by a sudden pang of nostalgia. His little girl had grown up, and he had been so preoccupied that he had failed to notice the young woman who had blossomed into a bewitching beauty, capturing the undivided attention of every gentleman who stood in the entryway, waiting her approach.

Trager's silver-gray eyes were fixed on Serena as she floated down the steps, mesmerized by the picture of perfection she presented. The gown displayed each swell and curve that lay so temptingly beneath it, and its rich color accented the vivid green of her eyes. A wry smile spread across his lips as his attention focused on the creamy flesh of her breasts that rose and fell with each breath she took. Trager felt the rise of desire, remembering the feel of her soft skin beneath his hand, the taste of her sensuous lips on his. And for a long moment he was content to be just another of the many pairs of eyes that rested on the bewitching goddess who stood above them.

Serena glanced down, singling out Olivia, and bit back another ornery smile when she noticed that Olivia was envy green around the gills. Olivia might have thought she could maneuver Serena, but she had sorely misjudged her stepdaughter.

Mitchell took the opportunity to announce his daughter's appearance, since every man in the hall was entranced. A proud smile came to his lips as he moved toward the bottom of the stairs. "And this, gentlemen, is my daughter, Serena."

Serena nodded graciously when she heard her father's voice, giving up her game of revenge for the moment. She lifted the front of her skirt and started down the last flight, her eyes circling the entourage of red uniforms and the faces that sat above them. But she fumbled on the face that was framed with raven hair and sported a rakish smile. Serena swallowed air, caught her heel on the step, and felt the color gush from her face like water bursting from a broken dam. She muffled a gasp as she lost her balance and teetered precariously in midair. A strong arm encircled her waist to halt her fall and then remained as support as her wobbling legs took her to the last step.

Her lashes fluttered up to see the expression chiseled on the bronzed features of Trager Grayson's face. The look assured her that he was well aware of what had caused her composure to come unraveled like a ball of string on a downhill roll.

"A serving maid?" he mocked dryly as he leaned close to her ear, as if to quietly insure that she had recovered from her near fall. "My, but you are a deceitful little chit. And there you were trying to pry information out of *me*."

When he deposited her beside her father and faded back into the crowd of admirers, Serena collected her scattered composure and then glanced between Trager and Olivia, hoping to catch some discreet glance that alerted her to the fact that there was more to their relationship besides new acquaintances. But Trager, like Olivia, guarded his thoughts, revealing nothing of what was running through his mind.

"Serena, the man who came to your rescue was Trager Grayson," Mitchell said, introducing them, aware that the lithe gentleman had saved his daughter the embarrassment of ending sprawled on the stairs in front of their guests.

Pasting on one of her most charming smiles, her gaze filtered through the crowd to settle on Trager. "I am happy to meet you, Mr. Grayson."

Since he and Serena were the center of attention, Trager took the opportunity to return to her side. "Please call me Trager," he insisted as he pressed a kiss to her wrist. Slowly he raised his head, his eyes penetrating her like silver daggers, warming her with such intensity that she felt a blush rise in her cheeks, replacing the color loss that had occurred when she had first recognized him.

For once in their brief acquaintance she was in command, and she used it to her advantage. All eyes were upon her as she smiled sweetly and aimed her question at Trager, knowing he would be unable to weasel out of answering this time. "And what is your profession, Mr. Grayson . . . besides rescuing damsels in distress?" she inquired, arching a perfect brow.

His smile indicated that she had successfully managed to maneuver him into a corner, twisting his arm behind his back until he was forced to explain himself. Serena noted the slight twitch of irritation in his jaw before he camouflaged his annoyance with her.

"I am the owner of a shipping fleet, a captain, who commutes to the mother country with merchandise to trade." He sighed heavily, looking a bit more uneasy than Serena had ever seen him, and then continued, "That is, until the Patriots looted and burned several of my family's ships and storehouses because of my political beliefs." His gaze strayed to Colonel Powell and his aide, Lawrence Hill, and then Trager allowed a faint smile to graze his lips. "John has been helping me get in touch with willing investors who are interested in seeing our trade with England return to its previous state and aid in putting our family's business afloat."

A ship's captain who had run aground, Serena mused. But why had he been so evasive with her? Did he think that she would have thought less of him because he was floundering, that he had suffered beneath the hands of radical Whigs? Suddenly, Serena felt very cruel for embarrassing Trager in front of all these distinguished officers. Her ploy had gained her the information she sought, but she had damaged Trager's pride in the process. If he had known what was coming, he probably would have let her fall on her face in front of the crowd, and she really couldn't have blamed him.

Serena's attention returned to Mitchell as he slipped his arm around her waist and displayed his proud-father smile.

"Serena has been filling in for us at the district school until we can locate and interview a suitable instructor."

"And I think I have found him," Serena insisted, taking the opportunity to praise the young man she had become so fond of these past few days. "His name is Nathan Hale, a very knowledgeable young Dutchman who would be an asset to this community and its children."

Serena frowned slightly when her eyes strayed to Trager for a split second, noting the disapproving expression that Trager was unable to mask before it evaporated into a carefully blank stare.

"You have been praising him for the better part of a week," Mitchell teased, "but have you convinced him to come for an interview?"

From out of nowhere, Brandon appeared, wedging himself between Serena and Trager. He pressed a kiss to her cheek and then focused his attention on Mitchell. "I hope Serena has used her feminine finesse on this Hale fellow. I would like to see my fiancée at home preparing for our upcoming wedding, instead of standing at the head of her class," he announced, his tanned face beaming.

Serena flinched when Brandon spouted off his remark, but the wheels had been set in motion. Serena muttered under her breath when she saw Olivia's face light up like a candelabrum. Mitchell's grip tightened about her waist to give her an excited squeeze, and Serena felt like a captive who had been tied to the mast of a sinking ship. She had hoped to inform Brandon tactfully that the marriage was off before he could make the announcement, but he had blundered in and blurted out the arrangements, which would now have to be canceled.

"I am so pleased that Serena has finally consented to marry you, Brandon. I was beginning to think this daughter of mine would never find a suitable mate. I think a toast is in order." Mitchell directed Serena and his guests to the refreshment table in the ballroom and urged his daughter and soon-to-be son-in-law along with him.

Serena's eyes settled on Trager, finding him propped against the door casing, a thoughtful frown creasing his brow. She fought back the urge to explain the situation to him, but then, why should she? Trager didn't give a fig about her. It was only his wounded pride that was showing again, she told herself. Trager had been caught off guard, thinking that she had trifled with him, just as he had attempted to use her to satisfy his lusts. Perhaps it would be good for him to have his male pride deflated a bit, she decided.

She was paying little attention when Mitchell raised his arm to toast the upcoming marriage, and then she forced a smile as the guests filed past to congratulate her on her choice of mates. Only when Brandon took her in his arms did she bury her wandering thoughts and focus her attention on the young lieutenant who swept her across the dance floor. Serena resigned herself to the fact that she would be forced to play the charade for the night.

Trager watched the captivating young beauty waltz around the ballroom with her soldier, amazed at the twinge of jealousy that stabbed him between the shoulder blades. Why did he feel so betrayed? He had no claim on that ornery little wench. She was bewitching, he admitted to himself, but there were other attractive women in the world and he had had his share of them. And yet, there was something intriguing about her feisty spirit. She had amused him when he thought her to be a serving maid who had swiped her master's fancy steed and stolen off in the afternoon to swim in the cove. She had been a lioness who had come at him with her claws bared, but at times she had been as gentle as a kitten, her kisses as soft and thirst-quenching as a summer rain. Trager shook his dark head, attempting to dissolve his whimsical thoughts, but as soon as his eyes anchored on Serena, he was lost again. Now he viewed her from an entirely different angle. She was a shrewd little chit who owned the cove she swam in and the prize stallion from which she had toppled. And in a matter of minutes she had forced him to divulge his purpose to half a regiment of soldiers and the influential magistrate—her father. And then, before he had recovered from her first prank, he had had to listen to Lieutenant Scott's announcement that he had claimed this captivating, deceptive vixen as his fiancée. Trager felt an unfamiliar rage surging his veins. It was only that Serena had turned him every which way but loose, he told himself. He was not accustomed to being outmaneuvered, especially by a woman, and it went against his grain.

Deciding on distraction as a cure for his suffering, Trager made a fast sweep of the ballroom, singling out a woman of comparative beauty—Olivia Warren. He took her in his arms, focusing on the seductive smile that played on her lips. No wench was worth worrying over, Trager told himself, not even that green-eyed enchantress. He had enough on his mind without dawdling over Serena. Besides, she had played her game with him, leading him to believe that she was no more than a maid who had no attachment to another man. The ornery chit! She deserved that skinny-legged lieutenant.

Serena felt a twinge of irritation gnawing at her when she glanced past Brandon's shoulder to see Olivia curl her hand around Trager's neck, drawing him into her clutches. So it was as she had suspected. They *were* lovers. It was obvious from the way they were ogling each other. Serena gritted her teeth. Damn that witch! Couldn't Mitchell see what Olivia was doing? He deserved more respect than for Olivia to flaunt her lover right under his nose!

"Don't you think your gown is a bit daring, love?" Brandon questioned, dragging Serena from her pensive musings. "I couldn't believe my eyes when I walked in to see every man in the hall leering at you."

A shallow smile touched her lips. "My dress is no more revealing than Olivia's or any other woman's. I'm beginning to think that you believe in double standards," she rebuked, casting him a disapproving glance. "'Tis perfectly fine with you if other women wear provocative gowns, but you would have me dress as a saint."

"'Tis just that I want your beauty for my eyes only," Brandon parried as he drew her closer, inhaling the sweet feminine fragrance that hovered about her. "I do not want my fiancée peddling her wares before a houseful of lusting beasts."

As if he wasn't one himself, Serena mused sourly. She had seen that lecherous look in Brandon's eyes that night at the brothel when he latched on to that doxie and propelled her toward the stairs. Brandon

Scott was a hypocrite. Serena could stand no more of his suffocating nearness. He was only showering her with attention because he had an audience to impress. If they had been alone, he wouldn't have come within five feet of her. Serena found his touch repulsive and she pried his hand from her waist. She had played his charade as long as she could stand.

"I'm going out to the terrace for a breath of fresh air," she informed him, her tone cold and clipped. When Brandon made a move to join her she raised her hand to halt him. "Alone."

As she breezed past one of the servants who held a tray of champagne, she retrieved a glass and then aimed herself toward the terrace. Serena breathed a sigh of relief and then gulped her drink, focusing her attention on the swaying shadows, wishing she could become one of them. So far, this night had proven disastrous. Brandon had made his announcement before she could inform him that she had changed her mind; Trager Grayson had appeared to unravel her composure, and Olivia had attempted to seduce her lover on the dance floor.

Her footsteps took her the length of the terrace and back again, trying to walk off her nervous energy, but nothing helped. She felt like a bomb looking for somewhere to explode. If only she could talk with Nathan. He had such a soothing affect on her. Perhaps she should have told him about her feelings for Trager and his entanglement with her step-mother. Nathan might have offered her advice, something which she desperately needed at the moment.

"So, at last I have located the future Mrs. Scott, the daughter of New York's most wealthy and influential Loyalist." Trager's husky words rolled over her, a mocking edge on his voice that attempted to and succeeded in annoying her.

Serena wheeled toward the sound, reluctantly noticing the way the moonlight danced on his raven head, keenly aware of his muscular physique, and aroused and agitated by his presence. "And I suppose you came to the ball this evening to beg money from my father," she retaliated, her tone matching his. "Did you intend to sweet-talk Olivia into asking my father for funds in your behalf, expecting him to invest in the rebuilding of your family's faltering fortune?"

Trager strode toward her, his silver eyes pinning her back against the terrace railing. "I do not depend on women to do my talking for me." His tone was sharp, slicing across her carefully controlled composure like a double-edged sword.

"So it *is* money you are after," she accused, bravely tilting her chin to meet his penetrating gaze. "I'm glad you didn't know who I was. You probably would have attempted to get to my father through me instead of his infidel wife."

"You're a witch, Serena, and your words are as vicious as a snake's bite," Trager growled as he roughly grabbed her to him. "You mistrusted my intentions from the beginning. I bought you this gown because I thought you owned nothing but rags." He scoffed bitterly down at her. "Little did I know that you could well afford to replace your entire wardrobe with gowns that would put my meager offering to shame."

"You gave me the gift to lure me into your bed," she snapped, wincing in pain as his lean fingers bit into the tender flesh of her arm.

"And you toyed with me behind your fiance's back," he countered, a tight smile thinning his lips. "So that was why you were window peeking that night. You wanted to see if Lieutenant Scott was playing your own game, as well. Where do you find the gall to criticize your stepmother when you flirt about the countryside, trying to attract *me* to amuse yourself?"

Serena reacted without giving the consequences a thought. Her hand cracked like thunder against his cheek, evoking an enraged growl from Trager. A tingle of fear flew down her spine as he glowered at her.

"And I have no doubt that you also seduced your young schoolmaster, enticing him to take the job so you can keep him at your beck and call on those lonely nights when your future husband has traipsed off to the brothel."

Serena was itching to strike him again, but she couldn't worm her hand from his viselike grip. Instead, she stood fuming, outraged by his slanderous remarks. He was putting her in the same class with Olivia, and Serena sorely resented it. No other insult could have cut so deeply.

"How dare you insult me, you worthless beggar. I

should have my father throw you out of this house," she hissed venomously, reminding Trager of a snake poised to strike.

"He isn't man enough, nor is your mealy-mouthed fiance," Trager smirked arrogantly.

"Let me go!" Serena railed, certain she would come unglued if he continued to hold her.

"Not yet, witch," he muttered as his head moved deliberately toward hers. "Not until I know if Scott's kisses affect you the same way mine do. Do you ache for him the same way you desire me when I hold you in my arms?"

Her denial and protest were muffled beneath his breathtaking kiss. Trager pulled her full length against him, crushing her breasts against the rock-hard wall of his chest. His racing pulse thundered against her bare flesh, beating in frantic rhythm with hers. Serena was set to deny the fact that he could set a fire blazing in her blood, but her body refused to acknowledge the lie, leaving her trembling in his encircling arms, her lips parting to allow his tongue free access to the recesses of her mouth.

Trager's hand slid along the trim column of her neck and then he tilted her head back, his eyes focused on her kiss-swollen lips. "So that is the reason you once asked me to kiss you as if I was madly in love with you," he speculated, his tone quietly insulting. "You were experimenting to see if Scott was man enough for you. He failed the test, didn't he, Rena?"

Serena gasped indignantly, annoyed that he had

uncovered her dark secret. And then his mouth slanted across hers, stripping her breath from her lungs. A white-hot fire shot through her as his hand dipped beneath the silk and lace to capture the taut peak of her breast. The ache of desire burned to her very core, and Serena despised herself for allowing him to affect her so. She didn't want to respond to his touch, to enjoy the feel of his sleek, muscular body pressed tightly to hers. She wanted to despise Trager and all he represented. But her body, as if it possessed a will of its own, moved closer to the flame that burned her inside and out, thrilling to the pleasures his caresses evoked. Serena cursed herself a thousand times as she surrendered to the sensations that rocked her sanity. It was humiliating enough that he realized that Brandon did not satisfy her, but for her to yield to his skillful embrace was a devastating blow to her pride. Lord, what strange magic did this man weave over her when he took her in his arms and kissed her with such penetrating thoroughness?

"What the devil is going on here?" Brandon halted abruptly when his gaze fastened on the embracing couple who stood among the shadows. Fury blazed in his eyes as he stalked toward them to drag Serena away from Trager. "This is my fiancée, and I will have no man molesting what is mine," he growled.

The faintest hint of a smile found the corner of Trager's mouth as he eyed the steaming lieutenant. "And you can have her." His tone was bland, showing no evidence that passion had gripped him moments earlier. Serena was amazed at his ability to turn his emotions off and on so quickly while she still wobbled and gasped for breath. "The two of you are a perfect match," Trager went on to say. There was an undertone of sarcasm in his remark that made both Brandon and Serena jerk their heads up.

"You will answer for your verbal and physical abuse, sir," Brandon snapped, his body trembling with rage.

One dark brow arched in wry amusement. "Are you suggesting a duel, Scott?" Trager chortled as he sauntered away and then paused to give Brandon the once over, finding nothing impressing or frightening about the man. "Forgive my bluntness, but if you are foolish enough to take arms against me, you will find yourself the recipient of a well-aimed bullet. What use would a cold corpse be to this hot-blooded vixen you intend to marry?"

His insult stung like salt on an open wound. Serena lunged at him, but Brandon hauled her back to his side, holding her in place while she entertained the idea of slitting his miserable throat.

"Keep your distance from Serena or you will regret it," Brandon challenged from a safe distance.

Trager studied the man who hid behind a woman's skirt and laughed out loud before he walked away, throwing his comment over his shoulder. "My only regret is that I didn't keep my distance from that fire-breathing witch in the first place. Save your empty threats, Scott. Like a bee, I know when a rose is void of nectar. I won't be back to be pricked by her thorns."

Serena was seeing red, furious crimson red, and she thirsted for blood—Trager's in particular. She was certain she would have reduced herself to smoldering cinders if she hadn't gotten a grip on herself that instant. If Brandon was such a coward that he wouldn't deck that arrogant scoundrel for insulting them, Serena would have to defend her own honor while Brandon, who possessed none, had no reason to feel intimidated. She twisted from Brandon's grasp and stormed up behind Trager, grabbing his arm to detain him.

"Grayson." Her tone was honey-coated and she surprised herself by refraining from shouting at him.

There were times when it was necessary to fight fire with fire and, by damn, Trager had lit her torch. When he arched a curious brow and turned back toward her, Serena gave him the sound portion of her fist and a good piece of her mind while she had his attention.

"Perhaps Brandon can endure your insults, but I cannot," she spat at him as she massaged her aching knuckles. It was a gratifying pain, one she could easily endure.

The blow to his jaw stunned him. He was shocked that Serena could pack such a wallop for one so petite. The stars circled his head as he stumbled back to keep his balance. He gazed down at her, his stinging jaw sagging in disbelief as he listened to the rest of her tirade.

"If you ever come near me again, you can expect the same type of reaction. The only kind of retaliation a cur like you deserves is a solid blow to the jaw. Perhaps it will knock some sense into you and you can remember to curb your own vicious tongue the next time you are tempted to slander someone's good name."

Serena peered back over her shoulder at Brandon, who still had not come to his own defense, glowered at Trager, and then gave them both a cold shoulder that was capped with ice. She swept back into the ballroom, pasting on an enchanting smile, pleased with herself for putting both men in their proper places.

Trager rubbed his sore jaw and grinned to himself as he watched Serena glide into her father's arms, waltzing across the room as if nothing out of the ordinary had happened. He shot a quick look to Brandon, who seemed to have swallowed his tongue along with a mouthful of teeth.

"If you think you are man enough to keep a tight rein on that honey-haired hellion you have selected for your wife, I suggest you reevaluate your capabilities and your marriage proposal," Trager advised before leaving Brandon to himself and his spinning thoughts.

"Where have you been?" Mitchell inquired of his daughter. "I thought you and Brandon would be dancing every dance."

"Papa, Brandon and I . . ." Serena strangled her words as Trager's towering figure appeared beside her father.

"Excuse me, Mitchell," Trager began with a

courteous smile. "I wanted to see if your charming daughter was lighter on her feet on the dance floor than she was on the stairs." A hint of mockery glinted in his eyes as his gaze slid to Serena momentarily, causing her to bristle like an angered cat.

Mitchell relinquished his hold on Serena, deposited her in Trager's arms, and returned his grin. "I think you will find that my daughter can follow your lead with little difficulty. She is a product of the British court, educated in England's finest finishing schools, and taught the technique of dance by private tutors," he boasted.

When Mitchell had bowed and taken his leave, Serena glared into the amused gray eyes that fell upon her in open appreciation. "Did you return to insult me?" she muttered, trying to control her volatile temper.

"Nay, Serena, I came to offer my apology." His words were soft, his grasp upon her becoming a light caress. When relief spread across her exquisite features, he added, "To you, but not to that uniformed milksop you intend to marry. He isn't good enough for you."

"And I suppose you think you are?" she smirked, her chin tilting to regard him closely.

He nodded affirmatively. "I daresay that I am more qualified to handle a little spitfire like you than Scott is," he insisted, offering a statement of fact rather than a boast.

"And fortunately for you *and* Brandon, I am in no need of a husband. I don't intend to marry Brandon.

I, too, have realized that I could not be content with him. The two of us have too many conflicting ideas."

Her words brought her more tightly against him, his manly fragrance encircling her senses, making her forget how furious she had been with him moments earlier.

"I am relieved to hear you still have your wits about you," Trager breathed as he nuzzled against the top of her silky blond head. He felt Serena wince and glanced up to see Brandon weaving his way through the crowd toward them. A wry smile parted his lips as he watched her stare at her now ex-fiance. "Would you prefer that I leave you alone to give Scott the heartbreaking news that he has just set a record for short engagements?"

Serena nodded mutely and then forced a smile as Trager retreated.

Brandon's fingers bit into her waist as he drew her into his arms. "If I ever witness another scene like the one I viewed on the terrace, I will deal very severely with you, Serena." His voice was low but threatening, rolling over her like thunder.

Serena did not appreciate his ultimatum, especially when he had bypassed the chance to pick on someone his own size. He chose to intimidate her rather than Trager, the man who had taken outrageous privileges with her. But Trager was right. Brandon was a milksop, and the longer he glared at her, the angrier she became.

"But you see nothing wrong with dallying with the trollops at the brothel," she flared, her green eyes spitting sparks hot enough to ignite a forest fire. "You have no right to criticize me for being in another man's embrace. You are a hypocrite, Brandon."

He gasped, recovered, and then leveled her a hard gaze. "You have been spying on me?" When she nodded affirmatively, Brandon cursed under his breath. "Your behavior is beneath contempt, Serena," he scolded.

"No more than yours," she countered, her tone as acid as his. "And I do not intend to . . ."

"Lieutenant, may I dance with your lovely fiancée?" Colonel Powell inquired, bringing quick death to what had every indication of becoming another revolutionary war.

Brandon wasted no time in depositing her in his superior's arms and then disappeared into the crowd, much to Serena's relief. Her gaze faltered on Olivia, who was turning her charm on Lawrence Hill, the colonel's aide. John's eyes followed hers and then he smiled when he noticed who had captured Serena's attention.

"Olivia is a disarmingly attractive woman," John remarked before focusing his undivided attention on Serena. "'Tis rare to find two such captivating women who bear the same name."

Serena displayed a wan smile, wondering if any man could resist Olivia's sultry beauty. Obviously the colonel, as well as his aide, were taken with Olivia. Serena could only hope that Olivia had taken her warning seriously when she had insisted that she would not set foot out of the house until Olivia had relinquished her lovers.

When several of the officers began to filter from the room, the colonel escorted Serena to the refreshment table and followed the flow to the study. Serena glanced over to see Anna Morgan standing like a wallflower, looking self-conscious and very out of place. It had been rude of her to leave Anna alone, but with all that had happened so quickly, Serena hadn't seen Anna arrive.

"Is that the best smile you can muster?" Serena teased as she edged up beside Anna. "This is supposed to be a celebration."

Anna's tension eased when she met Serena's lively expression. "But how would the rest of your guests feel if they realized that there was a Whig sympathizer in their midst?" she queried as she leaned close, taking care not to be overheard.

Her shoulder lifted in an unconcerned shrug. "Just don't talk politics with them if you wish to avoid being recognized." A mischievous grin caught one corner of Serena's mouth as her eyes flickered down the exquisite gown her friend was wearing. "You certainly do that dress more justice than I did," Serena admitted. "And you look very attractive, despite that apprehensive expression on your face. Do try to cheer up and enjoy yourself."

"And let me congratulate you on your engagement," Anna responded, forcing a wider smile, only to have it fade when she noticed the way Serena's face had fallen. "Is something amiss?"

"Aye," Serena admitted as she heaved a frustrated sigh. "I had intended to tell Brandon that I had serious misgivings about the marriage and that I did not want to make the announcement this evening, but he blurted out the news before I could stop him."

"Has someone else captured your attention?" Anna teased.

"Nay," Serena lied through her teeth, knowing that that someone was Trager Grayson, a man whom she detested and yet found devastatingly attractive.

Anna eyed her skeptically. "You are not speaking to some shallow officer's wife," she reminded Serena. "I have not forgotten our last conversation, when you informed me that the Devil was nipping at your heels."

Serena glanced uneasily about her, uncertain that she wanted to rehash that discussion, but Anna was fishing for information.

"It's that notorious-looking rake you were dancing with earlier," Anna predicted. "The one dressed in black velvet. He is a magnificent specimen." A taunting smile slid across her lips. "And don't tell me you hadn't noticed."

"I hadn't."

Anna laughed out loud and pointed an accusing finger, but carefully lowered her voice to continue, "I could feel the vibrations as I leaned against this wall, Rena. I saw the way the two of you were looking at each other."

"Those were murderous glares you misinterpreted," Serena protested, trying to sound indifferent, but Anna was quick to detect the edge in her voice.

Anna rolled her eyes and then sent Serena a withering glance. "Don't be so stubborn, Rena. Every other woman in the ballroom has been ogling him and whispering about his striking good looks. Even *I* will admit that the man has a certain charismatic charm that is impossible to ignore, and *I* wasn't dancing in his arms."

"Very well, I agree that he is dashing," Serena replied, her voice holding a hint of sarcasm. "Now, will you quit harassing me? I have more important matters on my mind besides falling head over heels for a rogue."

"Perhaps," Anna agreed, biting back a grin. "But all the same, the man is on your mind, and I would venture to guess that he has been since your accident." Her eyes flashed devilishly, making Serena uneasier by the minute. "Imagine my surprise when your father stopped by to thank me for allowing you to spend the night at my home when you were caught in the storm." The smile that Anna had carefully smothered burst free, blossoming on her lips when Serena swallowed her breath. "Not to worry, though." Anna patted Serena's trembling hand. "I covered for you. After all, that is what friends are for, as you once reminded me. I told your father that I enjoyed your company that stormy night, but it does leave one to wonder just where you managed to hide from the storm . . . and with whom."

Reluctantly, Serena allowed a sheepish smile to surface and she glanced at the far wall, averting her

CAROL FINCH

eyes from Anna's mocking gaze. "You always were a wizard at prying the truth from me," she said begrudgingly and then hastily added, "but nothing happened between us. Trager only tended my injury."

"The gallant knight rescued a lady in distress," Anna laughed, enjoying watching Serena fidget like a nervous cat. Never had she seen Serena go to such lengthy measures to protect her interest in a man. But then Serena had never found one to match her intelligence and high spirit, Anna reminded herself . . . until now. After observing the confident way Trager Grayson carried himself, Anna was willing to bet her hard earned money that Serena had been sorely tempted by that outrageously attractive dark-haired devil. "Your will power is very commendable."

Serena had endured as much taunting as she could stand. Although she enjoyed seeing Anna's face light up for the first time in a month, Serena wished it wasn't at her expense. And yet, Serena recalled the way she had unmercifully teased Anna when she returned from England to find her friend married to the same man to whom she had awarded a black eye and had sworn she would eternally detest.

"Don't press your luck *or* my good disposition, Cinderella," Serena warned, flashing Anna a sugar-coated smile. "If you don't get a tight rein on that tongue of yours, you might find yourself turned into a pumpkin before the stroke of midnight. I will inform Colonel Powell that there is a Whig in our midst and you will be tossed out on your ear."

146

Anna chuckled, her eyes dancing with mischievousness. "Your secret is safe with me and mine is safe
with you. Forgive me for teasing you, but I couldn't
resist. I feel more reckless and alive than I have in
ages." Her expression sobered. "I meant no harm,
Rena. You know that. I count you as one of my
dearest friends."

"All is forgiven." Serena offered a peace-treaty
smile and fondly squeezed Anna's hand. "Just don't
harp on the subject of Trager Grayson. I have
another matter that requires immediate attention."

As Serena picked up the front of her skirt to walk
away, Anna touched her arm to detain her. "I think
you have made a wise decision. I don't think Brandon
is the right man for you."

Serena had heard that once too often that night,
but the comment did not rile her when Anna made it.
"And I'm not certain that there is one on all of God's
green earth who is suited for me," Serena admitted
with sudden sobriety. "I have yet to find a man with a
skimpy list of faults."

There was a merry twinkle in Anna's eye. "But one
never knows when she will find love staring her right
in the face."

"While you hold up this wall, dreaming up clever
quips, I think I will see to this business of disengag-
ing myself from one Lieutenant Brandon Scott,"
Serena insisted before sweeping across the room.

Chapter Nine

Serena positioned herself by the door of the study, hoping to draw Brandon's attention, but she was caught up in the conversation about the events of the war. The colonel had informed his captive audience that General Howe and his troops had taken Harlem Heights that very afternoon and had sent Washington and his so-called army of Patriots retreating north with their tails tucked between their legs.

Colonel Powell eased back in his chair and sipped his brandy, his smile fading as another thought crossed his mind. "Although we have routed this unorganized force, we still must contend with marauders who have been antagonizing us. The legendary Captain Montclaire has been ransacking our coast, destroying ammunition and supply houses." John sniffed distastefully and squirmed in his seat. "I have put a high price on his head, but we have gained very little information about him, and he is as elusive as the shadows. How he continues to sneak past our watch points and destroy our supplies has me baffled." His gaze strayed to the door to see Serena hanging on his every word. "Is there something you wanted, my dear?" he inquired as he twisted around in his high-backed chair.

She had intended to speak with Brandon until she became engrossed in the conversation. "Nay," she informed him with a charming smile. "I was only interested in what you were saying."

"We are talking politics," Brandon insisted, his irritation mounting on top of an already smoldering pile. "I think you should join the women."

That did it! Serena's finely tempered patience snapped. "Am I to understand that you gentlemen do not think a woman to be intelligent enough to talk politics?" Her voice dripped heavily with sarcasm as her gaze circled and paused on each face.

Colonel Powell offered her a patronizing smile that burned Serena to the quick. It reminded her of the expressions that Brandon had a nasty habit of bestowing on her when he attempted to brush her off without being offensively rude.

"We do not mean to insult you, Miss Warren," the colonel said carefully, watching a spark of irritation ignite in her emerald eyes. "But these are matters that would only clutter your lovely head."

Serena drew herself up and strolled into the room, her eyes recircling the group of clustered officers. "I do not appreciate the antiquated logic that a woman's purpose or her mental capacities do not exceed menial household management, that she is incapable of making important decisions or voicing her opinions on matters of state." Serena was gathering steam, fueled by the shocked faces of her captive audience. Only one face among them did not register surprise at her outburst. Trager sat calmly in his chair, sipping his drink, a wry smile hovering on his lips. "I do not appreciate being shooed away as if I had no right to listen or interject an occasional comment."

"Serena, that is quite enough!" Brandon snapped as he bolted to his feet. He felt it his obligation to silence her, to put her in her proper place, since she was his fiancée. "You are meddling in men's affairs."

She smirked and then pounced on his choice of words. "*Men's* affairs? I assure you that war affects women as well as men, Brandon. The whole lot of you leave me to wonder if the Patriots do have a very reasonable complaint. You seek to stifle and exclude them, just as you intend to cast me off because I am a woman. You intend to make your decisions and then force your opinions on me without allowing me a voice. The Crown has treated the colonies with the same inconsideration, making them bear the burden of taxes, oppressing them as if they were slaves. Perhaps if the shoe was on the other foot, you noble gentlemen would feel the pinch."

"Serena, mind your tongue!" Mitchell gasped, certain he was about to suffer his first heart seizure. He knew Serena would never hesitate to spout off if she witnessed an injustice, but he had not expected her to carry the matter to such extremes. "If you were not among friends your words might well be considered blasphemous.''

Although Serena realized that she had waded in way over her head, she felt that what she had said needed to be voiced. She had a mind of her own and she did not appreciate being ostracized as if she suffered from the plague.

When Brandon stalked toward her, his face darkening in a scowl, Serena held up her hand to halt his advance. ''And before you chastise me, I wish to inform you that our marriage is off. You need not feel embarrassed. You have not been castrated in front of your fellow officers.'' Her smile was all too innocent, her tone so sweet that it took a moment for her sugar-coated remark to take effect.

A delayed gasp erupted from the group of men, but Serena didn't care. The time had come for her to declare her own independence, and she was anxious to be rid of Brandon and his narrowminded opinions, once and for all. ''You need not assume responsibility for me, Brandon. I am quite capable of defending myself. As a matter of fact you have continued to overlook that point since the beginning of our relationship. You made a serious mistake by asking for my hand and I made a gross error in judgment, thinking I could portray the empty-headed doll you wanted for a wife.'' Serena curtsied graciously and blessed the group with a blinding smile. ''Good evening, gentlemen.''

Jaws were swinging from their hinges as Serena swept out of the room. Serena was certain she could have heard a pin drop and it would have sounded like a ton of lead falling through the floor. Brandon was hot on her heels, breathing fire down her neck when he caught her arm and spun her around to face his angry snarl.

"I swear you have taken leave of your senses," he growled furiously. "You'll be sorry you humiliated me, Serena."

Her chin tilted courageously, a mocking gleam in her eyes. "I doubt it," she disputed. "I will be gloating over it, Brandon. You are a lily-livered sap who has done his best to keep from defending his beliefs. You would have been perfectly content to let the British do your fighting for you. If the Patriots had been the stronger force I would not be the least bit surprised to see you swayed toward their convictions, thinking you could sit idly by without becoming directly involved in the skirmishes."

Brandon's scowl blackened like the dark clouds of a threatening thunderstorm. Infuriated, he backhanded her across the face, sending her reeling. "Damn, you little bitch!" he hissed. "I wish your father could have seen the folly of sending you to those fancy finishing schools. Now you think yourself high and mighty. I fear your father has created a monster." Brandon wagged a lean finger in her face as she brushed her hand over her stinging cheek. "Don't think you have heard the last from me, Serena. Only out of respect for your father do I resist the temptation of wringing your damned neck."

As Brandon wheeled away and stalked back to the study to reinstate his good name, Serena flew toward the door before she burst into tears. Damn that man and damn her for losing her temper and allowing her tongue to run away with itself. What a mess she had made of things. The entire evening had been a nerve-wracking journey in which one catastrophe led into another.

When she stepped onto the porch she let her breath out in a rush, brushed back the tears, and attempted to maintain her composure. Her eyes flew to the stables, and impulsively she walked down the steps to order her stallion saddled.

Serena swung onto Sandpiper's back, determined to forget the scene that kept flashing before her eyes. She had made her point with the British officers, but, no doubt, it would cost her dearly. Her father rarely raised his voice with her, but she had the uncomfortable feeling that she would be forced to listen to Mitchell rant and rave before the sun shamefully raised its head the following morning. If she was lucky, the world would come to an end before the night was out and she would be spared his wrath.

After a reckless ride, Serena drew her winded steed to a halt and hopped to the ground to stare across the quiet cove. The moonbeams skipped across the water's surface, and Serena was hypnotized by the pacifying setting that spread before her. The temptation was too great and Serena yielded to the impulsive urge to cleanse her soul. In a matter of minutes she had shed her gown and waded into the cove, breathing a sigh of relief. Laughter bubbled from her lips, remembering the stricken look on Brandon's face when she had pegged him as a coward. Although she had intended to put him in his place, she hadn't meant to verbally crucify him in front of his superior officers. But then, her irritation had snowballed into an avalanche. Ah well, she rationalized, giving the matter a moment's consideration, it was best that Colonel Powell realized that he had gained no prize by enlisting Brandon's services. He couldn't sniff his way out of a feed sack. What use could he have been to the British as a scout? The thought of Brandon, a gun-shy weasel, ducking into the brush and then turning tail at the first sign of trouble brought another round of uproarious laughter sailing across the cove as she splashed in the water. Washington's key weapon was having Lieutenant Brandon Coward Scott on the Redcoats' side.

The sound of cracking twigs made Serena swivel her head around, searching the shadows for an intruder. A tall silhouette appeared among the brush and moved deliberately toward her, and Serena relaxed when she recognized Trager's face. The moonlight sprayed across his handsome features, his devilish smile glowing in the darkness.

"Have you come to lecture me on my abominable behavior, Mr. Grayson?" she inquired before he could open his mouth to utter a word. "Save your breath. I know my remarks were outrageous, but once I started I simply could not stop myself." Serena chortled again, her reckless laughter flowing toward him like the incoming tide.

He strode to the water's edge to bow before her. "I

CAROL FINCH

have come to praise Caesar, not to bury him," Trager
assured her, his own laughter lifting to be carried out
with the breeze.

Her brow quirked, a curious smile hovering on her
lips as she appraised his muscular physique. "You
do not share their opinion that a woman's place is in
the bedroom and kitchen and never in political
gatherings?"

"I have never been one to dictate to a woman, but I
would have advised you to use discretion had I
known you intended to mortify the British officers,"
he pointed out, his gaze wandering over her exquisite face. "I am left to wonder if you have disturbed a
den of rattlesnakes."

One bare shoulder lifted in a shrug. "Perhaps I
have, but at least I am rid of Brandon Scott. It always
did take a bright flare to gain the man's attention."

"I think Colonel Powell's opinion of Scott
dropped a notch. I heard his aide remark that Scott
would not be a valuable asset to the cause if he could
not even control his woman."

"Then my outrageous tantrum has served a useful
purpose," Serena murmured as she leisurely swam a
wide circle. "Powell has seen Brandon for what he
really is."

A long, silent moment passed while Serena continued her midnight swim. "Are you coming out?"
Trager questioned impatiently.

"Nay," Serena breathed contentedly. "'Tis far too
enjoyable to think of coming ashore."

The rustling of clothes drew her puzzled frown and

156

she gasped when she glanced back to see Trager's sleek, virile body emerge from the shadows. Serena knew the proper thing for her to do was turn her head, but her gaze was glued to Trager, admiring his muscular body. Mesmerized, she watched him move toward her, her heart pounding so furiously that it sent ripples across the water.

"Trager, keep your distance," Serena warned when she finally came to her senses. "I'm not wearing a stitch and you're . . ."

It was too late. His arms encircled her waist, molding his hard body to hers. His familiar touch set her on fire, and Serena feared that steam would be rising from the water at any moment.

"When a sea siren calls, a man cannot refuse the temptation," Trager rasped before his lips captured hers in a searing kiss.

Nor could *she* resist the feel of his hands on her bare flesh or the rakish smile that hung on one corner of his mouth when he lifted his raven head. Serena was in a reckless mood, and her merry giggle erupted from beneath another scalding kiss.

"Have you no shame, sir? Your reputation will be ruined if anyone discovers that you are consorting with me."

Trager traced a lean finger over her flawless features, hypnotized by the mischievous sparkle in her eyes. "Damn, but you're tempting." A sudden frown plowed his brow when the moonlight illuminated the bruise on her left cheek. "Did Scott do this?"

"Aye, but it doesn't matter," she insisted as she

looped her arms around Trager's neck, toying with the damp hair that curled at its nape. "I suppose I had it coming after I called him a lily-livered coward to his face."

"It matters to me," Trager muttered angrily. "Now I wish I had accepted his challenge. I would derive excessive pleasure from putting a bullet through his heart."

"It would have been a waste of good ammunition," she replied with a careless shrug. "There is no need for you to feel obligated to avenge my honor. After my outburst tonight, I fear I have very little left." A guilty smile traced her lips as she met his solemn gaze. "And I fear I have foiled any chance you might have had of obtaining a contribution from my father for your business venture. He will be in no mood to discuss finances after I have shamed him."

"Then I shall be forced to extract payment from your lovely hide," he insisted, flashing her another roguish grin.

Serena brazenly returned his smile and then realized that love *was* staring her right in the face. Aye, that was the emotion that had been playing havoc with her thoughts these past few weeks. She had fought those feelings like a trooper, but to no avail. Trager stirred something in her that she had never realized existed. The sensations had been unfamiliar and she had denounced them, trying to dislike his confident manner. But it was no use. She had never been so drawn to a man, never ached to feel those passionate sensations until Trager had come into her life.

Her lips parted in invitation, knowing that she had stepped so far out on a limb that night that she could not avoid the fall. It seemed to follow that she should yield to the tantalizing feel of his embrace. It was sinfully wicked to be standing waist deep in water, clinging to a man who was wearing the same suit he was born in, but the Devil had been sitting on her shoulder all evening, and Serena had already allowed him to have his way with her.

"Make love to me, Trager," she whispered. "Teach me the meaning of passion. Show me the ways of lovers."

Trager drew far enough away to stare into her exquisite face, bewildered by her request. "Do you know what you're saying?" he cross-examined her, having one hell of a time controlling the overwhelming desire to ravish her without giving her the opportunity to withdraw her brash proposition.

Her laughter tickled his senses, sending a rash of goose pimples skitting across his skin, intensifying his need of her. "Strangely enough, I do," she assured him as her index finger traced the chiseled lines of his face.

"And you will not claim that you have been unjustly abused when the dawn reflects new light?" he persisted. Trager was between a rock and a hard spot. If Serena awoke in the morning regretting their tryst, Trager might feel the whip on his back when Serena informed her father that she had been seduced in a vulnerable moment. But Lord, if he couldn't appease this maddening craving for this enchanting vixen, he would be suffering in his own private room in hell.

Her brow had a mocking tilt as she regarded him for a quiet moment. "Do you think I would point an accusing finger at you and then declare that you took advantage of me?" She chortled softly and gave her head a denying shake. "Nay, my handsome rogue, you will not suffer because of me, and I ask no more than tonight. You are free to go your own way without fearing that I will make unreasonable demands on you." Although she realized that she had fallen in love with Trager, she knew that he did not return her affection and that she, in good conscience, could expect no more of him.

"You have made me an offer I cannot refuse," he murmured huskily.

His hand wandered freely over her hips and his kisses traced a searing path to the peak of her breast. Serena felt her heart catapult to her throat and then tumble down to hammer against her ribs as his tongue teased the taut peak. His touch wove a black-magic spell over her, scattering logic, making her ache to know the complete fulfillment of his love-making.

Trager scooped her up in his arms and carried her to shore, his eyes anchored on her, studying the expression on her face. Her lashes swept up to see the desire that burned like liquid silver in his eyes. She smiled softly as she traced her finger over his high cheekbones and then followed the crows' feet that sprayed along his face. Her hand fanned across the rock-hard wall of his chest and then wandered over his hip, reveling in the strange new emotions that crept in from the shadows of her heart. The sensation exceeded physical attraction, and Serena knew that love had molded itself around her soul.

As he stretched out beside her on their discarded clothes, Serena held his unwavering gaze. "Love me as if there were no tomorrow, as if I were the only woman you have ever held in your arms."

It was a vain request and she knew it, but she wanted their moment together to be more than two people appeasing passion, more than physical attraction.

Trager peered into her face, his expression solemn. "Touching you burns away all other memories, as if no other woman existed. I have been obsessed with taking you since I first saw you," he murmured huskily.

His mouth lightly caressed hers, drinking fully of her response, losing himself to the heady sensations that swam around him. A muffled groan intermingled with the sounds of night as he rediscovered every exquisite inch of her body. His hand trailed from the peak of her breast to her trim waist and then descended to her thighs, leaving quivering sensations in the wake of his exploring touch.

Serena felt herself sinking as if she were melting into a soft, puffy cloud. His caresses were like a massage, releasing the nervous tension, leaving her pliant and responsive. For that moment in time, nothing mattered except the feel of his hands on her flesh. It was sweet torment, and Serena sighed as his caresses found each sensitive point, making her body tingle with anticipation. And he continued to arouse her to the point of reckless frenzy, his hands flowing over her flesh until she arched to meet his seeking hand. She was aching and breathless, yearning to satisfy the burning desire that splintered her sanity.

"Rena . . ." His voice trembled with a passion that threatened to blaze out of control.

"I want you." Serena drew his dark head to hers, hungry for his kiss, but as his hard body covered hers, parting her thighs with his muscled hips, she gasped and tensed beneath him.

His soft, reassuring words eased the pain, and she relaxed as his skillful caresses glided over her buttocks. He moved within her, slowly at first, but Trager could no longer control his maddening need. He plunged deeply within her, releasing the emotions that surfaced like smoldering lava. Her body moved in rhythm with his as passion's fire spread through her veins. She couldn't think; she could only respond to the wondrous sensations that consumed her. She was living and dying, skyrocketing toward the distant stars without leaving the secure circle of his arms.

And then they were gripped by indescribable senstions. He was a part of her, touching her heart and soul, as if their separate identities were lost in that split second that pursued and captured time. Serena discovered a world that defied reality. It was like a forbidden dream that she had never imagined existed. It was a long, breathless moment before she drifted down from her lofty perch, still warm and intoxicated by the rapturous pleasure of his lovemaking. Serena gazed up at the sea of stars, knowing she had touched each one and was now content to remain in his arms. As Trager drew a ragged breath and rolled beside her, Serena glanced at his shadowed face, a puzzled look in her eyes.

"Trager?" Her voice held a hint of question, but for the life of her, she couldn't remember what she had intended to say. At the moment, murmuring his name was enough.

His arm slid beneath her breast as he drew his knees up behind hers and cuddled against her. A low chuckle erupted from his chest as he rested his chin on her shoulder. "I have been living with the misconception that lovemaking required two experienced partners. Again I find myself eating crow, witch." His lips found the pulsations of her neck and he sighed contentedly. Her innocent response had driven him to the brink of insanity, amazing and satisfying him. "This exquisite body of yours was made for love. You have the power to tempt a man and drive him mad with desire."

A mischievous smile caught one corner of her mouth as she squirmed to her back to peer up at his chiseled face. "Then show me some proof of your words," she challenged.

Trager swallowed his breath. "Again . . . now?" He rolled his eyes in disbelief. "Brazen wench," he chided playfully. "Have you no shame? First you shock the Redcoats, and now you are attempting to seduce me for the second time tonight."

Serena enjoyed taunting him. For once she had turned the tables on him. Her hand wandered across the bronzed lines of his face and then trailed down the dark furring on his chest as she blessed him with a provocative smile. "Are you refusing me? Perhaps I should search elsewhere for a man who can satisfy me."

"I doubt that any mortal man can keep this witch content, except the Devil himself," he smirked as he brought her hand to his lips.

"I had guessed you to be Satan, disguising himself in the form of a man," Serena mocked lightly.

Abruptly, Trager pulled her to her feet and led her to the shore, his arm gesturing to draw her attention to the water's surface, which glowed like silver in the moonlight. "The river Styx," he informed her with a husky chortle. "Come my wicked witch, 'tis time we cleansed this evil from your soul and took you home."

"I don't want to go home," Serena said whimsically, her gaze drifting with the waves that curled toward shore to erase their footprints.

Trager leaned close to her ear, his breath caressing her cheek. "Am I to understand that you have used me as a distraction?"

"Would you be incensed if I admitted that to be true?" Serena inquired, knowing she was not about to tell the dashing rake that she had lost her heart and head in a moment of recklessness.

His hand slid around her waist as he led her into the water, his smile broadening to show even white teeth. "Nay, I was happy to accommodate you." His dark brow lifted suggestively. "And do not hesitate to summon me again when you desire distraction."

Their careless laughter floated away in the breeze as they sank into the water, boldly touching each other in the familiar ways of lovers, sharing kisses that threatened to burn out of control even though they were submerged in the stream.

Beneath the low-hanging branches, a figure lurked in the shadows. A pair of discerning eyes narrowed while Serena and Trager embraced in the moonlight, oblivious to all that transpired about them. Silently, the silhouette retreated without making a sound to alert the couple to the fact that they had been watched.

Finally, Trager mustered the will to emerge from the cove and don his clothes. He would have been content to spend the night with this intriguing wench. She had amazed him with her daring remarks to the British and pleased him with her unequaled passions. Trager had foolishly thought that once he had possessed her, the obsession of conquering her would be satiated. But he had sorely misjudged his reaction. Serena left him hungering for more.

When he had fastened the stays of her gown, he slipped his arms around her, pulling her back against him. All playfulness evaporated when the fresh, clean scent of her captured his senses, and he began having serious misgivings about taking her home.

"Serena, I want you to come away with me."

A frown knitted her brow as she glanced up at him. "Are you planning to leave?" Her voice held a hint of disappointment.

He nodded slightly. "I have obligations that need my attention."

And she had obligations here, she thought to herself. Did he expect her to drop everything and follow him, becoming his paramour until he tired of her? Pride made her tilt her chin. Although she loved him, she was not foolish enough to think Trager felt any deep emotions for her. He spoke of want and need, but he was not the type of man to become involved in tangled affairs.

"Tonight just happened, Trager. Nothing has changed. I still intend to find a man to whom I can profess my love, and who returns my deep affection. I cannot change who and what I am, and I have no intention of becoming your temporary harlot."

"These are troubled times," Trager coaxed. "Tomorrow is uncertain. I have always followed the philosophy that a man and woman must take pleasure where they find it without attaching strings."

Serena stepped away and stared off into the distance. "And I seek a lasting love that can withstand even war and destruction. When the world crumbles and falls at my feet, I want one lifeline to cling to." She turned to face Trager's hard expression. "You and I are like two ships passing in the night. When the dawn comes we will go our separate ways, doing what we must to survive. Perhaps you can trip from one shallow affair to another, but I cannot."

"You're too damned stubborn for your own good," he muttered as he shrugged on his jacket. "And you are clinging to childish dreams, Serena. I have yet to find a love that masters storms at sea or the tortures of war," he added cynically.

"Perhaps that is because you are not wise enough to admit that love can make you stronger when you do not have to stand alone," she parried, issuing him a challenge.

"Admitting to loving a woman is a weakness," Trager argued in a pessimistic tone. "Once a man allows a woman to occupy his thoughts, he endangers his cause. Love distracts a clear-thinking man, and he falls to the wayside to wither and die."

"And I suppose you imagine yourself to be a man of purpose," Serena sniffed caustically. "I would have labeled you as a wandering vagabond who travels where the wind takes him."

A wry smile pursed his lips as he offered her the reins to her stallion. "It is apparent that you and I do not see eye to eye, either."

"Nay, we do not," Serena agreed as she pulled into the saddle and then looked down her nose at him, wishing she hadn't surrendered to him in a moment

167

of weakness. She would probably live to regret her folly. "Goodbye, Trager. I think it wise that we part company here and now."

"Serena?" Trager grabbed the rein before she could gallop away and then stared her straight in the eye. "I won't be back again. Perhaps 'tis for the best that we forget this night existed."

A haughty smile grazed her lips as she tugged on the reins and turned Sandpiper toward home. "'Tis already forgotten. I doubt that I will even remember your name when dawn comes to clear my head."

Trager could not name the cause of the spark of irritation that chipped at his temper, but he was aware of its existence as he marched up to detain Serena. "I will not be easily forgotten," he insisted. "I was the first man to teach you the ways of passion, and you will find yourself comparing others to me." A wry smile hung on one corner of his mouth as he gained control of his composure and continued in a tone that lost its unpleasant edge. "When another man takes you in his arms it will be *my* face that materializes before you. And you will hunger for *my* kisses, Serena."

Her chin tilted a notch higher and she sniffed derisively. "My, but you are arrogant. You may have been the first, but you won't be the last. It would have made no difference who followed me here tonight, I would have surrendered." Childish vengeance spurred her words, seeking to chisel away at his self-confidence. "It could even have been Brandon or the colonel's aide. You see, tonight I was no more particular about who satisfied my needs than you are. I had a taste of your way of life, and now I know for certain that I want no part of it."

Trager flinched as if she had slapped him across the cheek and he stood frozen to the spot as she galloped away. Damn that ornery witch. Why had he allowed her to creep beneath his skin? She was nothing but trouble, a vixen who could stir each and every one of his emotions, leaving him simmering like a pot of stew on an open fire. Trager growled under his breath and stalked toward his horse, determined to forget Serena Warren existed. But then, as his eyes strayed to the silhouette that disappeared into the night, he was haunted by her bewitching smile and the way the moonlight had glistened in her emerald eyes. His mouth tingled as if she had pressed her sensuous lips to his, offering herself to him, taking more from him than he had intended to give.

His eyes turned to chips of granite as he aimed himself toward New Rochelle. She was only a woman, he told himself. And he would make no attempt to see her again. The vow seemed empty, and Trager was thoroughly disgusted with himself for tampering with her. He was not in the habit of deflowering virgins, and that minx had been armed with thorns. The man who married Serena Warren was letting himself in for a taste of hell, Trager decided. She possessed a passion the likes of which he had never known, but her words had a vicious under-bite. Aye, it would take a strong-willed man to conquer that little spitfire, and he had not the time or patience to tame her. Let some other fool hobble her.

Serena breathed a sigh of relief when she turned to the house to find that the hall had emptied and most of the guests were in the ballroom. As she started up the steps, Olivia appeared above her, wearing her prim and proper smirk. Serena squared her shoulders, lifted the front of her skirt, and moved toward her room, but Olivia blocked her path.

"The gossip is buzzing after the outrageous scene you made." Olivia looked down her nose at her stepdaughter. "Really, Serena, I would never have believed you could have stooped so low."

"Oh?" Serena forced a shallow smile that did not reach her eyes. "Why should it surprise someone like you, Olivia?" Her gaze ran the full length of her stepmother, a hint of contempt following in its wake. "You have not only stooped, but you have found yourself flat on your back. I consider adultery far worse than voicing one's opinion."

Olivia's hazel eyes snapped fury, her lips curling maliciously. "You little bitch, I have had my fill of your accusations."

Finally, Serena had broken Olivia's cool facade. Her hateful sneer fit her better than her presumptuous smiles, Serena thought to herself. "And I think it hypocritical for the pot to be calling the kettle

170

black," Serena parried as she brushed past Olivia, leaving her smoldering and cursing under her breath.

Serena barely had time to catch her breath before she was assaulted by her father, who waited in the hall. Had she known she would have to storm the manor and fight her way to her room, she would have used the tunnel.

"I want to speak to you, young lady." A disapproving frown plowed Mitchell's brow as he grasped Serena's arm and propelled her into her room.

Serena averted her gaze, studying the thick carpet beneath her feet, as if something had suddenly drawn her attention. "Papa, I'm sorry I behaved so badly. I don't know what devil possessed me, but I regret that I allowed my tongue to outdistance my brain."

When she finally peered up at him, Mitchell's frown transformed itself into a look of concern. "What happened to your face?"

"Brandon struck me," she murmured as he carefully inspected her bruised cheek.

Mitchell gasped incredulously, his eyes as wide as silver dollars. "Why?"

"Because I called him a coward," she admitted.

Her father grinned in spite of himself. "I had begun to notice that flaw, but I attempted to overlook it. Ever since I recommended him to Colonel Powell, Brandon has been dragging his feet. I am beginning to think he would rather someone else fight his battles."

171

"Aye," Serena agreed as she touched her tender cheek. "Until it comes to abusing women. Then he prefers to see to the matter himself."

"And I cannot stand by and watch you suffer. Perhaps I do not know the young lieutenant as well as I thought."

"Nay, you don't," Serena was quick to affirm. "I could spout a list of odd quirks that he possesses."

"Well, the matter is over and done." Mitchell strolled toward the door and leaned heavily upon it. "And I have only a few words of advice to offer on the other incident." His gaze was somber as he stared at his daughter. "Although I admire your spirit, 'tis not wise to voice such strong opinions with the Redcoats. You have ruffled their feathers and one day you might need a favor from them. If you bite the hand that feeds you, the British will be hesitant to offer protection and assistance."

Serena did not argue the point. She had said more than enough for one night. As she sank down on the bed her thoughts strayed to Trager and his curse. First loves were not easily forgotten, but she was determined to do so. Someday there would be another man to take his place, one who would erase his memory, the feel of his strong arms about her, the taste of his drugging kisses. And tomorrow would be the first day of the rest of her life, she told herself. She had declared her own proclamation of independence, and she began to understand the feeling of pride that filled the Patriots' hearts and bolstered their spirits. No man would call himself her master, and certainly not that arrogant rake, Trager Grayson.

As Serena stretched out in the darkness, his taunt came to haunt her. A pair of silver-gray eyes formed above her, glowing with passion and then sparkling with amusement. What was so intriguing about him? What made him so different from all the others? Serena took the time to analyze him, hoping his flaws would surface, like cream coming to the top. Nothing fazed him. He was calm and confident, in command of every situation.

Serena flounced in bed, seeking a more comfortable position. If only Trager wasn't so damned handsome, if only his kisses did not ignite a wildfire in her blood. But he wasn't the only fish in the sea, she reminded herself. Other men would make her yearn to rediscover passion. Trager would not be back again, and she must forget what they had shared, as if the moment had never existed. The exquisite feelings that had consumed her when they were one, touching the distant stars, would fade . . . Serena squeezed back the thought as a tingle of pleasure flew up and down her spine. She was going about this all wrong. Trager Grayson? He was just a man. He had no special powers over her. Serena smiled to herself and fluffed her pillow. This was more to her liking. By dawn she would barely recall his name. Tomorrow . . . she mused drowsily. The bright light of day would come to outshine the memories and erase the shadows of the night when she had surrendered to an emotion she should never have experienced in the first place. She had made a mistake, but she would put the past behind her and begin again, careful not to make the same error twice. She would profit from her experience instead of dwelling on past mistakes, she mused as she yielded to the darkness that hovered about her.

While Serena relaxed in slumber, Trager sat upon his bed at the inn with a half-emptied bottle of brandy as company. A dark scowl was stamped on his handsome face as he raised his glass to throw down another drink. His eyes took on a faraway look as he stared at the opposite wall. He had gone directly to the brothel to seek out a wench who could satisfy him, but the moment he took her in his arms, her dark hair had become sun-kissed tendrils of gold, her eyes a mysterious shade of green that could not disguise Serena's lively spirit. Trager had been shocked by the lingering vision and had cast the wench aside, fleeing from her room as if the Devil himself was nipping at his heels. Now he sat alone in his chamber, detesting the haunting silence and the vision that kept emerging from the bare wall. How dare that little hellion deny that their moonlight tryst would hold any special memory. *He* was the one who could turn his emotions off and on as easily as snuffing out a candle.

Through blurry eyes Trager grasped the neck of the bottle, wishing it was Serena who dangled from his hand. He was tempted to choke the life from her for informing him that it would have made little difference who made love to her. The thought burned its way to his very core. Trager sloshed another drink into his glass and scowled as it overflowed, dripping on the crotch of his breeches. Dispensing with the glass, Trager turned up the bottle and chugged the brandy, choking as it burned its way to his belly. He would drown the thought of that captivating vixen, he vowed to himself.

When the quiet rap on the door reached his ears, Trager muttered at the interruption and wove his way across the room, feeling he was moving in slow motion, numbed by the effects of the liquor, but still not immune to the effects of Serena.

Roger Grayson sized up his older brother, who stood propped against the door. His raven hair was tousled, his shirt gaped to reveal the dark furring on his chest, and his pants were noticeably stained. Roger grinned amusedly as he studied the man he had looked up to all of his life. At that moment, Roger found very little to admire. Trager looked as if he had tangled with a grizzly bear and lost.

"May I come in?" Roger sauntered into the room without waiting for a reply.

"Do I have a choice?" Trager grumbled as his brother parked himself in the chair and raised his amused gaze.

Roger bit back a grin as Trager started across the room and stubbed his toe on the nightstand, knocking himself off balance. Trager cursed under his breath as he sprawled on the bed and slopped brandy in his face. When Roger guffawed, Trager flashed him a silencing glare, but his brother refused to take the hint.

"I think perhaps you have had enough to drink for one night." Roger reached over to retrieve the bottle that dangled precariously between Trager's thumb and finger. "I expected you to be hugging a woman rather than a brandy."

His remark did not set well with Trager. "When I want your advice I'll ask for it," he snapped harshly.

Roger shrugged off the rebuke and took a small sip of brandy to wash away the dust from his throat. "I brought news that might interest you . . . that is, if you are sober enough to comprehend it." He arched a quizzical brow and waited for Trager to prop himself into a sitting position.

"Out with it, Serena," Trager commanded tersely.

"Serena?" Roger did a double take. "Who the hell is Serena?"

Trager scowled sourly at his slip of the tongue. "A witch. Now tell me what you have come to say. I'm ill-tempered tonight."

A wry smile caught one corner of Roger's mouth as he surveyed his disheveled brother who sat upon his crumpled throne. "I think I would prefer to hear about this witch who has cast her spell upon you," he taunted.

Trager heaved an impatient sigh. "I'm waiting, little brother. What is so damned important that it could not wait until tomorrow's meeting?"

Roger resigned himself to the fact that he would be unable to pry information from Trager. But then, that didn't surprise him. Trager had always been close-mouthed, revealing little of his thoughts. "I fear my news is not pleasant and it will not improve your disposition."

As Trager eased back against the headboard of the bed, he listened to the information. And Roger was correct. The news did nothing to ease his sour mood.

Chapter Ten

As the children filed from the schoolhouse, Serena released a sigh and gathered her books. Life was back to normal after the ball the previous weekend. Brandon had left with Colonel Powell and his aide, Lawrence Hill. Mitchell had forgiven her impudence and she had seen nothing of Trager, but then she hadn't expected to. And Serena and Olivia were tolerating each other, avoiding any confrontation.

Serena smiled secretively as she stepped outside to catch sight of the man who was propped against the outer wall of the school. When Nathan glanced at her, Serena displayed a wider smile.

"I thought I had seen the last of you," she remarked as she walked past him to place her armload of books in the buggy.

"And I thought you would be relieved to be rid of me," he speculated as he fell into step behind her.

Serena cast him a reproachful frown. "Certainly not, Nathan. I count you as a dear friend. You know that."

Nathan took her hand and placed an affectionate kiss to her wrist. As he rose to full stature, he winked down at her. "One of your *many* gentleman friends," he added with a chuckle.

"Not as many as you think," she retorted. "I seem to be one of those women who repels rather than attracts men." Her lashes swept down and she smiled sheepishly. "I have been accused of having a razor-sharp tongue when I am angered."

"Have you had a falling out with the mysterious man in your life?" Nathan pried. "Who is this rake who has captured your heart?"

Her emotions were masked behind a carefully blank stare. "There is no light and love in my life," she said simply.

Nathan flashed her a skeptical grin. "I may not be as astute as other men, but I can see through that lie," he insisted.

Serena heaved a sigh. Perhaps she could rid her thoughts of Trager if she talked of him with Nathan. "Aye, there is a man . . . was a man," she corrected as she toyed with the sleeve of her gown. "But Trager and I . . ."

Nathan's head jerked up. "Trager?" he broke in before she could finish her sentence.

"Trager Grayson. Do you know him?" Serena frowned quizzically at the odd expression that surfaced on Nathan's face.

He stared off into the distance. "Aye." His voice was low and he seemed very preoccupied with his thoughts. "I met him a few weeks ago."

"So did I." Serena was striving for an indifferent tone. "He was also a guest at the ball when I startled the British officers."

Nathan chuckled, recalling the story she had given him. "And you thought Grayson to be a very striking and attractive man," Nathan predicted.

"I try not to think of him at all," she insisted and then heaved a sigh as she stepped into the carriage. "I would prefer to think of your taking the position as schoolmaster here."

Nathan focused his full attention on the comely blonde perched on the buggy seat. A rueful smile slid across his lips as he met her vibrant green eyes. "I'm afraid I must decline, Serena," he said softly.

Her spirits hit rock bottom. Serena had hoped Nathan would take the job and accept a room in their home. In one short week, Nathan had become like the brother she had never had, someone to share her thoughts with, without wondering if her words would be passed among the village gossips.

"Is there nothing I can say to change your mind?" Her gaze was pleading, so much so that Nathan was forced to swallow over the lump that had suddenly collected in his throat.

Finally, he gave his head a negative shake. "Nay, Serena, as much as I enjoy your company, I have decided to return to New York. There is a great deal going on there. And history is in the making . . . I want to be a part of it."

A tear formed in the corner of her eye as she peered down into Nathan's young face. "I hope you find what you are looking for, Nathan, but I will miss you terribly. Words cannot express the fondness I have for you."

Nathan grasped her hand, giving it a loving squeeze. "If things could have been different, if these colonies were not split with dissent . . ." Nathan expelled a frustrated sigh. "What I am trying to say is that I highly regard your friendship and that if I stayed, I would find it impossible to leave." A faint smile skitted across his lips and then disappeared as he glanced down at the dusty toes of his boots. "I think you know what I'm hinting at, and we both know that it would be a mistake."

Serena understood his insinuation. They had grown fond of each other, but Nathan was pledged to another woman and possessed a desire to see his share of the world. "I will make no more demands on you," she assured him with a muffled sniff. "But if you pass this way again, I will be anxious to see you."

He nodded slightly and then stepped back as Serena fought back a sea of tears and took up the reins. Her eyes were on Nathan as she popped the horse and sent him on his way. Nathan stood motionless, and their gazes remained locked until the distance between them left them no more than silhouettes.

Serena had the strange feeling that there was more that Nathan wanted to tell her, but something had stopped him. And why was he curious about her reaction to Trager Grayson? Emotion swam about her, derailing her train of thought. It was as if the world had slid out from beneath her, and she succumbed to the tears she had carefully held in check. Nathan was leaving. Trager was gone. Mitchell would replace her at the school and she would have nothing but idle time on her hands. What was she to do with herself?

Her eyes lifted to the gray haze in the sky and she could find nothing cheerful to preoccupy her. Perhaps she should have gone with Trager. There was nothing to keep her here now. Serena tossed her head to discard that preposterous thought. Following Trager Grayson would solve nothing. He was a man desperate for money, and there was no telling what extremes he would take to get it. He was cynical when it came to affairs of the heart, and she was a fool to think she would ever mean more to him than a moment's pleasure.

When Serena walked into the house she was drawn by the sound of muffled voices that filtered out from the edges of the closed door of the study. Serena frowned, wondering who was with her father. It was not Olivia, because Serena had seen her riding when she came over the last hill before reaching the manor. Serena shrugged and continued on her way to change into her riding habit. Perfect timing, she mused. Olivia should be due back at the house after Serena left. Lately, they had avoided each other, coming and going without confrontation, and Serena could not have been more pleased.

Serena paused at the top of the stairs to see Olivia rap on the closed door and then disappear inside.

What was going on around here, she wondered curiously. Since she had been teaching she had been excluded from household activities and didn't have the faintest notion who was conferring with her father or why Olivia was allowed to sit in. Mitchell rarely invited Olivia to his private meetings. She made herself a mental note to question her father that evening, hoping to learn what had transpired that afternoon.

Sandpiper was feeling his oats as Serena gave him his head to thunder across the meadow. She grinned at the high-spirited steed, who was having difficulty holding himself to a walk when Serena tugged on his reins. He pranced and sidestepped, his nostrils flaring in anticipation of another run. Serena leaned against his powerful neck and urged him to his swiftest speed, thrilling to the sound of his hooves pounding the ground.

This was just what she needed—an invigorating ride to clear the cobwebs from her brain. She breathed a contented sigh as the wind whipped by her face, and then she pulled the pins from her hair, letting it billow about her like a cape of gold, loving the feel of Sandpiper's muscular body beneath her, giving her strength.

As the sun made its slow descent across the hazy sky, Serena turned her steed toward the stables and then frowned when she saw her father and Olivia climbing into the phaeton. She nudged Sandpiper to a trot and then pulled him to a halt to peer at her father's solemn expression.

"Papa, where are you going?"

"I have an important meeting in New York. Olivia and I will be staying the night. Serena, I . . ." Mitchell frowned and bit back his words as he glanced at Olivia, who sat perched beside him like a regal queen. "We will discuss the matter tomorrow evening," he assured her, his tone holding a hint of frustration.

As the phaeton rumbled away, Serena stared puzzled at it. What the devil was going on around here? Mitchell seemed annoyed with Olivia. Wishful thinking, no doubt, she told herself. Serena swung down from the saddle and wandered toward the house, wondering how she was to amuse herself while she rattled about the empty mansion.

The creak of her bedroom door brought her awake with a start, and she squinted to make out her father's slumped form as the lantern light in the hall cast a shadow on his face.

"I had given up on you," she greeted him drowsily. "I thought you had decided to stay another night."

Mitchell grimaced as he gazed at his daughter. It had been his intention to tell her of the reason for his trip to New York and of the incident with Olivia, but he didn't have the heart to spoil her night's sleep. The news would have her pacing the floor, and, as impulsive as she was, Mitchell wasn't certain what her reaction might be.

"I only wanted to inform you that we had

returned," he said quietly.

"What did you want to discuss with me?" she inquired as she propped herself up on one elbow and stared at his weary face.

"We can talk tomorrow," he assured her with a tired sigh. "It has been a long, grueling journey, and I'm exhausted. I'll see you in the morning."

As his footsteps retreated, Serena frowned curiously. Something was brewing. She had noticed the underlying apprehension in her father's tone, but obviously he was not ready to reveal the dilemma that weighed heavily on his mind. Serena yawned drowsily and squirmed to her side, letting sleep overtake her.

Somewhere in the night a vivid dream consumed her, one that had come too often of late. She had attempted to block out the lingering memory of Trager, but she could only gain meager success during her waking hours. When the darkness closed in on her she could see those incredible gray eyes, eyes that could burn through her to her very core, filling her with a need that had sprouted and grown to consume her private thoughts. His kisses had been branded on her mind. She could almost feel his sensuous lips playing on hers, smell that manly fragrance that hovered about him. Why did his memory invade her dreams, granting her no peace? Why couldn't she forget the feel of his skillful hands working magic on her flesh, enticing and arousing her to sensuous heights that left her hungering for fulfillment?

Serena climbed from the depths of drowsiness and flinched as her tangled lashes swept up to see the looming shadow above her. Her shriek of alarm died beneath the calloused hand that clamped over her mouth.

"Don't wake the whole damned house," came the husky whisper. "I'll release you if you promise not to make a sound."

Serena nodded slightly and then waited until Trager removed his hand. "What are you doing here? How did you get in? I thought . . ."

Trager brought quick death to her rash of questions, his scalding kiss silencing her and assuring her that their previous encounter had been no dream. Trager was bending over her, holding her in his arms, making her forget the harsh words that had passed between them.

When he finally raised his head, Serena blurted out her next question. "Trager, how on earth . . ."

"Dammit, be quiet," Trager snapped, his voice hushed but insistent. "I'll explain later. Right now you must pack your belongings. You're coming with me."

He had already drawn her to her feet before she could protest, but once she had collected her wits, she raised a rebellious chin and refused to budge from the spot.

"I will do no such thing. I told you I wanted nothing more to do with you. 'Tis over and done, and I want to forget we ever laid eyes on each other."

Trager heaved a frustrated sigh, glanced about the

dark room, and then aimed himself toward the dresser, careful not to stumble over the furniture that sat like a maze to trip him up. "Believe me, I have toyed with that idea myself. I ought to leave you here to stew in your own juice," he muttered sourly. "Get your bag, Rena. We haven't time for a lengthy argument."

"Time?" Serena's brows creased into a puzzled frown as she watched Trager rummage through her dresser, randomly tossing her undergarments into a pile. "You are not making any sense."

"I'll explain later." His tone registered impatience. "Just grab some gowns and get dressed," he instructed. Still Serena hadn't moved. He marched toward her, staring down into that exquisite face that had captured his thoughts, tormenting him when he had been doing his damnedest to shut her out of his mind. But he kept seeing those bewitching features surrounded with tendrils of silver-gold. Against his better judgment he had come back for her, and, as he had feared, seeing her stirred the emotions he had spent night upon endless night attempting to bury. "If you value this lovely neck of yours, you will do as I say without questioning me."

There was an urgency in his gaze that she could not understand, but she accepted it with blind faith, much to her own surprise. Trager would not have come back unless he sensed danger. But why should she be on a collision course with trouble? Wordlessly, Serena grabbed an armful of gowns and tossed them into the bag Trager held in his hand. With no regard for modesty, Serena retrieved her breeches and shirt and shrugged them on while Trager watched, his gaze roaming over her. Serena ignored the warmth that spread through her veins, determined to keep her mind on the seriousness of Trager's words. And then her jaw sagged in bewilderment when he stepped over to the panel that led to the hidden staircase. He grasped her hand and uprooted her from her spot, urging her down the steps in dangerously impatient strides.

"How did you know about the tunnel?" She fired the question at him and wormed her hand from his. Suddenly, she didn't trust him. She was suspicious, and none of the pieces of the puzzle fit together. Her greatest danger was Trager himself.

"Later, Serena." Trager yanked her with him before she could retreat up the steps. "You will have all your answers when we are a safe distance from here."

"Where are you taking me?" Serena was frantic. Her father's uneasiness had piqued her curiosity, and now Trager was dragging her away without an explanation.

"Somewhere they can't find you." Trager shoved her ahead of him, keeping her moving at a swift pace.

"They?" Serena eyed him even more skeptically.

"The Redcoats." He grabbed her shoulder and then wedged himself between the rocks to inhale a fresh breath of air, ridding his senses of the musty smell of the tunnel.

"But I have done nothing wrong," she insisted as

Trager drew her outside with him.

"The Loyalists are of a different opinion." Swiftly, he walked to his horse and pulled Serena up behind him. His muffled curse floated back to her, and she flinched at the sound of hoofbeats echoing in the silence of the night. "Damn. They came sooner than I expected," he mused aloud.

Serena's eyes flew wildly about her, seeing the band of men that galloped toward the front of the manor. Trager cautiously moved around the slope and reined the steed toward New Rochelle. When he had put a good distance between them and the British soldiers, he lifted Serena to the ground and hopped off to tie her bags on behind the saddle.

"I think we're reasonably safe now." He stared off into the darkness, his ears pricked to detect any unfamiliar sounds in the night, his keen gaze studying the swaying shadows.

"I want an explanation and I want it *now*!" Serena demanded tersely. "You have been behaving strangely. Why are those soldiers looking for me?"

Trager grasped her shoulders, holding her at arm's length, his expression grim. "Serena, the British have captured Nathan Hale in New York City."

His announcement hit her like a hard slap in the face and she gasped to catch her breath. "Captured? Why?" She could barely force the words from her lips.

He looked her square in the eye, seeing the confusion on her lovely features. "He has been accused of being a Rebel spy."

"A spy?" Serena was certain that if Trager hadn't had a good grasp on her she would have crumbled at his feet. The tears welled up in her eyes as she met his solemn gaze. "Oh, God," she choked.

He nodded affirmatively and then drew her closer when she broke into a sob. Serena clung to the only stable force in her shattered world, crying like a child. Things were moving too swiftly. The events of the night had come like an ambush to knock her feet out from under her.

"Nay, not Nathan. I've got to go to him. I have to explain to the British that he is only a teacher seeking employment."

"You can't, Rena." Trager's voice was quiet as he nuzzled his chin against the top of her head, feeling her tremble in his arms. "There is nothing to be done for him now. My brother informed me that the officers were becoming suspicious of him because he was spending his evenings wandering among the troops instead of searching for the job he claimed to be interested in acquiring. I tried to find him to warn him, but he was taken to Howe's headquarters before I could get to him."

Serena pushed away from the hard wall of his chest, her lashes sparkling with tears. "I can tell the general of my friendship with him and plead for his life. My father has influence and he . . ."

"That will only help to tighten the noose around his neck," Trager cut in. "After the remarks you made in front of the British officers last week, you are also under suspicion. Someone has made the connection between you and Nathan. Those soldiers were coming to take you to Howe." His words were slow and deliberate, trying to explain the gravity of her situation. When she stared incredulously at him, her jaw sagging, he gave her a shake, sending her hair tumbling wildly about her. "Do you understand what I'm saying? You have been named as part of the conspiracy."

Serena couldn't believe what she was hearing. Who would have given her name to the authorities? "That is preposterous."

"One of your Loyalist friends has stabbed you in the back," Trager muttered. "Someone is itching to see you hanged on the gallows alongside Hale."

"Hanged?" Serena nearly strangled on the word. "They intend to hang Nathan?"

His gray eyes locked with her wide green ones. "That is the punishment for spying. Nathan has confessed. The British found maps of their encampments around New York and other informative notes stashed in the soles of his boots."

"Nathan only carried European maps, ones that he had made from memory to aid in his teaching," Serena defended him hastily. "I saw him working on them. His notes were in Latin, historical information for his lessons, nothing more."

Trager gave his head a negative shake. "Nathan was clever, but General Howe closely inspected those maps. Although Nathan had labeled them as important points in Caesar's campaign in Gaul, they closely resembled the position of British troops in

New York."

Serena swayed toward him as the world spun furiously about her. Trager hooked his arm beneath her knees and set her atop his horse. When he pulled up behind her, he took up the reins and held her quivering body tightly against his.

"I have a place for you to stay until I can transport you to safety. When I return from my meeting we will cross the British lines."

Serena stared straight ahead as the steed galloped toward New Rochelle. She saw nothing, heard nothing except Trager's words over and over again. And then suddenly she remembered her last conversation with Nathan. There was something he had wanted to tell her. Was that the unspoken message in his eyes? Serena choked, on another sob. She could not allow the British to hang him without attempting to go to his aid. Nathan was a dear friend and she would not allow this unjustice to befall him.

"Trager, take me to him," she commanded, her trembling voice strengthened by determination.

"Are you mad?" Trager snorted derisively at her ridiculous request. "General Howe would have you in the cell next to Nathan's before you could utter a word in his defense. Someone has betrayed you, Serena. Can't you get that through that stubborn head of yours?"

"I want to see him." Her chin tilted defiantly as she glanced back into Trager's chiseled features, which remained unrelenting.

"You ask the impossible," he insisted. "You may

as well request that I fly to the moon and bring you back a slice of it." His voice dripped with sarcasm as he bent his gaze to her for a split second and then focused his attention on the path he was blazing across the countryside. When she squirmed in his arms, he tightened his grasp on her, keeping her chained to him. "Dammit, woman. I am trying to buy you precious time and save your hide. My association with you could well put a rope around my neck, and I do not relish the idea of staring at the world while I dangle from a tree branch!"

When Trager finally pulled the winded steed to a halt, Serena frowned dubiously. She stared at him and then at the brothel where she had found him and Brandon late one evening.

"Why are we stopping here?" she queried.

"I'm stashing you here for safekeeping. No one will think to search for a proper lady in this abode," Trager explained as he dragged her reluctant body from the saddle. "Ellen will have a room for you until I return from my meeting."

"A meeting in the middle of the night?"

Her eyes were riveted on him, blatantly mistrusting his intentions. There were still too many unanswered questions bouncing off the corners of her mind, and she failed to see Trager as her knight in shining armor. He didn't look the part, she mused as he tugged on her arm and forcefully propelld her to the back of the brothel.

Ellen appeared a few minutes later and held up the candle to light the way through the hall and up the back staircase. Trager ushered Serena into a dark room and then stepped back into the hall to speak with Ellen. Serena pressed her ear to the door, her heart hammering so loudly in her head that she could barely make out their words.

"I need a favor," Trager said urgently. "The British have put a high price on her head and are anxious for information about her. I want you to keep her here until I return."

"Did anyone see you come in?" Ellen queried in a hushed tone.

"Nay, I don't think I was followed."

What was he planning? Before she could find an answer the knob turned and Serena was forced to back away from the door.

"Ellen will take care of you until I come back." When Serena edged cautiously away from him, he frowned. "Are you all right?"

"I'm not staying here," she informed him, her tone cold and clipped.

"And I am not offering you a choice," Trager countered, a distinctly unpleasant edge on his voice. "Consider yourself my prisoner until I have decided how to handle this matter." His tone rolled over her like thunder, ominous and threatening as he marched toward her, only to have her retreat. "I stuck my own neck out to fetch you from your home. Now behave yourself."

Serena shrieked as he reached for her, but her struggles were all for naught. Trager yanked her to him, holding her captive in his tight embrace. When she attempted to scream for help his mouth swooped down on hers, silencing her with a kiss that stripped the breath from her lungs. Serena squirmed for release and failed, but she was determined not to melt beneath his ravishing kiss. He was attempting to seduce her into submission, and she was hell-bent on defying him. But when his hands began to roam possessively over her hips, she felt her resistance drooping, despite her willful thoughts. His touch became a light massage and his kiss was persuasively arousing, slowly eating away at her defenses. Why did he have such strange power over her, she wondered as her arms instinctively curled over his shoulder, assuring her that she had lost the battle of mind over body.

When he raised his dark head, a satisfied smile skitted across his lips, a hint of devilishness sparkling in his silver eyes. "Now be a good girl and don't cause Ellen trouble. I will be back as soon as I can."

As the door closed silently behind him, Serena wilted onto the edge of the bed, baffled and bewildered by the events that had swept her from pleasant dreams to a frantic flight. Only now, in the darkness of her room, did she have the chance to grapple with the information Trager had given her. Nathan captured as a spy? She let her breath out in a rush. It was too incredible to believe. A frown plowed her brow, and her heart stopped when the all too vivid picture of a man hanging from the gallows came to torment her. God, she couldn't allow that to happen to Nathan. He was like a brother, a friend

196

who had shared her innermost thoughts.

But how had Trager gained this information? Was his brother a British officer? Who was Trager meeting in the middle of the night? Serena inhaled a deep breath and collected her wits, all of which had been randomly scattered during their wild ride to New Rochelle. Trager was desperate for money, and he had been rubbing shoulders with the British. Now her heart was thundering against her ribs as the pieces of the puzzle fell neatly into place. The money-hungry mongrel had pointed an accusing finger at her and intended to hold her captive until the British put a higher price on her head. He was holding her for ransom, money that would put his faltering business back on its feet! He had attempted to distract her by informing her of Nathan's precarious predicament, not giving her time to wade through the facts and assemble them. That unscrupulous blackguard! And how had he known about the secret entrance to the manor? Could Olivia have discovered it and met him there for their trysts? Was Olivia in on this scheme? Had Olivia talked Trager into disposing of her when the situation presented itself? The questions were buzzing through her head so quickly that Serena was having difficulty matching answers.

She nervously wrung her hands in her lap and attempted to get a tight grip on herself. Perhaps it had been Brandon who had betrayed her, and Trager was only making the most of the moment. Brandon had been furious with her for voicing her opinion in front of the British and for rejecting his marriage

197

proposal. Had he linked her with Nathan for spite? She well remembered how he had backhanded her, his eyes spitting fury. And he was in New York, having the perfect chance to spill the information to General Howe. Or was it Colonel Powell? Had he become suspicious of her after that night? Her thoughts circled back to the faces she had seen that evening in the study and she frowned again. Trager had been sitting there grinning devilishly while the other men swallowed their tongues. No doubt, the wheels of his brain had been turning, devising a scheme that would grant him the money he desperately needed to keep his ships afloat. Perhaps Trager had thrown suspicion on her and then dragged Nathan down with her.

Their faces rose above her, taunting and tormenting her. Serena experienced a feeling of paranoia. It could have been any one of them or *all* of them who had conspired against her and Nathan. Trager could even have consented to spy for the British, free to wander at will, serving a double purpose, becoming a mercenary to see his desired end.

Panic gripped her. She had fallen into his trap! Trager was not her champion; he was a henchman for the Loyalists. He sought to gain her trust, expecting her to follow along like a lamb led to slaughter. No doubt, he intended to confer with the British patrol that had come to her home, collect the bounty, and then come back to feed her to the wolves.

Her eyes flew wildly about the room. She had to escape before Trager returned. Damn him! He thought his kisses would scatter her logic, leaving her to play the lovesick fool until he returned to deliver her to the Redcoats. Damn him to hell and back. That merciless mercenary! He cared nothing about her or Nathan. Serena bolted to her feet and rushed to the door, only to find that Ellen and Trager had locked her in.

Get a grip on yourself, Serena scolded, but her body was shaking like a leaf in a windstorm. Inhaling a deep breath, she tried to gather her unraveled composure and collect her thoughts. Calmly, she glanced about the room, reminding herself that this was no time to lose her head. She had to be deliberate and methodic if she was to escape with her life. Her gaze came to rest on the window and she frowned thoughtfully. She walked back to it, quietly lifted the pane, and stared down from her second-story prison. There was nothing but wooden shingles—no lattice, no ivy, nothing but a long fall that would surely break her neck. Again her eyes swept the room and then flew back to the door. With a hopeless sigh, Serena sank down on the bed, toying with the bedspread. A slow, devious smile worked its way to the corners of her mouth.

Chapter Eleven

Trager flicked the dust from the brim of his hat and heaved a tired sigh while he waited for Ellen to open the back door. He was exhausted, having covered ground at breakneck speed that night. Now he was anticipating lying beside that golden-haired vixen, feeling her velvety flesh molded to his. It was to be his reward, he mused as Serena's bewitching face hovered above him like a specter in the night. A witch, he thought as a faint smile skimmed his lips. She left a path of destruction behind her, and Trager had been caught in her wake, mesmerized by her beauty, amused by her fiery temperament, and aroused by a memory that had not faded even when he attempted to wash it from his mind with a bottle of brandy. The world wasn't prepared for a woman like her. Serena was intelligent, quick-witted, and too far ahead of her time to be appreciated. Her outspokenness, although admirably brash, had her stewing in her own kettle, and Trager couldn't deny that she deserved it.

His head jerked up as the candlelight splintered between the door and its casing. "'Tis about time," he teased. "If you had tarried much longer, you would have found me asleep on your doorstep."

Ellen smiled apologetically. "Forgive me, love. 'Twas a long night. Business booms during a war." There was a seductive twinkle in her eyes as her gaze flooded over Trager, not missing the smallest detail of his virile form.

Trager ignored her blatant proposal and wedged past her, his eyes lifting to the dark stairway. "Did the wench cause you any trouble?"

"Nay, I haven't heard a peep out of her. The poor little twit was probably so terrified by being here that she couldn't find her voice to scream for help, not that it would have done her any good," Ellen smirked. "People in this establishment have learned to mind their own business and keep their noses out of matters that don't concern them."

"Poor little twit?" A low chuckle erupted from Trager's chest as he took the candle and led the way up the steps. "That wench can fight like a sailor and is the proud owner of a razor-sharp tongue. She has cut more than one man down to her size by verbally abusing him. I must admit I'm surprised that she didn't scream the walls down around you after she had time to collect her wits. She was dazed after I filled her with shocking information."

Ellen snickered as they walked side by side down the hall. "Or maybe you have misjudged her, love. She has been as quiet as a mouse." She offered the key

202

to Trager and then retracted it, a persuasive smile on her lips. "Perhaps you would prefer to come to my room first. Seems to me that you could use some rest. No need to disturb the wench."

Trager flashed her a rakish grin and caught her hand as it wandered over his chest, knowing full well that she didn't expect him to sleep when he crawled into her bed. "First things first, my dear. Perhaps later," he added with a wink.

Her bottom lip jutted out in an exaggerated pout. "Your mind is on that blond-haired chit," she speculated. "'Tis a pity, love. She can't hold a candle to me and you damned well know it."

He bent to press a light kiss to her lips and then grasped the key she had tucked behind her back. "Nay, she can't hold a candle to you," he agreed softly. "But that is because the little spitfire burns her candle from both ends. Later, Ellen. I have important matters on my mind."

Reluctantly, Ellen turned away, disguising the envy in her eyes. She had been strongly attracted to Trager since the moment she had seen him stroll into the brothel. Never had a man made such a strong impression on her. And yet, she could sense that Trager was not the type of man who appreciated possessive women. He valued his freedom and avoided commitments. Ellen was certain that his connection with the Warren wench was only business and temporary fascination. Even Serena, as attractive as she was, could not capture the heart of Trager Grayson.

"Until later then, love," she murmured softly.

Trager watched in silence as Ellen moved silently away and then unlocked the door. When he walked into the room and squinted in the darkness, his smile of anticipation evaporated. "Damn!" he swore under his breath when he spied the makeshift rope that had taken Serena to her freedom. She had tied the bedspread and sheets together to make her escape. No wonder Ellen hadn't heard a peep out of her. Serena had spirited off into the night, cackling at her own cleverness, no doubt, Trager predicted as he wheeled and stalked back into the hall. That troublesome minx. He should have tied her to the bedpost. It had been a foolish oversight on his part, he scolded himself as he took the back steps two at a time in his haste to find Serena.

His gaze circled the dark alleyway, but she had vanished into thin air. From that moment on he would give the wench full credit for ingenuity. He wouldn't trust her out of his sight until he had deposited her in the hands of his superiors. And she would damn well pay for being such troublesome baggage, he thought bitterly as he stepped into the stirrup and reined his weary steed toward the path that led from town. Fate had frowned on him when he had met up with that wench. Just where in the sweet loving hell was he to look for her? Finding Serena would be like searching for a needle in a haystack. Trager heaved an agitated sigh. He did not have time to sort through a pile of straw. Dammit, that vixen had an uncanny way of turning good fortune into disaster.

From beneath the low-hanging branches, Serena yawned and rubbed her weary eyes as she peered at autumn's dawn, feeling a mixture of betrayal and forbidden love. How could she have fancied herself in love with Trager? He was her enemy, and she was an outcast. As the golden light filtered through the trees, Serena nudged her stolen mount through the brush and then gasped when a surly old man unfolded himself from his bed on the ground, grabbed his musket, and turned it on her.

"Whatcha doin' 'ere?" the old man snapped as he glared at the intruder.

His gaze flooded over the ragamuffin who sat atop her steed and then he grinned when he realized the waif was a woman with smudged cheeks. Her linen shirt barely camouflaged the high peaks of her breasts and it took a great deal of effort for him to drag his eyes up to her grimy face. But on closer inspection he was not disappointed. Her features were bewitching, soft and creamy, or would be once she had the time to wash her face. A rim of gold protruded from the edge of her cap, and Egan could imagine that those lustrous tendrils would feel like silk in his calloused hand.

Slowly, he lowered his weapon and gestured for her to step down. "Ye look like ye could use a little somethin' to drink and eat. Ye've 'ad a rough night, 'aven't ya?" he speculated, judging by the tired circles under her eyes and the snags on her clothes.

Serena gave the stubble-faced man a long, measuring look. He was dressed in buckskin and stood only a few inches taller than she. Although he was a crusty old man, there was a hint of kindness in his eyes. When he finally cracked a smile, she saw he was missing several teeth, and Serena grinned in spite of herself, feeling no fear of him. After all she had been through that night, she doubted that anything could frighten her. She was numbed by her experiences.

"Aye, I could use some food," she admitted as her gaze circled the small camp that was nestled in the trees. "But I haven't the money to pay you. You see I'm . . ." Serena fumbled for an excuse, but she was not forced to explain her appearance or her reasons for being alone and penniless.

Egan Hadley waved his hand for silence. "No need to 'splain, lass. Jest plant yerself on a soft spot and I'll fetch ye some vittles." He waddled over to retrieve a pouch from his knapsack and Serena bit back another grin, reminded of a duck scurrying away. "'Ow about a 'ot cup of tea?" Egan glanced over his shoulder as Serena sat down cross-legged in the grass. "I got me own special blend that will make ye fergit yer troubles."

Serena nodded agreeably. "I would be grateful for such a potion."

As Egan crouched by the dwindling campfire, he added a log and then poured water from his canteen into the pot that sat above the glowing coals. Serena frowned curiously as Egan sprinkled the contents from a pouch into the water.

"Is that your concoction of tea?" she queried as she massaged her aching muscles.

"Aye." He sent her a smile. "'Tis me own 'ighly flavored combination of natural 'erbs and spices. Since the price of imported tea is 'igher than a moonraker sail, I've taken to mixing me own blends." He sat back on his haunches, his bushy brows narrowing over his dark eyes. "Me name's Egan Hadley. What's yers, lass?" he inquired, quickly changing the subject.

Serena silently debated giving her name. After all, she was a fugitive with a price on her head. Egan could very well be a bounty hunter like Trager.

"Alaina Simpson," she replied. It was the best she could do on such short notice. "I was a servant at a manor east of New Rochelle." If she was going to give him a lie, it might just as well be a whopper. The bigger the better, she decided instantaneously. "I could not endure the master of the house." Her nose wrinkled distastefully. "He was an exasperating old man with the foulest disposition. I'm going to stay with my aunt in New York until I can find suitable work elsewhere."

Egan thoughtfully rubbed his bristled chin and eased onto the ground to prop his elbows on his knees. "I don't think it wise to be traipsin' 'round New York jest now. Them British are crawlin' all over the place. And the tales I've 'eard 'bout what they do to defenseless women.'' Egan sadly shook his head. "Well, it ain't a story fit fer a woman's ears.''

Serena discarded his warning and pounced on his previous remark. "I assume you don't approve of the Redcoats in these colonies.''

His shoulder lifted recklessly, making the fringe on his buckhide jacket dangle around him. "I ain't fer 'em or 'gainst 'em. I don't much care what they do as long as they leave me be. I keep to meself and don't bother nobody. I 'spect the same from the Rebs and Redcoats.'' When Egan noticed the water had boiled he strained the tea into a cup and offered it to Serena, along with a strip of dried beef. "It ain't much, but it'll keep yer belly from talkin' to ye all day.''

She graced him with an appreciative smile and took a cautious sip of the steaming tea. It had a strange undertaste to it, but Serena didn't complain. She was thankful for the nourishment. While she nibbled on the beef and drank her tea, Egan eased back against an oak tree and extracted a reed flute from his pocket. The melody he chose was soft and serene and she relaxed for the first time since Trager had kidnapped her, listening to his quiet tune as the sun arched across the autumn sky.

"More tea, lass?'' he inquired when he noticed she had drained her cup.

"Aye,'' Serena extended the cup to him. "I would take a bit more if you can spare it.''

When her cup had been refilled, Serena downed it to quench her thirst after chewing on the beef. A feeling of drowsiness overcame her. She had gone without sleep all night, and, once she had relaxed, her weariness caught up with her.

Egan frowned in concern and tucked his flute in his pocket. "Ye look a little pale, 'Laina. Are ye feelin' 'lright?"

Serena nodded drowsily. "'Tis just that I haven't had time for sleep."

Egan gestured toward his pallet. "Why don't ye lie down and catch a few winks? I ain't plannin' to break camp 'til later." He rose to his feet and grabbed her horse's reins. "I'll take yer mount to the creek fer a drink while ye rest."

As she stretched out on the fur quilts she smiled up at him. "Thank you, Egan. You are very kind."

He shrugged leisurely and returned her grin. "T'ain't nothin'. Ye jest rest and I'll wake ye when I'm ready to leave."

When she was left alone, Serena closed her eyes, thankful that she was no longer required to hold them open. It had become an effort. In a matter of minutes she had fallen into a deep sleep that was void of dreams. Trager wasn't there to haunt her as he had been so often. There was nothing but peaceful silence and she was drifting on a boundless sea.

Egan's face split in a devilish grin when he led the steed back to camp. His low chuckle settled about Serena, but she couldn't hear it, nor did she see the wicked gleam in his dark eyes as he knelt down to give her a sound shaking.

"Ye shouldn't have taken that second cup of tea, lass," he told his sleep-drugged companion as he dragged her lifeless body from the ground and tossed it over the saddle like a feed sack.

Egan secured Serena to the horse, saddled his own steed, and picked his way through the woods, whistling a merry tune as he went.

Trager let his breath out in a rush as his gaze swept the surroundings. He had come to the conclusion that Serena had headed for New York to seek out Nathan, but he had ridden hard and had seen no sign of her. Damn that witch. Perhaps she had grabbed her broom and had flown over the treetops to reach her destination. Now his search would have to wait. He was due at another meeting, one that could not be avoided. Trager reined his steed south, but his eyes kept skimming the area, hoping to catch sight of that honey-haired hellion who had skillfully managed to elude him.

Several horses were tethered in front of the shack when Trager arrived. As he walked inside he nodded solemnly to the man who sat around the table sipping brandy.

"We thought you had changed your plans without informing us," Roger remarked as he surveyed Trager's tired, drawn face. "You look like hell. What have you been up to?"

Trager frowned at his brother's rude observation and tossed his hat aside. "I've had a busy, but unproductive night," he grumbled as he parked himself in the empty chair and threw down the drink that awaited him. "What news have you brought with you?"

Roger eased back in his chair, tipping it on its back legs like a rearing stallion, and sighed disgustedly. "Bad news," he admitted. "It was as you predicted."

Trager grimaced, knowing full well what his brother meant. "When?"

"This morning," Roger responded disheartenedly. "General Howe issued the order and it was carried out at dawn."

A stilted silence fell over the room and Trager stared at the bottom of his empty glass. "The rest of us stand to suffer the same fate," he said solemnly. "We have no choice but to evacuate the area until things have cooled down. This place will be crawling with soldiers by nightfall."

After listening to the rest of the information Roger gave him, Trager grappled with the news, sorting out the events of the day, none of which were encouraging. His own report would not be a cheerful one and he was not anticipating talking with his superior. Good news was hard to come by these days, he thought dismally.

His gaze settled on Egan Hadley whose wry smile stretched from ear to ear. Trager frowned, finding no amusement in the situation. Egan looked like the cat that swallowed the canary, his dark eyes twinkling with deviltry.

"Spit it out, Egan," Trager barked. "Do you find some demented irony in all of this?" His tone dripped heavily with sarcasm.

Egan nodded affirmatively. "Ye must 'ave spent a long night all fer naught, but I've 'ad a bit of good fortune."

Trager rolled his eyes, summoning more patience, but he had depleted his supply. "If fate has smiled on you, share it with the rest of us. We could use a lift."

The old man gestured toward the back room of the shack, grinning outrageously. "I've got a little surprise fer ye, cap'n."

Burning with curiosity, Trager unfolded himself from the chair and strode over to the door. His jaw swung from its hinges as his gaze circled back to the spry old man who stood behind him. "Where did you find her?"

The word *her* brought the other two men to attention and they all congregated around the portal to peer at the sleeping beauty who was curled up on the cot.

Roger grinned as he craned his neck to see around Trager's broad shoulders. "Who is she?" His tone registered aroused interest.

Although Trager's eyes were glued to Serena, he replied. "That, gentlemen, is Serena Warren, the lady with a steep price on her head."

"So this is the witch you were ranting about not too long ago." Roger tossed his brother a mocking smile and then carefully assessed Serena's shapely figure and angelic face. "And she looks to be well worth the sum," he commented with a chuckle. "Damned tempting."

Trager raised a dark brow as he dragged his gaze

from Serena and settled them on his lusting brother. It shocked him to realize that he felt so protective of the same wench he had been considering strangling since she escaped him. "The price or the wench?" he questioned, his reproachful frown warning Roger to plug his eyes back in their sockets and reroute his wolfish thoughts.

Another broad smile cut into the craggy features of Roger's face. "Seems to me that a man couldn't lose either way."

Egan snickered as he strained to see his captive between the shoulders of the men who blocked his view. "Ye should've 'eard the crock she fed me when I met up with 'er. Told me she was a runaway maid lookin' fer a new employer and that she was goin' to New York to stay with 'er aunt."

Trager brought his index finger to his lips to shush Egan, frowning at his loud voice. The faintest hint of a smile bordered his mouth when he observed the eager pairs of eyes that flowed over Serena. He was reminded of four of the seven dwarfs who stood gawking at Snow White. And she was like a princess in a fairy tale, he mused as his gaze anchored on the delicate features of Serena's face. As much as he hated to admit it, this wench's bewitching features deserved their admiration. She had the body and face of a seraph, but she could also breathe the fire of dragons. She was an enigma, a walking contradiction who could entrap a man and then burn the pants off of him before he could put a safe distance between them. And Trager, who should have known better than to tamper with her, was entranced in her spell. His thoughts drifted back to the present as Egan continued in his overly loud tone.

"She won't be rousin' fer 'while yet, cap'n," he insisted.

Trager eyed the crusty old man skeptically. "How can you be so certain of that?"

Egan broke into a toothless grin as he patted the pouch in his pocket. "I slipped some of my potion in 'er tea. Sleepin' beauty don't even know where she is or 'ow she got 'ere. Since she didn't recognize me from that night ye brought 'er to the shack to wait out the storm, I took advantage of 'er. And I knew ye was goin' after 'er." His shoulder lifted in a leisurely shrug, sending fringe dangling about him. "I thought I would save ye the trouble of findin' 'er."

Trager's silver-gray eyes glistened with amusement. Leave it to Egan to sedate her so that she could not protest being hauled to the shack, he thought to himself. 'Twas a shame Trager hadn't considered such a method. He could have saved himself a good deal of trouble.

"But when she wakes, she will be breathing fire and come at us with her claws bared," he predicted.

"It ain't likely," Egan disputed. "She's tied to the cot."

"Breathing fire?" Roger cut in, his tone laced with skepticism. "She reminds me of an angel lying there so still. I think I have fallen hopelessly in love with this sleeping beauty you have incorrectly labeled a witch."

214

"Looks can be deceiving," Trager insisted as he closed off the men's view and returned to his chair. "Beneath that enticing body and exquisite face lurks the soul of the Devil's advocate."

"Are you entertaining the idea of handing her over to Howe and taking the reward?" Roger wouldn't have doubted it after glancing over to see the sour look on his brother's face.

Trager downed another brandy and stared at the bare wall. "My first impulse was to extract my revenge after uselessly tracking that wench across the countryside half the night and most of the morning," he grumbled and then swung his attention to Roger. "I want you to take the men and ride to White Plains. I'll catch up with you tomorrow."

A wry smile caught one side of Roger's mouth as he bent his gaze to Trager. "I'll be more than happy to escort Serena to New York, if that is what you have decided to do with her," he offered.

"No doubt you would," he smirked, "but *I* intend to see that Serena pays the piper."

"Are you referring to Howe or yourself?" Roger frowned thughtfully as he brushed his hand over the five o'clock shadow on his chin. "Could it be that this wench has caught your fancy? You have gone to great efforts to retrieve her."

Trager released a derisive snort and poured himself another drink. "Nay," he denied, his tone more emphatic than he intended. "'Tis just that I think she might serve some useful purpose."

Roger hadn't swallowed a word of it. "It seems to

me that you are very protective of her. Never have I seen you stew over a wench the way you have with this one. You were drinking yourself into a stupor over her not too long ago and it leaves me to wonder if . . ."

Trager's fist hit the table, rattling the glasses. "That will be enough on the subject of Serena," he broke in, flashing Roger a silencing frown. "You have a long ride ahead of you and I suggest you get moving."

Although Roger unfolded himself from the chair and retrieved the extra glasses from the table, his taunting smile remained intact. "Give my regards to the lady and tell her she has a secret admirer. I have a feeling we will be meeting again."

Trager flung his arm toward the door, his annoyed frown cutting deep creases in his bronzed features. "Out with you! You are sorely testing my patience, little brother!"

Roger swaggered toward the door and opened it to allow the other two men to precede him. "I have noticed a definite change in your disposition of late." He gestured his head toward the back room and then he grinned broadly. "I still think your black mood has more to do with this wench than the war."

"Out!" Trager's booming voice rolled over him like thunder and Roger slammed the door behind him before he aroused the full wrath of the lion who was growling at him, his snicker wafting its way back to Trager, who was pouring himself another drink to drown his irritation.

Chapter Twelve

When Trager heard the sound of retreating horses, he eased back in his chair and breathed a weary sigh. Roger had a bad habit of teasing him, and the subject of Serena was an extra-sensitive matter, one that Trager preferred not to discuss at all. His thoughts halted abruptly when he heard something crash to the floor in the adjoining room. Wearing a curious frown, he rose and went to inspect the cause of the disturbance.

Serena cursed under her breath and fought the ropes that held her captive in the same shack where she and Trager had spent the night during the storm. What in heaven's name was she doing here? She remembered nothing except falling asleep on the ground before Egan Hadley . . . damn him! That devious old coot! Why had he taken her prisoner? Was he some demented lech whom she had grossly misjudged? Her breath froze in her throat as the door swung open and Trager Grayson's massive body filled the entrance. A devilish grin hung on one corner of his mouth, and Serena itched to claw that intimidating expression off his face. He leaned his arm against the door casing and gave her the once over, twice.

"So at last sleeping beauty has awakened. I had considered bestowing a loving kiss on you to rouse you, but after giving the matter careful consideration I wondered if I might run the risk of turning myself into a toad," he commented caustically. His gaze fell to the nightstand, which lay on its side, assuming Serena had knocked it over during her tantrum.

"You cur!" she spat at him when she finally found her tongue. She strained against the ropes, wishing she could leap at him with her claws bared.

"Tsk, tsk." Trager swaggered toward her and then bent to replace the nightstand as he sadly shook his raven head. "Is that any way to talk to the man who rescued you from the jaws of death?" he mocked dryly.

"Rescue me from death so you could feed me to the wolves when it would benefit you." Her green eyes blazed with enough heat to ignite a forest fire, her penetrating gaze drilling into him, hoping to leave him in a pile of dusty ashes at her feet. "You're a heartless mercenary, Trager Grayson. You are an informant for the British," she accused, her tone as condemning as her glower. "It was you who pegged Nathan as a spy and then gave them my name, intending to collect a bounty when you delivered me to them."

Trager was quick to take offense when she glared

at him as if he was some slimy serpent that had just slithered out from under a rock. "How in the sweet loving hell did you jump to that conclusion? If that had been my intent I would have collected the reward and *then* informed the Redcoats where they could locate Hale's accomplice," he snorted derisively as he towered over her, watching her breasts heave with every angry breath she took. "I would have washed my hands of you then and there and I would have gone my merry way, toting my reward and gloating over my success." He looked down his nose at Serena, his lips thinning into a tight smile. "Each time I attempt to portray your knight in shining armor I find myself criticized for my efforts. I swear you are the most ungrateful chit I have ever had the misfortune of stumbling onto."

His protest knocked the wind out of her sails. Perhaps she had leaped to the wrong conclusion and yet . . . Serena eyed him suspiciously. Why should she trust Trager and where the devil was Egan? Surely he must have been in on the plot to capture her.

"Where is that weasel Hadley?" Serena demanded, her gaze locking with Trager's, watching for any hint that he was about to bless her with another of his honey-coated lies.

"He delivered you to me and went on his way," Trager replied blandly.

"Why did he drug me?" It had only taken her a moment to realize that the tea had been heavily laden with some sleep-inducing potion that had put her out like a lantern light in a wind storm. "I have never seen the man before in my life and he couldn't have known who I was unless he had some devious connection with you."

"Ah, but he has seen you," Trager countered as he sank down beside her to wipe the smudges from her cheeks. When Serena jerked away as if repulsed by their physical contact, Trager dropped his hand away. "He was here the night you fell from your horse. It was his voice you heard in the other room. He knew I was looking for you and presumed that I had not yet found you." Trager sniffed disgustedly. "Little did he know that I had you under lock and key until you spirited off into the night." He braced his arms on either side of her and leveled his gaze at her. "Because of you I have spent a fitful night and I am sorely in need of sleep."

"And I know how cranky you can be when you haven't had your nap," Serena shot back at him, her tone dripping with sarcasm.

"Me?" Trager choked on his breath. "Where does a fire-breathing witch find the gall to complain about *my* disposition? I am as even-tempered as the day is long," he boasted, a slight smile chiseling away at his hard features.

Serena scoffed up at him. "Don't wrench your arm patting yourself on the back."

"And don't snap at the hand that feeds you," he advised, flashing her a wider grin. "I am offering you protection from your enemies."

Her brows formed a dubious frown over her

narrowed eyes. "And I am not at all sure that I shouldn't count you among them," she mused aloud.

His breath came out in an exasperated rush. "Where did you come up with this hair-brained notion that I planned to hand you over to the Redcoats?"

"From your own confession," Serena answered. "You admitted that you were in dire need of money. How was I to know how low you would stoop to secure your funds?"

"Upon my word, woman, you could have given me the benefit of the doubt," he said indignantly. "Why didn't you confront me with your suspicions instead of running off into the night? You have a bad habit of flirting with danger and, under the circumstances, you could have found more than you bargained for."

"You have never been one to explain your motives. Why would I expect that you had suddenly changed?" she retaliated.

Trager sighed heavily. "I suppose I have given you little reason to trust me, but I was in no position to divulge information."

The condemnation faded from her emerald eyes as she watched the chiseled lines of his face soften considerably. "And are you now?" she questioned point blank, taking advantage of his mellowed mood.

"I am cautious by nature, Serena," he confessed as he tunneled his fingers through the sun-kissed tendrils that sprayed about her face. "I am never certain if you will turn on me when my back is

221

turned. 'Tis difficult for me to tell where your true loyalties lie. Your father is a British magistrate and yet you defied the Redcoats by voicing your opinions for the cause of independence. 'Tis a perplexing problem for me to tell which side of the fence you stand on."

Her lashes swept down to shield her from his probing gaze. "I am torn between my respect for my father and my allegiance to my countrymen. I was born and raised in these colonies and I feel we have every right to complain about the injustices. Nathan once said . . ." Her eyes were wide and apprehensive as she halted in midsentence. "We must do something for Nathan. After all that has happened I almost forgot that he faces severe penalty."

A grim expression seeped into his bronzed features. " 'Tis too late, Rena. . . ." His voice trailed off as his gaze lifted to the sooty window that made the world appear a dreary shade of gray. "The Redcoats asked him to become a double agent, but he refused. They hanged him this morning." His face twisted in a vengeful scowl. "If I could get my hands on the man who betrayed him I would see the fiend pay for his treachery," Trager gritted out. "I hope to see Nathan's death avenged."

Serena squeezed her eyes shut as the tears trailed down the sides of her cheeks. Trager wiped them away and then untied her hands. Her arms came around his neck, accepting the shoulder that he offered. Serena buried her head against his solid strength, letting her frustrations and grief wash away in the sea of tears that sprang from her eyes.

"I don't know where to turn or whom to trust," she choked out. "'Tis come to the point that I must guard my words, and I cannot tell friend from foe." Serena could not seem to get a grip on her emotions. She was sobbing hysterically. It wasn't like her to come apart at the seams, but her world had shattered like crystal, crumbling in a thousand pieces at her feet. "I cannot go home, I cannot stay here. . . ."

Trager cupped her chin in his hand, raising her face to his, seeing the tears that glistened on her long lashes. "You're coming with me, Rena. 'Tis too dangerous for you to remain here."

Serena would gladly have accepted his offer if she thought he cared, even a little, but he felt no more than an obligation, as if he were taking in a stray pup who had nowhere to call home. "That is impossible, Trager. I am not your responsibility. I can take care of myself."

His mouth narrowed in a hard line. "I said you were coming with me and that is the beginning and end of it." His tone held a hint of finality that expected no dispute.

"Nay." Her gaze locked with those stormy pools of silver.

Trager expelled an exasperated sigh. "Serena, I swear you are the stubbornest woman I have ever met. If I told you *not* to take a flying leap off a cliff, I think you would do it just to spite me."

Her eyes mellowed and a faint smile touched her lips. "'Tis only that I know I would be in your way.

You have important matters on your mind and little time to take me under your wing."

He folded her in his arms and placed a light kiss to her sensuous mouth. "But the arrangement does have its advantages." His brow arched provocatively. "It will be a long, cold winter. We could keep each other warm," he murmured against the curve of her neck.

Serena pressed small but determined hands to the rock-hard wall of his chest, dodging his next kiss. "I won't be your whore, Trager," she informed him tersely. "I have very little left, but I still have my pride and I find myself clinging very fiercely to it."

"Then perhaps you would consent to be my wife." The words were out before Trager realized he had spoken them and, for the life of him, he couldn't imagine what possessed him to make such an offer. He was a confirmed bachelor, taking pleasure where he found it, avoiding tangling bonds, content to enjoy more than one woman's bed.

Serena drew far enough away to eye him skeptically. "Why would you want to wed me?"

His shoulder lifted in a lackadaisical shrug, giving him time to think a moment before he responded. "Why not? It would make a respectable woman of you." It was a lame excuse, but it was the best he could muster, since he was still wondering why he had made the proposition in the first place.

"Respectable?" Serena scoffed at his flimsy reasoning. "A respectable woman would not consider marrying a scoundrel and a rogue." Her brows knitted into another suspicious frown. "What could *you* possibly have to gain, or I for that matter?" She knew Trager well enough to realize that there was method in his madness. He was a deliberate man, taking advantage of every situation, twisting it to suit his purpose. But what was his motive? Serena still wasn't quite certain that she trusted him.

Trager looked her straight in the eye, his expression sober. It annoyed him that she had rejected his offer, even if it was impulsively given. He could name a handful of women who would pounce upon the opportunity to become his wife. But Serena was behaving as if the idea of taking his name was distasteful. The nerve of that wench! He had risked his own neck to rescue her from the British and spent a sleepless night trying to track her after she eluded him. The *least* she could have done was to let him down gently. But nay, Serena was questioning his motives and turning up her nose at his proposal. He was certainly a better catch than that weasel Brandon Scott.

"And what, pray tell, can you possibly stand to lose?" he countered, his tone carrying a hint of sarcasm. "You are wanted by the British and you have nowhere to take refuge. Surely marrying me would be a notch above hanging from the gallows."

Unfortunately, she stood to lose her heart and watch it be broken in two by a man who was cynical of commitments to women. And if worse came to worst, she could stay with her aunt and uncle in Connecticut. Although they were staunch Loyalists

225

they would never turn on their own flesh and blood, or would they? It was the only place she could think of to go, but she was leery about dragging the rest of her family into this matter.

While she was grappling with her thoughts, Trager untangled himself from her and rose to pace the floor. Serena took advantage of his silence, deciding to voice her objections without being distracted by the feel of his strong arms about her.

"We hardly know each other," she pointed out, groping for another excuse to reject his proposal.

"You know me as well as any other woman does," he parried, canceling her argument. "That will come in time. After all, we will have the next few years to become acquainted."

His caustic tone did nothing to ease her apprehension. "I'm not at all sure I want to know any more about you. You are a rather suspicious character. What I might learn about you could make you even less appealing." Serena's emotions were being twisted and turned and she was walking a fine line between loving him and doubting his concern for her. With Trager, she never really knew where she stood or what was running through that complex mind of his. After Nathan's capture and her kidnapping she was leery of everyone, especially Trager, who still refused to explain himself.

"I'm going to be completely honest with you, Serena," Trager said as he paused from his pacing to stare down at her. "It may prove disastrous, because I'm not at all certain I can trust you with the information."

Serena sat up on the edge of the cot and rubbed her wrists. "Then it seems that we do have one thing in common," she remarked a bit sarcastically. "We share a mutual mistrust and, in my own defense, I assure you that I have never been one to spread gossip. I anxiously await hearing the *truth*." Her emphasis on the last word drew Trager's harsh frown.

"I intend to give you the truth, but I am wary of you because you have a habit of speaking your mind," he reminded her and then wagged a lean finger in her face. "If you don't guard your tongue, you could tie a noose around my neck—and I value my hide."

Her solemn gaze locked with his. "I have learned my lesson, Trager—the hard way. I won't betray you. I only hope you can honestly return that vow."

He sent her a long, measuring look and then nodded in agreement. "Very well, I will tell you the whole of it." He clasped his hands behind his back and went back to his methodic pacing. "I am not a ship-builder seeking investors. My business is sound, although inhibited by the British fleet. The money I have collected in this charade will serve the Patriots' cause. I am the captain of a group of men known as Grayson's Rangers, one of whom is Egan Hadley. We have been obtaining information about the British, just as Nathan attempted to do." Trager turned squarely to face her, watching her jaw sag in amazement. "I report directly to General Washington, who is having one hell of a time holding ground. The British have routed us out of New York and we must make a strategic stand or admit defeat. Any information we can gain will benefit the general. My men have infiltrated the British lines, but after this business with Hale, the Redcoats have become more cautious. We have been forced to withdraw from the area and retreat to White Plains to rejoin the troops until things have simmered down.''

So he was a spy, Serena mused, but not for the Loyalists as she had first suspected. And if Trager had not alerted the Redcoats to Nathan's activities and her connection with him, who could it have been?

Trager read the question in her eyes. "Now that you know that I was not the one who betrayed you, we must consider the other possibilities. It could have been Scott, Powell, or even his aide," Trager speculated. "Any of them had much to gain . . . for instance, a promotion for Scott, who was furious with you after the incident at the ball." A long moment passed while Trager stared at some distant point, wondering if he should voice another of his suspicions. Finally, he decided it was the time for complete honesty and he blurted out his thoughts, since they weighed heavily on his mind. "And it might have been your father. After all, he is a died-in-the-wool Loyalist, a magistrate for the Crown, sworn to serve his cause. I heard several of his remarks at the party and I know he is as strongly *against* the Patriot cause as I am for it. It would not be the first time this war has turned a family against each other."

Serena gasped, appalled that Trager would suggest such a preposterous notion. "My father would never betray me," she snapped.

"But would he lie for you and forsake his cause?" Trager countered as he focused his full attention on her.

He had planted the seed of suspicion and Serena took a moment to ponder the possibility, even though she chastised herself for doing so. Mitchell had been very secretive about his trip to New York, and she recalled the rueful expression on his face when he had returned last night. Had the British interrogated him, testing his loyalty? Had he been forced to explain about her relationship with Nathan? Could he have incriminated her against his own will?

Serena thoughtfully chewed on her lip and then slowly let out her breath. "I could never believe that my father would purposely hurt me."

"Nay, perhaps not purposely," Trager agreed, "but he could not lie when there were witnesses to attest to the fact that you had spoken against the Crown and mentioned your friendship with Nathan." Trager glanced down to study the bare floor beneath his feet. "My brother says your father was in New York a few days ago, conferring with the British officers. I fear that somehow he was involved."

Serena didn't want to think of it. It had to be someone else who had exposed her. Mitchell would never sell her out. A frown captured her features as another thought crossed her mind, one that had bothered her since Trager had appeared in her room. Perhaps Trager was baiting her, trying to pry information from her.

"How did you know about the secret entrance to our house? I am the only one who has used it and I have told no one. And what were you doing on our property that day we met at the cove? How well do you know Olivia? Were you her lover?" Serena surprised herself by firing the questions at him, but they had been just beneath the surface, tormenting her thoughts. Once they burst free, they flowed as coldly and swiftly as a spring-fed river.

A wry smile parted his lips as he ambled over in front of her, only to have her scoot warily away. Suddenly, they were right back where they had started. "My grandparents built that tunnel for my brother and me. We spent many hours escaping from imaginary enemies when we came to visit."

"The Widow Gravitt was your grandmother?" Her eyes were wide with disbelief.

"Was and is," he affirmed. "She lives with my parents in Connecticut." Trager's grin broadened to encompass his dark features. "And when my parents built their home, they included a similar escape route, just in case *their* grandchildren ever came to visit. And in reference to your stepmother, I have never laid a hand on her, except to dance with her at the ball."

Trager took her hand and pulled her into the circle

of his arms. "I am not your enemy, Rena, nor have I ever been. Now, will you accept my protection or do I have to carry you off kicking and screaming?"

"Are you still offering marriage, or have you reconsidered?"

"Nay, the offers stands as it was made," he murmured, lost to the enticing scent that wrapped itself around his senses and to the addictive taste of her kisses.

When he raised his dark head, Serena nodded compliance, but not without reluctance. She was furnishing her own private room in hell by marrying a man who had no belief in love. Serena had the sinking feeling that she would live to regret it. "Then I shall come peaceably, but I still have reservations about wedding you."

He chuckled softly, his breath warm against her cheek. "Do you see me as some monster, Serena? Have I ever harmed you?"

"Nay, but I have met more than one wolf dressed in sheepskin," she insisted just before his mouth swooped down on hers, drowning her misgivings in a sea of sensations that washed over her each time Trager took her in his arms. She could claim to mistrust him, but she could not deny the powerful attraction she felt for him. She was drawn by this strange force, submitting to her own desires as well as his. Trager was her weakness, a venom that had poisoned her blood, she tried to tell herself as his hands flowed over her like a gentle massage. Her sigh echoed in the silence as Trager drew the shirt from her shoulders, leaving her flesh exposed to the silver flame of desire in his eyes. His gaze warmed her skin like heated coals and a path of fire blazed over her as he reached out to touch what his eyes had boldly caressed.

"I want you, Rena," he rasped, his voice husky with mounting passion. "You have been on my mind since I first saw you swimming like a mythical mermaid in the cove, the sun dancing in your hair, the water flowing over your skin. You are the forbidden fruit that makes life sweet. I knew I should have turned and walked away that day, but I was drawn like a bee to nectar, craving the taste of your kisses." He drew her down with him to the cot, his hands caressing and rediscovering every inch of her skin, branding her as his possession. "My fascination with you is a hunger that I cannot seem to appease. Each time I touch you I want more, satisfied for the moment, but strangely discontent." His gaze held a hint of incredulousness as he moved toward her. "What spell have you cast upon me, witch?" he mused aloud as he sought the sweetness of her sensuous lips, drowning in the intoxicating taste of her kiss.

His lips left hers, seeking her breast, teasing its pink peak to tautness as his hand curled about her shoulder to capture the other mound. Serena trembled beneath his skillful fondling and then felt herself surrender all over again as his free hand wove intricate patterns across her abdomen. A slow, consuming fire spread over her as his lips returned to hers, his breath ragged and impatient.

His devouring kiss and wandering caresses sent the world spinning furiously about her, and logic fled the whirlwind of emotions that churned within her. She was hot and cold and breathless, aching to satisfy the shameless need he had instilled in her. As his knowing fingers found the soft flesh of her thighs, Serena knew the sweet torture of his lovemaking had returned to haunt her. All the forbidden memories of their night together emerged to intermingle with these new, wild sensations that held her entranced.

Serena heard him groan as he pressed his bold manliness against her hip, but his voice sounded a thousand miles away, as if he were part of a distant, hazy dream. The rapid beat of his heart thundered in frantic rhythm with hers, like the drumming fingers of impatience. His need for her was as great as her need for him, she thought dizzily. Although he didn't love her, they shared a passion that could pursue and capture time, blocking out the harsh words that had passed between them, leaving them drifting in a world that was ablaze with maddening sensations and hushed words of desire.

Her lashes fluttered softly against her cheeks as she yielded to the exquisite feel of his hands and lips on her flesh. She was like clay in the hands of a master craftsman, arching to meet his probing fingers, holding his head to her breast as his tongue traced lazy circles around each taut peak, Another breathless sigh escaped her lips as his hand retraced its

CAROL FINCH

route across her belly and then descended to her
thigh, leaving in its wake a path of deliciously
indescribable sensations that dissolved all thought
from her mind. She was like a puppet dancing on a
string, moving only on command.

When he stirred beside her, her lashes swept up to
see the heated glow of passion in his smoky eyes as he
lifted himself above her. The corded muscles of his
arms and belly tensed as he forced himself to keep his
distance. He wanted her, but he didn't want her. The
first time he had made love to her had melted the wall
of ice around his heart, and he was leery of these
strange new emotions she evoked in him. Serena was
different from other women, silently taking more
than he ever intended to give. Was he afraid of her?
He stared down into her exquisite face, seeing desire
ripple across those spellbinding pools of green.

Her hands fanned across his chest and then
wandered lower, leaving him trembling from the
overwhelming want of her. He caught his breath as
her fingers traced a tantalizing trail over his hips and
then brazenly folded around him to return the
pleasure he had given her. Her lips fluttered across
his skin like a butterfly skimming the earth, lightly
touching and arousing him. Her kisses and caresses
were playing havoc with his sanity and Trager knew
he had lost the battle of will. He could claim that this
vixen meant nothing to him, but his body yearned to
experience again those same unmatched sensations
that he had discovered that night when she had
surrendered to him. The taste of her honey kisses had

234

remained on his lips and the memory of their lovemaking had come uninvited to his dreams.

Finally, Trager could stand no more of her stirring caresses. He didn't want her. He didn't need her, but he had to have her or go out of his mind. She had ignited a fire that burned him inside and out, defying reasoning, awakening a desire that raged like a fierce, disturbed lion. A guttural groan echoed in his chest as his sleek body covered hers, seeking to appease a craving that had left him hungry and dissatisfied since Serena had ridden away in the night.

Serena clutched him to her to meet his hard, driving thrusts, giving herself to him, becoming his possession for that one timeless moment when nothing mattered except the feel of his solid flesh molded tightly to hers. They moved in flowing rhythm, scaling passion's mountain, finding new, unequaled sensations awaiting them at each crest. And then they were climbing higher, gazing at the far horizon from their lofty perch. Their souls touched and intertwined like the hands of time, making Serena tremble and cling tightly as the wild sensations sizzled their way to her core. Somehow, she had transcended the physical bounds of passion, soaring like an eagle, experiencing a freedom she had never known.

And then her breath caught in her throat as a nerve-tingling tremor shook the roots of her sanity. It was wild and sweet and maddening. She couldn't breathe. She couldn't think, swept up in emotions that sparkled like heated sunbeams on her skin. It was as if she were living and dying and Trager was taking her still higher.

A whimpering moan drifted from her lips, and she was deafened by the thundering beat of her own heart as it drummed in her ears. She dug her nails into the hard muscles of his back, clutching at the one man who had the power to make her forget that another world existed beyond the tight circle of his arms.

"Trager . . ." His name quivered with emotion until it died beneath his searing kiss.

He shuddered above her, drawing her even closer as they melted beneath the fires of passion. Slowly, his heart returned to its normal beat, but Trager could not muster the strength to move away. He propped himself up on his forearms and gazed into her perfect face, mesmerized by the glowing depths of emerald green. He had been to hell and back that day, searching for this elusive vixen, but *he* had become *her* captive, entangled in her silky web. What strange emotion had wrapped itself around his soul when he peered into her eyes? There was something compelling in her smile, something he could not resist. It was like wading into quicksand, knowing there was no escape, being drawn by some overwhelming need that could override logic.

Trager brushed his thumbs over her flushed cheeks as a lazy smile slid across his lips. "Rena, I . . ."

The loud rap at the door had him cursing under his breath, and he wasn't certain where he found the energy to move so swiftly, but he was on his feet, grabbing his scattered clothes before the knocking ceased. Serena moved just as quickly, donning her clothes in a split second. Her wide, apprehensive gaze flew to Trager, who silently motioned for her to find some place to hide, or better yet, disappear into thin air.

Leaving one side of his shirt draped on the outside of his breeches, Trager moved toward the door, his keen eyes sweeping the cabin, assuring that the intruder would think that he had been alone. When his gaze strayed to the back room, Serena was nowhere to be seen. A wry smile touched his lips. The witch had most likely transformed herself into a fly to buzz away undetected, he thought as he grasped the doorknob and leaned heavily upon it, making one last inspection before answering the knock.

Brandon Scott's jaw sagged when the door swung open to reveal the tousle-haired, sleepy-eyed man who propped himself against the door. The smell of brandy wafted its way toward Brandon and he squinted into the dark room to see a glass and an empty bottle sitting on the table. "What the devil are you doing here, Grayson?" he questioned as his gaze settled on his carelessly dressed companion.

"Catching up on lost sleep . . . until you interrupted me," Trager drawled as he ran his fingers through his ruffled hair. A rakish smile cut into his tired features as he raised a suggestive brow. "The lady who entertained me last night wasn't interested in sleeping, and when I stumbled onto this abandoned shack I could not resist falling into bed . . . alone, for a change."

Brandon craned his neck to see the disheveled cot in the adjoining room and then barged inside, glancing back to see that Trager was still squinting at the bright afternoon light. "I suppose you have heard that Serena Warren is wanted for treason," he blurted out and then carefully observed Trager's reaction.

Trager yawned and then frowned, as if the information had taken him by surprise. "Nay, I hadn't. I'm sure her father must have been shocked when they came to take her away."

"She has curiously disappeared before we had the opportunity to question her about her association with Nathan Hale, the Patriot spy."

"Spy?" Trager's head swiveled around to look Brandon right in the eye. "And Miss Warren is his accomplice?" His voice held a hint of astonishment, and then he frowned when he noticed the newly acquired patches on Brandon's uniform. "I see that you have been promoted since last we met," he observed.

"Aye," Brandon replied and then quickly cut to the heart of the matter. "Have you seen Serena?"

Trager gave his raven head a negative shake. "Nay, not since the night she planted her fist in my jaw." He rubbed his cheek and broke into a smile. "She certainly packs a wallop. That wench *is* dangerous."

Brandon's eyes darkened suspiciously. "And that was the last time you saw her?" he persisted.

Trager shrugged and then decided to admit to his second meeting with her at the cove. He could have sworn Brandon knew more than he was letting on, and this was not the time to lie. "I did see her later that evening before I rode back to New Rochelle," he explained. "But that was the last association I had with the wench. Thank goodness for that." Trager chuckled lightly.

Brandon studied him for a long, silent moment and then nodded his acceptance of his confession, his eyes still glowing with a hint of irritation. "Serena will pay dearly for being a traitor when I catch up with her," he muttered bitterly. Nodding abruptly, Brandon marched toward the back room to insure that Trager was alone and then strode back to him. "If you hear or see anything of Serena, I expect you to notify me immediately."

Trager smirked at Brandon's rigid stance and his demanding tone. "I don't intend to get within ten feet of that little witch, but if I hear of her whereabouts I will inform you," he promised, his gaze sobering for Brandon's benefit.

A smug grin slashed across Brandon's features. "There is a reward for her capture. Perhaps the funds you could obtain will make you more eager to seek her out."

Trager's eyes lit up like a candalabrum. "How much?"

The inquiry assured Brandon that Trager was a hard-boiled mercenary whose only interest in Serena was physical and financial. Although he had been furious with Trager for kissing Serena, Trager's reputation was that of a wandering vagabond who used women for his own pleasure and then discarded them when he tired of their charms. "Enough to set one of your battered ships afloat," he said dryly.

As Brandon wheeled and stalked back outside to join his men, Trager remained by the door, not daring to move or breathe until the Redcoats had disappeared over the hill.

"It was *him*."

Trager nearly jumped out of his skin when Serena's harsh voice resounded about him. He glanced over his shoulder to see her standing behind him, her eyes fixed on the retreating soldiers, her expression twisted with bitterness.

"You scared ten years off my life," he chided as he closed the door and wheeled to face her. "I didn't hear you crawl from your hiding place. I swear you are as silent as a cat when you sneak up on a man."

His gruff remark brought a mischievous grin to her lips as she sized him up and down. "Perhaps *I* should be the spy instead of you. Of late, I have acquired a knack for disappearing acts."

He returned her devilish smile as he hooked an arm around her waist, pulling her full length against him and then wishing he had kept his distance. Touching her always sent his thoughts wandering in a lusty direction. "One of your many exceptional talents, my dear," he admitted as his lips sought hers of their own will.

The familiar feeling flooded over her as his mouth slanted across hers. Serena swallowed her breath. Heaven help her. Only a fool would fall in love with a man like Trager—a tumbleweed who went where the wind took him, holding a woman in his arms until he had appeased his desires and then releasing her when another wench caught his eye. If she married him, she would have to learn to accept his wandering ways, never knowing who had enjoyed his skillful kisses while they were apart. But she couldn't marry him—because she *did* love him. She frowned at her twisted logic. It made little sense, even to her, but in her heart she knew she could never take the vows and watch Trager treat her the way Olivia had abused her father. If she didn't love him so, she could endure such an existence and feel no regret in marrying a man who offered protection when she desperately needed it.

Trager felt her reluctance and withdrew, staring thoughtfully at her. "What's wrong?"

Serena backed from his embrace and stared at the blank wall. "I have decided to return home and face the consequences. Once I explain . . ."

"What?" Trager gasped in disbelief. "You may as well sign your own death warrant. You heard what Scott said. The British are itching to get their hands on you. They will make an example of you, just as they did Nathan. 'Tis not the time to play the martyr, Serena. As you recall, Joan of Arc tried it and look what it got her—scorched." Trager cupped her chin, a mocking smile slanting across his lips. "I don't think charred black would become you, either."

She slapped his hand away, an angry spark in her eyes. "Perhaps not, but my fate would be no worse than if I married you. I intend to wed for love, not for your protection."

Trager rolled his eyes toward the ceiling and paused in thought when he spied a spider feasting on a fly. How very similar was his fate, he mused disgustedly. Tangling with Serena brought him constant trouble. "And you may not live long enough to see that whimsical dream come true," he scoffed cynically when he finally returned to her train of thought and followed in its tracks. Trager heaved a frustrated sigh and then tossed her a withering glance. "First you insist that you won't come with me unless we are man and wife. So I proposed, and now you insist that you won't marry me because you don't love me. I wish the hell you would decide what you expect of me."

"I didn't say I didn't love you," she corrected and then bit her lip, wishing she had held a tight rein on her tongue.

He raised a dark brow and allowed a rakish smile to skim his lips. "Could it be that you have somehow managed to fall in love with me, Serena?" he questioned point blank.

Serena presented her back to him and proudly tilted her chin. "Certainly not."

His husky chuckle floated about her, assuring her that he was skeptical of her adamant protest. "Would you find it such a detestable predicament if you actually did love me?" His arms curled around her waist, drawing her back against the hard wall of his chest, feeling her tremble beneath his touch. Trager traced a path of taunting kisses along the curve of her neck as his hand wandered higher to slip inside her shirt, cupping her breast.

"Aye, I would," she insisted as she attempted to still the arousing sensations that gushed through her veins. Serena set his hands from her, but Trager was not to be put off, using his superior strength to keep her in place. "You have many faults, Trager. I would expect your fidelity, and you don't even know the meaning of the word."

"Perhaps you could teach me," he murmured against her shoulder, sending a rash of goose pimples skipping across her skin. "With your experience in instructing, I might become one of your outstanding students."

He was teasing her and she didn't appreciate it. He was making a mockery of the marriage institution. "'Tis a proven fact that it is virtually impossible to teach old dogs new tricks," she retaliated in an intimidating tone.

"Old dog?" Trager released her as if he had been stung, annoyed by her biting insult and her emphasis on the word *old*. "You talk as if I am a doddering old man who shuffles along with the use of a cane." His dark brows formed a hard line over his steel eyes, his features turning to granite. "I think you missed your calling, witch. You should have become a doctor, since you can cut a man to the quick with that scalpel you call a tongue!"

A self-satisfied grin blossomed on her face and Trager scowled, noticing how well she wore it.

Serena had hit upon an exposed nerve, and since she had the knife in his back she decided to give it a quick twist. It was spitefully wicked of her, but oh, so gratifying. She stepped back and thoughtfully rubbed her chin, giving him the once over.

"Nay, you are not decrepit, but then you are not the picture of youth either," she pointed out.

Trager drew himself up in front of her like a puffed toad and cast her the evil eye. "And the *last* thing you need is some bungling schoolboy who would fall for your deceitful charms. You would have the poor lad wrapped so tightly around your finger that he would never come unwound. He would be so damned hen-pecked that I would expect to see him molting twice a year!"

"I am not a dominating woman!" she fiercely protested, her chin tilting a notch higher.

Trager snorted derisively. "Aren't you?" His brow quirked as he crossed his arms over his chest and looked her up and down. The look he gave her was worth a thousand words, none of them complimentary. "That is precisely why you and Brandon called off your engagement. You were having a power struggle over who would wear the pants. You had him stripped to his unmentionables with an audience of high-ranking officials as witness."

Serena gasped at his insulting tone and reacted impulsively. Before she could slap his face, Trager caught her wrist, holding her arm in midair.

"You need a man who can keep you under

244

control," he insisted as he easily bent her arm behind her back and pulled her to him, proving his strength and domination. "Obviously Scott could not foot the bill. He demanded your obedience, but he was not man enough to earn your respect."

"And I suppose you think you are," she flared, detesting him for manhandling her. It went against her grain to have him hold her so easily in place, especially when he had that smug, self-righteous grin plastered on his face.

"You *are* looking up to me, aren't you?" he taunted unmercifully.

"Only because it is physically impossible not to," she muttered bitterly, her tone showing evidence that she was annoyed with her handicap.

"Admit it, vixen." His voice was softer now, the mocking edge evaporating. "You are in love with me. You wouldn't have seduced me that night at the cove if you weren't," he speculated.

"Nay," she argued, afraid to speak the truth. "I only intended to seek pleasure in your arms. There will be other men and I will respond to them as easily as I did to you. Despite your arrogance, you will not be the only man who arouses me." Childish vindictiveness spurred her remarks, wanting to strike out and hurt him before he could hurt her.

Her denial of the magnetism between them found another sensitive nerve and Trager winced as if she had stabbed him again. A dark scowl captured his features, making his silver eyes turn a stormy shade of gray. "Two can play your game, Serena," he growled into her defiant face. "I refuse to allow you to return to your home. You will become my wife and your fate will be far worse than what the British planned for you." His hand bit into the tender flesh of her arm as he yanked her to him, his harsh words hot against her cheek. "I will hear you beg for my caresses. No man can satisfy you the way I can, and you will find that another man's kisses make a poor substitute. You can fight these tormenting feelings the rest of your days, witch, but I venture to guess that one day you will yearn to sleep in my arms."

His threat echoed about her as his mouth swooped down on hers, sealing his vow with a searing kiss. Serena had the sinking feeling she had once again allowed her tongue to outdistance her brain. Why had she spoken so cruelly to him? To protect her stubborn pride, she thought to herself. Now their marriage would become a constant challenge—a battle of will and wit, as if there wasn't enough war in the world. Damn, she had instigated a private battle between them. And yet, somehow she would find a way to keep him loyal to her, bringing him back to her each time he strayed. She would make him love her, she mused determinedly.

Her arms slid around his broad shoulders, her fingers tunneling into the raven hair that lay at the nape of his neck. Serena molded herself to him, feeling his rising desire. She would tempt and taunt him, driving him mad with want, making their time together more than a reckless tryst. The feel of her lips playing on his would be branded on his mind, she vowed as her tongue sought the recesses of his mouth. Her hands wandered across the drumming beat of his heart and then slipped inside his shirt to trail along the band of his breeches. She smiled to herself as he groaned and clutched her closer, pressing his hard manliness against her thigh.

Despite her own aroused state, Serena wormed from his embrace and flashed him a smile that was slightly mischievous and yet carefully innocent. "I will wed you, Trager Grayson," she announced as she traced her index finger over his full lips. "But it remains to be seen which one of us will be conquered by the bonds of matrimony. You are a man of experience in the ways of love and, no doubt, it has become an unconscious reaction with you to take a woman in your arms." Her delicate brow quirked as he frowned in an attempt to predict her point. "But these experiences are new to me. Loving a man brings a fascination that I have only begun to appreciate. Somehow I don't imagine that experimenting with other eager lovers will be such a distasteful existence." A devilish grin alighted on her features when Trager's face fell like a rockslide, and she bit back a spiteful chuckle. "Do not be surprised if I take to this arrangement without complaint."

Trager muttered under his breath as Serena sauntered away to collect her belongings. Damn that little witch. Torture was what she had in mind for him. He had taught her the meaning of passion and now she needed no instructor. She had become a seductive tease, and he was painfully aware of how his own men had gawked at the sleeping beauty, their lusty thoughts printed on their faces in bold letters, his own brother included. If she set her mind to it, she could have all of them begging for her affection, and she would give it, just to spite him. Damn, but he was going to have his hands full controlling this vixen. Perhaps he should wed her and stash her away in a convent for safekeeping. The idea was to his liking, and he smiled wickedly at the thought.

Her eyes narrowed as she studied the flicker in his eyes. "What are you planning, Trager?" she demanded to know, uneasy and wary of the way he was looking at her.

His smile widened to show even white teeth as he strode into the adjoining room. "'Tis time to ride, my dear. My men are expecting us at White Plains."

Serena watched his broad shoulders shaking in amusement as he swung open the door and waited for her to join him. She would have given a king's ransom to know what was running through his complex mind.

As they journeyed to White Plains, Trager remained close-mouthed, sitting behind her on the steed, wearing that silly damned grin that grated on Serena's nerves. As they rode, Serena began having misgivings about challenging Trager. She was only a novice and Trager was a professional at maneuvering people.

What a fool she had been to think that she could burrow her way into his hard heart. She would need a chisel and the perseverance of Job. Why was it that she managed to stumble from one disaster to another? Serena grappled with that question all the way to White Plains, but still she found no answer.

Chapter Thirteen

Trager smiled approvingly when Serena emerged from one of the bedrooms in the mansion where General Washington had set up headquarters. Her pale pink gown gave her an angelic appearance, but still she managed to retain that fiery sparkle in her eyes, assuring any man who looked upon her that there was more to this lovely golden-haired enchantress than silk and lace.

Serena glanced uneasily about her, knowing what was in store for her. Trager had informed her that General Washington had requested an audience with her as soon as she had ample opportunity to make herself presentable after her long journey.

After Trager led her to the study, he backed away and then closed the door behind him, leaving Serena to confront the man she had heard so much about. She swallowed over the lump that had collected in her throat and then thankfully sank down into the chair Washington offered to her. His keen eyes made a critical survey of her as he eased back into his seat at the desk.

"Captain Grayson has informed me of your friendship with Nathan Hale and the incident that has made you a fugitive in your own homeland." A wry smile pursed his lips as he focused his full attention on the nervous young woman who sat poised to break and run. "The captain also told me about the patriotic oration you made to the high-ranking officers." He chortled softly and shook his head. "My dear Serena, if all my would-be soldiers had your gumption we would send General Howe retreating to the shore and set him adrift in the Atlantic. Your feisty spirit is commendable."

Serena smiled sheepishly as the tension drained from her body, and then her expression sobered. "Had I known what would happen to Nathan I would have attempted to take Howe's officers captive and deposit them on your doorstep." She could not contain the bitterness that seeped into her voice, but she also doubted that Washington would begrudge her her whim.

Washington nodded thoughtfully, assured that his first impression of Serena Warren was correct. She was a vibrant young woman with more than her share of courage and spunk. "And I wouldn't have been the least bit surprised to see them there had you and I met at an earlier date," he complimented, gracing her with a warm smile. He propped his forearms on the desk and leaned toward her. "Our cause is in jeopardy, Serena. We are shamefully outnumbered and untrained. Although Captain Grayson and his rangers have brought me valuable information about the position and strength of the British troops, I know that there is much you could tell me. I know of your father and I also realize that you have been caught in the middle of this conflict. But out of respect for Hale, I would ask that you divulge any information that you might have gained."

Her gaze dropped to her lap like a kite that had taken a headlong dive without a breath of wind to sustain it. "You are forcing me into a very awkward situation, General," she murmured as she nervously toyed with the folds of her silk skirt.

Washington sighed heavily. "I realize that, but I was hoping that you had been swayed toward the cause of independence after what has happened to you. I do not ask you to betray your father. 'Tis only that we are in dire straits, hounded by the Redcoats on every side. Any information, no matter how insignificant it might seem to you, could aid in our strategy. I need to know how they think, what they anticipate from us."

Serena strangled on her breath. She could envision her father sitting before General Howe, facing the same dilemma. Had Mitchell been forced to divulge information about his own daughter? Had General Howe doubted Mitchell's loyalty because his daughter had spoken against the Crown?

The rap at the door interrupted them and Serena was thankful for the intrusion, giving her time to gather her wits. A young officer stepped into the room, glanced discreetly at her, and then bent his gaze to the general.

"Sir, Major Baldwin has just arrived and insists that he confer with you at your earliest possible convenience," the corporal stated in a businesslike tone before his gaze strayed back to Serena.

Washington nodded agreeably and bit back a smile as he watched the awestruck corporal gawking at Serena. "I will see him now." After the corporal exited, he stared at Serena, aware of her hesitation. "If you find that you wish to continue this discussion, I will be anxiously waiting."

Serena rose to her feet and forced a meager smile before moving toward the door. A frown creased her brow as she brushed shoulders with the man who entered as she left. There was something familiar about him. She had seen him before, but where?

Her thoughts came to an abrupt halt when she spied Trager accepting a shower of kisses from a young woman.

"Oh, Trager, I'm so happy to see you again. Roger told me I would find you here. It seems an eternity since . . ." Clarissa Baldwin's voice trailed off in midsentence when she leaned back to see that Trager's attention had flown over her head. Her blue eyes narrowed as she twisted around to see the shapely blond in the stunning pink gown standing like a queen in the hall. Her green eyes were throwing sparks hot enough to ignite a forest fire. Clarissa smiled to herself, determined to stake her claim on Trager. If the wench had any designs on him, Clarissa intended to rout any of her romantic inclinations before they could take root. Although her competition was bewitching, Clarissa knew how to tempt and satisfy a man. She had been practicing her technique since she was old enough to distinguish the difference between men and women. Keeping a possessive grasp on Trager, Clarissa blessed Serena with a radiant smile and then turned her attention back to Trager.

"I'm famished, love. I have discovered a quaint inn on the outskirts of town. Would you consent to accompanying me? We need to catch up on lost time." There was a provocative glimmer in her blue eyes and a raspy edge to her voice that assured Serena that there was something between this sultry, sable-haired woman and Serena's frivolous soon-to-be husband.

Serena felt a rise of color in her cheeks as a wave of jealousy flooded over her, turning her eyes a darker shade of green. She stood there smoldering, expecting Trager to inform his clinging vine that by nightfall he would have a wife.

Sporting a rakish smile, Trager glanced at Serena and then nodded his consent to Clarissa. "I would be more than happy to accompany you, my dear."

So that was to be his game, she muttered under her breath as she watched the striking couple stroll out the door. Left to her own devices and furious that Trager had abandoned her, Serena glanced about her and then marched outside to inspect the rebel troops. A frown knitted her brow when she spied Egan Hadley propped against a tree. It was his fault that she had been recaptured in the first place, and she intended to give him a good piece of her mind.

"Good afternoon, Miss Warren," Egan greeted her with a toothless smile.

"Is it?" Serena gave him a cold shoulder, complete with icicles. "I hadn't noticed."

The glare she gave him was potent enough to wilt a normal man, but Egan was thick-skinned and merely snickered as he unfolded himself from the ground. "Ye ain't holdin' a grudge 'gainst me, now are ye? 'Twas fer yer own good to be hauled back to the cap'n, ye know. If them Redcoats woulda caught up with ye, there wouldn't be nothin' left of ye."

Serena wasn't certain that marrying Trager was the lesser of the two evils. Indeed, it would have been less torturous to be hanged and have her misery ended. All that she and Trager seemed to have in common was that they were wrong for each other. But then, Serena had to admit that Brandon hadn't been right for her, either. Perhaps no man was, she mused, disheartened. She was a misfit, incapable of finding the perfect mate. And she had a bad habit of letting her tongue have free rein, leading her from one conflict to another.

Her pensive musings were interrupted when a long shadow fell over her. Her head jerked up to see a dark, attractive soldier who made no attempt to disguise his admiration. There was something oddly familiar about him, but then Serena had experienced that same sensation when she had brushed past Baldwin on her way out of Washington's office.

"Trager has left you alone? I'm beginning to doubt

the man's sanity." Roger's smile was contagious, and Serena found herself returning it without making an effort. He offered her his arm and then gestured toward the surrounding area. "Would you like for me to show you around camp?"

Why not, Serena asked herself and, finding no reason to decline, accepted his arm. If Trager could traipse off with his lover on the eve of his wedding then she could damned well stroll through camp with a dashing soldier. When she glanced up into his sun-bronzed face, a hint of a question rippled in her eyes and Roger smiled knowingly.

"If you find me a bit familiar, 'tis because I am Trager's brother, Roger. I saw you at the cabin before we rode to White Plains, but, of course, you were sleeping off Egan's potion."

Serena scrutinized his handsome face, noting the resemblance, but she was quick to see that Roger's features were not carved from granite, as his brother's were. Time and cynicism had not eroded away the gentleness from his face, and his eyes were a warm brown, unlike the stormy gray pools Trager possessed. She was so busy comparing the two brothers that she tripped over the hem of her skirt and fell unceremoniously into Roger's arms, her face coloring three shades of red before she could fight down the profuse blush.

Roger grinned as he held her securely in his arms, instantly aroused by the feel of her shapely body pressed to his. "Would you think it too forward of me to admit that I have been wishing I had met you first?"

"I'm sure Trager shares your wish," Serena responded as she pushed away and steadied herself on both feet.

"Oh?" His brow quirked as his hungry gaze ran the full length of her, lingering overly long on the swells of her breasts. "Then why has he asked me to fetch a clergyman for your wedding?"

"'Tis his way of offering me protection, nothing more," Serena murmured as she fixed her eyes on some distant point, striving for an indifferent tone.

"Had I known his intention, I would have offered my services, my lady," Roger assured her.

Serena stopped in her tracks, her lashes sweeping up to peer into his tanned face. "But you and I have only met. Why . . ."

His hand enfolded hers and brought it to his lips, assuring Serena that both Graysons had a charismatic charm that was difficult to ignore. "Have you not heard of love at first sight, Serena? If you find marrying my brother to be distasteful, consider your alternative. I am willing to offer you far more than protection." His face was dangerously close to hers, his lips parting, his eyes holding her captive.

Trager propped his chin on his fist and picked at the plate of food that sat before him, absently listening to Clarissa's conversation, nodding occasionally when she paused to ask him a question. Why the devil had he consented to accompany Clarissa, leaving Serena on her own? It was a foolish mistake, knowing Serena as he did. There was no way of telling what that woman would do if someone wasn't around to keep a watchful eye on her. She was impulsive, unpredictable, following whims without giving them second thoughts.

The longer he sat in the inn, the more uneasy he became, wondering what surprise he would encounter when he returned to headquarters. He had intended to make Serena jealous by leaving with Clarissa, but there was no consolation in annoying Serena when his thoughts kept straying to that mere wisp of a woman who had managed to turn him every which way but loose. In time he would tire of that little firebrand, he told himself, and then he would seek out Clarissa.

"Trager?" Her bottom lip jutted out in an exaggerated pout. "I haven't seen you in more than three months and you are very inattentive," she scolded. "What is the matter with you? Before we were separated I had your undivided attention."

His shoulder lifted in a noncommittal shrug. "I've had a lot on my mind," he said lamely.

Her hand brushed over his knuckles, a seductive smile settling on her lips. "Perhaps you need something to take your mind off your worries."

Trager withdrew his hand and rose to full stature, drawing Clarissa up beside him. "Aye, perhaps I do, but I have an important matter to attend this evening."

Clarissa pouted all the way to the carriage, agitated by his blatant refusal to share her bed. She had her sights set on winning him, and she was accustomed to having her way.

"Will you come to the inn later this evening to see me?" she pressed, disguising her irritation behind a pretentious smile. "We could have the night to ourselves. Papa has to leave again soon."

He glanced down at her attractive face, smiling apologetically. "Another time, Clarissa."

Her temper got the best of her. "I will not be cast aside, Trager," she flared, her lips curling in annoyance. "You know how I feel about you and that I have been faithful to you. I think you owe me a little consideration."

Faithful? The wench had more beaux than the army had volunteers. Trager chuckled at her fit of temper and outrageous lie. "There is a war going on, love," he reminded her glibly. "If you weren't so spoiled and eager to amuse yourself, you would realize that business comes before pleasure."

Clarissa bit back the sarcastic remark that waited on the tip of her tongue. The way to Trager's heart was through patience and understanding. He was not the type of man who could be maneuvered or pressured. If she bided her time he would come to her and then she would make him realize that she was meant for him. She could have had any number of men, but she wanted Trager, and he was worth the wait.

"Very well," she breathed defeatedly, knowing she was not about to surrender. She would only ease off for the moment. "I will wait until you return . . . and most anxiously." She reached up on tiptoe to press a kiss to his unresponsive lips and then displayed her forlorn smile. "Goodbye, my love."

Trager discarded all thoughts of Clarissa the moment his foot hit the carriage step and he settled himself on the seat. There was much to be done and time was short.

With a thoughtful frown stamped on his face, Trager marched into the hall to find Serena, but Angus Baldwin grasped his arm to detain him. "Where have you been these past months, Captain? Clarissa knew where you were stationed until August and then you suddenly dropped out of sight."

Trager had little use for Clarissa's father. He seemed more interested in working his way up the ladder of success than aiding the cause of independence. "Washington has been keeping me busy," Trager commented, carefully avoiding details.

"Where?" Angus prodded.

"I do not mean to be rude, Major, but I am pressed for time."

Angus dropped his arm to his side. "I thought you might be interested to hear what I had learned about the man who betrayed Hale. The two of you were friends, weren't you?"

"Who?" Trager stared long and hard at him.

A wry smile hung on one corner of the major's mouth. "Perhaps we can sit down later and have a long talk when you are not so rushed," he baited.

Trager was quick to realize that Baldwin was not

about to divulge any facts without an exchange of information. He was a snoop, constantly weaseling facts out of anyone who was loose with his tongue.

"An excellent idea, Major. Now if you will excuse me, I am already late for an appointment." Trager took the steps two at a time, wondering if Baldwin's information would amount to only a hill of beans, as it usually did.

Serena had seen Trager walking toward the mansion and muttered to herself. It was obvious that Trager intended to seek pleasure wherever he could find it, married or not. He would make a mockery of wedlock, and she would have no part of it. She loved him enough to let him go, even if it broke her heart. It would mend in time, she told herself as she nervously paced the chamber.

When she heard footsteps in the hall, she inhaled a deep breath and waited for Trager to appear in the doorway. She had rehearsed her speech, but the words were more difficult to produce when she faced him than they were when she spoke to her reflection in the mirror.

Trager halted in his tracks, his devouring gaze roaming over the pale yellow gown that accented each shapely swell and curve that she possessed. His eyes came to rest on the low bodice of her dress, watching her full breasts rise and fall with each anxious breath she took.

"Rena, you will make a lovely bride," he rasped,

his silver eyes traveling over her like flames that burned each inch of exposed flesh they touched.

Serena struggled to maintain her composure as she observed his virile form and ruggedly handsome features. For a split second she selfishly wished that he wasn't so strikingly attractive and that women were not magnetically drawn to him. If he had had a plain face and an average physique perhaps he would not stand out in the crowd. But as luck would have it, he stood poised like some Greek god to be admired by more women than she had known in her lifetime.

"And you will make a handsome groom," she reluctantly admitted and then hurried on before she forgot her memorized speech. "But not for me. I have been giving this matter serious consideration all afternoon and I have come to realize that wedding you would be a disastrous mistake. Since I have made more than my share, I choose not to stumble into another."

His dark brows plowed a frown across his forehead. "We have been through this before, Serena," he grumbled sourly.

"At the time you refused to listen to the voice of reason," she countered, gathering more steam when her first remark set him back on his heels. "I would be a jealous, demanding wife, and you would continue to be as you are—a frivolous vagabond who uses women to appease your voracious lusts and then discards them in your quest to acquire a long list of conquered hearts."

"And you are a headstrong woman who does not

need a man to lean on, but rather one to walk all over," he retaliated in an intimidating tone. "A lesser man would find himself lying facedown in the dirt with your footprints on his back." The faintest hint of a smile found its way to one corner of his mouth as he swaggered toward her. "Think of it this way, my dear. By marrying each other, we can save two other poor souls from eternal misery."

He was making light of this discussion and Serena didn't appreciate it. "You can jest if you like, Trager, but I have decided not to marry you," she insisted, her chin tilting determinedly.

His eyes held a glint of hard steel as he towered over her like a stone mountain that cast a foreboding shadow over her. "You can come quietly or be forced, but you will bear my name and the vows will be consummated before this night has ended."

Their gazes locked and clashed. "If you force me to marry you I will not come willingly to your bed," she shot back at him, biting her tongue to keep from shouting the walls down around him. "Would you rape your own wife on your wedding night?"

A devilish grin settled in his sun-bronzed features, carving crows' feet from the corners of his eyes. "I will demand my husbandly rights," he assured her, his tone softer as he reached out to trace his index finger over her stubbornly set jaw. "You have yet to find the experience distasteful, and I can be a very persuasive man when I intend to have my way."

His remark only reminded her that Trager had only one purpose for women. He could turn on the charm when he wanted something, whispering empty words to see the end he desired. Why had she fallen in love with such a callous, uncaring man? Because she was every kind of fool, she thought dismally. His head came deliberately toward hers and Serena clamped a tight rein on her emotions, determined to remain unaffected by his persuasive kiss. His lips caressed hers, his warm breath threatening to kindle a fire that could burn out of control. Serena stood like a stone statue, picturing him as some hideous beast whose touch repulsed her, refusing to be swayed from her decision.

The sharp rap at the door was perfectly timed, and Serena breathed a constricted sigh of relief when Trager abruptly released her to answer the knock. As the door swung open, Roger peered around his brother's broad shoulders to assess the shapely blonde who had been on his mind all afternoon. He let loose with a wolfish whistle as his eyes floated over her in possessive fashion.

Roger ignored his brother and moved to Serena, his arm encircling her waist as he bent to press a kiss to her swollen lips.

"What the hell is going on here?" Trager demanded to know as he watched Roger behaving as if he had staked some claim on this fiery little minx.

"Did you and Miss Baldwin enjoy your meal?" Roger inquired when Trager's harsh words reminded him that he was not alone with Serena.

"Nay, I was too preoccupied wondering if anyone had thought to keep an eye on Serena," he grumbled and then glared at his brother who still had not released his grasp on her.

Roger's grin was as wide as the Hudson River. "I was only too happy to keep her company."

Trager's heavy brows plowed a deep line over the narrowed slits of his eyes as his gaze swung to Serena, noting the smug expression on her face. What deviltry was she brewing?

"Do you want to give him the news or shall I?" Roger queried as he shot a quick look to Serena and then peered at his brother.

"Tell me what?" Trager glanced back and forth between them, becoming angrier by the second. His temper had a short fuse, and, between his miserable afternoon, Baldwin's baiting, and Roger's tormenting game, his composure was coming dangerously close to unraveling. "One of you better explain what the hell is going on!" he demanded sharply.

"Serena has consented to marry me this evening," Roger announced, a pleased smile encompassing all of his handsome features.

The news hit Trager like a doubled fist in the belly, knocking the wind out of him. "What?" His condemning gaze anchored on Serena. So the little tart had cast her bewitching spell on Roger, he mused bitterly. She was turning brother against brother, using Roger as her savior before discarding him when he had served his purpose.

"I thought the arrangement would be more to your liking," Serena commented and then huddled closer to Roger as Trager drew himself up like a panther preparing to strike. "I will still bear the name of Grayson and your obligation will be only in a brotherly sort of way. It seemed that you were more interested in Miss Baldwin." Her tone became even, showing no hint of emotion. "I realized that your marriage proposal was a noble attempt to protect me and when I confided in Roger, he offered to replace you, giving you the freedom to pursue Miss Baldwin."

Trager exploded. Nothing had gone as he had anticipated. This new twist caught him off guard and he could barely collect his scattered wits to speak. "Dammit, you barely know the wench!" he blurted out, glaring at Roger as if bats had taken up residence in his belfry.

"But I like what I see," Roger argued, his appreciative smile lingering on Serena. "And she has assured me that she is fond of me. More than one marriage began with a mutual admiration."

Trager opened his mouth to speak but no words formed on his lips. His plan to make Serena jealous had backfired in his face, and he was the one who was sprouting the horns of an envy-green monster. Serena would have Roger wrapped so tightly around her dainty finger that he wouldn't be able to breathe, Trager thought angrily. His brooding silver eyes riveted on Serena, cold and unrelenting.

"You are marrying *me*," he ground out.

Roger stepped between them, deflecting his brother's

hard glare. "She has made her choice. I should think you would be relieved that you do not need to assume the responsibility for her. You yourself referred to her as troublesome baggage," Roger reminded him.

Trager's gaze slid back to Serena, remembering that she had not succumbed to his kiss as she had that afternoon in the shack. Was he losing his touch or had he met his match with this vixen? Lord, the wench was twisting and stretching his logic until he couldn't think straight. He was itching to shake some sense into both Roger and Serena, furious that she had pitted his own brother against him as a rival. Damn that deceitful witch! He should have handed her over to the British and taken the bounty for her lovely neck!

"Aye, I did claim her to be troublesome baggage," Trager agreed, "but I do not intend to unload her on you. Now leave us alone, Roger. Serena and I have matters to discuss."

"Nay." Roger raised a proud chin, but found himself grabbed by the jacket and propelled out the door. When he wheeled around to barge back inside, Trager slammed and locked the door in his furious face. "Open up!" he shouted as he beat on the door.

"Go away before I do my talking with my fist, Roger," Trager snapped back at him. "Serena is marrying me and I will hear no more of it!"

"If you mistreat her, I promise you will have hell to pay," Roger vowed and then stalked down the hall. A wry smile spread across his lips and then Roger bit back a chuckle. He had spent a lifetime with Trager and he had come to realize that the louder Trager protested, the more determined he was to keep his possession. Aye, he may have referred to Serena as a thorn in his side, but he couldn't get that bewitching vixen out of his blood. Trager wanted her, Roger mused as he ambled down the steps, but Trager would probably be the last one to realize it.

Trager scowled as he focused his smoldering gaze on Serena, annoyed that he had spent his last few minutes of bachelorhood arguing with his own brother and his bride-to-be. He should have been soaking in the tub, contemplating his fleeting freedom, regretting his decision to take a wife. Instead, he was in Serena's room, fighting for a woman who had brought him nothing but trouble. Was nothing sacred, he asked himself as he met her defiant glare. Had it come to the point that a man could not enjoy one moment of peace before he tied the knot around his neck? Other condemned men were granted a last request or a moment of silence before they faced their destiny.

"I'm going to bathe and change," Trager announced and then wagged an accusing finger at her. "And you damned well better be here waiting when I return. I do not intend to be humiliated by being left standing alone on the altar."

"You don't trust me?" Serena's delicate brow arched mockingly before she strolled to the window, already devising a plan of escape.

"You have given me little reason to," he insisted before he whipped open the door and stormed out, deciding that he needed an ice cold bath to cool his blazing temper.

When the sounds of his leaving had echoed and died in the silence, Serena grabbed her belongings and hastily tossed them in her bag. With her heart pounding in anticipation she eased open the door and then flinched when she noticed the tall figure looming by the portal.

A knowing smile grazed the young corporal's lips as he watched the look of disappointment spread across Serena's lovely features. "Are you planning to leave before the wedding?" he inquired, a hint of amusement in his voice.

Serena returned his grin with one that was touched with guilt. "Aye, I had considered it." She looked him over thoroughly and then arched a curious brow. "I don't suppose it would be worth my time to bribe you."

"Nay, I'm afraid not, Miss Warren," he replied. "Captain Grayson assured me that he would have my head on a silver platter if I allowed you to pass through this door."

A spark of irritation flashed in her eyes. "Then perhaps you should be the one to marry him," she muttered sourly. "You seem to have more fear and devotion to him that I have." Her gaze slid back over her shoulder, planning her alternative method of escape.

"Grayson also posted a soldier below your window," the corporal informed her, biting back a chuckle. "I'm sorry, Miss Warren. I fear the only way you can escape from this room is to walk to the altar on General Washington's arm."

Serena slammed the door in the soldier's face and stomped her foot. Damn that Trager. He was bent on making her miserable.

Chapter Fourteen

Like a lamb being led to slaughter, Serena gulped over the lump in her throat and accepted the arm General Washington offered. When they had descended the stairs Serena paused to see the large ballroom of the mansion lined with officers who craned their necks to see her approaching on the general's arm. Her father would have had a fit of the vapors had he known the rebel general was standing in his stead and that she was about to become the wife of a Patriot spy. Lord help her. Hell had come to swallow her up, and Serena's knees buckled with the thought.

Washington smiled sympathetically and offered a supporting arm on her waist as he ushered her forward. "It will be over soon," he assured her softly. "And you have chosen a fine man, one whom I trust and admire."

His words fell on deaf ears. Her attention anchored on Trager, who stood beside his brother. His silver-gray eyes revealed nothing of his thoughts and his dead-pan expression left Serena to wonder if he saw her at all. It seemed to Serena that he was mentally preparing himself for his own funeral, rather than his wedding, and she shared his sentiments. If weddings were supposed to be the happiest day of a woman's life, she had been shortchanged. She was miserable, contemplating the notion of spinning on her heels and making her break for freedom. This was madness, all this pomp and circumstance for a loveless marriage. And there was Roger, smiling tenderly at her after he had abandoned her in her hour of need. But then she reminded herself that even Roger could not confront Trager and emerge the victor. No man could withstand Satan when he was breathing fire.

As Washington relinquished his grasp on her, Serena flinched. Trager drew her up beside him, his steady hand folding around her trembling fingers. Serena concentrated on the clergyman's words, but they whirled around her head and then escaped her. It was as if she were in a daze, half dreaming, half aware of what transpired about her.

Trager's rich voice echoed about her and rebounded off the walls to come at her from all directions. When the preacher stared at her, expecting her to repeat the vows, she peered dumbfoundedly back at him. The words were lodged in her throat, lost to the sound of her thundering heartbeat. Trager nudged her, but still no words formed on her lips.

A hushed murmur spread like wildfire through the congregation, and again Trager jabbed her in the ribs. The instinct to flee overwhelmed her and Serena wheeled to follow the impulse, but Trager caught her to him, his features chiseled from granite, a tight smile thinning his lips.

"Damn you, you have me cursing at my own wedding," he hissed, only loud enough for her to hear. "Speak the vows or you will surely wish you had."

His fingers bit into her waist like a clamp that threatened to crush her ribs if she dared to disobey. Serena winced beneath the bruising pressure. "I do," she managed to choke out, but she didn't. Why was he torturing her? He didn't love her.

Trager lifted the veil from her face, his mouth slanting across hers to seal the vow with a kiss. He drew her quivering body to his, branding her as his possession with a roomful of soldiers as witnesses. It was too late to flee. She was Trager's wife and she would have gladly relinquished her position to the first woman who expressed a desire to take her place.

"May I kiss the bride?" Roger tapped his brother on the shoulder and then pried them apart. "After all, I was the *best* man. Perhaps even better than the groom," he added as he shot his brother a hasty glance.

Roger gave Trager no time to reply to the barb. He pulled Serena into his arms, taking away the small breath she had managed to grasp when Trager had released her. And then she was passed around the room like a single mug of ale in a crowd of men who were dying of thirst. She could have sworn half of them had not been within ten feet of a woman in six months, and she found herself ravishingly kissed and nearly squeezed in two.

When Major Baldwin bent his head toward hers, Serena backed away to have a better look at him. There was something oddly familiar about him, but where could she possibly have seen him?

Trager picked that moment to appear beside her, offering her a glass of champagne, which she thankfully accepted, despite the donor. She peered at Baldwin over the rim of her glass, trying to place his face. And then it suddenly came to her from the shadows of her mind.

Baldwin had been at one of the meetings in New York the previous summer when she had accompanied Mitchell and Olivia. Although she hadn't met him, she had seen him meandering among the large crowd, rarely more than a few feet away from General Howe. She would never have noticed him had he not been following the commander like a pup. Was he a spy for the Revolutionists? Had he infiltrated Howe's headquarters? Serena eyed him warily. Howe was no one's fool. If Howe allowed the man near him it was only because he had been carefully screened.

Serena nodded slightly to Baldwin and then walked away. When Trager came up behind her, she glanced up, her expression sober.

"I want to see Washington . . . alone," she demanded. When Trager did a double take and eyed her dubiously, she added, "It is imperative that I speak with him immediately." The urgency in her voice drew his concerned frown, and he nodded.

Her lashes swept up as Washington entered the study and closed the door behind him. "Sir, I fear that you have a Tory among your troops, perhaps a spy for the Crown," she announced, cutting to the heart of the matter.

Washington's jaw sagged from its hinges and then he slammed his mouth shut as he wilted in his chair. "You are making a serious accusation, Serena," he reminded her solemnly.

Serena squared her shoulders and stared him straight in the eye. "I have seen your Major Baldwin with General Howe. I know that the general is a cautious man when it comes to choosing his companions . . . almost to the point of arrogance. Did Baldwin come to you offering his services or was he hand-picked for his duties?"

Washington frowned hard in thought. "He came as many others have, voicing their desire to give their time and talents for our cause. We do not have the strength of the British and we are in no position to be particular. We are desperate for aid and information."

"Then it would not surprise me if Baldwin is working as a double agent," Serena speculated. "If he has gained Howe's confidence, he could be playing this war to his advantage."

"You are asking me to believe that the man who has brought me information on the position of British troops would betray us at the drop of a hat?" Washington gasped incredulously.

"I am asking you to watch him closely," Serena corrected. "I sincerely hope I am wrong, but if I am right, Baldwin could do more harm than good. For it is as you have said, your cause stands on wobbly legs and his betrayal could well be disastrous."

Washington eased back in his chair and studied her for a long, silent moment before nodding for her to take her leave. "Please send Trager to me, Serena," he requested. "I want to discuss the matter with him."

As Serena swept from the room she wondered if Washington respected her enough to put stock in her suspicions. Why should he? They had only just met. But intuition bade her to be wary of Baldwin. Did Washington intend to cross-examine Trager about the credibility of his wife? She knew Baldwin was Clarissa's father—Did she mistrust him simply because of Clarissa's involvement with Trager? Serena was wishing she hadn't been so hasty in confronting Washington with her suspicions. Perhaps she should have allowed herself to digest her misgivings and decide if her motives ran deeper than an attempt to single out an unwelcome weed.

She was not able to pursue her wandering thoughts. Roger wedged his way through the crowd and offered her another drink. She downed it as if it were water and she was parched.

His smile made his dark eyes glow with amusement. "Shall I fetch you another?" Roger queried.

"Aye, why not." If it would help her through this night, she would drink the entire punchbowl and

278

float away on a senseless sea of dreams.

Serena swallowed another sensation of apprehension as Roger disappeared in the crowd. Would Trager be furious with her for daring to approach the general, accusing one of his officers of treason? Had she reacted in the same fashion as the mysterious person who had linked her with Nathan?

Forcing a feeble smile, Serena accepted the drink Roger placed in her hand. As the evening wore on the thoughts returned to haunt her. Serena found herself clinging to a glass of champagne, becoming numb to the entire day of torment. Her concern with Trager and Washington vanished and she became reckless as the heady sensations encompassed her. Her laughter floated about the crowd of soldiers gathered about her. She was still amused by their behaving as if they had not laid eyes on a woman for an eternity. They openly gawked at her, vying for her attention, and she responded, giving them the blinding smiles they ached to see.

Heaving a frustrated sigh, Trager stepped out of Washington's office and let his eyes circle the crowd, finding his new wife the center of attention. His first impulse was to retrieve her, but he saw Roger standing off to himself, watching the room of soldiers who waited for Serena to finish her drink before she was swept back onto the dance floor.

"Roger, I want to apologize," Trager began, clearing his throat to gain his brother's attention.

"There is no need." Roger slowly turned to study Trager's hard features. A devilish smile worked its way across his face. "I knew you would win out. You always do."

"And you do not hold a grudge?" Trager pressed, baffled by this sudden change in Roger's behavior. He would have bet his fortune that Roger was ready to fight for the troublesome wench.

"Nay. As they say, all is fair in love and war."

A skeptical frown creased his heavy brow as he stared Roger down. "I have the uneasy feeling that I've been had," he mused aloud.

"If you hadn't been behaving like the gallant hero who rose in defense to claim his possession, you might have noticed earlier." Roger chuckled as Trager's eyes turned to smoldering silver. "It does my heart good to know that for once in my life I have outwitted you, big brother. If I had married Serena you would never have forgiven me, and nothing would have been right between us." His expression sobered. "Aye, I would have been content with that captivating vixen, but I was not foolish enough to think that I could have won her heart. I only hope . . ." Roger halted in midsentence as Clarissa Baldwin approached them, her eyes flashing sparks that were aimed at Trager.

"So this is how you think to repay me for my loyalty," she hissed furiously, oblivious to the fact that Roger had backed away to fade into the woodwork. "How dare you treat me this way, Trager."

His gaze weighed heavily upon her, wondering

why he had been attracted to her in the first place. She was spoiled and demanding, and as fake as fool's gold. Her only interest in him was the pleasure he could provide in bed and a fortune that could keep her in silk and furs.

"I married Serena because it suits my purpose," he said harshly, his voice so cold and remote that Clarissa winced, wondering if she really knew him at all. "I do not need your permission and I'll be damned if I intend to ask for it."

Serena had fearlessly made her way toward Trager when she had spied Clarissa, but after hearing his remark she retreated to her crowd of admirers, attempting to mask the pain that twisted her soul. He had married her to suit his purpose? What was his motive? Did he intend to use her, to maneuver her for his cause? Serena accepted another glass of champagne and tried to drown her troubled thoughts, wishing she could transport herself a million miles away from Trager.

A hush fell over the soldiers and Serena frowned at the sudden silence, certain her musings would be heard by one and all. Trager's cold voice cut through the air, slashing her composure to shreds.

"I think you have caused enough disturbance for one night."

Her lashes swept up to see Trager moving bodies out of his way to reach her, his unrelenting gaze drilling into her. Mustering her courage, Serena raised her glass in mock toast, preferring to offer a curse. "Come join us in a drink," she insisted.

Trager discreetly observed the glazed look in her eyes and muttered under his breath. Clarissa had done nothing to lighten his dark mood, and Serena's intoxicated condition had colored his disposition pitch black. "It appears that you have been celebrating enough for both of us." He clamped his hand around her arm and uprooted her from the spot, propelling her toward the door. "Did you intend to choose a lover from that eager group of swains or was it your scheme to taunt them and then leave them lusting through the night, wondering what pleasure awaited the man who sampled your charms?"

His biting insult rolled off her like water off a duck's back. She had partaken so much of the bubbling brew that she had finally reached the point of recklessness. "A woman always has a tender place in her heart for men in uniform." She shrugged and then took another long sip of champagne. "And I was celebrating your absence."

Trager scowled as he ushered her up the steps. "I swear you are nothing but trouble. I have not enjoyed a moment's peace since I met you. Now I find myself chained to a woman who has more admirers than the night sky has stars."

"I was more than willing to let you keep your precious freedom." She tried to focus her eyes on his sour expression, but the task was becoming more difficult. "Just why did you marry me, Trager?" she inquired, still confused by the remark he had made to Clarissa.

"That is one question which will undoubtedly

torment me for an eternity," Trager muttered as he stepped onto the landing and stared at the second flight of stairs.

He was impatient with Serena's snail's pace and annoyed at the evening's turn of events. Sweeping her up in his arms, he stalked up the steps and did not set her to her feet until they were alone in her room.

His abrupt movement sent the world careening about her and Serena clutched at the lapel of his jacket to keep her balance. "It wasn't necessary to carry me across the threshold. I would have preferred to walk the last mile on my own," she chided.

Her slurred words made Trager roll his eyes heavenward, as if summoning more patience, but there was none left to draw upon. "In your condition it would have taken the rest of the night to scale that mountain of steps and reach the honeymoon suite."

Honeymoon suite? Her gaze circled the room and she sniffed distastefully. She had dreamed of her wedding night on a few occasions, but this did not meet her expectations. Here she was, virtually held captive in the Patriots' headquarters, wed to a man who didn't give a damn about her. This was hell, pure and simple, she decided. Her fate was to be bound to Trager Grayson, a man who might have been everything she would have dreamed of, but wasn't because he had a heart carved from stone.

As Serena wove her way across the room to study her reflection in the mirror, Trager shrugged off his jacket and tossed it over the back of the chair. His gaze was fixed on the tempting blonde who had haunted his thoughts for over two months. Roger was right about her. She had the face of an angel and the body of a goddess. It was little wonder that men flocked about her. She was impossible to resist. And yet, she was no seraph, he mused as he watched her brush out her silky hair. Beneath that spellbinding exterior lurked a witch with all the mischievousness of Satan himself. She had been sent up from the fires of hell to torture him during the middle of a war, tearing at his sanity, making him crave the taste of her kisses, ones that melted on his lips like summer rain, leaving him to hunger like a starved wolf. And then she had managed to embroil herself in a pack of trouble. Although he knew he should have left her stewing in her own kettle, he had leaped to her rescue. A noble deed, he thought to himself, but the repercussions of his chivalry had been disastrous.

Trager shook his raven head, trying to break her spell, but her image came at him again. He could envision her in the cove, her velvety skin glistening with water, her flawless features captured in the afternoon sunlight. And then the memory of that night in the shack flooded over him, remembering how she had clung to him in fear of the raging storm. Never again had he seen such terror in her eyes. She possessed but one weakness, as he did. His was Serena, a witch-angel who turned him every which way with her quicksilver moods. He was like a man on the rack, torn by his duties and twisted inside and out by his desire to tame this unpredictable vixen.

His eyes met hers in the mirror, lost to the glow of

the candlelight that was reflected in those fathomless emerald pools. It was as if he were staring across a boundless ocean, knowing the waters were rough and treacherous. Involuntarily, he moved toward her, drawn like a moth to a flame, despising his weakness for this woman who could take him to heaven or hell without his knowing where he was going until he was there. His arms encircled her small waist, the scent of jasmine infiltrating his senses, clouding his thoughts as he bent to press a kiss to her bare shoulder. His hands moved upward to linger on the full swells of her breast, bringing an ache to his loins, even when she shrank away from his touch. "You are the Devil's daughter," he rasped, his voice heavily laden with disturbed desire. "You begrudge me this night, making me fight my way through your defenses like a man who pursues the thorned rose. Your beauty is beyond compare, but you have the ability to prick a man's soul, even if he comes to you wearing a suit of armor."

Serena turned in the prison of his encircling arms, staring deeply into his silver eyes. "I am but a woman," she insisted, her voice trembling slightly. "And I too have my needs, ones that you cannot understand or fulfill. You offer nothing but the moment, like a restless wind. And then you will go your own way, and I cannot depend on you to return."

Trager was having difficulty containing his churning emotions. This was not the time for argument and yet he had blundered into one. "We have spent too long resisting each other, Rena," he murmured as he cupped her chin in his hand. "For this one night, give yourself to me as my wife. Let me make love to you as I yearn to do. And when I kiss you do not turn away from me. I ask for this one night, seeking to know what it could truly be like between us. Is that asking so much?"

His voice was soft and persuasive, washing away her resistance. The look in his eyes had mellowed, and for once she could see a hint of vulnerability. It shocked her to see it on the face of a man who always reminded her of a stone mountain. Her heart melted, the love she had so carefully protected spilling forth. For this one night she would show him what it could be like between them if he could offer more than fleeting affection. She would give him a night to remember, one that would be branded on his mind each time he found another woman anxious to offer him pleasure.

A quiet smile curved her lips as she worked the buttons on his shirt and brushed her palm across the thick matting of hair on his chest, feeling the accelerated beat of his heart. Using the techniques he had taught her and devising some of her own, she became the seductress. Her hands slid over the lean muscles of his belly and then ascended to push the shirt from his shoulders. His flesh quivered and then relaxed beneath her light touch as her caresses wandered over him. Serena reached up on tiptoe to press her lips to his and then traced a trail of kisses along his neck.

His eyes were upon her, warming her like a silver flame as she shed her gown and chemise. She stood shamelessly before him with her blond hair spilling over her breasts to curl temptingly around their taut peaks. She would make him want her, she told herself as she took his hand and led him to the bed. Serena knelt beside him, her hand tracing the hard line of his jaw, meeting his heated gaze.

"I will love you as you request, taking you into my heart, cherishing our time together," Serena whispered as her caress descended across his chest to follow the thick hair that trailed over his abdomen. "Is this what you desire of the woman you have made your wife, her love and blind loyalty?" Her tangled lashes swept up, peering thoughtfully at him while she continued her arousing massage. "Is it my soul you seek, sir, as well as my heart?"

Serena enjoyed touching him, feeling his powerful body beneath her hands, knowing that she could affect this man who carefully guarded his emotions. If only he could offer her more than passion, more than the physical pleasure a man and woman could share. Her loving touch was proof of her feelings for him, and Trager responded, his quiet moan shattering the dimly lit silence.

She was driving him mad with desire, her possessive caresses gliding over his rough flesh, making him aware of the contrast. Serena was all woman—soft and sensuous. And she had learned how to please a man, leaving him hungering for the taste of her kisses, making him ache to mold her flesh to his. Trager could stand no more of her arousing fondling. Her touch had sizzled its way to his very core like a bolt of lightning that sparked each nerve ending along its path.

His mouth opened on hers as he pressed her to her back, ravishing and savoring the sweet essence of her kiss. His hand fanned across her trembling flesh, bringing her to the same fervent pitch of frenzy. His caresses roamed possessively over every inch of her flesh, leaving her burning with a passion that defied logic. Serena felt herself gliding on wings of fire, towering toward rapture's pinnacle. And yet the flames that singed her skin could not touch her soul. It was bound by no mortal form, uninhibited and free.

His lithe body covered hers, and she arched to meet his hard thrusts, moving in perfect rhythm. He plunged deeply within her, seeking ultimate depths of intimacy, driven by an overwhelming urge to claim her as his own. Serena wondered wildly if she could endure the sweet agony of it all. She was again living and dying, trembling with pleasure as he took her higher, transcending the boundaries of reality, spiraling in the star-studded sky.

And then a soul-shattering sensation rocked her, sending her tumbling from her precarious perch. Serena clutched him closer, as if she would cling to the moment forever, reveling in the indescribable feelings that consumed her. It was as if she were suspended in midair and the world had stopped spinning. Time ceased to exist for that one magical moment.

As he shuddered above her, whispering raspy words against the column of her neck, Serena learned the meaning of contentment. Her love for him swelled in her heart and she thought it would surely burst. The forbidden words rolled from her tongue before she could bite them back.

"Trager, I do love you. . . ."

He drew her into the tight circle of his arms, nuzzling his head against her silky hair, inhaling the aromatic fragrance of her that had become a part of him. Trager traced a warm path of kisses along her shoulder and then released a sigh as their hearts slowed their frantic pace.

When Serena fell asleep in his embrace, her arm flung across his chest, her face pressed against his shoulder, Trager smiled tenderly. His lips grazed her satiny cheek as he raked his fingers through the silver-blond tendrils that sprayed across his pillow. As the candlelight flickered and faded into dark silence, Trager drew a deep, shuddering breath and closed his eyes.

Serena never ceased to amaze him. One moment she could be breathing the fire of dragons and in the next instant she could become an angel, taking him to heaven. She was constantly moving, ever changing, hovering just out of his reach and then descending to grant him the essence of what dreams were made of. And just when he held a sunbeam in his hand the warmth evaporated and he stumbled in the darkness, groping to recapture that split second of pleasure.

Trager groaned at the direction his thoughts had taken. Serena had crept beneath his skin, burrowing her way into his heart, chiseling away at his sanity. And when she had chipped his soul in two jagged pieces, what then? He would be half a man, he told himself, worthless to his countrymen and to any other woman. Committing himself to Serena would be his downfall. Men who stumbled and fell in love were vanquished foe, tied to the apron strings of a woman, no longer driven by a single cause. Lord, what madness had led him to take Serena as his wife? Trager was beginning to doubt his sanity. He should have handed her over to Roger along with his blessing. Damn, he didn't like this attachment that had begun to creep in from the shadows of his heart. She was right about him. He thrived on the freedom to come and go when the wind changed direction. He had spent a lifetime following a wandering star.

Heaving a frustrated sigh, Trager squirmed to a more comfortable position and then realized how tightly he was clinging to this mere wisp of a woman who slept peacefully beside him. Even while he told himself that his need for Rena was purely physical, he was drawing her closer, as if to protect his possession.

When she stirred slightly, her breasts pressing against the naked wall of his chest, his determined thoughts flew out the window. He sought her sweet lips and groaned as they melted against his own. Aye, it was madness, he told himself over and over again as his hands wandered over her pliant flesh. But in time he would tire of her and the tender feelings would fade. Yet, for now, he would enjoy the splendor of her embrace.

He came to her in a hazy dream and Serena responded as she had earlier, holding back nothing. His gentleness sent her floating on puffy clouds of pleasure, drifting toward the far horizon with no desire to return.

"I must leave you, Rena," he whispered as he smoothed the tangled tresses from her face. "Washington has ordered me to keep an eye on Baldwin. And he has heard rumors that the British are eager for another confrontation." His lips brushed lightly across her cheek and then he drew away.

Serena sighed and reached out for him, but he was gone from her side, leaving her curled beneath the quilt, savoring the warmth that had kept her in a contented cocoon.

"I have information about the man who betrayed Nathan. I cannot bring him back for you, but I will avenge his death," he promised her.

And then he was gone before the autumn dawn spilled into the room. Serena bit back the tears, feeling alone and unwanted. He had whispered words of how she had pleased him, but he had not returned her confession of love. He had only accepted it, leaving her to suffer, wondering what she could expect when he returned.

A tear found its way to the corner of her eye and then trickled down her cheek. Serena surrendered, letting her emotions flow unchecked into her pillow. His face appeared before her and Serena forced away his memory, but it came again, granting her no peace.

Chapter Fifteen

October 28, 1776

October dragged on at a snail's pace for Serena as she mustered smiles that were only skin deep. She was concerned about Trager, knowing he had gone back behind enemy lines, seeking revenge for Nathan's death, fishing for information from careless-tongued Loyalists.

Although Roger had come to her rescue, lifting her waning spirits and offering his lighthearted grins, Serena felt incomplete and helpless. She desperately wished to see her father, to confront him with the suspicions that Trager had put in her head. She had to know that her own flesh and blood had not betrayed her. But the risk of returning home made her hesitate. She had become fond of her own neck over the past twenty-one years and was not anxious to see it stretched past its limit. Trager's insistent warnings had finally gotten through to her and she had not given way to her impulsiveness.

"One of the soldiers who has just arrived with a regiment of reinforcements would like to speak with you," Roger informed her as he stepped up beside Serena, who stood on the stoop, staring off into the distance.

His gaze ran down the full length of her shapely figure. Try as he might he could not conceal the longing in his eyes. Trager had asked him to keep a watchful eye on Serena while he was away, but it was a torturous task, especially when he continued to see her as a desirable woman, instead of his sister-in-law. Roger had given her up because he had sensed the attraction between Trager and Serena. If it had been anyone but his brother, he would not have backed so gracefully away.

Her brow arched curiously as she glanced up at Roger. "One of the soldiers wants to see me?" she repeated.

"Aye, he saw you earlier this morning and recognized you," Roger explained as he leaned against the supporting beam, his eyes making another slow sweep of the yellow silk gown that made such a tantalizing wrapper for a tempting package. "James Cortney tells me that he is a former acquaintance of yours."

Cortney, her predecessor at the district school, she mused as her gaze swept the men who milled about the camp. "Where is he?"

Roger directed her attention to the far end of the rows of tents. "You can find him stretched out in the last tent." Roger threw her a hopeful glance. "Will you consent to have lunch with me after you have seen him? I want you to ride into the village

294

with me."

Serena flashed him an agreeable smile that melted him into his boots and then descended the steps. "It will be my pleasure, Roger."

"Nay, it will be *my* pleasure . . . and pain," Roger mused aloud as his longing gaze followed the graceful sway of her hips. The taste of the kisses he had bestowed on her had lingered on his lips, and again Roger found himself wishing his last name was something other than Grayson.

When Serena glanced back at him, peering quizzically at the expression on his face, Roger laughed at his own misery. "Do you know how difficult it is for me to remember that you are married to my brother?"

Serena stared at the gold band on her finger, a certain sadness in her smile. Why couldn't it have been Roger who had stolen her heart? "No more difficult than it is for me to forget that I have made a mistake," she speculated, her tone deflated. "I think fate has frowned on both of us, Roger. I know I deserve to suffer my sins, but you are the unblemished bystander whom I continue to call upon when my spirit fails me."

"And the same one who would be struck down by a bolt of lightning if the lady knew what was blazing across my mind at this very moment," Roger chuckled, making light of a difficult situation.

Her lashes swept up to see the glow of desire in his eyes and it broke her heart that she could not return the affection mirrored in his gaze. "If I were granted three wishes, my first one would be to wed a man who possessed all of your admirable qualities."

His lips parted in a smile. "And what of your other two wishes, my lady?"

Serena grinned spitefully, a devilish twinkle in her eyes. "I would turn Trager into a frog."

"And the third?" he prodded, chortling amusedly at her vengeful whim.

"He would find himself eternally treading water with not one lily pad to climb upon to catch his breath."

Roger cackled at her words and the diabolical gleam in her eyes. "Vicious witch," he teased, loving the way her feisty spirit sparkled in each and every exquisite feature.

"Aye, so I have been told," she murmured as she turned her attention toward the tent that housed James Cortney.

Serena walked to the far end of the camp and peered inside to see two men sprawled on the grass floor. "James?" she called softly.

James pried open one eye and then propped up on one elbow, smiling drowsily at the lovely young woman. "Hello again, Serena. 'Tis good to see a familiar face." He rolled to his feet and strolled outside to inhale a breath of fresh air. "I was surprised to see you in camp this morning. I had heard about your connection with Nathan Hale, but the rumors flying from New Rochelle were that you had vanished into thin air." James's gaze held a hint of awe. "'Twas very brave of you to stand up for your beliefs when surrounded by Loyalists." He ducked his head, sighing humbly. "I was not as courageous. I kept my convictions to myself until I joined the Rebel ranks."

"'Twas not courage that spurred me," Serena admitted sheepishly. "'Twas only that I lost my temper and spouted off when I should have held my tongue. It would have been wiser to have kept my thoughts to myself."

James smiled sympathetically and then fondly squeezed her hand. "You have endured great tragedy, Serena. I admire your strength."

A frown formed on her delicate features, bemused by his remark. There was no reason for him to bestow such praise on her. She had done nothing spectacular.

"I was grieved to hear about your father," he continued. "Although he and I differed in opinion, he was an honorable man. I feel no animosity for a man who stands firm in what he believes in, even if he and I are on opposite sides of the war." A sad smile touched his lips as he bent his gaze to Serena. "It must be difficult not to be able to return home to pay your respects."

Was? Why was he speaking of her father in past tense? The color drained from her cheeks and her legs buckled as if they had suddenly turned to jelly. No words formed. Her thoughts were spinning in confusion as she stared bewilderedly at James Cortney.

"I only heard the news last night. Have the authorities found the man who killed your father?"

Serena spun away, her eyes flying wildly about her.

Mitchell was dead, killed by an unknown assailant? Her mind screamed in denial, tears threatening to cloud her vision. The words Trager had uttered before he had left her came back to haunt her. He had called her the Devil's daughter. Was he trying to tell her that Mitchell was the one who had betrayed her? Had Trager avenged Nathan's death by taking her father's life?

"Serena?" There was concern in Cortney's voice. "My God, you didn't know, did you?" He would have sooner cut out his tongue than to be the one to give her the news.

She glanced back at him, her eyes wide with torment. And then, without saying another word, she dashed across the compound, fighting back the sea of tears that threatened to flood over her. She grasped the porch railing for support and then determinedly scaled the steps to her room, sobbing hysterically until she cried only dry tears.

Her head jerked up as the rumbling of a cannon shattered the silence. The frantic voices in the hall brought her to attention and Serena hurried to the window to see a cloud of smoke and dust rolling toward the mansion. The Rebel army was under attack! She flinched as the door slammed against the wall to reveal Roger, his face as cold and hard as the expression she had often seen on Trager's features.

"Come on, Serena. We must find cover. Trager would never forgive me if you sustained even a scratch." When she made no move toward him, he stalked toward her to uproot her from her spot.

"Damn, we weren't expecting an attack until tomorrow. I intended to have you safely tucked away before the fireworks began."

Trager. The mention of his name sickened her, but she had no time to relive the fierce emotions that gripped her when she pictured Trager murdering her father. Mechanically, she hurried to keep up with Roger's impatient pace as they wedged their way through the chaotic crowd that had gathered in Washington's headquarters.

The sound of whistling cannon balls had Serena taking the steps two at a time when her thoughts circled back to the emergency at hand. Roger urged her through the front door and into the trenches, keeping a protective arm about her.

It was as he had feared. General Howe was pursuing the Patriots before they could prepare themselves. The scouts who had returned to camp had attempted to second guess the Redcoats, expecting them to wait until dawn before besieging the camp. But apparently, Howe intended to bring the rebels under his thumb before they could retreat to a stronger fortress.

Serena shuddered as she peered up over the trench, seeing score upon score of British soldiers appearing in the distance. It was as if the world had crumbled about her and she had taken a headlong dive into hell. The cannon fire had set several buildings ablaze and Serena squeezed her eyes shut, refusing to watch her life flashing before her. And then, in the split second that she had regained her composure, Roger shoved her facedown in the dirt as a musket ball sailed past her.

"Dammit, stay down," Roger scowled as he rolled beside her and thrust a musket in her hands. "Can you handle this thing?"

Serena nodded mutely as she clutched the weapon to her.

"Then use it. We need every marksman we can find." His gaze fastened on her, intensely somber. "I hope you possess as much spunk as Trager claims you have. You're going to need it."

Trager gritted his teeth and stashed his flintlock beneath his jacket as he peered at the man who lay sprawled before him. The lifeless form still held the pistol in his hand and had left Trager no choice but to defend himself. Trager wrapped his hand over the wound on his left arm and swore under his breath.

When he had confronted his would-be assassin with the accusations, the man had become furious, cursing Trager for cross-examining his motives. Trager had intended to take him to Washington . . . alive; but too late he realized that only one of them would walk away from the confrontation.

His ears pricked to the sound of footsteps and he cast one last glance at the still form before leaping to his horse, leaving a cloud of dust at his heels.

Dawn feathered across the horizon as Trager drew his steed to a halt and swung down, heaving a weary sigh. Nothing had gone according to plan and the worst was yet to come—facing Serena. Damn, he would have given anything if he could have spared them both the agony.

His rap on the back door was answered within only a few minutes and Ellen gasped in concern when she saw the bloodstain on Trager's arm.

"Trager? What has happened?" Ellen urged him inside and quickly closed the door behind him. "You're bleeding."

"'Tis only a superficial wound." He shrugged slightly as his gaze lifted to the top of the stairs, knowing a soft bed awaited his weary bones. Two days and nights had passed without a moment's rest and Trager was sorely in need of sleep. "Are the Tories about?" he questioned softly.

Ellen gave her head a negative shake. "It's been a quiet night. No one here will recognize you." She gestured toward the steps, offering a supporting shoulder for him to lean upon. "I'll dress your wound and then you can sleep in my room. You look as though you could use some rest."

Trager waited impatiently while Ellen gathered her supplies, cleansed the wound, and bandaged his arm. He was anxious to return to White Plains, to face the general and Serena. Perhaps when it was over and done he could relax without seeing Serena's tortured face materializing before him. Lord, he hated to be the bearer of more bad news, but of late, it seemed there was no other kind.

Ellen's experienced hands fanned across his chest

in a gentle massage. "Is there anything else I can do for you, love?" she questioned softly. Although she knew she should leave him alone, the temptation of staying with him was too great.

Trager closed his eyes as her lips found his, wanting to forget everything that had occupied his thoughts the past few days. He didn't want to see Serena's face hovering above him as Ellen pressed wantonly against him. But she had come uninvited as she always did, destroying the pleasure he anticipated when Ellen offered herself to him. Trager twisted away and turned his back on Ellen, listening to her disappointed sigh echo in the stilted silence.

"'Tis that Warren wench, isn't it?" Ellen murmured as she trailed her index finger over the width of his shoulders.

Trager groaned, every muscle in his body rebelling as he stretched beneath the sheet, seeking a more comfortable position. "Just let me rest in peace. I am in no mood to be interrogated," he commanded, his voice harsher than he intended.

Ellen edged away from him, her eyes fixed on the muscled form that lay in her bed. It infuriated her that Trager refused her caresses. He had never turned her back on her until that Warren woman cast her evil spell on him. Silently, she cursed the vision of the blond-haired vixen who had routed her from the arms of someone who possessed every unique quality that she desired in a man.

Trager's sooty lashes fluttered up when he heard the door close behind Ellen, staring pensively at the wall. How he wished he had never laid eyes on Serena. She had entangled his complicated life, confusing his thoughts. Was there no peace to be found as long as the two of them remained on the same continent? He heaved a frustrated sigh and then flinched when he leaned too heavily on his bandaged arm. Damn, he should have deposited Serena in Roger's arms when the opportunity presented itself. Roger would have found that his devious plan had backfired in his face, and for the first time in his life Roger would have learned the true meaning of trouble. But it was too late, Trager mused drowsily, he was hobbled and handcuffed with that captivating little misfit and hell knew no fury worse than being bound to a woman he didn't want but couldn't live without.

Flouncing in bed, Trager groaned at the direction of his thoughts. Lately he seemed to have a one-track mind, and all roads led back to Serena. He wanted to close his eyes and dream just one peaceful dream that didn't revolve around windswept tendrils of gold and dancing green eyes. Aye, even a nightmare would be less frightening, he decided as he pulled the pillow over his head and determinedly gritted his teeth, thinking of anything that came to mind that had no resemblance to the bewitching rose who kept an aggravating thorn lodged in his side.

While Trager was begging for sleep Serena was discovering a new dimension of hell. The sky was choked with gray smoke and the earth shook as if it had split asunder. If there were to be a tomorrow, Serena would have been greatly surprised. The siege had dragged on from day to endless night, leaving Serena huddled against the earth wall for protection, fighting for her life, standing shoulder to shoulder with grimy-faced Patriots who had no choice but to defend themselves against the well-armed British troops.

Serena wiped her smudged cheek on the torn sleeve of her gown and reloaded her musket, her shoulder aching from the kick of the weapon, her ears ringing from the sound of muskets exploding beside her. Her tears were long dried, and Serena had put the past behind her, intent on a single purpose—surviving.

And then her long-awaited prayer was answered, but Serena found it ironic that her second greatest fear had saved her. The heavens opened and thunder exploded across the sky, drowning out the sound of British cannons. The rockets' red glare was replaced by jagged bolts of lightning and the pounding rain hindered the advance of the Redcoats. A thankful smile spread across her lips as the siege was muffled by the thunderstorm.

Roger grasped her arm and shuffled her along with him. "We're retreating," he informed her hurriedly. "Washington intends to move north while the storm protects us."

Serena nodded mutely and then glanced down to see her soiled gown clinging to her as tightly as her own skin. Her hair was a muddy, tangled mass of what had once been carefully manicured tresses of honey-blond. At the moment she could have cared less if she looked like a dirty ragamuffin. She had survived. If she had lived through the Redcoats' attack, she could endure any catastrophe—even Trager's treachery.

As the rebel officers shouted their orders along the troops who lined the trenches, Serena gazed about the wrecked camp and then sidled against Roger's drenched jacket as lightning streaked across the heavens. Only now did she realize she had traded one nightmare for another. Terrified, she swung into the saddle of the horse Roger had retrieved for her and then gouged the steed in the ribs. The horse reared, his hooves pawing the air, his eyes wide in fright as another rumble of thunder exploded about them. Like a streak of lightning, the horse galloped across the compound with Serena holding on for dear life, oblivious to all except escaping from the hell that had held her captive.

"Serena!" Roger's voice died as another clap of thunder shook the ground.

Serena's heart was hammering against her ribs so furiously that she could barely draw a breath. And she rode on in the pouring rain, praying that her flighty steed would not deliver her into enemy hands. Enemy? Serena choked on a hysterical sob. The entire world had become her foe—the British, Trager, the Patriots. . . .

Where could she go to seek asylum? Nowhere, she thought dismally, huddling against her mount's neck as the sky blazed with white fire. There was nowhere she could run *to*; but she must run away *from* her treacherous husband and an entire army of Redcoats who were swarming over New York like mad hornets.

The sound of hoofbeats tapped at her tormented musings, and Serena swallowed air. Frantically, she reined her steed from the muddy path and slid to the ground, huddling in the brush, hoping the intruder hadn't seen or heard her. She squinted in the darkness, afraid to move or breathe, waiting until she was alone on the road.

Trager's keen gaze scanned the darkness, certain he had heard another rider approaching, but the path was empty and the pounding rain had made it impossible to spot the tracks of another steed.

After grappling with his thoughts, he had dragged himself from bed and swung back into the saddle, knowing he could not sleep until he had seen Serena. He had seen the smoke of the cannons in the distance and had discovered the meaning of fear, wondering if Roger had managed to tuck Serena safely away before the battle began.

Again his sharp gaze circled the area, but he saw and heard nothing except thunder and rain. He pressed his knees to his steed's flanks and urged him into a fast clip, vowing that he would have Roger's hide if he hadn't kept a watchful eye on Serena. He stared upward as the heavens blazed with silver, reflecting the hard gleam in his eyes. Only a few more miles and he would know how Serena had fared during the siege, he told himself as he pulled his cap around his ears to ward off the beating rain.

When the hoofbeats had faded into the distance, Serena led her mount from the brush and climbed into the saddle, thankful that the lone rider had not discovered her. Her grimy face was set in a determined frown as she nudged her horse in the opposite direction of the rider who had come dangerously close to seeing her. But where could she go, Serena wondered as a feeling of despair closed in on her. She was alone and unwelcome on every doorstep. What had she done to deserve such misery? The tears streamed down her cheeks, mingling with the driving rain. And she rode blindly onward, not knowing where she was going . . . only that she was running away from Trager and a battle that had left her with haunting memories.

When Trager had circled White Plains, avoiding the British, he sought out Washington to deliver the news. The general's dark mood blackened with Trager's discouraging report. Trager had confirmed Serena's suspicions about Major Baldwin, who had been accepting money from the British for his information about Rebel tactics. He also told Washington that Howe intended to pounce on the Rebels, forcing their surrender before they sought winter quarters. Fortunately, the winds of fate had hindered Howe's strategy, and he was up to his ankles in mud, deciding not to pursue the retreating Rebels.

After Trager had been dismissed he sought out

Roger, muttering under his breath as he wedged his way through the chaotic mass of soldiers who fumbled in the darkness. As he shoved bodies out of his way, his gaze searched the silhouettes. Where the hell was Roger?

"Has anyone seen Roger Grayson?" he demanded to know as his gaze swept a group of huddled soldiers.

"I believe he and Egan Hadley were sent on ahead to find a new campsite," one of the soldiers offered.

"What about Serena?" Trager fired the question at the shivering soldier.

The smudge-faced private shrugged. "Don't know where she is. We haven't seen anything of her since the general gave orders to retreat."

Damn. Where could that little minx be? Trager searched the fleeing silhouettes as lightning dawned in the night sky. Where could Roger have taken her? There was naught else for Trager to do but search out his brother.

Heaving a frustrated sigh, Trager wheeled and stalked back to his horse, his foot finding a deep puddle. He cursed as he shook out his soggy boot and then splashed his way north, shivering from the chill of the pouring rain and exhausted from pushing his body to the limit. Could anything else go wrong? Trager wondered bitterly as he fought his contrary steed. It seemed the world was the darkest just before it turned pitch black, he thought, discouraged as he massaged his aching arm.

*   *   *

Washington and his faltering army retreated north toward Peekskill, intending to withdraw into New Jersey before they lost what was left of the Patriot forces, who were already dangerously close to collapse. Trager had spent two days searching for his brother and still had not spotted any of his men. As he sat sprawled by the campfire, staring off into space, a movement in the brush beside him brought him to his feet. As Egan Hadley ambled toward him, Trager replaced his pistol and frowned at the lackadaisical grin that was plastered on the old man's stubbled face.

"We was wonderin' when ye'd come prancin' in," he remarked, his tone holding a hint of amusement as he assessed Trager's sour expression and unkempt apparance.

Trager flashed Egan a disdainful glance. "If you were so all-fired anxious to see me, you should have marked your trail," he retaliated.

Egan scratched his bushy head and flashed his commander a toothless grin. "I didn't say we was eager to see ye, just that we was 'spectin' ye."

"Where's my brother?" Trager asked as his gray eyes swept the brush.

"Over yonder," Egan replied, gesturing to the east. "Would ye like to finish yer coffee before I take ye to 'im?"

Trager kicked dirt over the fire and doused the embers with the remainder of his cup. "Nay," he snapped impatiently. "Lead on, Egan."

As they wove their way through the trees, Trager peered into the distance, spotting his brother sitting with his head bowed, his shoulders slumped. Trager frowned in concern. He didn't like the way Roger held himself, lacking his usual self-confidence. Something was wrong. Trager could sense it. And without asking, he knew it pertained to Serena.

He swung from his saddle and stalked toward his brother, waiting an impatient moment before Roger braved a glance. "Well, where is she?" he demanded.

Roger forced a meager smile. "Is that the best greeting you can muster, big brother? You could at least ask me how I fared during the battle."

Trager's finely tempered patience snapped, his eyes glistening like hard steel. "You know how irritable I can be when I haven't had my rest. My steed and I have become Siamese twins these past several days, and I don't appreciate traipsing all over the country to learn where you have stashed Serena. I must speak with her immediately. Now where the hell is she?" Trager's voice had risen testily, reaching the point of shouting into his brother's weary face.

Trager was well aware of the discreet glances that flashed back and forth among his men and he scowled at the long pause. "Well, dammit, what did you do with that little termagant?"

Roger rose to his feet, his gaze solemn. "Serena fought beside us in the trenches and then galloped off in the storm before I could stop her." When Trager growled furiously and cocked his arm, Egan bear-hugged him and Roger retreated. "I wanted to follow her, but the general ordered us to seek out a suitable location for the troops. It was mass chaos and there was no time to stop her."

He broke Egan's hold and stalked toward his brother, bellowing into his face. "You allowed her to ride alone in the storm? She is scared to death of them." Trager muttered under his breath and clenched his fists at his side, fighting the temptation to plant his knuckles in Roger's foolish face. He wanted to strike out at someone, anyone, to ease his frustration and fear.

Roger stared incredulously at him. "Serena fought like a trooper under British fire and you are concerned about her being alone in the storm? I think some of those raindrops must have seeped through the seams of your skull to rust your cogs," he snorted derisively.

"And that's another thing!" Trager wagged a lean finger in his brother's face. "What the hell were you thinking about? *You* seem to be the one lacking sense. You should have had her tucked away before the British attack," he countered, his tone cold and accusing.

"I had intended to do just that, but they came upon us from all directions," Roger defended himself hastily. "We had anticipated the attack the following morning."

"And you waited until the last minute to stash her." Trager could well imagine that his lovestruck brother wanted to spend as much time with Serena as possible. Like a fool, Roger had allowed desire to override reason. Damn him! "I thought I could depend on you, but apparently I have made a gross error in judgment," he scowled as he wheeled away, staring off into the sunrise, seeing nothing but red. He was fuming, frustrated, exhausted, and had a long ride ahead of him.

"Trager," Roger's quiet voice filtered into his troubled thoughts. "Serena knows about her father. One of the men from the area told her. He came to me before we broke camp and apologized for mentioning it. He thought she already knew." There was a long, tense pause and then Roger slowly released his breath. "I'm sorry I forced her to endure the siege. I was afraid to let her out of my sight until the last possible moment."

"Damn." Trager stalked toward his weary steed and then muttered another round of epithets. He had intended to be the one to inform Serena about her father, to explain what had happened. Where could she have gone? Had she returned to her home or fled during the storm, unsure of her destination? His hard silver eyes scanned the countryside, wondering which direction to rein his horse. If only he had learned to second guess Serena, he thought whimsically; but she was as unpredictable as the wind, unsure of her own direction or reaction until the moment was upon her. Only God knew where to find that thorny, windswept rose.

Part II

Chapter Sixteen

Jonas Landsing glanced up from his desk to study the round, stooped woman who shuffled into his law office with the aid of her cane. The dowager was dressed in black silk from head to toe, her heavy dark veil camouflaging her graying hair and wrinkled features. Her spectacles sat on the bridge of her nose, barely visible through the dark lace, and Jonas frowned in concern as the woman wobbled and then collapsed in the chair. She drew the dog she kept on a leash to her side and then reached down to pat his head. The mutt snarled as Jonas came to his feet and started around the desk. Jonas took a cautious step backwards when the mutt displayed his sharp teeth and issued a warning growl.

Swallowing hard, Jonas decided it would be wise to greet the old woman from behind the shield of his desk. He eyed the mutt, which looked to be part wolf—the part that possessed a grizzly disposition and flesh-eating fangs. The evil-eyed mutt seemed satisfied with his decision and sank to the floor when

315

Jonas wilted in his chair.

"What can I do for you, madam?" Jonas's tone was polite, but showed signs of uneasiness.

"I have come for information." Voicing one sentence sent the feeble old woman into a coughing spasm, and with a gloved hand she drew her handkerchief from her purse and covered her mouth. When she had managed to draw a shallow breath she eased back in her chair and stroked the dog's head, soothing his concern. "I have come to see about the arrangements for burying my son. I have been told that you are in charge of Mitchell Warren's estate."

Jonas stared at the dowager in disbelief. "You are Veronica Warren? I was under the impression that you were in England."

Veronica noddled slightly, wheezed, and then cleared her throat. "I sailed to the colonies when my granddaughter, Serena, returned last year and have been staying with my daughter in Connecticut." She coughed again, sniffed, and then drew a ragged breath, as if the effort of speaking was physically exhausting. "Because of the revolution I have not dared to sail home," Veronica explained, her raspy voice making it difficult to understand with its heavy British accent. "Now I have been tormented by the death of my only son and the loss of my granddaughter to the Rebel cause." Veronica broke into tears, her slumped shoulders shaking as she sat with her head bowed, clutching at her handkerchief.

A wave of pity flooded over Jonas as he watched the feeble old woman succumb to her grief. The dog whined and laid his head on Veronica's lap, as if he too offered sympathy. It must have broken the old woman's heart to learn that her son had been killed and that his murderer was still running free. To make matters worse, her granddaughter had been labeled a traitor and a disgrace to her family.

"Did Marlena accompany you to New Rochelle?" Jonas questioned softly.

"Marl*ene*," Veronica corrected, muffling a sniff. "Nay, her husband, Edmund, has been bedfast for several months, and Marlene was afraid to leave him. I have come alone."

Jonas nodded thoughtfully, another wave of pity washing over him. "I have seen to tomorrow's arrangement, Mrs. Warren. And if there is anything I can do for you, do not hesitate to ask. Mitchell and I were good friends and I want you to come to me if you need assistance."

Veronica grasped the arms of her chair and slowly rose to her stooped stature, weaving as she leaned heavily on her cane. Pausing, she glanced back at the lawyer when she remembered what she had intended to ask. "Will you be at Mitchell's home for the reading of the will?" When he nodded affirmatively, she coughed and then forced out another question. "My daughter-in-law seems to have fled the house. Can you tell me where to find her?"

"Olivia has traveled to New York."

"To stay with her mother?" Veronica inquired.

"I'm not certain. She said she would inform me when she was settled," Jonas explained. When Veronica teetered precariously, he scrambled from his chair, but was again discouraged from coming to her aid when her bodyguard lunged at him, displaying his jagged teeth. "Mrs. Warren?" His voice held concern for her and himself.

Veronica braced herself on a nearby chair and sputtered for her breath. "It grieves me that Olivia would abandon Mitchell in his darkest hour. I cannot forgive her for that."

Jonas frowned as he watched Veronica tremble and wheeze. "Are you certain that you can bear this funeral? Perhaps we could postpone . . ."

Veronica held up her quivering hand and gave her graying head a negative shake. "Nay, Mr. Landsing. I will endure the morrow. Then I can rest. If you need me, you can find me at Mitchell's manor."

After Veronica and her mangy bodyguard had disappeared from sight, Jonas sank into his chair and heaved a dismal sigh. The dowager seemed so frail and ill that he wondered how she could survive her son's funeral without collapsing. No doubt she had been forced to make the long journey, since she was the only relative to pay respects to Mitchell. Damn Patriots, Jonas muttered to himself. They had torn Mitchell Warren's family to shreds. And Serena . . . Jonas raked his fingers through his hair. He could not believe that she had turned traitor. She was an impetuous young woman who had filled her father's last days with misery as he wondered what had become of her. And then he had been cut down before he learned of her whereabouts.

Veronica accepted the driver's helping hand, urged her dog into the carriage, and then waited for the coachman to assist her up the step. Once inside, she settled herself on the seat and patted the empty space beside her. Barron took the invitation, his tail wagging as he eased down beside the dowager to rest his head on her lap, his sad eyes raised to meet the heavily veiled face that was covered with a sea of tears.

Her ragged sigh filled the coach, and Barron whined as he nuzzled against her, content to remain her devoted companion no matter what trials lay ahead of her.

Veronica eased the door shut, her gaze scanning the quiet hall of Mitchell's mansion. The ride to and from New Rochelle had drained her, and she was aching to shed her shoes and sink into the most comfortable chair in the house. She made her way into the parlor, laid her coat over the back of the sofa, and then sat down in the red velvet rocker to stare thoughtfully at the bare wall above the mantel.

A wry smile touched her drawn features as she discarded her shoes and propped up her feet. At least she had eradicated that dreadful portrait of Olivia. That had been the first item on her agenda when she discovered the woman had abandoned Mitchell three days before his death. Molly had informed her that Mitchell and Olivia had argued and that she had packed up and left. At least his last days had been peaceful ones, Veronica mused as she laid her head back against the rocker and removed her veil, smoothing the gray hair away from her face. If only Mitchell could have known what had happened to Serena, he could have faced his death, she thought to herself. Poor Mitchell; he deserved more, but fate had a cruel way of twisting itself around him.

When Molly turned the corner and noticed Veronica, she gasped at the round old woman who sat toasting by the fire. "I didn't hear you come in." Molly came to her, smiling fondly at the old woman's wrinkled features. "Shall I fetch you a hot cup of tea to ward off the chill?"

Veronica nodded agreeably and then glanced at her dog, which lay contentedly beside her, his head resting on his front paws. "And bring along a treat for Barron. His ribs are still sticking through his hide. We must put a layer of fat on him or he won't survive the winter." Her comment left her coughing, and she peered up to see the worried expression on Molly's face. "Run along and fetch the tea and quit fussing over me. I shall live to see this through and I fully intend to be alive and kicking when you return."

"Are you shore you wouldn't prefer to take yore tea in yore room? Mayhap a hot bath and a short rest would help you gain yore strength," Molly suggested.

Veronica waved her away with a weak flick of her wrist. "Just the tea, Molly. I have yet to muster the strength to move from this chair."

When Veronica was left alone with her thoughts, she sighed and stared into the fire, mesmerized by the curling fingers of flames that darted across the logs, casting dancing shadows on the dark stones of the hearth. The previous week had been a nightmare. Her journey had drained her physically and emotionally, her spirits scraping rock bottom. It was as if the world had crumbled about her and she could barely make the effort to step over the rubble and pull her life back together.

As Molly returned to the room, Veronica lifted her spectacles to wipe away the lingering tears and then frowned when she noticed the apprehensive expression that had settled on Molly's plain face.

"Is something amiss, Molly?" Veronica inquired, uncertain that she could face another crisis at the moment.

Molly's gaze strayed over her shoulder as she set the tea beside Veronica and then nervously wrung her hands. "There is someone here to see you. Are you up to company or shall I send him away?"

"Is it Jonas Landsing?" she questioned. Her eyes returned to the hypnotic fire, caught in the spell of the weaving flames.

"Nay, mam,' 'tis Trager Grayson."

Veronica grasped her tea, the cup and saucer rattling as she set it on her lap. "Give me a moment to compose myself and then send him in," she instructed and then choked on her breath.

After recovering from another coughing spasm she leaned down to retrieve her shoes and then replaced the veil over her tearstained cheeks. Molly waited by the door and motioned to Trager when Veronica nodded that she was prepared to greet him. An odd tenseness came over Veronica as she listened to the click of his boots on the tile and then stared at the immaculately dressed gentleman who approached her.

"Mrs. Warren, I do not mean to impose on you, but it is imperative that I contact my wife," Trager blurted out without bothering with introductions.

His gaze made fast work of assessing the dowager whose eyes fastened on the fire without bothering to acknowledge his presence. She stared straight ahead, her attention seemingly more concerned with the fire than with her companion. Her heavy veil disguised her features, but he could detect a hint of gray hair and the rim of her spectacles that reflected the dim light. Something about her reminded him of Serena. Trager muttered under his breath. *Every* woman had begun to remind him of that missing minx, anyone between the ages of eight and eighty. She had materialized from the swaying shadows, showing herself and then eluding him, driving him mad wondering what had become of her. He found himself searching the faces of crowds, intent on finding a pair of sparkling green eyes and a face of unmatched beauty. Trager was at the end of his rope. If Veronica Warren could not direct him to her granddaughter then he was at the point of giving her up for lost. He had spent the past few days searching every nook and cranny, but Serena had disappeared into thin air.

Veronica started to speak, but her intake of breath ignited another coughing spasm. Once she had recovered, she eased back in her rocker and focused her gaze on the glowing hearth. "So you are Serena's new husband," she presumed, her voice graveled and raspy.

Trager strained to catch her quiet words through her heavy British accent. "Aye," he affirmed. It was obvious that the old woman could not have cared less about meeting a new member of her family. "Can you tell me where I might find her?"

Trager made the mistake of closing the distance between them. His abrupt movement brought Barron up on all fours to issue a warning that the intruder was not to come within ten feet of his mistress. Barron bared teeth that glowed like ivory against the light of the hearth, assuring Trager that he made no idle threats. Veronica made no attempt to call off her snarling mutt, and Trager stood as still as a stone statue, not daring to annoy the wolflike dog or his cantakerous old mistress. What a sourpuss, Trager mused as he reassessed Veronica's darkly clad figure, which bordered on overweight. It was little wonder that Serena had such a fiery temper after living with the likes of this cranky dowager for six years.

"I was under the impression that my granddaughter did not wish to see you, not now or ever again," Veronica said hoarsely and then choked on her breath, muttering at the inconvenience of her ill health. A gloved hand moved toward Barron's treat of raw meat and then offered it to him. "Come, Barron, this will be more appetizing than this man's bony ankle."

Although the dog was eager for his meal, he kept a watchful eye on the intruder, who was cursing under his breath at Veronica's biting jibe.

"I demand to see Serena," Trager insisted, his patience nearing the end of its short fuse. He would have been more delicate with the dowager if he had thought her nasty disposition was attributable to her failing health, but he had the feeling she would have been as irascible even if she was as fit as a fiddle.

"Demand?" Veronica mocked in her crackling voice. "Mr. Grayson, do not issue me ultimatums. I am the only one who can tell you where my granddaughter is hiding and I will decide *if* and *when* you will be granted an audience with her."

Stubborn old woman, Trager grumbled to himself. Serena had inherited her obstinacy from her grandmother, no doubt. "She is my wife and I have every right to see her," Trager reminded her slowly and deliberately.

Veronica turned her head to stare up at Trager's awesome figure, raking him up and down with her eyes from behind her heavy veil. "And from what Serena tells me, the marriage was a grave mistake, one which she should have avoided entirely. I agree with her. Your whirlwind wedding is as distasteful as matching Barron with an alley cat."

The woman didn't mince words, Trager thought as he heaved a disgusted sigh and attempted to clamp a grip on his faltering patience. "Madam, I do not wish to annoy you, but . . ."

His explanation was interrupted by Veronica's distasteful sniff. "You already have, Mr. Grayson. You have disrupted what had every indication of being a quiet, restful evening."

Her remark set his teeth on edge and impulsively he took a bold step forward, only to have Barron bolt to his feet, reminding him that he was coming dangerously close to having his legs chewed off. Lord, he was itching to clamp a muzzle on both of them. Drawing himself up rigidly in front of Veronica, Trager made an attempt to be civil.

"'Tis imperative that I speak with Serena as soon as possible. I have been to hell and back trying to locate her. If this was not such an important matter, I would not be so persistent."

Her veiled gaze carefully measured him, doubting that Trager Grayson could be anything but pertinacious, no matter what the situation. Trager took the opportunity to study Veronica as critically as she was scrutinizing him, wishing he could clearly see her face and read the expression in her eyes. But the black veil camouflaged her wrinkled features, and he was itching to know what was running through the old woman's mind. Bitterness? A tragic sense of loss? Aye, he was certain of that. And hostility toward him, obviously. Serena's description of him had apparently earned him the old woman's contempt. He could sense it, but how he wished he could meet her eye to eye.

Veronica's hoarse chortle broke the strained silence. "You would like to see what lies beneath this veil, wouldn't you, young man?" she speculated. "I am an old woman, a little vain, perhaps." Along with her raspy admission came another choking spasm. When she had inhaled a weak breath, she settled herself in a more comfortable position and continued, "I prefer to bear my grief from behind a veil so that no one can see the wrinkles of age and the sadness in my eyes. And, in truth, I find myself mildly amused by the way you and others peer at me, wondering if I look as hideous as your imagination allows you to think." She paused a long moment, drummed her gloved fingers on the arm of her rocker as she stared at the hearth, and then heaved a weary sigh. "If I permit you to see Serena, you must promise not to upset her. She is a fugitive in her own home, and she greatly suffers the loss of her freedom and grieves the loss of her father. At the moment she fears her own shadow and trusts no one. Common sense warns me that seeing you will only distress her further and there is no telling what she might do if you pressure her now."

There was no telling what that wench might do . . . ever, Trager thought to himself, but he bit back the sarcastic remark that sat on the tip of his tongue. "There is much that she does not understand about the events that have brought her this misery," he said carefully. "I hope that what I have to tell her will ease the pain she bears."

The dowager gripped the arms of her chair and struggled to her feet. When Trager unconsciously made a move to assist her, she raised a weak arm to halt him in his tracks. "Stand your ground, Mr. Grayson. If you touch me Barron will think it his obligation to cut you down to his size and, I assure you, he can and will do it," she rasped as she balanced herself in a slumped position and then clutched her cane to hobble toward the hearth.

Trager waited an impatient moment while Veronica warmed herself by the fire, but he couldn't contain his plea indefinitely. "Madam, please tell me where to find Serena. I cannot rest until I have seen her, to explain . . ."

Veronica's head swiveled around, practically throwing her entire body off balance, and she braced her hands on the mantel to keep from falling into the blazing fire. "I have insisted that she remain in hiding until after Mitchell's funeral. I fear the Loyalists will be swarming, expecting her to pay her last respects to her father. I have forbidden her to see anyone until this matter is closed. If you wish to see her then you must have patience. It will be two weeks before she returns."

Trager released an exasperated sigh. Two weeks? Lord, the world could come to an end before then. "But I . . ."

"Those are my terms, Mr. Grayson. Take them or leave them," she challenged and then dismissed him with a feeble flick of her wrist. "My journey to town and your visit have drained what was left of my strength. I must rest now. Molly will see you out."

He might as well plead his case to a stone wall, Trager thought resentfully as he spun on his heels and strode away, listening to Veronica succumb to another fit of coughing. The dowager was as receptive to his needs as the British Crown. Two weeks?

Damn. In a fortnight Serena's hatred and mistrust would destroy the frail bond that had just begun to grow between them. He would wear out two good mounts, riding back to give his information to Washington and then flying back to explain to Serena on the appointed day her stubborn grandmother had allowed him an audience. It was little wonder that Veronica's husband was dead and buried. Trager was certain the old woman had dragged him there and shoved him in with both feet.

"Mr. Grayson?" Veronica's strained voice drew his quizzical frown. "How goes the war?"

"Splendidly for the Tories and miserably for the Whigs," he replied, his tone carefully indifferent.

Veronica nodded thoughtfully. "Then perhaps I might be granted safe passage home when this business is done," she mused aloud.

"Aye," he murmured before he disappeared into the hall. And he would be only too happy to insure her passage and to have that meddling old woman out of the way. He and Serena had enough obstacles to overcome without having that persnickety dowager as a stumbling block.

When Veronica heard his fading footsteps and the front door closing behind him, she hobbled into the hall and gestured to Molly to assist her to her room and her anxiously awaited bath.

"I think you should spend the morrow in bed until time for the funeral," Molly advised as she wrapped a supporting arm around Veronica and helped her scale the mountain of stairs that led to her room.

"Mayhap you are right," she agreed in ragged breaths as she paused on the landing, staring up at the rest of the tedious steps. "Bring my breakfast and lunch to me in bed. I will need the rest if I am to endure what awaits the coming dawn."

A tear formed in Molly's eye as she tightened her grip on Veronica, who seemed near collapse.

Trager stood apart from the small congregation that had come to pay their respects to Mitchell Warren, his gaze settling on the dark-cloaked dowager and her bodyguard. He had mixed emotions about the woman, resenting her interference and reluctantly admiring her poise under these formidable circumstances that had been flung in her face, a face that had yet to be exposed to sunlight. And yet, when Veronica raised her bowed head and stared at him, he was curious to know if she shed real tears. She seemed so cold and hard at times that he wondered if she could even cry for the passing of her son. He had a knack of reading people's faces, a talent that had landed him the task of meandering behind enemy lines, picking up bits and pieces of information that would make Washington's task easier. But there was one woman who had him puzzled—Veronica Warren: the picture of declining health, with the forceful spirit of a mountain lion.

In silent reverie, Trager watched as Veronica turned, and, with pained steps, shuffled along the rock path to return to the manor. She paused and then motioned for him to join her. Trager frowned curiously and then closed the distance between them until Barron informed him that he was not welcome to take another step.

"Have you come to mourn Mitchell's death or to applaud his passing?"

Although her voice trembled with grief, there was an undertone of bitterness that Trager had no difficulty detecting. Her remark cut him to the quick, leaving a mile-wide gash in his flesh.

"Regardless of your low opinion of me, I did respect Mitchell and I have come to assure you that I am offering my support in your time of grief. I am the only family you have to lean upon at the moment, Veronica."

She stared at him long and hard from behind her heavy veil and then nodded a hesitant acceptance of his words. "Then come inside and share a drink with me," she invited before continuing on her way.

Trager fell into step behind her, keeping his distance when Barron growled to inform Trager that he was still an unwelcome intruder, as far as he was concerned. When Molly had taken their wraps, Veronica gestured toward the study.

"Mr. Landsing intends to read the will," she informed him and then brought her handkerchief to her mouth to muffle her cough. "Pour me a drink of brandy, Mr. Grayson."

His heavy brow quirked at her request, but he strode across the room to do her bidding. When Veronica had shuffled inside and slumped into her chair, he offered her the glass, extending himself so that Barron would not disapprove of their close contact.

Within a few minutes, ones that were spent in silence, Jonas Landsing strode into the room and settled himself in the chair across from Veronica, eyeing Barron as apprehensively as he had the first time the mutt had entered his office. As he unfolded the paper, he leaned forward on the edge of his seat and frowned thoughtfully.

"Mitchell made another will soon after Serena's disappearance," he explained. "'Tis much simpler than the other, but 'tis ironic that the benefactor is not present to receive her fortune."

Both Veronica and Trager frowned at his remark, wondering if Olivia had been granted the estate and Serena had been disowned.

"Mitchell refused to explain why he had suddenly decided to change his will, but he requested that his daughter, Serena, inherit the manor and his entire fortune. Olivia is to receive not a penny," Jonas continued soberly.

Veronica's mouth gaped in surprise, unable to believe that Mitchell had eradicated Olivia from his will, leaving only his vagabond daughter his heir. Not that she didn't deserve it, Veronica thought to herself, but she knew how devoted Mitchell had been to the young woman he had taken for his second wife. Her gaze hardened as if anchored on Trager, who remained expressionless. He was a master at disguising his emotions, and he didn't need a veil to hide his

331

chiseled features. No doubt, behind that carefully controlled exterior, he was laughing at the irony of inheriting a fortune, she mused bitterly.

"I will set up a fund for the manor and, since Mr. Grayson has informed me of his recent marriage to Serena, I have no choice but to put him in charge of the estate." Jonas forced a meager smile. "I know how distressed you are about your missing wife and this business about her being a Patriot sympathizer. It places you in a difficult position."

Veronica doubted that Trager was too uncomfortable. He rarely faced a situation that he couldn't command and come out smelling like a rose. She would have staked the Warren fortune on it.

After Jonas left them alone, Trager turned his full attention on Veronica, who had been pensively quiet since the lawyer's announcement. "Have you stashed Serena at your daughter's home in Connecticut?" he questioned point blank.

Her head rose slowly, viewing his probing gaze. "It seems that you have been busy prying information out of Jonas," she surmised, her raspy tone heavy with disdain.

"He told me of your long journey and was concerned about your health," Trager said glibly. "It did not require a crowbar to loosen those facts from his lips. He asked that I keep a watchful eye on you to insure that you did not overdo."

Veronica smirked, noting the lack of concern in Trager's voice. "You need not fuss over me, Mr. Grayson. I have been taking care of myself long enough that I require no assistance, especially from the likes of you."

"Thank God for that," he muttered half to himself and half aloud.

Her head swiveled around and Trager could feel the chill that had suddenly settled over the once cozy room. "I may be old and decrepit, but I assure you that I am not deaf. I suggest you keep a civil tongue in your head, young man, and remember your place."

His brow quirked, unwillingly admiring the old woman's spunk. "I always wondered why age gave people the right to speak their minds. Although most of us have been taught to respect our elders, I find it difficult to sit idly by and receive verbal abuse without retaliating." Trager bowed mockingly from his sitting position. "Forgive me, madam. Serena has often declared that I am no gentleman, and perhaps she is right. I find it difficult to take a tongue-lashing, even from you. But do not feel insulted. If I found myself in battle, facing an older man in hand-to-hand combat, I doubt that I would allow him to run me through either, merely because he was my elder."

A wry smile worked its way onto Veronica's face. How she loved to fence words with this rogue. "Then by all means, do speak your mind, Mr. Grayson. I find that parrying with you sharpens my wits."

Her voice, though hushed and hoarse, had lost its thread of contempt. He could sense that somewhere beneath that heavy veil lurked a faint smile. Trager leaned forward in his seat and braced his arms on his knees, taking advantage of her softer mood.

"Veronica, if Serena is staying with your daughter, I want to go to her immediately. There is much we must discuss and I . . ."

"She is not there," Veronica interrupted. "Do you think me such a doddering old fool that I would stash her in a place where the British might seek her out?" She did not wait for Trager's remark and hurried on before he could open his mouth to speak. "I have selected a most unlikely place for her sanctuary, one that the British would never think to look and that, Mr. Grayson, is where she will remain until they have given her up for lost." Painstakingly, Veronica pulled herself up on her feet and motioned for her companion to accompany her. "Come join me for dinner, Mr. Grayson. Perhaps the two of us can light upon some subject for a heated debate."

"I really should be going," Trager admitted, undecided about going another round with the cantankerous dowager.

Veronica leaned heavily on her cane and twisted around to peer at the handsome rogue who held his tricorne in his hand, absently toying with the triangular black hat. "Perhaps if we spend a little more time together, I might come to like you, and then I will reverse my decision to make you wait a fortnight to see my granddaughter."

Trager took the bait even though he knew he didn't have a snowball's chance in hell of improving her opinion of him. But being with Veronica and learning what made her tick could give him insight

334

into Serena's personality. Both women had a fierce pride and a stubborn streak that was a mile wide.

"As you wish, madam. Does this mean that I will be allowed to see you face to face while we dine?" he inquired, flashing her one of his notoriously blinding smiles.

"Nay, Mr. Grayson, I intend to wear my mourning habit for a full year . . . or until the angels come to fetch me," Veronica assured him as she hobbled across the hall to the dining room.

Trager bit back a wicked grin, wondering if it would be angels who retrieved the feisty old woman. More likely the Devil's left-hand man, he mused as he swaggered along behind her.

Before he could swallow his diabolic smile, Veronica detected it and paused to study him closely. "I know what you're thinking," she insisted, a hint of amusement rippling through her hoarse voice. "And you are probably right, young man. But if it's hell that awaits me, I think that is another reason the two of us should become better acquainted, since you will probably be positioned on the fire beside me."

Trager winced as if he had been singed and then gracefully recovered, offering her a courteous smile as he drew out the chair for her. "Touché, Veronica. Your point is well taken. If indeed we are to roast in hell together, we should become better friends."

Two days had moved along at a snail's pace and Trager had become impatient. He had discovered

335

very little after wandering in and out of New York. As darkness settled over the hills like a damp cloak, Trager, blurry eyed, paused to stare at the specter that materialized before him on the hill above the Warren mansion. Against the hazy sky he watched as a silhouette stirred upon the dark horizon. Could it have been Serena? Had Veronica stashed her right under his nose, keeping her hidden during the day and allowing her to roam at night?

Trager had been sitting at the pub that evening, listening to the yarns of drunken storytellers. He had scoffed at their preposterous tales, but either his eyes were deceiving him or there was a ghost lurking in these woods. The waning moonlight followed the caped specter until it disappeared among the trees and then recaptured the shadowed form as it wove and meandered down the slope.

He nudged his steed closer, squinting to make out the silhouette, but it had vanished in the chilly night air. A curious frown settled in his rugged features. He had to know whether or not the wild tales of ghosts and witches that were circulating about New Rochelle were products of overactive imaginations and an overabundance of liquor or . . .

Trager followed the path to the hidden entrance of the Warren mansion and silently made his way through the tunnel that led to Serena's bedroom. His curiosity was eating him alive. If Veronica was hiding Serena here, she might well be the cause of the fantastic accounts of phantoms haunting the countryside. Trager ran his hand along the panel near the fireplace and then cautiously poked his head inside. The room was empty, the bed showing no sign of use. A sentimental memory crept in from the corner of his mind and Trager was involuntarily drawn toward the bed, remembering the night he had come to rescue the golden-haired hellion from the British patrol. The sight of her lying there so peacefully had stirred and tempted him, but there had been no time to pursue his lusty thoughts. He had settled for a tormenting kiss.

If Serena was in the house, sooner or later she would come to bed and he would be here waiting for her. The hour was late and he was exhausted, and that in itself seemed the perfect excuse to stretch out on the satin sheets. After stripping from his clothes, he crawled beneath the quilts and stared up at the darkness, captured by another memory that had haunted him for nights on end. He could almost see Serena bending over him, her silky flesh glowing in the candlelight. On their wedding night she had murmured words of love as she offered herself to him. No doubt, it was her way of trying to entrap him, making him feel a fierce obligation to the bewitching woman he had taken for his wife. Her lips had melted like rose petals on his and he had drowned in the sweet fragrance that had overcome his senses.

Before he could fully pursue those arousing thoughts, Trager reminded himself of the turn of events that had sent her fleeing. He knew what she was thinking. Like a fool, he had voiced his opinion of Mitchell's guilt. Now she despised him and he couldn't really blame her. He had dug his own grave and had fallen headfirst into it. What a witless wonder he had become since Serena had walked into his life, turning it upside down. Washington was up to his neck in hot water, his troops deserting him after each British attack, and Trager was meeting himself coming and going, trying to locate his runaway wife and still supply Washington with the information he desperately needed.

A weary sigh escaped his lips as his lashes fluttered against his cheeks. He would catch a cat nap and then be wide awake to confront Serena if she appeared, he told himself drowsily. And then the darkness closed in on him and he was drifting, tormented by the sweet memory of Serena's pliant body lying next to his.

Trager flinched when he was startled from his dreams by the sound whack of a cane on his bare shoulder. "What the hell . . ."

He pried open one heavily lidded eye, trying to get his bearings, and then grumbled at the stooped shadow that loomed above him. Veronica struck him again, but with more force, and then glared at the bare-chested rogue who had crept into the bedroom to make himself at home.

"You have your nerve, Grayson," she snapped, her tone as cold and clipped as the Arctic wind. "What the hell do you think you're doing in this house?"

Her raspy, heavily accented voice sliced through

his sleep-drugged thoughts, bringing him awake as if a bucket of ice water had been thrown in his face. Trager attempted to sit up, but Barron's warning growl made him freeze in his half-propped position. He was going to have a difficult time explaining this one, he mused sourly as he stared up at Veronica's camouflaging veil. He would have preferred to give a bald-faced lie to an entire British regiment than to construe some flimsy excuse for wandering in uninvited and planting himself in Serena's bed. But then, on second thought, he had every right to be in his wife's room. He was a member of the family, unwelcome and disliked, but a member just the same. He and Veronica had made a stab at friendship, but there was much room for improvement, and he was certain that his foolishness would cause a serious setback.

Gathering his self-confidence, Trager clasped his hands behind his head and cast Veronica a casual glance. "Since we had become friends, and since this is my wife's room, and since I was in dire need of a place to stay for the night . . ." Trager knew he was pushing his luck, but he hoped his feeble logic would help him avoid another bruising assault from Veronica's cane. "I didn't think you would mind this slight imposition," he fumbled and finished.

Veronica could feel the steam rising from her high collar, after listening to the rake wade his way through his excuse. "The *least* you could have done was to inform me that you intended to spend the night," she flared, her tone no less angry and terse than it had been the first time. "Have I not enough on my mind without wondering if rapists and renegades have invaded this domain? Upon my word, Grayson, I cannot imagine where even *you* could find the gall to march in unannounced and climb into Serena's bed!"

Trager sought to smooth her ruffled feathers as she raised her cane. He flashed her a charismatic smile, but either it was too dark for the dowager to notice it or she was unreceptive to his charms. Whatever the case, he had the uneasy feeling that she was glaring a hole through him from behind her veil. "I'm sorry, madam. I did not want to disturb you at this late hour."

Veronica sniffed disgustedly. "And you thought that I might have been keeping Serena here, didn't you?" she speculated. "I can assure that I have found a safer hiding place for her. If you thought she might come up to her room to share this bed with you for the night, you are in for a long wait . . . a fortnight, to be exact." Her explosiveness brought a coughing spasm and it was a long moment before Veronica regained her composure.

"I will be leaving the area in the morning," he assured her quietly as he drew the quilt over his chest and turned on his side. "It will please you to know that I will not be returning until the day you have granted me an audience with my wife." His gaze drifted back over his shoulder, certain that Veronica was trembling with rage rather than old age.

"See that you are out of this house at an early hour or Barron and I will rout you out in a most unpleasant manner," she muttered as she pounded her cane into the floor.

When Veronica shuffled from the room and slammed the door behind her, Trager fluffed his pillow and squirmed beneath the quilts. It was most fortunate that Veronica would not be ruling the roost, he thought sourly. She would probably be trailing after him, hammering him with her cane for touching her precious granddaughter. Damn, he was tempted to strangle Serena for forcing him to put up with that persnickety old woman. Trager was certain he had stumbled into a rattlesnake den and Veronica Warren had been installed as the resident viper. Damn that old woman, she was becoming a pain in the neck, he muttered as he sought a more comfortable position and squeezed out the thought of her standing over him, striking him with her cane.

Chapter Seventeen

November 11, 1776

Serena sat at the kitchen table in Anna's modest home, impatiently drumming her fingers, waiting until Anna had tucked her boys into bed. The events of the past two weeks had festered until Serena was a bundle of nerves, hiding like a creature of the night to avoid being discovered and talking to herself in an attempt to keep from going mad. She was restless and disoriented, her identity lost to save herself from the hangman's noose. She had tried to convince herself that the civilized British would not take a woman to the gallows, but, after hearing rumors of renegade loyalists who raped and raided the countryside, she wondered if she would even have the opportunity to face General Howe and plead for mercy.

When Anna returned to the kitchen she heaved a tired sigh and sank into her chair, turning her attention to Serena, who was fidgeting in her seat. A faint smile touched Anna's lips, remembering how Serena had burst into the house that evening with an arm-load of staples to replenish her bare cupboards. There was an array of succulent meats that left Anna's mouth watering, and treats for her boys, which she had consented to letting them nibble on as bribery to get them into bed. Although Anna was back on her feet, earning a meager living for herself and her children, Serena's generous packages were welcomed with an eager smile.

"Would you like to tell me what is bothering you?" Anna offered as she observed her friend's apprehensive state. "You have been close to biting your nails since you burst in here."

Serena let her breath out in a rush, as if she had been holding it since she arrived. "I am to meet Trager tomorrow night," she blurted out and then gulped down her tea, trying to swallow her nervousness. Unfortunately, it rose again with her intake of breath.

A sly smile caught one corner of Anna's mouth as she arched a quizzical brow. "If you intend to dissolve this marriage, why did you consent to see him? A simple note explaining your plans would have been sufficient."

That was a difficult question, one for which Serena had no answer. Why had she agreed to meet Trager? She detested him for what he had done, and yet the moment she had laid eyes on him all those familiar sensations came back to haunt her. It took every ounce of determination she could muster to remain calm beneath the devastating effect of

Trager's presence.

When Serena did not reply immediately, Anna nodded thoughtfully. "You are still in love with him, aren't you, Rena? Even after all that has happened he still possesses your heart."

"But he murdered my father." Serena fought back the tears that lurked just beneath the surface. "What kind of future can we possibly have together with that dark cloud hanging over us?" she breathed in exasperation.

"You do not know for certain that it was Trager who took your father's life," Anna reminded her. "First you must listen to his explanation. You owe him that much."

Serena slumped back in her chair, knowing in her heart that Anna was right, but not so confident that she could face Trager without Veronica's concealing veil. It had been difficult to play the charade, but she had managed with the aid of the terrible grippe she had contracted from exposure to the storm. She had practically lost her voice and could barely draw a breath without succumbing to coughing spasms. The oversized clothes she had worn in disguise had been borrowed by Anna from her mother. With a few layers of padding, Serena had managed to camouflage her youthful figure with lumps and sags that fit a crusty old woman who was nearing her eightieth birthday. The heavy veil of gauze and lace had protected her face, but she had taken particular care to wear a gray wig and glasses, and had painted an array of wrinkles on her face.

She had hoped that when she put herself in the role of her outspoken grandmother she could hold herself aloof from Trager. It had helped immensely in dealing with him. Although he had claimed that Veronica could not earn his respect just because of her age, he was still a mite wary of the dowager. If Serena had cut him with some well-aimed jibe, Trager would have manhandled her. But he had yet to lay a hand on Veronica and, for that, Serena was thankful. His touch was dangerous and she feared that she would melt from it like a witless fool. Serena admitted to herself that she had spitefully badgered him, deriving a wicked pleasure in repaying him for the misery she had suffered at his hands. Clubbing him with her cane had been gratifying, especially when she knew that Trager, even though he was a scoundrel and a rogue, would never harm a hair on the old woman's head. True, he had obviously entertained the thought of strangling her on more than one occasion, but the single thread of decency he possessed had prevented him from following through with the dastardly deed. Serena was safe behind her dark veil, but it was unnerving to think of shedding her disguise and confronting him when she was still so vulnerable to the emotions that she had attempted to bury, emotions that rose like ghosts in the night to torment her dreams.

She had claimed to despise him the night she had returned after living through the nightmare of the battle in White Plains. Serena had sought refuge under Anna's roof, afraid to return to her own home, expecting Olivia to send a message to the Loyalists that Nathan Hale's accomplice had appeared on her doorstep. Charading as her own grandmother, Serena returned to the manor, relieved to learn that Olivia had evacuated the house. The next-to-the-last person Serena wanted to confront was her stepmother, knowing that she would not grieve for Mitchell. And the *last* person Serena wanted to face was Trager, but, to her dismay, he had come to turn her heart upside down all over again.

When he had appeared in the entrance of the parlor, his face tired and drawn, she had felt the ridiculous need to console him while seeking her own comfort in his arms. But in that same instant she had experienced the fierce, compulsive need to jab him with her cane. And then when she had returned to her room after roaming the darkness like a hunted beast that dared not show its face, and she had found Trager asleep in her bed, the temptation to lie down beside him had been so great that she had contemplated blurting out the truth. But something had stopped her. Perhaps it had been that charming smile he had flashed her, as if he could melt her into her shoes. Stubborn pride had made her square her shoulders and fling him a heated glare that would have burned both layers of skin off a normal man. It was easier to fire insults at him from behind her concealing veil than to confront him while he lay in her bed.

Serena had hoped that by giving herself time to heal she would be prepared to face Trager and demand that this mock marriage be dissolved, but a fortnight had elapsed and she was not one step closer to dealing with her emotions. They still lingered just beneath the surface, twisted and tangled with mistrust and that painful feeling of betrayal. How was she to make it through the night when she could not alight upon one sensation or the other, wavering between love and hate like a tightrope acrobat?

"Rena?" Anna's quiet voice filtered into her troubled musings and Serena glanced up to meet her friend's worried expression. "You owe it to yourself to talk frankly with this husband of yours. If he didn't care about you, he wouldn't have taken such pains to seek you out. He could have let you go and washed his hands of you, leaving you to manage on your own."

"He has only come because he has deviously devised some new technique to torture me," Serena muttered bitterly, refusing to be softened by Anna's logic.

"Nay, I think not. You know that he has discovered that you and I were friends, and that he came here twice to question me. How he discovered our close association, I do not know, but he must have done some fast footwork to come up with that information. He seemed very sincere and concerned about you."

Serena released a distasteful sniff and clasped her teacup tightly in her hands to still her nervous trembling. "He has an uncanny knack for digging up bits and pieces of information and gluing them

348

all together." Her gaze fell reproachfully on Anna. "And no doubt you were swayed by that devil who disguises himself behind a blinding smile. Trager can be very persuasive when he wants something, especially searching me out to torment me more than he has already."

"Then 'tis little wonder that Washington puts such stock in your husband," Anna remarked, hiding her smile behind the rim of her cup. "The man has the unusual ability of finding needles in haystacks. But, although I was tempted to tell him the truth about Veronica Warren, I held my tongue, knowing that it was not my place to inform him that the decrepit old dowager that had become a thorn in his side was also his stubborn wife."

Serena was in no mood to listen to Anna praise Trager. She had spent the better part of two weeks dwelling on his faults, molding him into some fiendish villain in her own mind. "Save your compliments," she demanded, her tone harsher than she intended. "My husband is no saint. He is a spy, a deceitful, underhanded scoundrel whose personality better fits his role than another I could name."

A sentimental tear crept into Anna's eyes. "He supports the cause my husband gave his life to defend. I have lost the love of my life, Serena," she said brokenly. "Don't throw away this love you harbor in your heart. You are making a grave mistake by attempting to bury your feelings for Trager. There is so little pleasure to be found these days. Amid all the tragedies, a woman must cling to each fleeting moment before it is lost to her forever." Anna reached across the table to grasp Serena's hand, squeezing it compassionately. "You *must* see him, Serena. You must confront him with your suspicions and talk them out. What if you are wrong about him? Could you live with yourself if you later learned that it was not his hand that took your father's life?" Anna wiped away the tears with the back of her hand and forced a meager smile. "Take the advice of a woman who would give anything if she could rewind the hands of time and relive all those moments with her husband, showing him in all the ways that lovers do that she adored him and the ground he walked upon. If I could have foreseen the future I would have cherished each of those moments and offered words of love more often. But now I have lost him, and I was not allowed to tell him that he took my heart with him when he died. Spare yourself that pain, Rena. At least learn the truth before you condemn him and break the vows you made when you wed him."

Serena's heart went out to Anna, who was breaking down now for the first time since she had lost her husband, shedding a sea of tears that she had carefully held in check while she put up a noble front for her children.

"See him," Anna pleaded between sobs. "Salvage your one chance to make amends or you will live to regret it. If Trager is guilty as you have accused him, then you will have been fair and just and you can let him go, free of conscience. But you *must* know the truth. Do not forget how you have suffered from lies and misconceptions because someone has accused you of conspiring with Nathan to aid the Patriots.''

Reluctantly, Serena allowed herself to be led to the door and shuffled out into the cold. "Very well, I will see him," she assured Anna, who broke into a thankful smile. "But only because you request it. I fear him, Anna. I do not think I can listen to him tell me how he murdered my father."

Anna braced herself against the door, staring at her cynical friend through tear-rimmed eyes. "But it is far easier to live with the truth than to go on wondering what happened. Good night, Serena. My prayers will be with you."

As Anna disappeared behind the closed door, Barron rose up on all fours, stretched, and then wagged his tail as his mistress ambled up beside him. Smiling fondly, Serena bent to brush a gloved hand across the dog's broad head and then walked off the porch. "Let's go home," she murmured to her devoted companion.

Barron trailed along beside her as Sandpiper ducked his head to face the brisk wind that foretold winter. There was a chill in the air that cut its way through Serena's cloak even though she had drawn it tightly about her. Tomorrow night she would face Trager. That thought sent a shiver down her spine and she huddled against her steed, urging him into a trot, letting him guard his own steps in the darkness. Her gaze drifted back to insure that Barron was keeping the pace and she smiled to herself as the dog trotted obediently at Sandpiper's heels. Barron had become a silent friend to whom she could verbalize her innermost thoughts. He had been lost and alone, just as she had been during the dreadful storm. They had found each other and huddled together to ward off the blowing rain and winds that whipped about them in the darkness. The dog had followed her, adopting her as his mistress, defending her so fiercely at times that she wondered if the mutt had discovered the meaning of blind devotion. Had he realized that she was a criminal, fated to be hanged, he might have sought out someone whose life wouldn't end after one careless move. But like a guardian angel he continued to hover beside her, wagging his tail each time she spoke softly to him, nuzzling against her to offer comfort during her blue moods.

After Serena had made her way up the dimly lit tunnel to her room, she heaved a frustrated sigh and stripped off her clothes. The darkness brought another round of forbidden memories, memories that ventured in at twilight and lingered until dawn. It was the thought of her wedding night. Her body tingled just as it had when Trager's exploring touch roamed over her, bringing rapturous sensations that she was trying not to remember. But his face was hovering above hers, his lips fluttering across hers in that sweet tempting way that could melt her defenses. Serena squeezed her eyes shut and commanded the image to evaporate, but a pair of silver-gray eyes penetrated her, chiseling away at her resistance. She could almost feel another of his feathery kisses playing on her lips, smell the manly fragrance of musk that wrapped itself around her senses when he nuzzled against her.

Serena tossed her head from side to side, denying the taunting emotions that bubbled and churned within her. She willed herself to see Trager for what he was—a liar and a rogue who only used others for his purposes, taking what he wanted from them and giving nothing in return, leaving them to suffer while he wandered like a tumbleweed, drifting in the wind while her soul was left to burn, shrivel, and waste away.

Damn him for hurting me, Serena muttered as she clenched her fist and slammed it into her pillow, giving way to the tears that flooded her eyes. She could not love a man like Trager, she told herself. Nay, it wasn't love at all. Ladies always had a weakness for outlaws, but once her fascination died, she would pick up the pieces of her life and go on without him, making her own way as she always had.

But when her determination faded and her dreams overshadowed her thoughts, Trager was there beside her, as he had always been, kissing away her willful defense, making her body respond to the exquisite feel of his caresses. She was lost to the ecstatic memory of a time that should have never been and would never be again.

Chapter Eighteen

The impatient rap at the door brought Serena from her silent reverie, as if a bolt of lightning had exploded beside her. She clutched the arms of her chair, waiting tensely for Trager's confident steps to take the tiled entryway and deliver him to the study door.

She cast a sidelong glance at the elegantly dressed rogue who filled the entrance. Trager's face was stamped with a determined frown that carved deep crevices in his chiseled features. He marched up in front of the old woman who was warming herself by the fire and addressed her with a curt nod.

"Madam, I trust my wife is here as you promised," he declared, dispensing with idle pleasantries since the dowager was rarely receptive to any.

Serena smiled beneath her veiled disguise. "Aye, she is here," she assured him hoarsely. "We both had hoped that you might have lost your way or reconsidered your decision to see her."

Trager gritted his teeth to bite back his caustic

retaliation, attempting to ignore the barb. "Is Serena in her room?" he persisted.

"Nay." Serena drew herself up and then resettled herself in a more comfortable position and Trager began to toy with the idea of whisking her up in front of him and giving her a hard shake, forcing Serena's whereabouts from her tight lips.

Clamping a tight grip on his composure and attempting to deal civilly with the cantankerous old woman, Trager forced a thin smile, finding the task painstakingly difficult. She wore heavily on his patience. "Then where might I find her?" He could sense that Veronica was delighting in agitating him, waiting for him to lose his temper so she could order him out of the house. "I have waited two long weeks to speak with my wife."

A gloved hand directed his attention toward the snifter of brandy that set perched on the table by the window. "Perhaps a drink would ease your tension, Mr. Grayson," she suggested in a raspy tone.

Trager's carefully tempered patience snapped like a string stretched far past its limit. "Dammit, I . . ." Trager swallowed his irritation and continued in a less hostile tone. "Thank you, Veronica. I could use a drink . . . although I would rather see Serena."

Serena overlooked his reminder of why he had come in the first place and flicked her hand toward the bar. "And pour this old woman one too while you are at it," she requested.

Trager could have sworn that he detected a hint of laughter in her hoarse voice. Veronica was enjoying antagonizing him. No doubt that had become the one demented pleasure in her otherwise dreary existence. Well, he would not allow that feisty old woman to creep beneath his skin, he vowed to himself as he strolled over to pour Veronica a stiff drink. If only he had a powder to mix with her brandy, he thought spitefully.

"You still do not like me, do you, Mr. Grayson," she inquired as she studied Trager's broad shoulders. "You think I am a meddling old woman. And I would also venture to guess that you wouldn't be the least bit distressed if I keeled over in my rocker and expired this very night."

Trager's raven head swiveled around to observe the perceptive old woman who attempted to voice his thoughts. It was amazing that she had come so close to pinpointing his lack of affection, especially when she was in one of her aggravating moods. After pouring himself and Veronica a drink he strode back to her and extended the glass.

"Do you actually think me to be such a black-hearted scoundrel that I would want to see you dead, madam?"

"The thought has crossed my mind," Veronica smirked before she drew her glass beneath her veil to take a healthy sip. The liquor burned its way through her throat and she sucked in her breath, choking on the strong taste.

Trager knelt beside her, concern etching his dark features, but he immediately retreated when Barron bounded from the other side of the chair to snap at him. "Veronica? Will you be all right?"

When she managed to take a breath she nodded affirmatively. "I had hoped the liquor would ease the aches and pains in this old body, but I fear the cure is as destructive as the affliction," she wheezed. In truth she had hoped the brandy would calm her nerves, helping her to deal with Trager, but she needed something less potent.

Trager's mood softened as he watched the frail old dowager sputtering. "Veronica, I want to apologize for intruding on you and going to Serena's room unannounced. 'Twas very inconsiderate of me to startle you."

She waved away his apology with an absent flick of her wrist. "No need, Mr. Grayson." Her tone registered indifference. "I derived pleasure from whacking you with my cane. I think Serena would have delighted in doing the same thing herself, had she had the chance."

Her candid remark set his teeth on edge. So they were back to swords and daggers again, he mused sourly. How could he be pleasant to that snippy old witch when she continued to bite at him like a rabid dog? It was damned near impossible, he decided.

"I have been indulging you, Veronica, allowing you to pick me apart like a vulture devouring her prey because you stand between Serena and me. But I am only a man, and I do not possess the patience of Job. I have agreed to wait until the appointed day as you requested and I hope that you will do the honorable thing by allowing me to see my wife." His tone was firm, his gaze unrelenting as he came to stand before the darkly clad dowager, deciding that now was the time to confront her, even if it meant having his leg chewed off by her vicious bodyguard.

After a long, stilted silence, the old woman nodded slightly. "Aye, you have kept your end of the bargain, and I will keep mine." Slowly, she pushed her way to her feet, grasping her cane in one gloved hand and her half-finished drink in the other. "Wait for Serena here," she commanded as she shuffled across the room. "I will send her to you in a few minutes." She paused at the door and twisted around to stare at Trager from beneath her veil. "I would suggest that you keep your distance from her, young man. She has become very suspicious and cynical—not that I blame her."

When Trager was left alone with his thoughts, he sank down in the rocker Veronica had abandoned, staring pensively at the fire. Would Serena accept his explanation or reject it as Veronica implied? A perplexed frown creased his brow as he watched the flames leap across the crackling logs. He could only hope that Serena harbored the slightest bit of affection for him; otherwise, he might just as well plead his cause to a rock wall.

Serena hastily shed her gown and padding and wiped the wrinkle lines from her face. Her hands trembled as she went about her chore, apprehensive about going back downstairs to face Trager without her disguise. Lord, why had she agreed to this? She must have weakened in a moment of madness, she decided as she shrugged on her gown and then peeled off her wig to brush out her hair. Satisfied with the reflection that peered back at her, Serena inhaled a deep breath and then let it out in a rush. Damn, she wasn't anticipating this confrontation. She would much rather be whipped than listen to Trager lie his way out of this predicament. First, she would hear what he had to say, and then she would inform him that she wanted the marriage dissolved at any cost. After all, she had made a promise to Anna and she would keep it.

With that determined thought in her mind, Serena locked Barron in the spare bedroom she had been using and walked down the hall, mentally preparing herself to greet Trager.

As Serena appeared in the doorway, the dim light hovering on her creamy skin, Trager rose to his feet, mesmerized by the vision of loveliness that was poised so cautiously by the door. It was as if she intended to break and run if she felt threatened. Trager could feel the electricity in the air, the shock sending a tingle across his skin. He had envisioned this moment, but Serena was far more captivating than he had allowed himself to remember. He had to will his body to keep the distance, but he could feel himself involuntarily moving toward her, aching to feel her silky flesh beneath his caress. Her dusty pink gown accentuated each of her alluring curves, and Trager remembered all too well the feel of her shapely body pressed closely to his. She had become an obsession with him, a woman whom he had yet to conquer. She had given her body to him, but she continued to hold her heart and soul just out of reach, fleeing from him when the opportunity presented itself.

When he made a move toward her, Serena raised her hand to halt him in his tracks. "Say what you have to say from where you stand," she ordered, her tone cold and clipped.

Trager bowed his head and formulated his thoughts before attempting to put them into words. "Serena, I know why you fled from White Plains and I know what you think of me, but . . ."

"Get to the point," Serena snapped briskly. "I do not intend to be manipulated."

"When I left you in White Plains, Washington ordered me to keep tabs on Major Baldwin's activities. And you were right about him. He was filling Howe with information about the Patriot forces. I confronted him when he came from Howe's headquarters and he became indignant, issuing threats and swearing that he would divulge my identity to the British if I did not allow him to continue with his underhanded activities. He also swore that he would alert Howe to your presence among the Rebels. I think he had been keeping that ace up his sleeve until the bounty on your head met his price." Trager frowned thoughtfully. "And now I am left to wonder if perhaps he had found some way to link you to Nathan. I told Baldwin that I would not compromise my beliefs for the likes of him and we both knew that only one of us would walk away. He pulled a pistol on me and I was forced to kill him. The shots drew the soldiers' attention and I had to flee before I was caught and questioned." Trager stuffed his hand in his pocket and sipped his drink as he turned to stare at the fire. "I rode to the manor and used the secret entrance to stay in your room, hoping the patrol would give up their search for Baldwin's assassin. I sustained a wound on my arm, and with the loss of blood and exhaustion I fell asleep in your room. The following morning I intended to speak to your father, to inform him of your whereabouts and test out my theory that he was involved in the scheme to connect you with Hale." He paused a moment, his attention returning to Serena, who had not moved a muscle but waited tensely to hear the sordid details of her father's murder. "During the night I was awakened by a gunshot. At first I thought I was dreaming, but then I remembered where I was and became suspicious of the sound. I did not kill your father," he told her solemnly. "When I walked into this study, he was lying facedown on the floor, and the front door stood ajar. I heard your maid coming downstairs so I hurried out the door before she caught sight of me, and then I attempted to seek out the murderer, but he had vanished in the night. I crept back to your room through the tunnel to collect my belongings and went on my way."

A tear formed in the corner of Serena's eye and trickled down her cheek as relief washed across her features. She *did* believe him, even though she had been certain that nothing he could say could convince her of his innocence. "And did you discover who betrayed Nathan?" she questioned point blank.

Trager nodded affirmatively. "Aye, in a round-about way. I learned that Nathan's cousin, Sam Hale, who is known as a Loyalist sympathizer and renegade, spotted Nathan at the Widow Chichester's Inn at dawn, just as he was about to depart to meet a friend who would take him by boat to Whig territory. Sam Hale alerted the British officers and had Nathan taken into custody." He let his breath out in a rush and then raked his fingers through his dark hair before his arm dropped loosely to his side. "I still have not learned who pegged you as Nathan's accomplice. But I would venture to guess that it had to be someone who attended the ball and who had something to gain by naming you for treason." His silver eyes strayed back to Serena, intending to be completely honest with her. "Only your father could have told me if he had anything to do with the bounty on your head, or who has now taken his life. Now I wonder if we will ever know for certain."

Sensing that her hostility toward him had dwindled, Trager quickly closed the distance between them, unable to deny the need to take her in his arms, to feel the exquisite warmth of her tempting body pressed tightly to his. He was aching to touch her, to brush his hands over her honey-gold mane, to inhale the sweet fragrance that could entangle his senses.

"I should turn you over my knee and give you a good thrashing for leading me on this wild goose chase," he murmured, his voice too raspy with desire to make her take offense at his remark.

If this was his idea of punishment Serena was certain that he had found a most effective method of torture. His sinewy arms encircled her waist, his breath warm against the rapid pulsations of her neck. He was tearing her in a thousand pieces, knowing she could never share his love. His touch was heaven and hell and she detested the wild sensations that danced across her skin. Serena was doing her damnedest to remain aloof, but that was asking the impossible. Every inch of her flesh smoldered and her body arched to make contact with the hard length of him. Her thoughts were careening, her senses contaminated by the sight, feel, and tantalizing aroma of him. It was almost too much to bear, Serena thought hopelessly. How could she speak her love for him as Anna had suggested when she knew he would take her heart and then recklessly toss it aside when he no longer had a need for it?

And then his lips descended on hers, hungry and impatient, draining her resistance, like a bee quenching its thirst on the nectar of a rose, leaving it empty and without value.

Trager dragged his lips from hers, a wry smile etching his rugged features as he traced the sensuous curve of her mouth with his index finger. "I can taste the brandy," he whispered, his gaze flowing over her face like a tender caress. "I'm surprised Veronica permitted you to partake of it."

"As a matter of fact, she was the one who suggested I drink to take the edge off this meeting with you," Serena replied, her voice quivering slightly. There was a mischievous twinkle in her eyes as her lashes fluttered up to meet Trager's wondering gaze.

"I would have guessed that Veronica would have been delivering a lecture on temperance, although *she* is not opposed to tipping the bottle now and then. It seems that she has one set of standards for herself and another entirely different for the rest of the world, and she does not hesitate to point out our shortcomings," Trager smirked.

"Veronica is her own woman," Serena countered, biting back another smile. "I think she has every right to say what she thinks."

"And there have been times in our short acquaintance that I have wished she had been struck dumb long enough for me to pick the barbs from my hide," Trager said absently, losing interest in conversation. Holding Serena was too distracting and the subject of the razor-tongued dowager was the least of his concerns. "I've missed seeing that fiery glint in your eyes." His breath became uneven as he bent his head toward hers, eager to taste another of her intoxicating kisses that left the brandy he had consumed earlier sorely lacking in flavor. "Lord, I've missed you."

Serena mustered her determination and pried his arms from her hips, putting a safe distance between them. "I thought perhaps you would have been pleased to be rid of me," she blurted out. "Your original purpose for marrying me was to protect me, but now that Veronica is here, she will grant me shelter."

Trager frowned at her sudden burst of independence. Damn, but this wench made a perfect model, posing with the American flag draped around her. The libertine rebel from head to toe, he decided as he looked her up and down. "But how long do you intend to hide behind Veronica's skirts?" he inquired, sarcasm dripping from his lips. "You dare not show your face in this neck of the woods, and Veronica has informed me that she intends to sail home on the swiftest ship afloat."

"She may be staying longer than you think," Serena shot back at him. "Veronica won't desert me if I need her assistance."

"You have no future here, Rena," he told her simply. "You need to be free to come and go as you please. If you stay here, hiding during the day, you will shrivel up and waste away. And I also fear that a close association with Veronica will only sharpen your tongue."

Serena looked him square in the eye, ignoring his insult in order to voice her thoughts. "I must stay to protect the manor. I have heard it rumored that the Patriots are becoming desperate for money and that they are not beneath selling the property of Loyalists who have lost their lives in battle or have migrated to Canada to avoid the war."

"Aye, 'tis true," he agreed, "but I can assure you that your father's estate will be spared, especially now that its ownership lies in my hands."

He moved nearer, clasping her small hands in his, staring down into her exquisite face, seeing the same expression that had haunted his dreams, half questioning, half answering, a mite suspicious and yet so very compelling. "I want you to come with me. There is much we must do and time is running short. Washington is contemplating the move to Valley Forge for winter quarters and my mission here is finished for a time. Howe intends to settle in New York, lolling in the lap of luxury, playing his gentleman's game of war. He is more the fool," Trager scoffed bitterly. "He could have had Washington backed against the wall if he had pursued us to Peekskill, but now he tarries and allows the Patriot army that wobbles on crutches to regroup and train."

He was playing a tug-of-war with her emotions. How tempting it would be to go with him, to sleep in his arms on those cold winter nights, to follow Anna's suggestion to cherish the pleasure granted to her. But to follow him was foolish. Loving him was madness. She wanted more than pleasure and passion, more than a cozy nest. It was all or nothing with Serena, and she possessed enough pride to settle for nothing if she had to make her choice.

While Serena grappled with her thoughts, Trager grasped her arm and propelled her toward the stairs. "Pack a few things for our trip. Washington is expecting my report by the end of the week, and we have a long ride ahead of us."

Mechanically, she moved along with his insistent step, part of her still aching to run away with him and another part determined to let him go alone. When they entered the room, Trager retrieved a small bag and began stuffing undergarments in it and then wadded up her dresses, hastily stuffing them into the pouch.

"Put on something that will not hinder you on our journey," he insisted, throwing her a quick glance, seeing that she was glued to the same spot where he had released her to begin the packing. "Serena." His tone demanded that she come to attention and then obey.

Her gaze swung in absent response, formulating her thoughts. Trager released an impatient sigh and came to her, deftly loosening the small buttons on the front of her velvet gown. What had begun as an urgent task became a leisurely chore as he exposed the creamy flesh of her breasts to his gaze. His weeks of longing overwhelmed him. Time was of the essence, and suddenly he didn't give a damn if the world crumbled at his feet as long as he could cradle this captivating vixen in his arms. All he had on his mind from the moment his knuckles brushed across the valley between her full breasts was taking her to bed. He had hungered and craved for weeks since she had eluded him, dreaming tormenting dreams that left him waking alone in a bed where he could have sworn Serena had lain beside him.

Her tangled lashes swept up to see the passionate spark that leaped between them, and her body trembled as the palm of his hand touched her rib. Deliberately, his fingertips fanned across her breasts and then glided up to push the gown from her shoulders.

"Can you see the want in my eyes?" he whispered

as his wandering caresses trailed along her back, rediscovering the feel of her satiny skin beneath his hands. She nodded mutely, hypnotized by the silver flame that burned its way to her very core, unable to protest, as she was in the habit of doing. "I don't think I can find the will to leave this room until I have appeased this maddening urge to possess you."

The faintest hint of a smile grazed her lips. He reminded her of a pleading little boy who begged for favors and who would have been brokenhearted if he were denied his whim. "You are my husband. What kind of wife would I be to refuse your rights?" Serena surprised herself with her reply, wondering why she was consenting when she would be forced to watch him withdraw and leave her side after he had made love to her. She must be mad, she told herself.

A rakish grin tugged at one corner of his mouth as he pushed the dangling gown over her hips, letting it slip to the floor like a pool of velvet and lace around her ankles. "And you do not condemn me for craving this delicious body of yours?"

Trager gave her no time to reply. His lips swooped down on hers as he clutched her to him, his tongue searching the recesses of her mouth with ravishing impatience. When he captured her in the tight circle of his arms, Serena felt her skin branded with fire, every nerve in her body tingling in anticipation. Her hands trailed across the broad expanse of his chest to curl over his shoulders, involuntarily responding to the magic of his touch. She could feel the corded muscles of his back flex and then relax beneath her caress. And despite her better judgment she found herself arching to meet his bold manliness that pressed against her thigh, thrilling to the feel of his magnificent body molded to hers, dizzy from the musky fragrance that swirled about her senses, longing for that one priceless moment that she had known in his arms.

His silver eyes shimmered with heated passion as he pressed her to the bed, and Trager caught his breath as her hair sprayed across the pillow like a cape of gold, enhanced by the shaft of moonbeams that kissed each silky tendril that flowed away from her face. He wrapped his hand in the thick curls, tilting her head back to accept another devouring kiss.

Trager propped his forearms on either side of her, mesmerized by the desire he found in those emerald pools. "Only now do I realize how much I have missed you, much more than I had thought," he mused aloud, wondering at the deep emotion that bubbled up inside him.

"Have you truly?" she whispered.

"Shall I show you how much?" Lord, she had entangled herself so tightly in his thoughts that he wondered if even an exorcist could rout her.

Her gentle hands framed his face, and Serena held her breath, fearing that he would see the love shining in her eyes as she peered up at him. If only she could have his devotion, if only she could touch his heart, she mused ruefully. "Aye," she murmured, her voice heavily disturbed with desire. "Show me proof of your need for me." She silently prayed to hear the phrase that could ease the pain that twisted her soul. "Love me, Trager."

His mouth slanted across hers in a strangely tender kiss that brought a tear to her eye. And then she gasped as his lips left hers to trail to her breast, his tongue circling the taut peak. Serena surrendered to the warm sensations that had her feeling that she was sinking into the mattress, relaxed and pliant beneath his skillful touch. His wandering caress captured the full mound of her breast and then traced an arousing path across her abdomen. As his hand glided lower to the softness of her inner thigh she heard the echo of her own sigh somewhere in the distance. And, as his knowing fingers aroused her to sensuous heights of pleasure, she was left to wonder if she could endure the sweet torture. He left her to burn as his caresses receded to her flat belly while his lips fluttered from one pink peak of her breast to the other. The fire spread until it had encompassed each tingling nerve and each quivering inch of flesh. Serena was suspended in the breathless moment, drifting like a weightless feather in the wind, unsure of her destination and unable to control her direction or scattered thoughts. All she knew was that she wanted him, if only for this one timeless instant, no matter what the cost or the pain that she might suffer when the clouds of passion had parted and she was left to deal with her folly.

Finally, she could endure no more of his sweet, agonizing fondling. She squirmed away, attempting

371

to return each maddening ounce of pleasure he had given her. A moan escaped his lips as her exploring hands trailed across the dark furring on his chest, following the matting of hair that trickled over his muscled belly. In the wake of her arousing touch came butterfly kisses that brushed lightly over his hips and tracked across his thigh as her hand folded around him. In such a short time she had become a devastating seductress, inventing new ways to bring him to the brink of insanity. Her gentle touch was exquisite rapture, an experience that even his dreams had not been able to capture. It was sinful the way she made him feel, her lips and hands touching him in the familiar way of a lover who knew each sensitive point on his body and could make him respond like a senseless puppet on a string.

And then, with ease, he lifted her above him to resume his fondling, his lips searing her flesh as his kisses wandered over her.

Serena was dizzy with desire. He was driving her mad with the want of him, his kisses tasting each inch of her skin, his caresses stroking her so possessively that she could barely catch her breath. And then a wild, budding ache that she was certain nothing could appease spread through her loins and she clutched at him, begging for him to claim her.

He rolled her to her back, his muscled hips sliding between her thighs. Impatiently, she arched to meet him, accepting his driving thrusts with eagerness. Trager was amazed at her abandon. And for the first time in his life he found himself afraid that he could not satisfy the wild longing that overcame a woman. Her lips parted in invitation, wanting him to take all of her, body and soul, for that glorious moment that pursued and captured time.

Their flesh was as one, their breath intermingling, their hearts beating in furious rhythm as he thrust deeply within her, seeking depths of intimacy. Serena was certain that the previous sensations had been passion's highest pinnacle, but she quickly realized that it was yet another crest that could not hold a candle to the one before. She was soaring, wrapped in such indescribable pleasure that tears sprang from her eyes. The love she felt for Trager blossomed in the corners of her mind and emerged from the shadows of her heart, consuming her as he moved within her, filling her with such pure emotion that she was sure her heart and soul would burst.

And then like a falling star that had blazed across the endless sky, burning and consuming itself, they glided back to reality, cradled in each other's arms, their bodies intertwined. In the aftermath of love, Trager tucked his legs behind hers, nuzzling against the golden curls that felt like satin against his cheek. His hand glided across her bare shoulder and then he clasped her fingers between his and brought them to his lips. He drew a ragged breath as his gaze followed Serena's to the window. He was tempted to pinch himself to insure that this had not been some fantastic dream. He could not remember the feel of another woman in his embrace, conjure up another face that could equal the perfection in hers. The thought of Serena overshadowed all lovers of the past. She was what dreams were made of. But what was so compelling about this vixen? A secretive smile brushed his lips. The list was too extensive to recite, but he found himself mentally thumbing through the many facets of her personality that continued to captivate him.

Trager commanded his body to move, but his strength had abandoned him. His lips feathered across her flesh and again she yielded to his touch without protest. Trager halfheartedly hoped that she would deny him, knowing that he shouldn't tarry with her.

"There is no hope for it," he breathed in dismay. "I fear someone must light a fire beneath me to rout me from this lair."

Stung by a mischievous impulse, Serena reached for the lantern to accommodate him, the heat of the dim flame singeing his bare hip.

"Damn!" Trager shrieked and withdrew at blazing speed to glare at Serena. "Your quicksilver moods have me miffed, witch," he muttered sourly. "One moment you have me burning with desire and in the next instant you attempt to set me afire!"

Her soft chortle floated over him as she bent over to smooth away his frown. "Rest your fears, my handsome rogue. I did not intend to scar your flesh. I only sought to obey your command."

When Serena tried to withdraw Trager grasped her arm, pulling her off balance. She fell into his waiting arms, her naked breasts crushed to the solid wall of his chest.

"Could it be that you have become submissive during our long separation, that you will eagerly give in to all of my whims?"

Serena fell prey to his winsome smile, content to play along with his taunt. "But of course, m'lord. Is that not the way of a dutiful wife?" she inquired, arching a delicate brow.

"Then tell me you love me, Rena," he requested, the playfulness evaporating from his voice, his silver-gray eyes probing deeply into the fathomless pools of emerald green.

She stiffened, afraid to speak the words that were trapped in her heart. Trager was toying with her again, intending to bolster his male pride, seeking to add her name to his list of conquered lovers. Her chin tilted proudly as she braced herself, pushing back as far as his captive embrace would allow.

"Nay, I cannot," she told him, avoiding his level gaze.

"You told me once," he reminded her quietly as his lean finger traced her kiss-swollen lips. "The night we wed you whispered words of love to me. Was it just a meaningless phrase?"

Serena did not need to be prompted and quickly offered an excuse for her folly. "'Twas the liquor talking," she insisted as she took advantage of his relaxed grasp and squirmed from his arms. "'Tis only that it seemed fitting at that moment that I should love the man I married. I must have been caught up in some romantic notion which grew from a childhood fantasy."

Had he really expected her to admit to love, he wondered curiously. Serena? The most independent woman he had yet to meet? The rebellious rose who was the essence of beauty but was heavily armed with thorns? Nay, of course not, nor would *he* admit to an emotion that was as elusive as the wind. During his wanderings he had seen lovers seeking to find what could not be had. More than once he had listened to confessions of love from women who were eager to claim his fortune. And he had watched Serena toy with Brandon Scott, clinging to the security of his proposal while she experimented with Trager. How long before her eyes would stray to another man, Roger, for instance? How long before she would yearn to satisfy her curiosity in the arms of other lovers? The thought burned him like a twisting knife in his back. The vision of Serena lying with another man painted much too vivid a picture in his imagination, and he scowled to himself as he squelched the image. Women were not to be trusted, he reminded himself as he rolled to his feet and stalked about the room snatching up his discarded clothes and hurriedly throwing them on.

Silence fell like a partition between them, and Serena frowned at the icy atmosphere that had suddenly invaded the room. The chill seemed worse than the brisk breeze that wailed at the window. It only took a moment for her to realize that once Trager's lust had been appeased he had no more use for her.

ECSTASY'S EMBRACE

Attempting to win his love was a futile battle, she thought, discouraged. Anna's well-meaning advice was of no use to her. It only pertained to a man and woman who shared deep feelings for each other, not to one-sided affairs like hers. Serena could sympathize with General Washington, knowing how it felt to lose one battle after another. She was entertaining the thought of raising the white flag of surrender when Trager grasped her hand and aimed her toward the secret passageway.

Serena set her feet, refusing to leave with him. "I am not going," she said flatly.

"The hell you're not," he snapped, glaring at her. Trager uprooted her from the spot and shoved her ahead of him. "Washington awaits."

Under protest, Serena found herself shuffled down the steps to the tunnel and gritted her teeth when she lost the circulation in her left arm, his grasp like that of a vise grip.

"You're hurting me," Serena hissed as she struggled for release.

"Then do not resist me," he shot back at her. "I'm in no mood for one of your tantrums."

As he hustled her along the footpath to his waiting steed, her gaze strayed back to the dim light in the window. "I don't want to leave Veronica," she blurted out, grasping for some excuse to remain behind.

"Veronica can take care of herself," Trager muttered as he swept Serena around beside him and gestured toward the pasture. "Call your stallion."

Serena shivered as she faced the cold north wind and drew her cloak tightly about her. When Trager nudged her, practically knocking her off balance, she whistled for Sandpiper and listened as the steed galloped toward her. A curious frown knitted her brow as Trager retrieved the bridle from his saddle bag and stalked toward Sandpiper.

"What are you doing?" she questioned bewilderedly.

"I'll ride him," Trager threw over his shoulder as he stuffed the bit in the contrary steed's mouth.

"He won't let you on his back." Serena informed him, biting back a wicked grin as Trager grabbed the steed's mane and swung onto his back.

A giggle bubbled from her lips as Sandpiper pranced skittishly, dancing in a tight circle. He suddenly flung his hind legs out behind him and ducked his head, intent on unseating Trager. Caught off guard and finding no handle to which to hang on, Trager flew through the air and landed with a thud and a groan. In pain, he twisted around to hear Serena call softly to her steed, and he muttered under his breath when Sandpiper came to her like an obedient pup, nuzzling fondly against her.

Trager swallowed his pride and rolled to his feet. "Damned nag," he growled, his face darkening in irritation. And then the last of his temper came unraveled when Serena broke and ran back toward the house. "You stubborn little minx!" Trager hooked his arm around her waist and whipped her up off the ground to stomp back to the horses. "I said you were coming with me and, by damn, you are!"

"Go to hell!" Serena fired back at him as she writhed and fought for escape.

"Save your curses, witch." Trager retrieved a rope and bound her hands and then swiftly unhooked his saddle and tossed it on Sandpiper's back, intending to tie Serena on her horse. "Come hell or high water, you're coming back with me."

Serena gritted her teeth as he set her atop her mount and muttered several epithets as he bound her feet in the stirrups. "You can't keep me tied up forever, Trager," she spat at him, her eyes flaring like torches. "The moment your back is turned I will escape. I will always prefer Veronica's company to yours."

"Lower your voice," Trager muttered sourly. "These woods are crawling with Redcoats. We're behind enemy lines and I don't relish the idea of losing my hide when they catch me in your company. For your information, you are still wanted for treason, and the price on your head rises with the dawning of each new day."

Serena clamped her mouth shut and squinted at the shadows. "Then lead on, Trager," she whispered bitterly. "You leave me little choice in the matter . . . for the moment."

Trager pulled his steed to a halt to stare at the irate woman. "Serena, if I left you behind, I could not sleep at night, wondering if you had been captured."

"Your concern is very touching." Her voice was heavily laden with sarcasm, her gaze raking him mockingly.

"Would it surprise you to hear that I care about what happens to you?" he questioned, his tone softer now as he stared at her silhouette.

"Aye, it would. I thought you considered me to be the albatross that hung around your neck, an inconvenience that hampered your cause," Serena admitted, voicing her private musings and then wishing she could have bit off her tongue when she noticed the wry smile that pursed his lips.

"But a very attractive and desirable one," he acknowledged before tugging on the reins and leading them into the swaying shadows.

Serena peered at the dim light of her window once again, vowing that she would escape and return to resume the role of Veronica, protecting her home and keeping a safe distance between herself and Trager. The moment he let his guard down she would pounce on him and flee from him, sparing herself the misery of a one-sided love that was tearing her heart in two.

Chapter Nineteen

The restless wind swept the countryside and Serena shivered beneath her jacket, wishing she was tucked beside a cozy fire, reheating the blood that moved through her veins like icy slush. Her time with Trager had been spent in strained silence. Despite her pleas, Trager refused to unchain her, eyeing her suspiciously, as if he expected her to leap at his throat each time he dared to turn his back on her. His mood had darkened with each dawning day, his eyes streaked with red, evidence of his lack of sleep. Not once had he looked at her with desire as he had that night in her room. Now his hooded gaze was as remote and cold as the winter winds. Each evening he curled against her to sleep, but she remained bound, unable to slip away in the cover of darkness or even stir in her sleep without making him flinch and clutch at her.

Serena had yet to understand why he was dragging her along with him. He had no affection for her and he was constantly muttering about what a troublesome lot she was. Her straying thoughts evaporated when she glanced up to see Washington's encampment in the distance. Her spirits sank to their lowest depths when she saw the tattered soldiers who wore the evidence of their last defeat on their faces and on their backs. Even Roger, who usually sported a lackadaisical smile, looked the worse for wear, she thought, as Trager brought her steed to a halt.

A perplexed frown creased Roger's brow when Trager swung from his saddle. Trager's unkempt beard and tousled raven hair made him appear ominous and forbidding, almost fiendish, with a scowl carving hard lines on his face. When Roger spied the ropes that wound tightly about Serena's wrists and ankles, his head swiveled around, his gaze anchoring on his brother.

"Have you made her your slave?" he inquired, his tone harsh with disapproval.

Trager's face was as hard as granite as he focused bloodshot eyes on Roger. "'Tis that I don't trust her. I have seen one too many of her disappearing acts, and I was in no mood to chase her to hell and back . . . again."

A wry smile worked its way onto the corner of Roger's lips as he gave his growling brother the once over. "Aye, I see your point. You do look as though you have been singed. It has left you a bit rough around the edges."

Another scowl cut crevices in Trager's stony features. "And I am in no mood for your taunts, either," he muttered, pinning Roger down with a reproachful glare. "Where is Washington?"

Roger gestured toward the mansion that served as the new headquarters. "Yonder sits the general, but his disposition is no better than yours. He has just returned from a conference with Lee."

Trager unstrapped his hostage and deposited her in his brother's hands. "Find quarters for Serena and do not let her out of your sight until I return," he barked before he spun on his heels.

"From army scout to nursemaid," Roger smirked. A smile traced his lips as he winked at his sister-in-law. "Others might think that I have been demoted, but I have no complaints. I only hope that you request a bath and a massage to bring the circulation back."

Trager had taken two steps, but then he wheeled around to flash Roger a glare that would have wilted anyone but his own brother. "You are sorely testing my patience, Roger."

"I wasn't serious," Roger shot back at him, losing his own good disposition after watching Trager buzz about like a mad hornet who was itching to implant his stinger in human flesh.

"You damned well better not be," Trager snapped before he spun around and stalked away.

Serena breathed a sigh of relief. It was as if she had been holding her breath these past two weeks while Trager breathed fire down her neck. His foul moods had become unbearable, and Serena often found herself biting her tongue to keep from lashing out at him. She knew it would only make matters worse, and the less she said to him, the better.

"I'm not certain which is worse, fighting the British infantry or enduring Trager's irascible temper," she mused aloud.

Roger smiled sympathetically as he curled his arm about her waist. "It seems that you have fared badly. I cannot imagine why he resorted to keeping you bound." He urged her toward the house, taking the distance slowly since Serena seemed stiff from her long ride. "I don't know what has come over Trager. He has been wearing a permanent frown these past months."

"'Tis because he despises me and this unwanted marriage is playing havoc with his temperamental disposition," Serena murmured.

She had given the matter careful consideration during her nerve-wracking journey with Trager. He resented her and the responsibility of providing protection for her. Trager had, in a moment of madness, attempted to do the honorable thing by marrying her. Now he realized that it had been a foolish mistake and he regretted his impulsiveness. He was a man of his word and he could not break the vow, even if it made both of them miserable. They both would have been much happier if he had allowed her to remain at the manor.

Roger frowned, grappling with her conclusion. "Nay, I don't think that is the cause, Serena," he speculated. "I had noticed the change last fall, but it has become steadily worse. I am beginning to think that Trager's problem is himself. He is having difficulty accepting the truth of the situation."

Serena kept silent, even though she wasn't certain that she followed Roger's train of thought. When Roger had escorted her into one of the bedchambers, she paused to offer him a weary smile. "You need not stay. I have no intention of trying to escape at the moment. All I desire is a hot bath and a featherbed to ease my aching bones and muscles."

"But, Trager said . . ."

She held up her hand to halt his objection. "You have my word, Roger," she promised. "I will cause you no trouble."

Heaving a resigned sigh, Roger gracefully bowed out and went back downstairs to order water for her bath. He swallowed his breath when he spied Trager, looking as sour as a lemon.

Trager's dark brows formed a hard line over the slits of his steel-gray eyes. "Can I count upon no one to do my bidding?" he grumbled. "When I give you a command it sails in one ear and escapes out the other."

"Serena gave me her word," Roger defended himself, his tone as crisp as his brother's.

"Her word?" Trager laughed bitterly and then barged past Roger, knocking him off balance. "I should have known that witch would turn her charms on you and you would melt into your boots." He took the steps two at a time to reach Serena before she could escape. "Can no man resist that wench?" he muttered to himself.

Serena gasped startledly and clutched her shirt to

her bare breasts as the door slammed against the wall, sending a trickle of dust filtering from the woodwork. Trager's ominous figure filled the entrance and he glared suspiciously at her.

"There is a common courtesy called knocking. I suggest you use it in the future," she snapped caustically.

Trager knocked on the opened door, his eyes gliding over her exposed flesh. The faintest hint of a smile hovered on his lips, the first one she had seen in weeks. "Forgive me, madam." He strode into the room and kicked the door shut with his boot heel. "'Tis just that I didn't expect to find the room occupied at all."

"Put your fears to rest. I do not intend to devise a plan of escape until I have had a bath and a nap," she remarked, her tone heavily laden with sarcasm. Serena shrugged her dressing gown on her shoulders and then busied herself with the chore of pressing out her wrinkled gowns. "My criminal mind functions best when I am clean and well rested."

His eyes wandered over her shapely backside, his lusty thoughts overriding his irritation with her. He was like a man on the rack, torn between his mistrust and his compelling desire for her. Didn't he have enough on his mind without worrying over this troublesome wench? Every moment he had spent with her during their journey had been torture, pure and simple. Each time he had touched her he had been shocked to realize how much he wanted her, even after he had spent long hours telling himself that she was no different from the others. He had willed himself to keep his distance from her to prove to himself that he still possessed the power of mind over body. Lord, how many times had he reminded himself that he was a man of discipline? At least a thousand, he decided. He could live without appeasing himself with a woman, even if this one he had married happened to be the most desirable, feisty, and stubborn vixen he had ever met.

He had gritted his teeth and clenched his fists to keep from ravishing her each night he nestled against her to ward off the winter chill, but passion's fire was burning him up inside, tugging at his sanity, making him even more determined to prove to himself that he could live without that captivating wench. But now, as his silver eyes flowed over the honey-gold hair that tumbled recklessly about her, he found his mind and body fighting their constant tug-of-war. He was well aware of what lay beneath her robe. Her skin was like satin beneath his touch, her kisses as drugging as fine wine. Two weeks of wanting boiled through his veins. The days of struggling with his emotions all converged upon him, and Trager was too tired to begin the struggle all over again. There were a few things in life that a man couldn't change, no matter how strong his will.

Serena's gaze slid over her shoulder and she frowned at the odd expression on Trager's bearded face. There was a faint glow in his eyes, an expression that she could not decode. "Is something wrong?" she questioned as she rose and worked the kink out of her back.

Trager strode toward her and lifted a stray curl of gold, marveling at its silky texture. "Serena, I . . ."

The knock at the door interrupted him and he scowled. "What is it?"

"The lady's bath water, sir," the corporal called from the hall.

His hand dropped limply to his side, knowing the moment had been destroyed. He could have sworn that if he took her in his arms at that moment he would have met with no resistance. Serena was staring quizzically at him, her features soft, her gaze welcoming him to break the wall of ice that had formed between them.

"Come in," he ordered, his tone deflated.

Trager waited silently until the tub was filled, parking himself in a nearby chair, watching her move gracefully about the room to collect her toiletries. And then, when they were left alone, her assault on his senses began again as she stripped from her robe, ignoring him as if he were another stick of furniture. He stared thoughtfully at the ceiling, only to have her bewitching image materialize above him. What was this little minx trying to do, tempt and taunt him until he was begging for her affection? And what stipulation would she attach to spending a moment of heaven in her arms? His permission for her to leave and return to the manor and Veronica? How long could he sit here, his body aching to touch her, before he surrendered? Damn, Washington should have had Serena capture the British forces.

Her subtle femininity would have had the whole lot of them down on their knees, waving flags of surrender. And how in the sweet loving hell was he to withstand this gnawing ache that chippd away at his sanity when he knew that she, above all others, could hold a man entranced when he was in her loving arms?

When he heard the water splash, his eyes involuntarily strayed to her. A contented smile played on her lips. Her blond hair was piled on top of her head, revealing the trim column of her neck where he had often felt the rapid pulsations when his kisses had wandered from her inviting lips. Her creamy flesh was beaded with droplets of water. She was incredibly seductive, and Trager found his footsteps taking him to her, drawn like a moth to a flame that would inevitably become his undoing. Damn her. She was crumbling his resistance, as if his defenses were built of straw. The guileless witch could not be content with entangling herself so tightly in his thoughts that she had left spider webs in his brain. Nay, she sought his heart and soul, as well.

Serena's lashes swept up to see Trager towering over her, and she arched a delicate brow when he glared at her. *Now* what had she done to annoy him? His constant scowls were wearing her patience threadbare. "How long do you intend to punish me?" she blurted out, unable to keep the silence. She had held her tongue for a week and finally it had broken loose. "Perhaps if I know how long I am to be your prisoner I can pace myself and salvage my sanity."

CAROL FINCH

"Punish *you*?" he repeated incredulously. "My word, woman, I could have sworn 'twas the other way around!"

Serena frowned at his distorted logic. "You hold me captive, leave me chained like a criminal on her way to the gallows, and *you* protest that I am tormenting you?" She laughed bitterly and then took up the chore of scrubbing away the layers of dust she had collected on her journey. "I think the dirt has filtered into the cogs of your brain, Trager, and it has clogged up the works."

"Has it now," he snorted derisively and braced his hands on his hips. When his eyes dipped to the rosy peaks of her breasts, he was derailed from his track of thought. Lord, help him, he couldn't think when his gaze faltered on that appetizing body of hers. Damn, what was the use? He had fought enough hopeless battles to last him a lifetime. Futilely, he threw up his hands in defeat. "I think 'tis time the two of us had a serious talk. I'm tired of this struggling."

Serena stared him straight in the eye. "Trager, why don't you release me?" Her lips trembled as she forced out the words. "You don't love me, and I seem to be an aggravating thorn in your side." A tear formed and trickled down her cheek to intermingle with the water droplets she had splashed on her face. "I have no wish to make you miserable and I cannot stand this strained existence much longer. Just let me return to the manor to seek sanctity."

Trager knelt beside her, puzzled by her confession. He had anticipated a ploy to gain his trust before she

390

demanded release. This new twist had him baffled. He had expected her to attempt to seduce him and then, in his vulnerable moment, she would make her escape. Thoughtfully, he took the sponge from her hand and busied himself with the task of washing her back. The feel of her soft skin beneath his hands sent a passionate spark leaping between them. Their eyes locked, their need smothering their reason. If he had hell to pay for succumbing to her charms, then he would gladly empty his pockets. He wanted her more than he had ever wanted another woman. He rose to his feet, his silver eyes smoldering as he fixed his gaze on her and shed his clothes.

A curious frown knitted her brow as she watched his garments fall carelessly to the floor. "Are you routing me from my bath, the one enjoyment I have found these last two weeks?"

He grinned rakishly as he sank into the tub and maneuvered his long legs on either side of hers. "Nay, madam." His voice was heavily drugged with desire as he reached out to trace the fine line of her jaw. "I am suddenly reminded of the mermaid I found swimming in the cove and of the night she seduced me."

Serena blushed slightly, soaped the sponge, and lathered his chest. "And you were certain that I intended to have you flogged when I came to my senses," she reminded him. "You didn't trust me even then, and I doubt that you ever will."

He caught her hands, staring deeply into her sea-green eyes. "Since the day I first laid eyes on you, I think you have spent your idle moments devising new ways to torment me," he rasped, the heat of his passion rising even though he sat waist deep in lukewarm water.

"'Twas not my objective," she assured him softly, averting her gaze, only to have it settle on the corded muscles of his arms, lost to the sensuous feel of his body wedged against hers.

Trager drew her closer, his breath whispering against her cheek. "And what *was* your fiendish purpose, Rena?" he inquired before his mouth slanted across hers, drinking in the intoxicating flavor of her kiss.

There was no time for a verbal response. His embrace sent her thoughts fleeing from the path of fire that blazed through her veins. All she had ever desired was to feel his powerful body molded to hers, to melt in the possessive circle of his arms, to share one rapturous moment with the only man who had managed to capture her heart.

When he finally raised his dark head, Serena ran her nails across the stubble on his chin. Taking the hint, Trager leaned out to retrieve the razor and then resettled himself in the tub.

"Let me," she requested as she took the razor from his hand.

One heavy brow shot up as he regarded her suspiciously. "You wouldn't, by chance, be entertaining the thought of using that on my throat instead of my chin, would you, madam?"

Serena flashed him a devilish smile, tested the

blade for sharpness, and then lifted his chin to scrape the beard from the side of his face. "The thought never crossed my mind . . . until now." With the quickness of a cat, she crouched between his legs, holding the razor to his throat, a wicked gleam sparkling in her eyes.

Trager flinched, and then remained as still as stone, realizing that the slightest movement could be his last. "I should have known better than to trust you," he muttered out the side of his mouth. "I wondered what devious plan was running through your mind. What a fool I was to be ambushed in my own bathtub."

This sudden feeling of supremacy spurred her on. For once she had Trager under the blade and she intended to keep him there. "Aye, you should have known better than to leap into this stewing kettle with both feet," she taunted unmercifully.

"Witch," Trager hissed, furious with himself for falling into her trap.

"Aye, I am a witch," she agreed, pressing the razor closer when he made a move to grasp her hand. "And you will obey as my slave or you will lose your head for your foolishness."

His hand dropped back in the water and he resigned himself to the fact that he would be forced to yield to any request she made, either that or have his head severed from his shoulders. But then again, it was dead weight. He had already lost his mind and all the sense he had prided himself on possessing.

"What price do you expect me to pay for saving my

neck?'' he queried, wondering if the cost would be worth salvaging his worthless head.

A deliciously mischievous smile blossomed on her face, encompassing each delicate feature. "Tell me you are madly in love with me and that you do not resent all the trouble I have caused you.''

Trager stared long and hard into her dancing green eyes. How much longer could he protect himself from the devastating effect of this woman? He had arrogantly thought that time would cool his craving for her. But nay, the bond had grown stronger, practically strangling him while he fought for release. He had become a ghost of a man, walking through life, fooling himself into thinking that he could exist without her. Now he was forced to swallow his pride and all the cynical remarks he had spouted off. He had lost every skirmish with Serena, avoiding defeat by retreating as Washington had done with the British. Perhaps the general could find the strength to go on suffering, but he could not. Love was a far more hopeless cause than independence, he rationalized. Even Washington had succumbed to love.

"You have taunted and tormented me for the last time," he murmured defeatedly. "I love you, Rena. God help me for admitting it, but I do.''

Serena's probing gaze held his for a long, silent moment. Her playfulness evaporated and she began to regret her impulsiveness. Making Trager confess to a love he did not possess gave her no satisfaction. She ducked her head and tossed the blade aside.

"Forgive me. I am ashamed of myself for forcing the lie from your lips. Let me go home, Trager. 'Tis the best for both of us."

When she started to rise from the tub, Trager grasped her hand and brought her back to him, a faint smile curving his lips. "I didn't want to need you. I didn't want to feel this fierce desire to protect you and keep you by my side, but I cannot fight these emotions any longer," he admitted as his fingertip traced the sensuous lips that always melted like rose petals beneath his kisses. "'Tis true, you know. I do love you."

She held her breath, not daring to believe that she had heard that confession from his lips. She had waited an eternity, knowing that it was only a whimsical dream. And now, when she ached to tell him of her feelings for him, no words formed. She could only stare at him, her mouth gaping.

He drew her to him, pressing the peaks of her breasts against the hard wall of his chest, folding her in his arms. "Have you nothing to say to that? You? The incorrigible witch who is daring enough to confront the British with her convictions? Don't you intend to gloat over the fact that you have drawn another soldier beneath your spell?"

Still Serena could not find her tongue. She was certain she had swallowed it.

Trager chortled lightly, feeling the tension draining from his body for the first time in months. Confession *was* good for the soul, he decided. And once he began, he could not seem to stop himself. "I have stumbled through affairs, finding no one who could occupy my thoughts or touch my heart. I have denied the existence of love because I considered the emotion to be a sign of weakness in a man. But because I have denied the truth to myself like a coward, I have become half a man." His lips covered hers in a strangely tender kiss. "Rena, the thought of losing you brings more fear than battling the Redcoats." A sheepish smile hung on one corner of his mouth as he cast her a discreet glance. "You must forgive me for the way I have been behaving. I am a novice at this sort of thing. Being a spy has forced me to hide my darkest secrets, and 'tis not easy to confess."

Serena was sure her heart would burst with happiness. She threw her arms around his neck, showering him with kisses and slopping water from the tub in her overzealousness. But she didn't care. Her soul was soaring.

"Oh, Trager. I love you." Her face radiated with pleasure. "I never thought I would live to see the day that you would come to me with that confession."

Trager pried her arms from his, chuckling at her amorous assault. "You once told me you loved me and then later you denied it. How am I to know if you are sincere, madam?"

"Don't tease me," Serena pouted, pulling a face at him and then breaking into a smile when she noticed the way his chiseled features softened when he gazed down at her. "You know I have never been able to resist you, even when I thought you to be a loathsome cad for spying on me at the cove and kidnapping me for a bounty."

After setting her to her feet, Trager grabbed the towel to dry her, his longing gaze flowing over her skin, finding himself oddly content with the task. Perhaps Roger was right. Being this lady's maid was a promotion,

"Do you know how beautiful you are?" There was a hint of wonder in his husky voice.

Serena curled her arms over his shoulders, her long hair tumbling down her back like a shimmering cape. "Nay, tell me," she giggled giddishly.

Trager swept her up in his arms and strode toward the bed, falling with her onto the mattress. "I prefer to show you."

The feel of his firm flesh molded to hers brought a warmth that aroused and excited her. His hands glided over her shoulders and along her hip in a leisurely caress, his eyes mellowing to a soft shade of gray.

"Serena, don't ever leave me again," he rasped just before his lips captured hers.

"I won't," she promised when he allowed her to draw a breath. "I can't, for you alone possess my heart and soul." Serena nuzzled against him. "Oh, Trager, I wish this war was over." A fearful tremor sailed down her spine when she tripped on the thought of losing him as Anna had lost her husband. She never wanted to be separated from Trager, not for a day, not for an hour, she decided as she met the adoring glow in his eyes. "I want to spend the rest of my life loving you. I don't want to share you with anyone, not even Washington.''

"Nor I, you," he assured her softly. "I'm entertaining the thought of singlehandedly sabotaging the British and deporting them all on my fleet of ships.''

If only it were that simple, she mused as she surrendered to the exquisite feel of his lips hovering on hers. And then all thought escaped her as his caresses sought and aroused each sensitive point of her body. His skillful touch took her to dizzying heights of pleasure, leaving her aching and breathless, impatient to appease the maddening craving. His kisses blazed a searing path along the column of her neck to her breast, his tongue teasing its taut peak, making her arch toward him. His hand stroked her flat belly, leaving her soft and pliant beneath his magic touch. And then his kisses trailed across her abdomen and Serena heard the echo of her sigh as she melted and surrendered to the exquisite sensations that flooded over her.

His caresses retreated to encircle her breasts, and Serena gasped to catch a breath before she was dragged beneath reality's surface, drowning in the sweet torment of his lovemaking. His touch could take her to the heights and depths of passion, and he seemed to have twice the normal number of hands, his caresses discovering every inch of her flesh, taking her to the brink of insanity. His knowing fingers found her womanly softness, and she moaned as he set her body afire with an unquenchable ache that she deliriously wondered if she could endure. His touch was heaven, his kisses as intoxicating as wine. Serena was certain she was dying in the splendor of his love-making. She didn't care if tomorrow ever came. Her world revolved around this raven-haired devil who possessed her body and soul.

And then a sensation that seared its way to her very core consumed her, and she clutched at him, begging him to take her, but Trager sent her spiraling higher and higher. When he lifted himself above her, her lashes swept up to see the sparkling passion in his eyes. Over and over again, she whispered the words of love that she had carefully protected those many months. The muscles of his arms bulged as his sleek body covered hers. Serena arched to meet his hard thrusts, reveling in the rapturous pleasures of becoming his possession. They moved in perfect harmony, like a melody of love that played only for them. No other moment had been as sweet or as satiating, and the memories of the past could not hold a candle to the blazing fire that forged their souls into one.

Serena could have sworn she had already viewed passion's highest pinnacle, until this glorious moment when they skyrocketed to the distant stars to explore a new universe that knew no time or space. The world was glowing like a radiant rainbow, and Serena sighed, clinging to Trager with her last bit of strength as they drifted back to reality.

As Trager shuddered above her, Serena buried her head on his chest feeling the thudding of his heart as it gradually slowed its frantic pace. A contented smile hovered on her lips as she withdrew from her hazy dream, hardly daring to believe that she had earned Trager's love, a love that meant more to her than life itself.

Trager propped his arms on either side of her, mesmerized by her unmatched beauty, fascinated by the way the light sparkled in her golden hair. He bent his head to taste her soft lips, lost to the feminine fragrance that had entangled his senses.

"Sweet Serena . . ." he breathed raggedly. "Lord, how I love you."

In the aftermath of love, they slept in each other's arms, reliving a dream that was full of promises for a bright future. They had each other and nothing could separate them. Love was the silken bond that would eternally hold them together.

Chapter Twenty

Stirred from his pleasant dreams, Trager grumbled when the impatient knock at the door refused to cease. "Go away," he ordered sluggishly as he curled against the soft, womanly body that was intertwined with his.

"The general wants to see both of us . . . now," Roger informed him, his voice holding a hint of amusement. Roger could well imagine what was going on behind the closed door.

"Give me a moment." Trager propped himself up on his forearm and called for the strength and will to leave his cozy lair, but his request was unanswered.

Roger barged through the door, despite Trager's remark, wearing a face-splitting grin. His gaze pivoted toward the bed while Trager tugged at the quilts, attempting to protect Serena from his brother's hawkish stare.

"Don't you have more sense than to burst in when you have been specifically instructed to wait!" Trager scowled as his brows formed a hard line above his eyes. He glanced down to see Serena squirming farther down in the covers, her face coloring hotly, and then turned his glare back on his brother as he parked himself in a chair, drinking in the sight of their carelessly discarded clothes.

"My, my, what a cozy scene," he snickered, his eyes dancing with wry amusement. "May I assume that you and my lovely sister-in-law are again on speaking terms . . . among other things?"

Trager's bare arm shot toward the door. "Get out, Roger." He was accustomed to his brother's taunts, but he had no intention of allowing Serena to be the brunt of Roger's jokes.

Roger unfolded himself from the chair and sauntered toward the door, his head turning around toward the bed. "I'll be waiting in the hall while you drag yourself away from Serena." His face beamed as he paused to lean heavily on the doorknob. "Don't tarry too long, though; Washington enlisted you in *his* services too."

Trager cast his brother a withering glance and then waited until the door closed behind him. When they were alone, Trager rolled away to don his clothes. "I'll be back as soon as I can."

Serena propped her head on her hand, her blond hair streaming over her shoulder to curl temptingly around her breast, a seductive smile pursing her lips. "Tell me, Trager, do I rank ahead or behind the general?"

He flashed her a rakish smile. Damn, but she looked enticing, her naked body glowing in the early

402

light of dawn. He fumbled with the buttons on his shirt. "At the moment, I would gladly turn all thirteen colonies over to Howe if I could spend just one uninterrupted day with you," he confessed and then bent to press a lingering kiss to her inviting lips.

A pleased smile settled into the exquisite lines of her face. "Then I am content in knowing that you would never leave me unless it was of ultimate necessity." Serena grasped his hand and brought it to her cheek. "I know I cannot have all of you until this war is ended, but I will be satisfied with what I have, and I do not begrudge Washington because I must share you with him."

With a great deal of effort, Trager aimed himself toward the door, wondering if Washington knew the full sacrifice he had made to answer the call.

A serene smile hovered on Serena's lips as she eased back on the pillow, staring up at the ceiling. A pair of silver-gray eyes peered back at her, warming her soul. At last they had a true marriage, she thought to herself. Only now had she begun to live and breathe. Strange what love could do. Serena felt as if she had the world in the palm of her hand. No obstacle was too great to overcome when she had Trager's love.

Her lashes fluttered against her cheeks and she yielded to the exhaustion of the long days she had gone without rest. It seemed that she had barely closed her eyes before Trager soundly shook her. Serena greeted him with a loving smile, but it evaporated when she noted the grim expression on his face. There was a combination of anger and resentment carved into his rugged features.

"Trager, what's the matter?" she questioned in concern.

"Washington wants me and my men to scout out the best path to our winter quarters. We are leaving this afternoon."

Her face fell, disappointment dulling the usual sparkle in her eyes. "That doesn't give us much time, does it?" she murmured as she brushed her hand across the empty quilts beside her, knowing how lonely she would be without him.

Trager hastily walked back to lock the door to insure that his ornery brother did not come barging in on them again. "I left instructions not to disturb us unless someone sets fire to the place. It seems we are to have another brief honeymoon."

When he had shed his clothes, he sank down beside her, the bed creaking with his solid weight. Just being near him was enough to kindle the flame of desire. This day was all they had, and Serena wanted it to be a memory that would keep both of them warm until they could again sleep in each other's arms.

Her eyes settled on the liquid pools of silver that reflected the late morning light. She reached out to trace her index finger over the sensuous curve of his mouth. Drawn to his warmth, she pressed her lips to his, quivering as he eagerly responded. Her hands fanned across the dark furring on his chest. When he impatiently reached for her she held him at bay.

"Relax, my love," she whispered. "I have no wish to rush this moment."

Trager eased back against the headboard, his dark brow quirking as his gaze flowed over the rosy peaks of her breasts and the trim curve of her waist. "Do you intend to drive me mad with this delicious body of yours, tempting and taunting me as you have in the past?"

"Aye, even more so," she assured him as her light caress trickled across the hard muscles of his abdomen. "And when some wench offers to keep you warm on these cold winter nights, the memory of this moment will be branded on your mind."

She had become a skillful temptress, Trager mused, as the white hot-fire of desire simmered in his veins. Her features were flawless, her hair shimmering like a cape of gold, her eyes as clear and green as priceless emeralds. Her skin was so soft and silky that it begged for his touch, and Trager could not resist trailing his hand across the trim column of her neck and down her bare shoulder. Her touch was like a massage, melting away the anxiety he had experienced when Washington informed him that he would be leaving Serena behind, as he had been forced to do a dozen times before.

A sigh escaped his lips as her kisses fluttered across his chest, her caresses exploring the taut muscles of his back, touching him in a familiar way. She set every nerve atingle, as in a chain reaction, passion consuming logic. He ached for her. His body, as if it possessed a will of its own, hungered to feel her soft lips on his and the arousing touch of her hands wandering languidly over his flesh. It was like a fantastic dream, one that sent reality fading on the far horizon. When she boldly caressed him, his heart thundered in his chest, nearly beating him to death with its frantic pace. His breath came in ragged gasps as she continued her sweet, torturous assault. Trager closed his eyes and mind to all except the tantalizing sensations that washed over him. Aye, she had invented a new meaning for the word *torment*, Trager decided as the echo of his sigh reached his ears. Sharing Serena's love was an intricate combination of heaven and hell. His want for her was driving him to the brink of his sanity. And yet, as if he were paralyzed, he seemed helpless to stop her delicious, maddening caresses.

She was his weakness, bringing him the one compelling emotion he had not been able to overcome. She was returning every ounce of pleasure that he had ever offered her in a most exquisite way. For the first time in his life he allowed his lover to take the full initiative, letting his heart and soul seep from beneath its protective coat of armor, lying vulnerable to her charms. Surrendering to this complicated vixen was like living and dying in the same breathless moment.

Trager groaned as her lips discovered every inch of his flesh, sending a path of fire blazing across his body. And then he was sailing toward some distant universe. The world he had known and commanded was lost in a haze. The feel of her lips on his skin, her hands weaving patterns on his lean belly, her breasts pressing wantonly against him brought a pleasure that no words could describe. Finally, Trager could stand no more. The fires of passion had consumed him, and he cupped her face in his hands, bringing her lips back to his, impatient to appease the maddening craving to make her his possession.

Trager lifted himself above her, his eyes glowing with love and desire. She arched to meet his hard thrusts, shamelessly giving herself to him. But she was *not* his possession, he thought as he fitted their bodies together like two pieces of a puzzle that made no sense at all until they were one, body and soul. He was a part of her, sharing an emotion that transcended time and space. Driven by impetuousness, he sought unattainable depths of intimacy until love's fire consumed itself. And then the world exploded in an array of vivid colors, like rockets exploding and then evaporating in the darkness as they tumbled from their lofty perch. Trager clutched her to him, shuddering beneath the overwhelming sensations that he had never realized existed until he had given his heart to this fascinating woman. No other woman could compare to Serena. No one else had ever brought a confession of love from his lips, but Serena had drawn out the words, and he murmured them over and over again. Although passion's flame was spent, the coals continued to smolder, assuring him that one touch, one kiss could ignite another fire.

Trager nuzzled his head against her shoulder and breathed a ragged breath. A tender smile brushed her lips as she toyed with the raven hair that lay at the nape of his neck. He had brought her a happiness that she had never dared to believe she could enjoy. The feel of his solid body pressed to hers was all the warmth she needed to survive the coldest of winter winds. When she was in the tight circle of his arms she was invincible, drawing strength from his love. Serena was content in knowing that he would never stray from her side unless duty called. And though it would, time and time again, he would return to her.

Her lashes fluttered up as the afternoon light filtered through the curtains that shut out the rest of the world. Trager propped himself up, staring thoughtfully at her. She raised a perfectly arched brow and reached over to smooth the frown from his rugged features, smiling adoringly up at him.

"What are you contemplating so seriously?" she inquired, her voice still raspy with desire.

Trager felt a twinge of regret stab at his soul. Loving her and leaving her was a torture far worse than death. Now that they had come the full circle, confessing their deep affection for each other, he knew he could never think of living without her. He began to understand his fierce need to protect her all these months. She had become so much a part of his life that he could not think of facing a day without her. She had his heart and soul, and the newness of it all had him clinging to the emotion that had brought him such delirious happiness. He had long denied this compelling force that drew him to Serena, but she had woven a spell over him and he had at last surrendered. And he resented being taken from her loving arms, spending long cold nights dreaming of

her while he was forging a path for the other soldiers
to follow.

"I was just thinking how miserable I'm going to be
without you. The days will seem an eternity . . . and
the nights even longer," he answered her.

A hint of sentimental tears lurked beneath the surface as Serena hugged him close. "I want to go with
you, Trager." The thought of being left behind came
to haunt her. "I don't think I can let you go . . . not
now."

Trager sighed heavily and then gave his raven head
a negative shake. "I have dragged you all over the
country and I cannot subject you to this trip. It will
be a grueling journey. Washington is ready to pull
back to our winter quarters at Valley Forge, and time
is of the essence." He laughed bitterly as he raked his
fingers through the tangled curls that dangled about
Serena's face. "General Howe has stabbed us in the
back with his proclamation that any Patriot who did
not reenlist would be forgiven his transgressions
against the Crown. We have only three thousand
soldiers left to fight for the cause of independence.
The rest have traipsed back home, accepting Howe's
generosity."

Her gaze dropped as she traced an intricate pattern
on his hard chest. "I'm sorry things look so bleak."

He cupped her chin, raising her eyes to his faint
smile. "Nothing worth having comes easily, Rena.
You and I practically started our own war, but
now . . ." His mouth slanted across hers in a tender
kiss and then he nibbled at her neck before he found

the will to drag himself away from the sweet fragrance that wrapped itself around his senses. "Now I would gladly walk barefoot through the fires of hell if I could acquire the same results."

Serena threw her arms around him, drawing him to her, feeling the loneliness closing in on her. "Oh, Trager, I wish we could go home and start afresh."

Her whimsical remark made him flinch and he held her at arm's length, staring solemnly at her. "Would you allow Nathan's death to be forgotten? I could have killed his cousin for turning him over to Howe. But Sam Hale knew that there were those who would have lynched him, and he surrounds himself with British soldiers who are honor bound to protect his worthless hide. Nathan gave his life for what he believed in and I cannot let his memory become meaningless. Nor can I refuse Washington when he so desperately needs the help of all those who are able to fight for the cause of freedom."

Serena ducked her head. She was being selfish, wanting to protect the fragile bond that had begun to strengthen between them. "I know, Trager, but . . ."

"Our time will come," he promised her. "And until then, we must make the most of each moment."

And then his hands flowed over her flesh, leaving a kindled fire to burn in the wake of his touch. Serena reveled in the sensations that surged through her veins, sizzling their way to her very core. His sleek body covered hers and she yielded, cherishing the fleeting moment, praying that one day they would take their place in the sun, warm and content to bask in their love.

The impatient rap at the door had Trager muttering under his breath. He was beginning to hate doors. His eyes flooded over her kiss-swollen lips and her creamy skin as he dragged himself away from her loving arms.

"Promise me that you will be waiting here for me when I return," he pressed as he hastily shrugged on his breeches and shirt.

An impish grin parted her lips. "Do you wish me to remain abed the entire time you are gone . . . just in case you should return unannounced?" It was difficult to act cheerful at the moment, but Serena was doing her damnedest not to burst into tears.

Trager smiled rakishly. "As long as you are here *alone*. I do not expect to come back to find that you have latched on to another willing soldier." His expression sobered as he gestured for her to cover herself and then strode toward the door. "I do not want you to even consider returning home while I am away. 'Tis too dangerous. Write to Veronica, if you must, but do not be foolish enough to go to her." Although he had begun to trust her, he knew that she harbored a desire to return to the manor and her grandmother. "I will take you to see Veronica when I return and the troops are settled at Valley Force."

"But Trager . . ." Serena had intended to tell him that *she* was Veronica, but Trager opened the door to allow his brother inside before she could finish.

Roger displayed a cheesy grin as he sauntered inside. "I seem to have the misfortune of appearing at the most inopportune moments," he remarked.

"Aye, that you do," Trager grumbled. "I think Mother may have overlooked the polishing of your manners."

"'Tis because you were always her favorite and I was shuffled out of the way to survive as best I could, using my own devices," Roger countered in a playful tone. His gaze strayed to Serena, lingering overlong on her bare shoulder.

Trager snorted derisively as he stepped between Roger and Serena, blocking the tempting view. "Mother spoiled you beyond repair," he insisted as he shrugged on his jacket. "*I* was the one who was forced to fend for himself, forfeiting my possessions to keep you from running and crying to Mother over little or nothing."

A reckless chuckle floated from Roger's lips as he retrieved his brother's bag and turned back toward the door. "I can see that we will have to have a lengthy debate on the subject of who is the favorite son during our journey. I think I shall save my rebuttal until later." He glanced back to see that Trager was paying very little attention, his silver eyes glued to Serena. "The rest of the men and I will be waiting downstairs while you are saying your last goodbye."

Serena swallowed over the lump that collected in her throat and attempted to blink back the tears that welled up in her eyes. "I shall miss you terribly," she murmured as she propped herself up on an elbow, her long hair tumbling over her shoulder. The hollow ache had begun to burn in the pit of her stomach, and she was certain the pain would not subside until he returned to her.

Trager quickly closed the distance between them and enfolded her in his arms, inhaling the clean fragrance of her hair, memorizing the feel of her satiny skin beneath his hands. "I intend to hold you to your promise that you will be here waiting for me, Rena. I want to walk back into this room to find you as you are at this moment, welcoming me with open arms," Trager whispered against her skin, sending a rash of goose pimples skipping across her body like a tidal wave.

Muffling a sniff, Serena leaned back as far as his encircling arms would allow and forced a smile. "I will be here."

"Come hell or high water?" Trager teased before he sought her soft lips, drowning in the intoxicating taste of her kiss, one that would have to sustain him during the torturous eternity that they would be apart. A long breathless moment passed before he withdrew to meet her tear-rimmed eyes.

"Come hell or high water," she assured him softly and then watched ruefully as he unfolded himself from the edge of the bed and backed away.

Quietly, Trager opened the door and disappeared. For Serena the silence was deafening, and she fought the overwhelming impulse to follow after him, knowing he would be furious with her for disobeying him. And yet, the loneliness was already gnawing away at her. Serena swung her legs over the edge of the bed, grabbed her robe, and hurried to the window to watch Trager swing onto his steed. Their eyes met, the message clear before he turned and rode away. Lord, what was she to do with her time while Trager was away, she wondered as she breathed a forlorn sigh. Her gaze followed him until he disappeared from view, and then she wept, succumbing to the tears that she had carefully held in check, aching for the man who had given a new meaning to her life.

Chapter Twenty-One

Three days after Trager had left her, Serena heard a commotion in the hall. Wearing a curious frown, she opened the door and gasped in delight as Barron scrambled between the legs of several soldiers who were attempting to rout him from the mansion. The mutt trotted toward her, his tail banging against the wall. Serena knelt to pet her devoted dog. He had trailed her from the manor when he discovered that she had abandoned him.

James Cortney strolled up to her and watched Serena hug her four-legged friend. "I assume that the two of you know each other."

"Aye." Serena came to her feet and peered up at Cortney. "He must have followed me from home. Barron thinks he is my bodyguard."

"He should make a fine one," Cortney chuckled. "He came barging through the door and tried to take a bite out of several soldiers who made the mistake of attempting to stop him from climbing the steps."

Serena ambled back down the hall with Barron

following at her heels. The lingering soldiers backed against the wall to let them pass, glancing warily at the dog that moments earlier had been growling and frothing at the mouth like a rabid beast. Cortney shook his head in wonder as Serena wove her way downstairs to find some scraps for her starved dog. Beauty and the beast, he mused as he followed in her wake, leaving a safe distance between himself and the mutt. Barron reminded him of a devil wolf, his eyes so black and penetrating that courageous soldiers stepped aside to let him pass.

James had become Serena's constant companion since Trager had left to find a safe passage for the troops through New Jersey. She seemed so sad and alone that he could not resist befriending her. It also helped to pass the idle hours before they collected their belongings and traveled to their winter quarters. James had become very fond of Serena and cherished her company, finding that he could converse on any subject with her. She was a very bright and knowledgeable young woman, to say nothing of her obvious comeliness. He had always been fascinated by her, but only now did he realize the full extent of her beauty.

When Serena had fed Barron, she glanced up to flash James the first honest smile she had displayed since Trager left her. "It amazes me that he could track me all the way to Peekskill."

James reached down to pat the dog and instantly regretted his impulsiveness when Barron paused from his meal to show James the length and sharp edge on his teeth. Jerking back his hand, he tucked it in his pocket, thankful his fingers remained intact.

"I get the feeling that this mutt would follow you to the edge of the earth," he commented.

"But the earth is round," Serena reminded him, flashing him a smile. "I should think a man with your education would know better than to make such a blundering remark."

James rolled his eyes as if he was perturbed with her, but in truth he delighted to see the return of color to her cheeks and the sparkle in her emerald eyes. "You are too keen-witted for me, Serena. I can see that fencing words with you could be disastrous. I think I shall strive to remain on your good side."

Serena curled her arm in his and then drew her cloak more tightly about her neck as they stepped off the porch to greet the crisp winter wind. "You know I count you as a friend," she said quietly. "I don't know what I would have done without you these past two days."

"If I had not been here, some other man would have gladly taken my place."

"You belittle yourself, James. I have always been fond of you, even before we met again at White Plains," Serena assured him.

"And I have always admired you from afar. I doubted that you wanted me bothering you. Besides, I would have had to fight my way through the flock of gentlemen who gathered when you made an appearance."

Serena laughed, a hint of bitterness seeping

through. "Now, most men avoid me like the plague. I have become a Rebel-Loyalist. I'm not certain that the officers here trust me—they wonder if I might turn on them, as Major Baldwin did."

A rueful smile touched his lips. "But those of us who are close to you know where your loyalties lie and that you would never betray us," James insisted. "Those who saw you fight beside them have given you nothing but praise."

"Thank you, James. 'Tis comforting to know that you care and that I am not shunned as an outcast." Her lashes fluttered up to see the fond expression in his eyes.

"If ever there is anything I can do for you, Serena, do not hesitate to ask," he encouraged as he drew her closer.

For a moment, Serena thought he meant to kiss her and she stepped away, attempting to keep the conversation light and casual. "I think I should check on Barron before he causes another disturbance among the troops."

James nodded slightly, a sheepish smile pursing his lips. He had come dangerously close to making a fool of himself. She belonged to Captain Grayson, and he would be furious if he learned that one of the soldiers had made advances toward her. "Aye, I suppose so," he murmured.

When Serena wandered back to her room, she heaved a frustrated sigh and sank down in her chair, absently reaching for the book she had retrieved from the library. Barron curled up at her feet, resting his head on his paws, content to bask before the fire. She glanced toward the window, seeing the dreary gray haze that reflected her mood. If only she had a purpose, something to occupy her instead of idly waiting for Trager's return, she thought.

The light rap at the door drew her from her pensive musings and she frowned curiously. "Who is it?"

"Roger." His voice sounded flat and Serena's frown settled more deeply on her face.

As the door swung open, Serena swallowed her breath. Roger's clothes were stained and ragged, his dark hair tousled, his expression grim. There was no gleam in his eyes, as if the fire of youth had been extinguished. Serena could sense that something was amiss.

"What's wrong?" she demanded to know without bothering with a greeting.

Roger came deliberately toward her and knelt before her, clasping her hands in his. When Barron bolted to his feet, Serena ordered him away, intent on what Roger had to say.

"Serena, we were ambushed by renegade Loyalists when we attempted to cross the river. We had not anticipated trouble but it was upon us before we could defend ourselves."

Serena tensed, afraid she knew what was coming next, trembling beneath Roger's comforting touch. Nothing could still her fears. Somehow she knew what he was going to say before he said it.

"Trager was leading us across the Hudson when they opened fire on us. He caught a musket ball and fell from his horse," Roger told her solemnly, a hint of tears lurking in his eyes. "The current was swift in midstream and the water was cold. . . ." He was trying to put it to her delicately, but the task seemed impossible. "Serena, I could find no sign of him after we retreated to shore. Egan and I searched the area, but we could find no trace of him."

"Nay." The word formed on her lips, but no sound came. No, not Trager too! First it had been Nathan, then her father, and now Trager. Dammit, it wasn't fair. Was there no justice, no lasting happiness? Something inside of her withered and died. Serena was instantly reminded of Anna's words about losing her husband. Serena had wasted precious time, fighting her love for him from the beginning, and now he was gone. Why had she protected her feelings from him? Perhaps they could have shared months of bliss instead of just a few fleeting moments before he was taken from her.

She threw her arms around Roger's neck and sobbed hysterically. She had been granted a small taste of heaven, only to have it snatched away from her before she could bask in the love of the only man who was bold enough to gain her respect and devotion.

Roger brushed his hand over her silky hair and cradled her in his arms, murmuring against her ear. "I'm so sorry, Serena. If I could have exchanged places with him, I would have."

For an eternity they clung together, afraid to let go, afraid to face the world without the man who was such an integral part of their lives. When Roger brushed away his own tears, he wiped Serena's moist cheeks, but the flow continued, spilling down the sides of her flushed face in a steady stream.

"I loved him so," she choked out. "And I cared deeply for Nathan and my father. Now they have all been taken from me. It seems that all I have held dear to me is cursed. I am to blame."

"Nay, Serena," Roger insisted, his voice cracking with emotion. "You cannot blame yourself for what has happened. 'Tis this damned war that cuts down the best of men." He held her at arm's length, his gaze probing her tear-filled eyes. "Trager would be disappointed in you if you admit defeat. He adored your strengths. That is what drew him to you. He knew you could stand alone and face every obstacle that came your way. You are a survivor, Serena," he told her firmly. "Don't let Trager down. Don't fall apart on me."

His words of encouragement did little to raise her spirits. She had lost the person who meant the most to her, and she was so very tired of searching for rainbows in a sky that was filled with smoke and exploding shells.

When she did not respond, Roger gave her a sound shake. "Listen to me. We are going to live through this, both of us. In time the pain will fade and we can remember him, cherishing the moments we shared with Trager . . . the good times, and even the bad. We have to stick together, Serena." His gaze dropped as he heaved a sigh and then lifted his eyes to see the fresh tears that glistened on her lashes. "I once asked you to marry me and I am proposing to you again. I know you can never feel the same deep affection you held for my brother, but I offer you my love and protection, just as he did."

"Nay." Serena adamantly shook her head. "I will only make you miserable, just as I did my father and Trager. I breed trouble and misfortune for those who dare to care for me." She muffled a sniff and then cupped her hands around Roger's stubbled cheeks. "Don't you see? I value your friendship, and if I begin to care more deeply for you it will destroy you. I have caused enough misery and I cannot take the chance of bringing this curse down on you."

"Serena, don't do this to yourself," Roger pleaded as he drew her to her feet and hugged her close. "You are not being punished, nor are those who lost their lives for the cause." He stepped away and then gave her trembling hand a loving squeeze. "I have to speak to Washington. He intends to break camp and travel as quickly as possible. You are going with me to Valley Forge, and once we are settled I am taking you to my parents' home and we will be married. I know this is what Trager would want."

Stunned, Serena watched him go. She didn't want to believe that Trager had perished and that she would never see him again. It wasn't true. It couldn't have happened. Trager was invincible, capable of overcoming any obstacle. And then the tears came, forcing her to accept reality. He had been taken from her and she would never share his love or find consolation in his arms. He was gone, her mind screamed at her.

Her gaze flew around the room. How could she remain here when the chamber held sleeping memories that would surely haunt her dreams? How could she look at Roger without seeing Trager? She could almost visualize Trager walking through the door, wearing that outrageous smile that always melted her heart. She could feel his strong arms encircling her waist and taste the drugging kisses that stirred a passion that she would never experience again. Trager had taken her heart and soul with him, and there was nothing left to offer Roger. She could only hurt him, pining for a love that had perished in battle. Roger had suffered enough and she would not bring him pain, not after the way she had destroyed Nathan, Mitchell, and Trager.

There was naught else to do but flee before Roger returned for her. She had to go home, back to the shelter of the manor, hiding behind the disguise of Veronica Warren. At least she would be safe and Roger could get on with his life. Determined to follow through with her plan, Serena hastily jotted a note to Roger and then collected her belongings. With one last glance, she studied the room where she and Trager had admitted their love for each other. A single tear formed and trickled down her cheek, the last of many that had flowed like a river.

Silently she crept away, with Barron following at her heels. Aye, Roger was right, she told herself. Time would ease the pain and she would find a way to live without Trager because she *must*. She had to survive the cruelties of war. That was all she had to offer to Trager's memory. And she would find a new purpose. For it was as Trager had said, the lives that were lost had to have a purpose. She would do what she could to aid the cause that Nathan and Trager had died to preserve.

One day she would even learn to smile again, she told herself. Perhaps in a hundred years, she mused miserably. Trager had taken every reason for happiness with him.

Serena reined her stallion south and allowed the crisp winter wind to follow at her back, pressing her onward, back to the meager existence of living with the fear of being discovered, back to the mourning gowns and shadowed veils of Veronica Warren. Serena was dead, unable to appear during the light of day, bound to the darkness, living like the haunted spirits that roamed the earth during the witching hour. She had nothing to anticipate and she could not dwell on the past. She had nothing left, Serena reminded herself as another tear froze on her cheek and chilled her to the bone.

From behind a veil of gauze and lace, Serena gazed out the window of her father's study, amazed at how bleak the world appeared to her. Depression had closed in on her. She had walked the empty halls, hearing nothing but her methodic footsteps, groping for some desire to continue this charade. Once or twice she had toyed with the idea of surrendering to the British. Hanging would end this unbearable misery of feeling so useless and alone.

Aye, she must be cursed, she told herself as she absently played with the tassel of the drape. Or was she a witch, as Trager had often claimed, causing grief to those she had cherished? Listlessly, she ambled toward Mitchell's desk and sat down into the chair. It was time to sort through her father's papers and put his business in order. Jonas Landsing had come to call on her earlier that afternoon, advising her to settle the estate. She had not told him of Trager's death, intending to handle the affair as if he was still in charge. Serena had agreed to see to the matter as Jonas had suggested, but it was difficult. So many memories of her father lingered with her.

Serena drew the veil from her head and smoothed the gray wig back from her face, a determined frown creasing her brow. Carefully, she sorted through the top drawer. After assembling her father's letters and ledgers, she read each and every one. When she had completed the first phase of her task, she arranged the correspondences and attempted to close the drawer, but it refused to settle into its normal resting place. On closer inspection, she found a paper lodged at the back between the drawers. Serena removed the drawer and struggled to free the paper without ripping it.

Her curious frown deepened when she noticed that

the letter had been written by her father and dated the day of his death. She pressed the wrinkled letter and slowly read its contents.

My dearest Serena,

It grieves me greatly that you have been accused of treason. I spoke with General Howe, inquiring about who had brought the matter to his attention, but he refused to name his source. I have pleaded your cause and claimed your innocence, but I fear Howe plans to deal harshly with you. My heart and thoughts are with you. No matter what has happened, you still have my love.

Serena wiped away the tears that came so easily of late and waited an impatient moment until her vision had cleared so that she could continue reading.

There is so much I want to say to you, and yet I wonder if this letter will ever find you. I should have told you of the brewing trouble when I returned from New York, but I could not find the right words. And now it is too late. At last I realize that I have been narrow-minded in my beliefs and too blind at times. You were right about Olivia, though I didn't want to believe it. She has asked me for a divorce. It seems that she has been seeing Colonel Powell behind my back. Perhaps I am a vain old man, but I will not grant her wish. Although she has left me, I intend to see that she bears my name and receives nothing of my estate when my time comes. It is just punishment for the way she has betrayed me.

I am leaving for New York to search for Olivia and speak with the general, hoping I can convince him to grant you immunity since he has proclaimed that Patriots who lay down their arms will be spared. I have begun to wonder if the person who betrayed you was . . .

Damn. Serena gritted her teeth. Who had interrupted his letter? Was it his murderer? And whom did her father suspect of being an informant for Howe? Clutching the unfinished letter, Serena sought out Molly to question her about Mitchell's activities the evening he was murdered. Molly told her that Mitchell had been working late in his office, but that he had sent her on to bed.

Curiosity was eating her alive. Serena had to know who had killed her father and accused her of blasphemy. She could not allow the murderer to go unpunished. If her father had intended to seek out Olivia and speak with the general, then she would have to go in his stead, groping for information that might lead her to those who had plotted against her and her father.

Perhaps she could draw some clues from Olivia or

John Powell. It would be difficult to get close to General Howe, but she had nothing to lose, she reminded herself.

When she informed Molly of her plans, the maid teetered and braced herself against the wall, her face as white as a sheet.

"You cannot take such a chance," she breathed in gasps. "If someone discovers your identity there will be no one left to manage this house. The Whigs will come to confiscate all the valuables and . . ."

"No one will touch this house." Serena did not sound very convincing, even to herself. Now that Trager was gone, she had no way of insuring that the manor would be protected from plunderers. And yet, what use was this mansion when there was no one who needed the home? If it would serve the cause that Trager had died defending, then the Patriots were welcome to it.

"But Serena, New York is swarming with Tories," Molly protested. "One false move and it could be yore last."

"No one will be suspicious of Veronica Warren. She has every right to be in British territory, especially since she is planning to return to England." A wry smile pursed her lips as she turned toward the stairs and easily took them without the cane she clasped in her hand. "Rest your fears, Molly. Veronica Warren is not about to let those sniveling Tories outwit her."

Molly was filled with reservations, but she followed behind Serena to help her pack for her journey. And

428

she couldn't help wandering if she would ever see Serena again. Serena was wading into quicksand, and it might well be the last time Molly ever laid eyes on her. Swallowing her fears, Molly collected the garments Serena needed for her trip and then watched in dismay as the carriage disappeared over the hill.

Chapter Twenty-Two

December 12, 1776

The wind whistled through the carriage window and Veronica Warren braced herself, summoning her determination to follow through with her plan. She had visited Dora Michaels, Olivia's mother, and had learned that her daughter was residing at British headquarters with her lover, Colonel Powell. It left Veronica simmering to think that Olivia would openly flaunt her affair so quickly after her husband's death. But then, after giving the matter further consideration, Veronica realized that Olivia was holding true to form. She was selfish and heartless. Her only goal in life was to please herself, no matter how many toes she had to tromp on to do it.

Wearing a grim frown, Veronica adjusted the veil over her face, grasped her cane, and clasped the groom's arm to descend the carriage steps. A nervous tingle flew down her spine as she slowly took the distance to the mansion where General William Howe and his staff had settled in for the winter. Strange, she mused as her gaze swept the area. It seemed very long ago—that first time she had come to British headquarters with Mitchell, anticipating the elaborate balls and feasts. So much had changed. Now she was wary, knowing that the pitfalls of her scheme could leave her dangling from a rope.

Veronica paused at the foot of the steps, playing on the young corporal's sympathy as she teetered and then barely caught her balance before stumbling on the first step. The soldier had been watching her hobble toward him and quickly came to her rescue with a supporting arm. Veronica leaned heavily upon him as she focused her attention on the massive oak door that stood between her and the general.

After she requested to see Howe, she waited an anxious moment for the corporal to return. As she paused at the study door, she heard a familiar voice and glanced to the top of the spiral staircase to see Olivia, adorned in all her finery, which had been purchased with Mitchell's money, perched like a regal queen, her laughter bubbling from her lips. Veronica gritted her teeth and resisted the urge to slap that arrogant expression from Olivia's face. How she detested that woman for what she had done to Mitchell. And then Veronica reminded herself that the revenge she had in mind for Olivia would ease these pent-up emotions that were begging for release. When Veronica finished cutting Olivia to shreds, the deceitful witch would drop her honey-coated pretense, revealing her true, vicious nature.

The corporal touched Veronica's arm, bringing her from her silent reverie, and urged her into the study to meet General Howe. Veronica's gaze strayed back to see Olivia and John Powell descending the stairs, and then she focused her attention on her role. She wobbled unsteadily on her feet, wheezed and coughed, and then collapsed into her chair, playing her charade to the hilt.

General Howe frowned in concern. "Mrs. Warren, is there something I can get for you? Perhaps you would like a drink."

Veronica nodded slightly. "Nay, thank you. There seems to be no cure for what ails me. My doctor has informed me that I must attribute my ill health to old age, and learn to live with my maladies as best I can."

Howe eased back into his seat and clasped his hands in front of him, staring solemnly at the heavily veiled dowager. "I was deeply grieved to learn of Mitchell's death. Mitchell served the Crown long and well. Now that the Rebel forces have evacuated New York for the winter, perhaps we can aid in your search for your son's assassin."

"You could help him most by dismissing these outrageous charges against my granddaughter," Veronica blurted out and then choked on her breath, hacking and coughing to draw out the general's sympathy. She intended to use every device to see her end result. After all, she had nothing to lose and everything to gain, she told herself. "I'm sure Mitchell died a haunted death, knowing that Serena had been unjustly accused of conspiracy and God knows what else!"

The general frowned thoughtfully as he watched the dowager overcome her spasm. "I know Mitchell adamantly protested that there was no connection between his daughter and the Rebel spy, but my informant had several witnesses who can attest to the fact that she spoke out against the Crown and openly admitted to her friendship with Nathan Hale."

"Rubbish!" Veronica pounded her cane on the floor to emphasize her point. "Serena has always been an impetuous child with a fiery temper. Those who did not know her well might have concluded that her loyalties were with those heathen Rebels, but Mitchell realized that her main complaint was that the officers were excluding her from their conversation simply because she was a woman. Serena's loyalties were always with her father. She loved him dearly." Veronica paused to wheeze and catch her breath. "The poor child has inherited her feisty disposition from me and I cannot condemn her for speaking her mind. I have seen enough of those simpleminded twits in England to know that I would never want Serena to behave as they do."

"Were you present at the party?" Howe inquired.

"Nay, but I made it a point to speak with several local friends and demanded to know exactly what my granddaughter said," she explained. "And I would hate to think that every remark *I* made would be taken so literally." Veronica chortled hoarsely. "I daresay that I would have been accused of crimes far worse than speaking against the Crown." She leaned toward Howe, staring at him through her black veil. "Now who is this witless wonder who has unjustly accused the poor child of treason?"

A reluctant smile bordered Howe's lips. Although the dowager was demanding and outspoken, he admired her spunk. He rather wished he had attended the ball, so as to know whose side of the story was correct. And he was a man who appreciated lively women, eager to take the challenge of conquering their wild spirits. If Serena was as high-strung as her grandmother, he would enjoy her company.

"Madam, as much as I would like to reveal my source to you, I fear I cannot. Just as you seek to protect and restore your granddaughter's good name, I must defend those who have the Crown's best interest at heart," he told her diplomatically.

"Poppycock!" Veronica sniffed distastefully. "I would stake my fortune on the fact that your informant had an ulterior motive. Snitches usually do. I have not met one yet who didn't expect compensation for squealing like a stuck pig."

Howe bit back another grin, wondering if he had just met an older version of Serena Warren. Veronica minced no words and was not afraid to speak her mind. "You may be right," he conceded, slowly turning his thoughts to the informant who had been so eager to point an accusing finger at Serena.

"You have issued a generous proclamation for those Whigs who fired upon our own men," Veronica reminded him. "What your informant claims that Serena has done, even though it is a bald-faced lie, I might add, is no worse than those soldiers who have cut down our own men with Rebel muskets. I hardly think that a careless remark about liberty and freedom for all, especially for women who have been dominated by overbearing men, is a criminal offense." Veronica's tone carried an under-bite of sarcasm, and she hurried on before Howe could interject a comment. "I still contend that killing British soldiers is the worst offense. And yet, you have granted hundreds of Whigs immunity if they lay down their arms and return to their homes."

General Howe was stumped. Veronica's logic made his course of action seem unjust, and he did not care to have the old woman spreading rumors that he was not capable of commanding an army because he could not determine his priorities. And she would have the story on the gossip vine by nightfall, he speculated. The dowager had lived to a ripe old age and she feared nothing. Howe even imagined that she would win her bout with death, determined not to let the angels come for her until *she* was prepared to depart. If she had a mind to plant a seed of contro-versy concerning his capabilities, she could damned well do it. The Warren name was influential in the colonies and in England, and Howe did not wish to step down from his position.

A long, pensive moment ticked by. The only sound invading the silence was the ticking of the elabor-ately carved clock that sat on the mantel above the hearth. Finally, Howe nodded agreeably. He had not backed down to Mitchell, but he softened to Veronica. "You have a well-founded point, madam. But I am still curious about Serena's connection with young Nathan Hale."

"They were friends, but my granddaughter did not know the young man's purpose until he had been captured. It came as a shock to her." Veronica leaned out on her cane. "I have discussed this matter with my granddaughter, and aye, I have kept her safely stashed away. If you decide to hang me for harboring a fugitive, then the two of us will walk to the gallows together," she insisted, raising a defiant chin.

"That will not be necessary, Mrs. Warren. I intend to drop the charges against Serena," General Howe said.

Veronica breathed a constricted sigh of relief. At least she had won the first round.

Howe propped his forearms on his desk, a look of determination etching his features. "And since I have agreed to grant Serena immunity, we will drop the matter of who pointed the accusing finger at her. That is my compromise."

Damn. She had lost the second bout, Veronica mused disgustedly, but she did not voice her objection. She needed the general's friendship and could not afford to push him completely against the wall.

"Agreed," she affirmed with a nod. "At least I can sail back to England knowing that my only grandchild will not face the gallows."

A slow smile worked its way across the general's face. "And I must admit that I am relieved that neither of you will be there. I pride myself in being fair, and it would have grieved me to hang a woman."

From beneath her disguise Veronica broke into a grin. Howe wasn't half as relieved as she was. After all, it was *her* neck they were discussing. Veronica decided to move on to the third reason she had come to New York City while the general was in a generous mood.

"I would like to see my daughter-in-law," she requested and then wheezed to remind him of her failing condition. "I have learned that Olivia is staying here and I wish to settle the matter of Mitchell's estate before I plan my passage to England."

"I believe that she and Colonel Powell intended to go out this morning. She seems to be a charming woman," he complimented, unaware that Veronica harbored the direct opposite opinion of her. "Olivia is a strong woman and has survived her loss with amazing strength."

Of course, she had, Veronica thought bitterly. Olivia had been relieved to learn that Mitchell was dead. It made it easy for her to pursue Powell. "Aye, so I have heard." Veronica strove to maintain a pleasant tone. "Mitchell wrote of her often, but we have yet to meet. You see, I only arrived in the colonies the week he died, and Olivia had already left for New York."

Veronica decided this lie better suited the situation. After all, if she had been staying in Connecticut as she had informed Jonas Landsing, she might have had the opportunity to meet Olivia. Veronica doubted that what she had told Jonas would reach the general's ears. News only traveled as fast as the swiftest horse, and Jonas seldom journeyed to New York.

"Oh?" The general frowned at the information. "I am sorry to hear that you arrived too late. It must have been tragic to learn about your son."

Veronica muffled a sniff in her handkerchief. "Very tragic. I had come to surprise my son, to meet my daughter-in-law, and to visit Serena. I had missed her terribly. Serena lived with me in London for six years during her schooling. The house seemed empty without her."

"Perhaps you can see her again before you depart. I will immediately draw up the papers for her release from these charges," he assured her and then produced a wry smile. "If she is half the woman her grandmother is, I should like to visit with her." The general's smile widened. "And I would be pleased to have you accompany me to the ball I am giving tomorrow evening. Perhaps you could meet Olivia and further entertain me."

Veronica was grinning devilishly beneath her veil. Things were working out splendidly. If she gathered one shred of information about Olivia, Brandon, or Colonel Powell, she would have served her purpose. "'Tis very kind of you, sir, but do not think that you must dote over me. I am not accustomed to having such an attractive gentleman requesting my company. This face is plagued with an assortment of wrinkles and this body with stiff bones."

Howe chortled lightly, his eyes twinkling in amusement. "But I would venture to guess that you have had your share of beaux flocking about you, vying for your attention. And even now, I would not be surprised to find men collecting about you. You seem to have a zest for life that attracts people, including myself."

Veronica allowed herself a short laugh. The general was attempting to charm her. She had heard that he was a ladies' man, and obviously he did not care about the woman's age. "You're a devil, General. You know the way to this old woman's heart. There is a young maiden locked inside this decrepit body, and I would be lying if I said I would not enjoy being escorted about on your arm." She paused a moment and then continued in a solemn tone. "But I cannot relinquish my mourning habit even for this grand occasion. I hope you will not begrudge my attire."

The general unfolded himself and walked around his desk to assist Veronica to her feet. "Madam, I will be pleased with whatever you wear. I find you enchanting company. And I wonder if my officers will be jealous that I have asked you to dine by my side and dance in my arms. They will be wishing that they could exchange places with me."

Veronica patted his cheek in a motherly sort of way. "You have wedged your way into my heart, young man. I am very particular about whom I befriend, but I count you among those I have chosen."

"As do I," he insisted as he clasped her hand around his arm and walked her toward the door. "I have a spare room upstairs, if you would like to remain at headquarters until you depart for England. I would enjoy having you here."

"'Tis very kind of you, general, but I have taken a room at the inn and I usually have my dog, Barron, with me wherever I go. He is very protective of me and I would not wish to chance having him take a bite out of one of our brave soldiers." Veronica chuckled and then fondly squeezed Howe's arm. "I would be dismayed if he, too, were accused of being a Rebel because he attacked a red uniform," she mocked lightly. "My family has suffered enough as it is. I do not wish to have my mutt persecuted as well."

Howe bent his gaze to the spry old dowager, unable to smother the smile that skipped across his lips. "You do not intend to let me forget that I have wronged your granddaughter, do you?"

"Nay, and you should also know that she had nothing but kind words about you in her letters. She wrote that she had met you when she came here with her father."

He halted in his tracks, a thoughtful frown creasing his brow. Somewhere in the corner of his mind he shuffled through his file of tempting beauties and finally conjured up the face of Serena Warren. Aye, she was a rare and lovely rose, he recalled. Strange, if he had remembered meeting her, he would have immediately discounted the accusations. Serena had a lively sparkle in her eyes, but she had the face of an angel. She had been hounded by officers who kept her busy dancing at the party he had given that evening. Aye, he thought to himself, perhaps his informant had had an ulterior motive for speaking against Serena.

Finally the general smiled sheepishly. "It seems that I have indeed caused your granddaughter unnecessary grief. Now that I think upon it, I recall that she was most gracious and charming, a compliment to the fact that you had a hand in her upbringing," Howe added with a charismatic grin.

Veronica steadied herself on her cane. "And I imagine that being in your company tomorrow evening will be one of the most pleasurable occasions I have enjoyed in years. 'Tis not difficult to see why King George and Lord North have placed you in such a position of authority, General. I must commend them on their decision when next we chance to meet."

"Please call me William," the general insisted as he gave her gloved hand an affectionate squeeze.

"And you must call me Veronica. Now that we are friends, it would not do to refer to each other by formal names," she said as she turned toward the door.

Howe was beaming as he watched Veronica hobble away. There was something compelling about the dowager. He was certain that having her around for the next few months until she could set sail for England was going to prove interesting. He had earned the old woman's friendship, but he pitied those upon whom she chose *not* to bestow her affection. Aye, watching the cantankerous dowager pick apart those who did not meet her expectations would be a delightful experience, and one which he would participate in vicariously, since his position demanded that he keep harmony among his staff and those who coveted his position.

After Veronica settled herself in the coach, she laughed happily to herself. The following night she would be wandering through the crowd on the general's arm and she would single out Olivia, slowly breaking her defenses. Subtle, endless torture was what Olivia deserved, Veronica mused spitefully. After all the misery she had caused Mitchell, she deserved such punishment. God forgive her for seeking revenge, Veronica mused as she squeezed her eyes shut and inhaled a deep breath. But after all the hell Olivia had put the Warrens through, she could not resist taunting that woman a bit.

Standing in front of the mirror in her room at the inn, Serena lifted the heavy veil and stared thoughtfully at her reflection in the mirror. It was becoming easier to put herself into the role of Veronica Warren, shutting out the memories of the past, as if Serena had never existed. It eased the pain of losing Trager, but she wondered if she could ever truly forget him and allow herself to love another man. Trager had meant the world to her. He had become her reason for living, and now she had turned to portraying her grandmother and seeking revenge on Olivia, clearing her own good name, and discovering who had murdered her father.

A tear formed in the corner of her eye and trickled down her cheek, taking part of the wrinkle lines with it. She had hoped that by directing her efforts toward new goals she could bury the past, but each time she stripped off her black padded clothing and washed away the painted wrinkles, the memories of what had once been came to haunt her.

Lord, how she missed the feel of Trager's loving arms about her, the warm, intoxicating taste of his kisses. Would she ever experience those same emotions with another man? Roger had offered to replace his brother, offering his love and devotion, but Serena had feared that he would remind her of Trager. She could not hurt him by living a lie.

Serena eased into her bed and shivered beneath the cold quilts. A hint of a smile grazed her lips as Barron hopped up on the end of the bed, turning a tight circle until he had made himself a nest in the quilts. As devoted as Barron was, he could not help ease the loneliness that encompassed her. Sleeping alone after lying in Trager's arms was torturous. Serena would awake from dreams, almost certain that Trager had been beside her. Why couldn't she face the truth? He was gone from her, and she must learn to accept the fact and get on with her life.

Clinging to that thought, Serena closed her eyes and begged for a dreamless sleep, but she was not granted her wish. The fantasies came as vividly as they always did, bringing a temporary sense of happiness and then despair when she woke to find herself alone. She was too impatient, she told herself. It took a great deal of time to forget the memories and let her soul heal. Time, she mused as she heaved a heavy sigh. That was one thing she would have an abundance of.

Chapter Twenty-Three

The British headquarters was full of activity when Veronica returned the following evening. Confident beneath her disguise, she stepped from her carriage to find the general's aide waiting for her and the general himself standing just inside the door at the head of the receiving line.

"Ah, Veronica, you are right on time," Howe observed, flashing her a broad smile.

"I pride myself on punctuality," Veronica told him. "I detest those who blame their tardiness on old age. Since I am a woman who has spent these last few decades fighting the clock and begging for borrowed time, I find it too precious and dear to waste."

William Howe nodded thoughtfully. Veronica had a point, and he had the feeling that she was not the type of woman who sat and stewed about her failing health. She was much too feisty to spend her last few days or months in her rocker. She would be in the thick of things, living her life to the fullest.

"Permit me to introduce you to my officers." William drew her gloved hand around his arm and patiently waited for Veronica to move alongside him.

After Veronica greeted the familiar faces of men she had met when she attended the affairs with Mitchell, she fastened her eyes on Olivia, who stood primly beside her lover, Colonel Powell.

"Olivia, I have a surprise for you," William began. "This is Veronica Warren."

Olivia's face whitewashed and it took her a moment to recover and locate her tongue. "Veronica?" she repeated cautiously and then dropped her hand from the crook of John's arm.

"Aye, I came from England for a surprise visit, but I arrived too late. 'Tis a pity that you were in such a rush to flee the manor...." Veronica let her carefully chosen words hang in the air as she glared holes in Olivia through her dark veil. "I had expected you to return for the funeral." Her raspy voice held a hint of disapproval.

"Well, I ..." Olivia floundered like a fish out of water. She had never expected to have to explain her actions to anyone in New York.

"You what?" Veronica asked sarcastically, prodding her on. "I am most eager to hear your excuse, my dear," she purred in a honey-coated tone, delighting in watching the last bit of color drain from Olivia's creamy features. "Imagine my dismay after the grueling journey at sea to find that you had abandoned Mitchell in his last hour." When Olivia reswallowed her tongue, Veronica grinned spitefully and then turned her attention on William. "Can you arrange for Olivia and her gentleman friend to sit beside us at the table? There is so much we need to discuss."

"Whatever you wish, Veronica," William agreed, biting back a smile as he watched Powell fidget in his boots.

Although Howe had wondered how John had snatched up Olivia so soon after Mitchell's death, he had never bothered to ask. Veronica had planted another seed of curiosity in his thoughts, and the seeds had begun to sprout when he noticed how uncomfortable the couple had become after being introduced to Veronica. Were they hiding something? Leave it to Veronica to weed out the sordid facts, he mused as he watched her hover beside them like a vulture intent on her prey.

"It seems that the colonel is to be commended for befriending you in your hour of need. 'Tis good that at least one of you can show a bit of compassion for another human being," Veronica continued, focusing her attention on John and then returning her veiled gaze to Olivia, who trembled like a leaf in a windstorm. "My dear, did you have to send out your mourning habit to be cleaned, or have you shed it *only* for this grand occasion?"

"Well, I . . ." Olivia stumbled again. Veronica had intimidated her with her rapidly fired questions, questions for which Olivia had difficulty producing answers, since she had been caught completely off guard.

"My, but, you are the shy one, Olivia," Veronica taunted her unmercifully and then gestured toward the next couple who waited in the receiving line. "Let us continue meeting your staff, William, and give dear Olivia the opportunity to catch her breath. She does not seem to think well on her feet. Perhaps she can find her tongue while we are dining." With a curt nod she edged past Olivia and John and then focused her attention on the next couple.

"I take it that you are not at all pleased with your Olivia's behavior," William remarked as he leaned close to Veronica to prevent being overheard.

"Oh, was I that obvious?" she questioned in mock innocence.

"I doubt that either of them missed the point," William assured her, breaking into a wry smile.

"Good." Veronica nodded slightly. "And now that I have inserted the knife in her back, I intend to give it a twist. I am not finished with her yet." Although Veronica attempted to keep the tone of contempt from her voice, it managed to wrap itself around her words.

"I do hope you do not have a stiletto with my name on it," William chuckled. "As quick-witted as you are, I do not doubt that I would buckle beneath the blade."

She patted his cheek and returned his laugh. "You are safe from this old woman's wrath, dear William. I do not intend to betray you, but I do plan to let my daughter-in-law know that she has fallen from my good graces by traipsing off to New York before Mitchell had his last rites read over him."

When William came to the end of the greeting line, he directed Veronica toward the dining hall and then seated her in her chair. Veronica muffled a giggle as she watched Olivia edge cautiously toward her. Her gaze lifted as Olivia hesitated a long moment and then, at John's insistence, planted herself in the seat beside Veronica. The dowager kept the silence until their meal was placed before them and waited until Olivia lifted the fork to her lips.

"How long had you been cuckolding Mitchell before he passed on?" Veronica queried in a hushed tone.

Olivia drew in her breath and choked on her first bite of steak. Unsympathetically, Veronica reached over to whack Olivia between the shoulder blades. The guests paused to stare at Olivia, whose face had turned as red as a beet, much to Veronica's delight.

"My, my, you seem to be having a rough time of it tonight, my dear," Veronica mocked lightly. "First you could not find your tongue to speak and now you seemed to have swallowed and choked on it. Have you ever considered having the vicious thing removed?" Veronica leaned close, hiding a vengeful grin. "Are you certain that you feel up to all this pomp and circumstance this evening? Mitchell wrote me that your family was not accustomed to money or to entertaining the upper crust of society. I suppose it makes you nervous to associate with the upper echelons, since you have come from the lower rung on the ladder of society."

Although Olivia had managed to dislodge the bite of meat that had nearly strangled her, she lost her composure after Veronica's barbed remarks. The split second before she almost lashed out at the wicked dowager, she remembered that all eyes were upon her. Olivia silently smoldered, itching to clamp her hands around that witch's throat and shake the life out of her.

"I have managed to adapt to this new life style," Olivia ground out, her tone harsher than she had intended, her hazel eyes simmering like an overheated tea kettle.

"Aye, you do seem to be a very flexible sort," Veronica acknowledged. "And I suppose you have bent over backwards for your colonel."

The insinuation hit Olivia like a hard slap in the face. She had been poked and jabbed so many times in the past hour that her nerves were frayed and her temper reached its boiling point.

"You vicious bitch," she hissed.

"Olivia!" John gasped when her voice rolled down the table like a tidal wave.

His face was splotched with embarrassment and shock. Never had he seen this side of Olivia. She had always been calm and in control, but Veronica's appearance had unraveled her composure.

"'Tis quite alright," Veronica said, her gaze glued to Olivia's furious face. "I understand that she has been under a terrible strain of late, and I am certain that her conscience is bothering her a wee bit. Mitchell always claimed that she was a temperamental sort, and I can see that he knew her well."

Olivia bolted to her feet, unable to sit by and listen to another of Veronica's insults, especially when no one else at the table could hear her remarks. Veronica had deviously made Olivia appear the culprit, and she felt like a spectacle in the center ring of a circus, as if Veronica was pitching daggers at her, making her a living target.

"Please excuse me." Olivia was striving for a civil tone, but her effort fell short. "I seem to have contracted a headache. I think I will return to my room to rest a bit."

As Olivia stomped out of the room, Colonel Powell followed after her, smiling sheepishly as he bid adieu to the other guests. When they were alone in the hall, he grabbed Olivia's arm and whisked her around to face him.

"Can you not conduct yourself in a proper manner in front of the general and his staff?" he questioned tersely.

Olivia gasped indignantly. "Did you expect me to sit there and endure that bitch's slanderous remarks? She has a vicious tongue!"

John urged her toward the winding steps. "Aye, that she does, but you must not allow her to creep beneath your skin, love."

"If you could have heard what she said to me, you might find yourself wishing to slit her throat," she muttered angrily. "That woman has come here with no other purpose than to torment me for leaving Mitchell and for . . ." Olivia bit her lip, turning wide

453

hazel eyes to John. "Can we go away for a while, just until she leaves for England? I do not think I can endure the next few months with her underfoot."

"Nay, we cannot. The general intends to plan his strategy for the spring campaign. He would not understand if I suddenly abandoned him."

Olivia heaved a frustrated sigh. How could she survive Veronica's presence without losing her sanity? Damn, that bitch, why had she shown up here? She was nothing but trouble.

"Did you perchance provoke Olivia's ailment?" William inquired as he arched a curious brow. Although he had not heard the entire conversation, he had picked up bits and pieces and knew that Veronica had needled her unmercifully.

Veronica chuckled hoarsely and then gestured toward the general's plate. "Eat your vegetables, William. Your food is getting cold."

William laughed out loud as several pairs of eyes fell upon him. He moved toward Veronica, his eyes dancing in amusement. "I do hope I am sitting on your good side. I have already informed you that I do not wish to suffer the same fate Olivia has experienced."

Fondly patting his hand, Veronica smiled beneath her veil. "And I have assured you that I count you among my friends. You are safe from this old woman's razor-sharp tongue."

"Unless I step out of line?" William guessed as he

scooped up a forkful of peas and obeyed Veronica's command to eat his vegetables.

"I suppose I might be tempted to draw your error to your attention." Her raspy voice carried a trickle of humor. "But I would not confront you as I have Olivia, since I have far more respect for you than I do for her."

"Perhaps I would be wise to discuss matters of state with you first . . . to prevent displeasing you," he said jokingly.

Veronica carefully drew a bite of potatoes beneath her veil, nibbled thoughtfully upon it, and then nodded affirmatively. "'Tis an excellent idea, William. I have been a great many things in my life, but never an advisor to the commander of our armed forces. I should like to experience that, too."

"Then I shall invite you to my next staff meeting," William assured her. "It should cause a stir among my officers."

"Perhaps it will promote their circulation."

Veronica was curious as to why the general had taken such a liking to her and it disturbed her that he had not been more inquisitive about her. Perhaps the fact that the war was going in his favor and that the Patriot troops had dwindled to a skeleton crew had eased his suspiciousness about his companion. It seemed the general was content to sit back and enjoy the luxuries of New York for the winter. He had not been as aggressive as Mitchell had hoped but had sat back on his heels when he could have wiped out the last of the Rebel troops. Whatever his reasons for accepting her and becoming complacent about his military objectives, Veronica was thankful. It made it easier for her to infiltrate his headquarters and seek out Olivia.

Her gaze circled the officers, and then she flinched when she noticed Brandon Scott, decked out in his flashy uniform, seated at the far end of the table. Odd, she thought to herself, Brandon seemed to have assumed a certain air of haughtiness and, knowing him as she did, she could not imagine what he had to be so smug about, the sniveling coward. Veronica could have told the young woman upon whom he was bestowing his attention that there was much ado about nothing where Brandon was concerned. Veronica made herself a mental note to single him out and repay him for the harsh way he had abused her.

The light touch of William's hand on hers brought her from her pensive musings, and she turned her veiled gaze to the general.

"Veronica, would you like to join me for a glass of wine in my study?"

She eyed him warily and then nodded her acceptance. When she had shuffled into the room on his arm, she sank into the chair and took the glass of wine and eased back to scrutinize Howe.

"Is there something you wanted to discuss privately with me, William?" Veronica coughed and sputtered and then brought the glass to her lips, anxiously awaiting his reply.

William smiled fondly, wishing he could see the face that was carefully hidden behind gauze and lace.

"You are very perceptive, Veronica. And aye, I am curious about your impression of my staff."

Her hoarse chuckle wafted its way toward him. "Do you think me to be a soothsayer who possesses the gift of prophecy, someone who can predict which of your men are excess baggage after only one meeting with them?"

"Nay," he said solemnly. "But I respect your opinions and I know that you will be honest with me. I appreciate that. A man in my position must be cautious of the people who surround him. Many lust for my position and others cater to me to gain favors."

Veronica frowned thoughtfully. How could she speak against his staff when she had deceived him far worse than the others? And yet, he had asked her opinion and he expected a candid reply from Veronica Warren, one that she was obliged to give.

"Perhaps it would be better if we postponed this discussion until tomorrow. After I have milled about for an entire evening, I can respond to that question far better than I can at this moment. There are several whom my instincts tell me are wolves in lambs' wool, social climbers who are more interested in their own success than the Crown's."

William nodded in agreement. "I have had the misfortune of having such a culprit revealed to me not long ago. Major Baldwin brought information about the Patriots for a fee, but I later discovered that he was supplying Washington with information, as well."

"And what became of him?" Veronica inquired, hoping that the identity of the man who had shot him was still a mystery to the British. Even though Trager was gone, she wanted nothing to taint his name.

"We found him shot to death and we are without a clue. But I would venture to guess that whoever confronted Baldwin had just cause for his action." His thoughtful frown evaporated as he focused his full attention on Veronica. "We will delay this conversation until tomorrow, as you wish." A warm smile pursed his lips as he extended his hand to assist Veronica to her feet. "Shall we dance the first dance? I believe the orchestra awaits us."

Veronica carefully laid her hand on the general's shoulder, staring up at him while they danced alone. When the music ended, Veronica gestured toward a chair.

"I believe I will sit the next one out, William. I must preserve my strength for our last dance. And I would imagine that your lady is tired of watching you dote over an old woman. Tell her that I appreciate the fact that she has shared you with me."

A wicked gleam flickered in her eyes when she spied Olivia standing at the refreshment table, gorging herself on spiked punch and tarts since she had been forced to bypass her meal. Olivia gulped over her pastry when Veronica hobbled toward her, and she braced herself for another bout with the meddling dowager.

"Are you feeling better, my dear?" Veronica

purred, her voice void of concern.

Olivia did not trust her tongue. The mere sight of Veronica incensed her and she only nodded curtly before grasping another tart.

"You really should not stuff yourself with those fattening treats," Veronica advised as she gestured toward the skin-tight dress of blue silk that daringly displayed Olivia's bosom. "If all of your gowns fit so snugly, you might split your seams when you strangle on your food."

Angry red made fast work of staining Olivia's cheeks. "What do you want from me, old woman?" she hissed venomously. "You have already embarrassed me and insulted me in front of my friends."

Veronica calmly studied Olivia, who trembled with barely contained fury. "'Tis time you paid the piper, Olivia. What you did to Mitchell was unforgivable, and as long as I live and breathe I shall never allow you to forget this injustice," Veronica insisted.

"Mitchell had his faults," Olivia defended herself, her voice rising testily. "But, of course, being his mother, you are blind to that fact."

"We all have our flaws," Veronica assured her in a deliberate tone. "But you have used Mitchell's shortcomings as excuses to justify your infidelity. You, Olivia, are no better than a common trollop."

"I am not!" Olivia protested and then bit her tongue, chiding herself for allowing the dowager to infuriate her again.

Veronica tossed her head and then chortled haughtily. "Perhaps you have fooled others with your pretense of charm and grace, but I can see right through you. I can see why Mitchell cut you out of his will. He did not want his hard-earned fortune to fall into tainted hands."

Colonel Powell wedged his way through the crowd when he saw Olivia, her face flushed, her claws bared, prepared to pounce on Veronica. He quickly maneuvered himself between them before Olivia could go for the old woman's throat.

"Come, Olivia, 'tis time we danced. Please excuse us, Mrs. Warren."

Veronica's soft chortle nipped at Olivia's heels as the colonel dragged her away. Her gaze swept the group of officers, looking for Brandon Scott, who was next on her list for questioning. Leaning heavily on her cane, Veronica shuffled toward him, her smile disguised behind her dark veil.

Brandon eyed the old woman warily and then forced a polite smile. "Are you enjoying the ball, madam?"

"Aye," she assured him in her hoarse voice. "And I have been most anxious to speak with you."

"Oh?" Brandon arched a heavy brow and then took a small sip of punch, studying her from over the rim of his glass.

"I have heard it rumored that you visited my son's home the day he was found shot to death." Veronica wasted no time coming to the point.

Brandon took a retreating step and glanced from side to side, hoping she had not been overheard. "Ah, well . . . I was there," he admitted. "I was grieved to hear about what happened to him. I only wish I would have been there to aid him in his time of need."

"Aid him?" Veronica sniffed distastefully, dropping all pretense of politeness. "I doubt that your presence would have benefited Mitchell. From what I have heard from various sources, you are not the type of man who comes to rescue people in distress."

"That source wouldn't happen to be Serena, would it?" he queried, eyeing the dowager suspiciously.

"Perhaps." Her shoulder lifted in a noncommittal shrug. "Would you mind telling me what you discussed with Mitchell during your visit?" She circled back to the previous subject, determined not to let him sidetrack her.

"I had come to inquire about Serena. We are still trying to locate her for questioning about her connection with the Rebel spy."

"The general has assured me that all charges against her will be dropped." Veronica watched him closely. "He has decided that his informant may have been too hasty in accusing her of treason."

"Oh?" Brandon's brow raised acutely and then returned to its normal arch. "I had not heard."

"Did Mitchell mention that he was expecting a guest that evening?" Veronica persisted, intent on dragging information from Brandon.

"I am afraid that I can be of little help, madam. I saw Mitchell that afternoon, but he did not inform me if he expected another visitor at the manor."

461

Veronica frowned thoughtfully when she noticed the medals that were draped on Brandon's uniform. "You have collected many awards for a man so young," she observed, wondering what the man could possibly have done to earn merit badges.

Brandon toyed with his medals and forced another shallow smile. "I do what I can for the Crown."

More likely as little as he could without getting dust on his boots or wrinkles on his uniform, Veronica mused resentfully. "Including slapping women who voice their opinions?"

His face lost all color. "Serena deserved to be punished for her slanderous remarks," he defended, his voice cold and clipped. "She is no saint. If you knew how she had . . ." Brandon clamped a tight rein on his tongue and swallowed the rest of the sentence. Veronica had an uncanny knack for putting people on the defensive and forcing them to say more than they intended.

"But it leaves me to wonder what kind of man abuses women," she commented, her raspy voice holding a hint of mockery. "It seems out of character for one who has so many medals dangling from his jacket. It piques my curiosity to know just how far a man like you would go to collect these trinkets." Veronica's probing gaze played havoc with his taut nerves. "Would it include tattling on Serena, ruining the Warrens' good name, and then doing away with my son so you could claim the position of magistrate?"

Brandon gasped at her accusations and then

clenched his fists at his sides, attempting to control his boiling temper. "You Warrens seem to have a great deal in common. 'Tis little wonder that Mitchell and Serena met with disaster. All of you have a vicious streak," he gritted out between clenched teeth.

Veronica maintained her composure, delighting in watching Brandon reduce himself to a pile of smoldering coals. "And you sought retaliation, since Serena cast you aside and Mitchell forced you to take a position in the British army. You had no desire to defend the Crown, did you?" Veronica curtsied slightly and then stepped back, muffling a snicker as she watched the steam rising from the collar of his red uniform. "Time will out your true nature, young man. Even this bright red jacket cannot disguise your yellow streak."

After she had left Brandon cursing under his breath, she wandered through the crowd to visit with the members of the general's staff. Her eyes kept straying to Olivia, John, and Brandon, watching them huddle together as if they were planning some devious scheme to do away with her. Veronica wondered if perhaps all three of them had plotted against the Warrens, since all of them had motives. But which one was responsible for which dastardly deed? Patience, she told herself. In time she would pry the information from them.

The sound of a familiar voice wafted its way toward her, and Veronica felt her knees buckle. She turned to glance behind her and suffered a shock that

463

made her heart skip several beats.

"Veronica?" Trager's dark brow arched curiously as he moved away from the young woman who clung possessively to his arm. "I am surprised to see you here."

The world was spinning furiously about her and she could not catch her breath.

"Trager?" Veronica breathed his name and reached out to him, but before she could grasp his hand she collapsed, her cane clanking on the tiled floor. The darkness circled like a looming vulture, and she was free of the ghost that had appeared from out of nowhere to torment her.

Trager scooped Veronica up in his arms the split second before she crumpled to the floor. Swiftly, he carried her through the crowd and climbed the stairs to put her to bed. He stared down at the veiled face in concern, wondering why the sight of him had caused her to faint.

What the devil was she doing at British head-quarters in the first place, he wondered as he settled her on the quilts. Thoughtfully, he studied her life-less form and then checked her pulse to insure that the devil had not come to claim another soul. The temptation to peer into the dowager's face was too great. He had spent weeks wondering what lay behind that heavy veil. Impulsively, he reached out to remove the gauze and lace.

Trager choked on his breath when he spied the strands of gold that crept from beneath the gray wig. Carefully, he removed the spectacles and brushed his hand over the painted wrinkles, watching them melt beneath his touch. "Damn that witch!" he grumbled under his breath. It wasn't enough that Serena had toyed with his heart and then abandoned him the moment his back was turned. Nay, she had purposely deceived him with another disguise, cutting him to the quick while she portrayed the cantankerous dowager. Was there no end to the misery this windswept rose could inflict on him? His hand wandered over her pale cheeks and then he jerked away, determined to feel nothing for this devious witch. Aye, he had loved her once, but those emotions had died. There was nothing left between them but a common name. Serena was no longer a part of his life, and he detested the memories that crept from the corners of his mind as he stared down at her, recalling the night he had returned to Peekskill.

He had limped into the bedroom and lit the candle on the nightstand, expecting Serena to be there waiting for him, but he had cursed under his breath when he found the room empty. Trager had been through living hell, fighting for his life. When he finally arrived at headquarters he found the camp had been evacuated and Serena had vanished.

Exhausted, he had collapsed on the bed and then had spied the note that lay on the pillow.

My dearest Roger,

I cannot remain here to make you miserable as I have made Trager. Too late I have realized that I was not meant to love. It only brings pain.

You will be much better off without me. Forgive me for not staying to say goodbye, but I could not face you again.

If we had met at another time and place perhaps we might have been able to make each other happy.

Do not worry about me. I will survive. My thoughts and prayers will be with you.

Always,
Serena

Trager had cursed under his breath and ripped the letter to shreds. Deceitful witch! He had realized that she had been playing with Roger's affection behind his back. All those words of love she had murmured while she had lain in Trager's arms were lies! She had used him and Roger to supply her with pleasure, but neither of them had touched her cold heart. God in heaven, how could he have been such a fool to think that vixen felt anything for him? Because she was the mistress of disguise, he had reminded himself bitterly.

His emotions had been twisted and stretched out of proportion and he had wanted to strike out at something. Impulsively, he had grasped the figurine that sat on the nightstand and hurled it against the wall. It had crashed into a thousand pieces, as did his dreams. He despised the angelic image of Serena that had hovered over him while he had fought his way through the strong current of the Hudson River. He had cursed that diabolic pair of emerald eyes that had glowed down upon him while he lay in a stranger's bed, recovering from his near escape from death. He had dragged himself from the jaws of hell, intent on returning to Serena, but she had been gone with the harsh wind that swept the countryside.

But it hadn't been enough for her to take his heart and wrench it in two. Nay, she had spitefully destroyed Roger, as well. Damn her! Trager had smashed his fist into the palm of his left hand and then cursed her over and over again.

Had she turned her charms on Roger the moment he had returned from the ambush and then left him hurting when she left him? How many other men had she taken to her bed while both of them were fighting for their lives? Trager had hated to venture a guess. Serena had deceived him at every turn, and he had fallen for her lies like a witless fool, believing that she honestly loved him, but, as she had professed in her letter to Roger, she was not meant to love. Aye, Serena was a witch with the powers of Satan, blinding men to her evil ways so they could not see the truth beneath her angelic appearance until it was too late.

That night he had vowed never again to put his trust in a woman, especially one as heartless and treacherous as Serena. He would use them to satisfy his lust, and then he would discard each of them when he tired of them. Never again would he speak of love, for there was no such emotion. It was only a foolish frame of mind. He did not need Serena and she didn't need him. Hadn't she told him that a dozen times? Why hadn't he listened? He should have known that she was only toying with him after he had watched her lead Brandon Scott around on a string and then humiliated him in front of his superiors. He should have realized how fickle she was when she agreed to marry Roger without even knowing him, spiting Trager by turning his own brother against him. Damn her to hell and back, Trager had scowled as he had flounced on the bed. He had been angry and exhausted, but he had been afraid to sleep. The darkness had always brought visions of Serena, and now they would haunt him. He didn't want to think of her, not ever again.

Then and there he had vowed that he would stumble onto that thorned rose and crush her in his bare hands. And he would tell her how he despised her for what she had done. He would reclaim his heart. He could look at her and see her for what she really was.

But she had come to him in dreams when he had not been able to keep his eyes open a moment longer. He had been too tired to conquer the visions that crept in from the corners of his mind. That night he had allowed Serena's memory to torment him, but when the new day dawned he had buried the bittersweet memories and had concentrated on his cause. From that moment on, he had had no wife. He had been determined to keep lovers, intent on erasing the thought of Serena and their time together.

She had betrayed him and lied to him. He had profited from his mistake with her. Now he was wary and more capable of defending himself against those who sought to destroy him.

Trager closed the door on the past, cursing himself for stirring the memories of that night. His expression hardened as Serena moaned and moved slightly.

Her lashes fluttered up to see Trager's scowling face hovering above her. Hesitantly, she reached out to touch him, wondering if this was yet another taunting dream.

"Trager?" she choked out. "It really *is* you. I thought you were dead." Tears scalded her eyes as she curled her arms over his shoulders, attempting to draw him close.

As if repulsed by their physical contact, Trager pried her hands from his neck and flung them away, his eyes boring into her like slivers of heated silver. "Wishful thinking on your part," he sneered at her. "Is that the story you have conjured up in your mind to convince yourself that it was perfectly all right to seduce my brother and then leave him too? You vicious bitch." His lips tightened as his fingers clamped around her neck, and it was all he could do to resist the urge to choke the life out of her.

"What?" Serena's mouth gaped, oblivious to the pain he was inflicting upon her. "It was Roger who . . ."

"You abandoned me and then him to hurry back to the manor to cloak yourself in this garb the minute I was out from underfoot, pretending that I had died in battle," Trager accused, glowering at her as if she were some horrid creature that had crawled out from under a rock. "You professed to love me to gain my trust. It was all a ploy. Your sole intent was to escape me, and you didn't give a damn how many lies floated from your lips or who you had to hurt to get what you wanted."

"Nay, 'tis not true," Serena protested as a sea of tears gushed from her eyes and flooded down her cheeks.

Trager snorted derisively. "Spare me the tears, Serena," he commanded, his tone as cold as the winter wind. "I am immune to all of your charades, even the pitiful dowager who attempts to play on her victim's sympathy."

"But, Trager, you do not understand. Roger . . ."

"Don't drag my brother into this," Trager interrupted. "I cannot blame him for falling for your charms. He was enamored with you from the beginning. Now, what are you doing here?"

Serena raised a proud chin, determined not to wilt beneath his condemning glare. "I intend to learn who killed my father."

"Are you mad?" Trager rolled his eyes and snorted in disbelief. "If the British discover your true identity you will be swinging from the end of a rope."

"Nay," she insisted as she propped herself up on her elbow. "I have convinced the general to dismiss the charges."

"Howe has fallen for this preposterous charade?" Trager laughed incredulously. "What spell did you

470

cast upon the poor man?''

"I did not mutter incantations," she informed him indignantly. "I only appealed to his sense of decency and to his logic, something you obviously know nothing about." Her voice was heavily laden with sarcasm as she returned his disgusted glare.

The insistent rap at the door made Serena flinch, and she quickly adjusted her spectacles and placed the veil over her face. "Who is it?" she questioned hoarsely.

"'Tis William. Aren't you feeling well, Veronica?"

Trager rolled his eyes and shook his raven head. "The two of you are on a first name basis? Christ, now I have heard everything."

"Come in, William," she offered as she glanced at Trager and then lifted a proud chin.

The door swung open and the general quickly closed the distance between them, kneeling at her side. "What happened?" he questioned, his expression mirroring his concern.

Veronica patted his hand. "I had a fainting spell, but 'tis nothing to fret over. It happens occasionally. I will be fine after I have a moment's rest." She gestured toward Trager. "Have you met another dear friend of mine? This is Trager Grayson. He came to my rescue when I collapsed."

Howe dragged his eyes off of Veronica and settled them on Trager for a split second before they returned to Veronica. He had seen the man on one or two occasions, but had not formally met him. "I am most grateful to you for coming to Veronica's aid. I have become quite fond of her and I do not want anything to happen to her. She is a joy and a rare treasure."

Trager silently discredited the general's praise, knowing damned well the wench was a pain in the . . .

"Trager attended Mitchell's funeral," she explained as both men stared down at her. "His shipping business has suffered greatly because of the Rebels. I was so impressed with him that I bought stock in his venture to rebuild his sailing vessels. They were destroyed by those dreadful renegade Patriots. It seems the Graysons have suffered as much as the Warrens in this unfortunate war."

"I am sorry to hear of your misfortune," Howe remarked as he glanced sideways at Trager and then returned his attention to Veronica, who was struggling to sit up.

After Veronica managed an upright position, she coughed and sputtered and then heaved a sigh. "Thank you, gentlemen, for coming to my rescue. 'Tis comforting to know that even an old woman can find knights in shining armor when she needs them." She curled her hand around the general's arm while Trager grumbled, watching Veronica charm Howe out of his boots. "Please help me down the steps, will you, William? I fear I have misplaced my cane."

Trager followed behind them, begrudgingly admiring Serena's gumption. She had barged into the British headquarters, befriended Howe, and had confirmed Trager's story so that the general would not be suspicious of him. He had expected her to blurt out his mission so that she could be rid of him once and for all. His gaze flowed over Veronica's well-rounded figure, knowing full well that beneath that padding was the shapely body of a woman who had long tormented his dreams. His emotions were churning inside him, torn between the bitterness of her betrayal and a memory that refused to die.

Determined to remain indifferent, Trager bowed out gracefully, leaving Veronica with the general to return to the young woman who had accompanied him to the ball. Although he swept Neoma Sykes around the dance floor, his eyes kept straying to Veronica, who had attracted a crowd. It galled him that she had successfully infiltrated Howe's staff while he had spent months gaining the confidence of the advisors. Obviously, Washington had made a poor choice. If he had asked Serena to spy, he would have collected every valuable piece of information he could ever hope to receive, Trager mused resentfully. Aye, Trager had been misplaced. He should have been a court jester, especially since he was adept at playing the fool.

Veronica forced herself to concentrate on her companions, but it was difficult when her thoughts settled on Trager. It hurt her deeply that he still mistrusted her and that he was bestowing his affection on the comely redhead. How well she remembered the feel of his arms about her. She had been so relieved to see that he had survived the ambush, but her elation had been smothered when he had spoken so hatefully to her. How could she explain when he would not allow her to get a word in edgewise and was too damned stubborn to listen? That had always been his worst two faults, she thought, discouraged. He guarded his heart as if it were fragile crystal, not allowing many people to truly know him. Damn that man. Did he really think she would confess to love him, turn to Roger, and then abandon both of them? Obviously he had a bolt loose in his brain, she thought to herself. And it would take a full set of wrenches to readjust his logic. He should have known that she could never love another after loving him.

The evening dragged on at a snail's pace, and Veronica kept glancing up at the clock, wishing she could return to her room to wallow in self-pity. It frustrated her to watch Trager charm his companion, and he made certain that she had a clear view. No doubt, this was his form of mental torment, assuring her that any affection he once had for her was dead and buried.

"Veronica?" William appeared at her side and extended his hand, urging her to her feet. "The last dance is ours," he reminded her. "Do you feel up to it?"

She nodded affirmatively and then slowly rose to her feet, accepting William's supporting arm and desperately wishing it could have been Trager's.

Chapter Twenty-Four

Serena heaved a despairing sigh as she adjusted the padding around her midsection and then pulled on her black gown. She had hoped to see Trager alone again, but almost two weeks had passed and she had watched him come and go from British headquarters with the lovely redhead on his arm. She had learned that Miss Sykes was the daughter of one of Howe's most trusted advisors, but Serena doubted that his interest in her was merely an attempt to gain information.

Trager had made it clear by flaunting his new lover that their marriage was over and that he wanted nothing more to do with her. Serena felt her heart twisting in two as she bit back the tears. She loved Trager, but he despised her. All this time she had believed him to be dead and had grieved for him. But this torture of watching him turning his charismatic smiles on Neoma was pure hell. Somehow she had to find a way to explain, to make him understand that she would never have left Peekskill if she had known that he had survived.

Her only consolation was that she had found some small success with Olivia, John, and Brandon. She had seized every opportunity to badger them, collecting bits and pieces of information, learning several interesting points that aided her in fitting the parts of the puzzle together. And there was much she could tell Trager about the general's strategy for his spring crusade to destroy the Rebel troops. But she had not been within ten feet of Trager since the night of the ball. Finally, she had decided to send a message to him, asking him to meet her after she returned from British headquarters that evening. Perhaps he would begin to believe in her again after he heard the information.

Painstakingly, she concentrated on the task of dressing, arranging the dark veil over her face, and attempting to squelch all thoughts of Trager for the moment. With Barron at her side, Veronica Warren emerged from her room and slowly took the steps to her waiting coach. General Howe had invited her to dine with him this Christmas Eve, and she had insisted that Olivia and the colonel join them, knowing that was the last place Olivia wanted to be.

Veronica had become impatient. She was itching to solve the mystery of her father's death and learn the name of the informant who had accused her of treason. Since she had yet to force a confession from Brandon, Olivia, or John, she had begun to wonder if she had been barking up the wrong trees. Perhaps her father's assassin had been a Rebel renegade who sought money and had been frightened off by Trager's appearance before he had had time to collect the loot. If the mystery did not begin to unravel at a faster pace, she was contemplating returning to the manor. At least she would not be forced to watch Trager flaunt another woman right under his nose.

Trager accepted the note from the messenger and then closed the door of his room, grumbling when he spied the signature at the bottom. Why did Serena want to see him? No doubt, she intended to fill him with more lies, attempting to melt his ire. But it wouldn't work, not this time, he told himself determinedly. He was no longer blind to her wily ways. Just because this was the season for giving did not mean that he would give in.

He had avoided her like the plague, spending his time with Neoma Sykes, a woman who offered her affection without touching his heart. But more than once he had been tempted to seek out Serena and more than a dozen times he had stopped himself. Trager had taken a solemn vow that he would keep his distance from Serena, pretending that she no longer existed, that she had no hold on him.

Angrily he stared at the letter and then ripped it to shreds, letting the pieces flutter to the floor, scattered and broken like the dream that had haunted him an eternity.

"Nay, witch,'" he muttered aloud. "I will not come to you tonight nor any other night. 'Tis over and done."

With that determined thought in his mind, Trager grabbed his caped top coat and hastily shrugged it on. Neoma had invited him to share their Christmas dinner, and he would not ruin his evening by winding up with that honey-haired hellion who disguised herself behind several layers of padding and a gray wig. Nay, this was yet another night that witch could amuse herself. He had learned his lesson, and only a fool would make the same error twice.

William Howe offered a smile when Veronica shuffled into the entryway to brush the layer of snow from her coat. "I thought perhaps you might have changed your mind after this weather took a turn for the worse."

"And miss spending Christmas Eve with you? Nay, even the snow could not keep me away," Veronica assured him as she allowed him to remove her jacket. "Did Olivia and John consent to join us for dinner?" She peered around his shoulder to see that the dining hall was empty.

"Aye, but I do not think that Olivia was particularly pleased with the idea," William chuckled lightly. "The poor woman is gun-shy after the way you have pinned her down these past two weeks." A thoughtful frown creased his brow as he glanced down at Veronica. "You have another purpose for hounding her, don't you?"

Veronica nodded affirmatively and leaned upon

her cane. "You are very astute, William. No doubt, that quality landed you the position of commander of our forces."

"And you don't plan to tell me what this is all about?" He arched a dark brow. "I'm deeply hurt, Veronica. I thought we had become close friends. Can't you take me into your confidence?"

Veronica affectionately squeezed his hand. "I have learned not to accuse someone of a deed until I know for certain that he is guilty."

"Guilty of what?" William frowned curiously.

"Of murder," she said simply and then hobbled toward the dining hall.

William choked on his breath. "Veronica, do you know what you are implying?"

"Aye, but as I said, I will not point an accusing finger until I know for certain."

Before William could continue cross-examining her, Olivia and John appeared from their room at the top of the stairs. Veronica paused to watch the wary couple move toward her. Her gaze anchored on Olivia's haunted eyes and then settled on John's drawn features. Veronica frowned thoughtfully. All this time she had wondered if Olivia was the culprit, but perhaps she had allowed her dislike for Olivia to contaminate her reasoning. Perhaps it was the colonel who had confronted Mitchell, demanding that he grant Olivia a divorce. And yet, she could not rule out Brandon, either. Damn, she could have convicted all three, since they all had motives.

"Wait a moment," William insisted as he spun on

his heels to hurry to the study. When he returned he drew his hand from behind his back and offered a gift to Veronica. "Merry Christmas. 'Tis a small token of my affection and friendship."

Veronica was deeply touched and saddened that she had not thought to purchase a gift for Howe. "I cannot accept this, William, for I have nothing to give you in return."

"Your presence here is gift enough," William assured her as he urged her to take the package. "You have given me your honesty and friendship, and these days both of those gifts are hard to come by. Now open the package."

Veronica bit back a denial. She had betrayed the general and it did not set well with her to realize that she had used him. At his insistence, she opened the gift to stare bewilderedly at a brooch that was studded with diamonds and emeralds.

"'Tis magnificent," she breathed hoarsely, and then fondly squeezed his hand. "Thank you, William. I shall always treasure the gift and our time together."

It was not difficult to see the envy in Olivia's eyes as Veronica pinned the brooch on her gown and took William's arm to walk to the dining hall. Intent on her mission, Veronica focused her full attention on the colonel after they were seated at the table.

"You are not looking well, John. Have you been unable to sleep?"

John forced a polite smile, even though the dowager's remark had set his teeth on edge. She was persistent, he mused sourly. Even this season had no effect on her. "Nay, I have had little difficulty," he lied. "I have been sleeping like a baby."

"Oh?" Her voice registered disbelief. "I thought perhaps your conscience might be keeping you awake."

"Why should it?" His voice cracked in irritation, despite his attempt to remain calm.

Her shoulder lifted in a shrug. "I thought perhaps you would tell us the answer to that."

Olivia slammed her silverware down on the table and bolted to her feet. Perhaps John could sit through another meal and allow Veronica to spoil their appetites, but she could not. She had pleaded with John to decline the dinner invitation, but he could not deny the general's request. Olivia had had her fill of Veronica's constant prodding. If she spent another evening with that bitch she was certain she would go stark raving mad.

"Excuse me. I have suddenly discovered that I am not hungry." Her harsh glare fastened on Veronica and then she nodded curtly to Howe.

As she swept from the room, John unfolded himself from his chair and followed in her footsteps. "Olivia, come back here."

Veronica pushed away from the table. "I think 'tis time that I had a private conversation with my daughter-in-law."

William nodded agreeably and then walked back to his study to sort through his paperwork while he awaited Veronica's return.

Cautiously edging up the steps, Veronica stared at the door, which was slightly ajar, and pricked her ears as the angry voices wafted their way down to her. She moved up a little further and obtained a clear view.

"Dammit, I don't know what has gotten into you, but I'm beginning to wonder if Veronica doesn't have just cause to harass you," John grumbled.

"The bitch is driving me mad," Olivia gritted out. "I am sick to death of catering to her. And I cannot endure any more of her badgering, innuendos, and insults. Do you expect me to sit idly by while she cuts us to shreds?" She clutched at John's jacket, raising a beseeching gaze to him. "Please take me away from her so we can be alone."

John jerked his arm from her grasp and glared at Olivia, whose behavior had evidently earned his irritation.

"Perhaps you should return to your mother's home . . . permanently. Maybe Veronica was right about you. You do not adjust well to rubbing shoulders with the upper crust."

Olivia's lips curled in a vicious sneer. "So you have tired of me and plan to cast me off," she concluded, her eyes glazed with fury.

"You are beginning to lose your fascination, Olivia," he told her bluntly. "I have spent more time taming your temper tantrums than enjoying your company."

Her indignant gasp sliced through the stilted

silence and Veronica leaned closer to hear Olivia's retaliation.

"You are not going to be rid of me that easily," she hissed, furiously. "After what I have done to insure that we can remain together I will not let you turn me out to live like a pauper with my mother."

John's brow knitted into a suspicious frown. "Now what are you ranting about?"

"Mitchell." Olivia drew herself up in front of him. "He cut me out of his will when I informed him that I was going to leave him. And then he spitefully refused to grant me a divorce so the two of us could marry. He left me no choice."

John swallowed his breath. "What are you trying to say, Olivia?"

"Mitchell swore that he would cut you down if I ran away with you. He intended to see that you received no more promotions. I had to kill him. He was a threat to us."

John gulped and backed away, repulsed by the woman whom he had foolishly thought he loved. But now he could see Olivia as she was, a vicious, self-centered woman who would allow nothing and no one to stand in the way of what she wanted.

"Get out of here, you little bitch," he spat at her. "I want to forget that I ever laid eyes on you, much less touched you."

Olivia's jaw swung from its hinges. "You can't mean that. We love each other."

"The sight of you sickens me, Olivia. If I had

known that you had killed your husband I would have handed you over to Veronica the moment she arrived. Now get out!" He flung his arm toward the door and swore under his breath, refusing to look upon her again.

"You will live to regret your decision," she assured him threateningly, her voice trembling as she spit out the words.

"I already do," he fired back at her.

When Olivia spun on her heels and yanked open the door to see that Veronica had been eavesdropping, her temper snapped. An enraged growl erupted from her curled lips as she charged at Veronica, itching to choke the life out of the woman who had destroyed her chance at happiness.

"Damn you," she hissed, her eyes spitting demented fire.

Veronica backed away, blocking Olivia's vicious blows with her arm, but Olivia hungered for revenge and her madness had given her unbelievable strength. She scratched and clawed at the black veil, determined to see the face of the dowager, to see the fear in her eyes before she killed Veronica.

Olivia shoved her backwards and then pounced upon her like a lioness devouring her prey, but John, hearing the scuffle, rushed from the room to pry them apart. Olivia's nails bit into Veronica's throat, stripping a layer of flesh from her neck as John attempted to step between them, taking the brunt of Olivia's furious beating.

John's forcefulness knocked Olivia off balance, and her shrill scream pierced the air as her foot slid from the landing. Veronica gripped the banister and gasped for breath as Olivia tumbled down the spiral staircase to fall in a lifeless heap. Simultaneously, the study door and the front door opened. William's eyes flew from Olivia to Veronica, who was being assisted down the steps by John. Brandon Scott stood in the opened door, his jaw sagging as his gaze followed the general's. His mouth thinned into a hard line when he realized that the dowager's constant harassing had caused Olivia's death. Damn her. She had meant to destroy Olivia and she finally had.

William knelt beside Olivia's still form and then glanced back at Brandon. "Take Veronica back to her room at the inn and stay with her to insure that she suffers no relapse after her experience," he ordered hurriedly.

Damn, Brandon would have preferred to ride to hell to fetch the Devil than to console the vicious dowager, but reluctantly he nodded to the general.

Although Veronica's head was spinning, she heard the general assure John that Olivia had met her death. Without protest, she allowed Brandon to whisk her out of the entryway and into the general's private coach. And then the world crumbled about her. Veronica burst into tears, despite her attempt to maintain her composure.

Brandon sat quietly beside her, offering no comfort, certain the dowager deserved to suffer and half hoping the shock of watching Olivia fall to her death would be too much for her old heart. Just in case Veronica did not realize that she was to blame, Brandon spitefully decided to make the point.

"'Tis all your fault," he assured her harshly. "You have been pushing Olivia since you first came here. I hope you are satisfied with the results. Now you have completely destroyed her. Would you like to return to finish off the colonel?" His voice was heavily laden with sarcasm. "Since you have made a disaster of this season, you might as well make the most of it."

Veronica winced, her tears halting as she swiveled her head around to glare holes in Brandon. "Mind your tongue, coward, or I will inform the general that you are wasted baggage in his headquarters."

When the carriage came to a stop, Brandon roughly yanked the dowager out beside him. "Don't threaten me. I will be tempted to avenge Olivia's death."

His lean fingers bit into Veronica's arm as he hustled her into the inn and up the steps, dragging her along beside him impatiently. Brandon shoved her toward the bed as a sneer settled into the lines of his face. "Wouldn't it be a pity if you died in your sleep after suffering such a shocking experience tonight?"

Veronica braced herself and swallowed the lump of fear that had collected in her throat. "Stay away from me," she commanded as she threateningly raised her cane to hold him at bay.

Brandon frowned at the sudden change in her voice, a voice that was all too familiar. He stalked toward the darkly clad dowager and ripped away her veil before she could stop him. Brandon gasped as he stared into Serena's face.

"You vicious bitch," he hissed furiously.

"Yellow-bellied coward," she flared as she raised a proud chin.

Brandon slapped her across the face and grabbed her arms to hold them above her head so she could not claw at him. He sank down on her belly to insure that she could not escape.

"Whore," he spat at her, his eyes spewing fire. "I have waited an eternity to get my hands on you. I stood on the shore that night to watch you throw yourself at Trager Grayson like a common trollop. And you cannot imagine how eager I was to capture you and return you to New York so you could hang beside your Rebel spy."

"*You* were the general's informant," she accused and then struggled when Brandon's grasp eased momentarily. "I knew it had to be you. Is that how you collected your medals, by tattling?"

Brandon's hands dug deeper into the tender flesh of her arms as a cruel sneer tightened his lips. "Aye, and I attempted to persuade Howe to take away your father's position as magistrate. He had no right to serve the Crown when he could not control his own daughter. And if it wasn't for him, I wouldn't be in this uniform. Mitchell recommended me for a position without bothering to ask if I wanted to join the forces."

"Nay, most cowards prefer to stand aside and watch," she hissed at him and then groaned as he slapped her across the cheek.

"And now you will pay." His voice rolled over her like thunder, ominous and threatening. "You freely offered yourself to a rogue who discarded you when he had used you. Now you will spread yourself beneath me like the whore you are." Brandon scowled down at her, venom dripping from his lips. "You could have claimed the position of my wife, but now you will learn the true meaning of whoring."

"The general will have your head if you lay a hand on me," Serena reminded him, frantically searching for a way to stop him.

His harsh laughter hovered above her. "I will probably be awarded with another medal when I inform Howe that Veronica Warren was a disguise and that you infiltrated the British headquarters as a spy." When Serena clamped her mouth shut, unable to retaliate, Brandon chortled wickedly. "It will be *your* head that he hungers for, my dear, not mine."

As he grasped the front of her gown and ripped it from her breasts, Serena writhed beneath him, itching to claw that fiendish grin from his face. Holding both of her arms with one hand, he roughly caressed her, and Serena squeezed her eyes shut, forcing out the thought of what he intended to do to her.

His knee slid between her thighs, and when Serena

attempted to scream his mouth descended on her, stripping her breath from her lungs. She twisted away, her cry of alarm cracking the silence. But Brandon's mouth captured hers again, his teeth biting into her lips until she tasted blood.

"I hate you," she cursed at him when he finally allowed her a breath.

"And I despise you, bitch," he hissed back at her, his lips curling in a contemptuous sneer. "I will derive great pleasure from stripping you of your dignity . . . and all else."

His hand left her breast to descend across her belly, tearing the gown from her hips. Serena struggled with every ounce of strength she possessed, realizing that she would fight to the death to keep from surrendering to his touch. The feel of his hands upon her was repulsive. And when he bent his head, his teeth nipping at the peaks of her breasts, she experienced a wave of nausea. God, how she detested Brandon.

As he lowered his heavy weight upon her, she heard the door crash against the wall. In a split second Brandon's body was tossed aside as if it were nothing more than a feed sack. Trager's furious growl cut through the air as he lunged at Brandon, whose expression registered shock and fear. Brandon was slammed against the wall, stunning him momentarily.

"You worthless cur!" Trager scowled as his fist rammed into Brandon's belly, causing him to double over from the well-aimed blow. "Keep your filthy hands off of her."

"She's nothing but a cheap whore," Brandon ground out as he clamped his hands around Trager's neck. "You of all people should know that."

Trager pried his hands away and then ducked when Brandon tried to swing at him. Brandon's breath came out in a rush when Trager grabbed him in a bear hug that was so tight that he could hear his ribs cracking beneath the pressure. With his hands braced against Trager's chin, Brandon pushed away and successfully managed to render a blow to his opponent's midsection. But his assault was like taunting a panther. Trager leaped at him, his enraged growl echoing in Brandon's ears. He knocked Brandon back against the wall, attacking him with several hard blows to his belly. It was as if Trager possessed the strength of three men and Brandon was helpless to defend himself. When he would have surrendered, he saw Trager's fist coming at him again. The room turned pitch black as he slid down the wall in an unconscious heap.

Trager insured that he would cause no more trouble. Then his gaze swung back to see Serena clutching her torn gown. His scowl settled in his chiseled features when he noticed the claw marks on her neck and the welts on the sides of her face.

"Did Brandon do that?"

Serena gulped for breath and then nodded slightly. "The claw marks are Olivia's. She tried to kill me after I discovered that she murdered my father," she explained, her voice trembling.

Trager came to her to inspect her scratches and bruises, his hand brushing lightly over her swollen cheek. Serena winced as he touched a tender spot and then lowered her eyes, afraid to meet the unconcerned expression on his face.

"Brandon was the one who informed Howe that I had conspired with Nathan. He told me that he even tried to persuade Howe to find someone else to fill my father's position."

"That comes as no surprise," Trager sniffed distastefully. When Trager realized that his hand was involuntarily caressing her face, he jerked away, reminding him that nothing had changed between them. As usual, Serena had embroiled herself in a bundle of trouble and he had come to her rescue even after he had been bound and determined not to see her. "Now what do you intend to do?"

Serena pushed up to a sitting position and gestured for Trager to turn his back. "First I intend to change my dress," she insisted. "'Tis too cold to go around half-naked." When Trager made no move to grant her privacy, she frowned at him. "Would you mind waiting outside while I dress."

His dark brow quirked as he crossed his arms on his chest. "I have seen you wearing less than this," he reminded her, his voice laced with mockery. "You do not have to fear being attacked again."

Serena cast Brandon a quick glance, assuring herself that he would cause no more distress, and then hastily stripped from her gown to don another black mourning habit.

491

"Just what did you want to see me about?" Trager questioned stiffly, focusing his attention on the bare wall, determined to remain indifferent to the sight of her shapely body.

"I have learned several things from the general that I thought might be of interest to you."

"My, but you have been a busy old woman, haven't you?" he smirked. Involuntarily, he moved toward her, his caress trailing along her arm to her shoulder. The familiar sensations swept over her, but Serena reminded herself that Trager was only taunting her. Her gaze swung away from him suddenly to see Brandon crouching, preparing to attack. Somehow he had silently managed to draw his sword, and Serena twisted around to protect his target—Trager's back. A searing pain burned across her arm as she deflected the blade and then she felt herself being thrown aside as Trager wheeled to meet his foe.

Vaguely, Serena remembered hearing the sound of furniture crashing as the two men wrestled on the floor. Although the world was whirling about her, she raised her head in time to see them struggling over the sword. And then a groan cut through the silence as Brandon felt the sting of his own blade. Trager untangled himself from Brandon and hurried to Serena, cursing himself for being caught off guard. He scooped her up in his arms and then laid her on the bed to doctor her wound, working quickly and silently, intent on his chore. The impatient knock on the door had Trager scowling under his breath. He replaced the dark veil to conceal Serena's identity and then twisted around to stare at the intruder.

The innkeeper's face turned white when he saw Major Scott lying on the floor in a pool of blood, his own sword penetrating his red uniform.

"What happened?" he gasped.

"This man attempted to kill Mrs. Warren," Trager explained. "I want you to send a message to General Howe. Tell him that Scott attacked this woman and that I am taking her home to recuperate from the wound she sustained from the major's sword."

When the innkeeper nodded and then turned on his heels to do his bidding, Trager stared long and hard at Serena.

"Why did you do it? You could have spared yourself the pain."

"He meant to kill you," she murmured and then sucked in her breath when Trager tightly wrapped a makeshift bandage over her arm.

"You should have let him," Trager muttered and then lifted her into his arms, taking his distance across the room in swift strides.

When Trager had situated Serena in the coach, he sent her groom back to the room to pack her belongings and then tied his steed behind the carriage. Serena shivered from the shock and the winter chill. And, try as she would, she could not stop her teeth from chattering. Her experience had left her nerves on edge, and Trager's standoffish attitude toward her had smothered what was left of her fighting spirit.

As Trager sank down on the seat beside her, a frown knitted his dark brow. "Are you all right?"

Serena huddled in the corner, drawing her cloak tightly about her. "I cannot stop shaking," she managed to say between her rattling teeth, knowing if they had been wooden partials they would have jarred loose and fallen to the floor.

Carefully avoiding her tender shoulder, Trager drew her against him, offering his warmth. "Rest now, Rena. 'Tis all over. You did singlehandedly what you intended to do. You have avenged your father's death and cleared your name."

"Nay, you came to my rescue. If not for you, Brandon would have . . ." Her voice trailed off as she squeezed back the tears.

"But I have no doubt that if I had not kept the appointment you would have managed without me," he assured her, his tone cool and indifferent.

Serena gave her head a negative shake and then nestled in his encircling arms. "Nay, Trager . . . and thank you. You spared my life."

"Then we are even. You saved mine."

A quiet smile grazed her lips as the tension flowed from her body and she relaxed in his embrace. And then she slept, content to relinquish her grasp on reality while Trager held her, keeping her from harm.

Trager eased back to seek a more comfortable position and then drew the lap quilt around them to ward off the chill. When he drew the dark veil from her face and removed her gray wig, her honey-blond hair tumbled free, spilling across her shoulder. The faintest hint of a smile found one corner of his mouth as he stared down at Serena. Her neck showed evidence of her struggles with Olivia and her cheeks were bruised from her encounter with Brandon. Trager lightly ran his fingertips over her exquisite features. Although she was exhausted and battle-scarred, she was still the most beautiful woman he had ever laid eyes on.

Heaving a frustrated sigh, Trager laid back his head and peered at the ceiling, fighting the senti-mental emotions that flooded over him while he held this vixen in his arms. He reminded himself that she had betrayed him with his own brother. She had lied to him, just as she had lied to Howe, convincing both of them that she was someone she was not. Trager clung fiercely to his pride, determined not to let his weakness for this woman destroy him. All those who had confronted Serena had met with disaster, while she seemed indestructible. Nothing could deter her from her cause, and she used every device to find suc-cess. She didn't need him. She had never needed him, and they would both be better off if they went their separate ways.

And then drowsiness overcame him and he involuntarily cuddled closer to Serena, giving in to the dreams that haunted his sleep. Her face rose above him, her soft voice calling out to him from across an endless sea. He was searching for her through the storms and cannon fire, reaching to grasp her extended hand, aching to take her in his arms and lose himself to the drugging taste of her kisses.

As the dawn's light filtered through the windows of the carriage, Serena's tangled lashes swept up and she saw Trager staring at her. There was still a hint of mistrust in the steel glint of his eyes. Serena pressed her hands to his chest, pushing away from him to maintain a sitting position. It was time that she accepted the fact that she had lost Trager's love. He had convinced himself that she had betrayed him and he was too stubborn to listen to reason. She had to learn to stand alone and to forget the past if she was to survive. She knew that the moment they returned to the manor he would leave her, making no more attempts to see her again.

"When you see Washington, tell him that Howe intends to attack Philadelphia and dissolve the Continental Congress during his spring campaign. They must move to another city to insure their safety," she insisted, striving for the same indifferent tone he had used with her the previous night. "Howe thinks that he can disrupt the Patriot cause if the Congress is no longer functioning, issuing proclamations to stir the people. He also intends to shift his headquarters to Philadelphia and expand the war to the sea. There will be three columns of soldiers flanking the colonies." Serena paused to take a breath while Trager's jaw sagged in bewilderment, wondering how she had dug up so much information in such a short amount of time. "General Burgoyne will move down from Montreal by way of Lake Champlain. St. Leger will march through the Mohawk Valley, and Howe was supposed to advance up the Hudson River." A wicked gleam flickered in her eyes as she reached beneath her cloak to produce a letter and then handed it to Trager. "But Howe does not know what Germain expects of him, because I intercepted the message. He will go on to Philadelphia and the Patriots cannot be blocked off."

Trager slumped back in his seat. Lord, if Washington had sent Serena to spy on the British in the beginning, the war would have been over and he would not have been wearing out good mounts traipsing across the countryside and back again. He rolled his eyes and then took the note to read the information once again.

"Washington will be very pleased with you," he said quietly and then drew back the window curtain to watch the sun peak through the clouds, seeing the Warren mansion appear in the distance.

Serena formulated her thoughts, took a deep breath, and then began. "Trager, I know what you think of me." Her eyes lifted to him, but he refused to meet her beseeching gaze. Her heart sank as she watched him stare off into the distance, reminding her of a stone mountain, hard and unrelenting. "But I do love you. I always have. I went to New York to avenge my father's death, 'tis true. But my other purpose was to aid the cause for which you fought. It grieves me to betray Howe, since I came to know and like him, but I wanted to help the Patriots and those who had died for the cause." She touched his hand, feeling him flinch from the light contact. "Whether you want to believe it or not, there has never been another man, and I doubt that there ever will be."

She was met with frigid silence that turned her soul to ice. And then Trager slowly bent his gaze to her, his eyes as hard as granite, his expression grim.

"I did not come to your room last night because you had information for me. I only came to retrieve something I had foolishly offered to you—my heart. I gave you my love, and although you betrayed me to search out Olivia and Brandon, you continue to protest that I have no just cause to discredit your word. It suited your purpose to believe that I was dead, that I would not survive when I knew you awaited me. 'Tis all that kept me alive," he told her harshly. "I fought my way back from the jaws of hell to return to you, and you had no faith in me. What will it be next time, Serena?" His smoky eyes glistened with mockery. "Will you be chasing some distant star when you steal off into the night to leave me behind?" Trager laughed bitterly and then shook his raven head. "Nay, Serena, I have no intention of tracking you across God's green earth, wearing my heart on my shirtsleeve. 'Tis over and done. I have heard enough lies to last me a lifetime. I intend to return to Washington to prepare to fight an enemy who wears only a red coat instead of a thousand disguises."

He stepped from the carriage and then strode over to untie his horse. Serena choked on her tears and died a thousand deaths as she stared at the hoofprints in the snow that marked his departure. How could she go on when he had taken her world with him? There was nothing but an empty house and broken dreams, ones that could never be mended.

Serena turned to peer at the mansion and then took the steps while her ears rang and her heart withered and died, the echo of his words coming again to haunt and torment her.

Chapter Twenty-Five

Roger slumped back in his chair, propped up his feet, and thoughtfully sipped his drink, hoping to warm his frozen insides. The accommodations at Valley Forge left a lot to be desired, and it was difficult to keep up his spirits when everywhere he looked were tattered soldiers and windswept shacks.

His days had become endless misery, waiting for Washington to formulate his plans and adjusting to life without Trager. It had been a month since the ambush and since Serena had vanished, leaving a hole in his heart. He had considered following after her, but Washington would not grant him a leave. Washington had become his overprotective father substitute, keeping Roger by his side. Roger assumed that Washington felt part of the responsibility for Trager's death, just as Serena did. But neither of them were to blame, Roger mused as he took another sip of brandy. If he had been paying more attention, if he had been in the lead instead of Trager . . . Roger breathed a dismal sigh. He had relived that moment a hundred times, wishing he could have altered the course of fate.

The sound of footsteps filtered into his silent reverie and he glanced up to see the slow twist of the door latch. Roger's heart stopped and the color seeped from his face when Trager materialized before him. The glass slipped from his fingertips and clanked on the dirt floor while Roger sat paralyzed, his jaw gaping, his eyes bulging.

"I thought you were dead," Roger choked out when he finally located his tongue.

"I was, but my condition improved," Trager smirked as he eased his weary bones into a chair, remembering that he had received the same reaction from Serena. Perhaps she *had* fainted because she really did believe that he was dead, he mused. At the time he had considered her behavior to be part of her lie, of her attempt to convince him that she had spoken the truth.

Roger roused from his shock and his gaze anchored on Trager's drawn face. "What happened? I searched every inch of that river after the ambush, but there was no sign of you."

Trager smiled tiredly. "The current swept me downstream until I lodged in some driftwood. I dragged myself out of the water and found my way to a farmhouse." He paused to rub his aching muscles and then continued. "After the old woman stitched me back together, she allowed me to stay until I had recuperated. I didn't have the strength to move. And, from what she told me, I must have flirted for quite a while with death.''

"Why didn't you send a message?" Roger felt his irritation rise. He had lived through hell, believing that if he had been more cautious he could somehow have spared Trager. And now here he was, not that Roger wasn't elated to see him, but dammit, Trager could have saved him a month of misery. "For God's sake, man, have you no sense of decency?"

"There was no one within ten miles, and the old woman lived alone. What did you expect me to do, order her to ride back to Peekskill?" Trager snorted derisively.

"No, I suppose not," Roger muttered and then gulped over the lump in his throat. "Trager, I told Serena that you had died." His voice was so quiet that Trager had to strain his frostbitten ears to hear him.

And then he waited. Trager had not allowed Serena to explain because he had become immune to her lies, but now he was eager to hear what his brother had to say.

Roger's shoulders slumped as he rested his forearms on his knees and peered solemnly at Trager. "When I returned to inform Serena about the ambush I asked her to marry me, to remain with me so I could protect her."

"How noble of you." Trager's lips dripped with sarcasm as he bent his gaze to Roger. "Did you intend to allow her the proper amount of time to mourn her not-so-dead husband?"

"I only wanted to protect her," Roger said, his voice registering indignation.

"Only?" Trager mocked dryly. "Come now, Roger, I know how you feel about that wench. You would have married her in the beginning if I had not claimed her first."

"But I knew she only loved you," Roger insisted. "And even though she thought she had lost you, she would not turn to me for consolation." Roger's gaze narrowed on his brother. "I knew she could never feel the same way about me as she did about you, but I thought I could live with that. Serena could not. She chose to leave. Serena felt responsible for your death. She had begun to believe that those she cared about would meet with disaster, like Nathan, her father, and you. . . ." Roger heaved a sigh and then stared at the toes of his worn boots. "She bears a heavy cross, thinking that she has cursed all those she loved, and she did not want to hurt me or attempt to live a lie."

Trager was pensively quiet, remembering how harsh he had been with Serena before he left her behind. He had not considered her feelings because he could not see past his own misery. He had successfully managed to stick his foot in his mouth, and it would take major surgery to have it removed. But dammit, when he had come back to Peekskill he had thought she'd abandoned him, lied to him to gain his trust, and then slept with his own brother on those cold winter nights. He had jumped to the wrong conclusion, never imagining that Roger could have given him up for lost. His reverie was interrupted when Roger came to his feet and strode up in front of him.

"You've got to find Serena. You cannot allow her to mourn your death," Roger insisted sternly. "'Tis my fault that she believes that you perished."

"Nay, I cannot go back to her," Trager murmured without glancing up at Roger. "And she knows that I am alive. I have seen her."

Roger's jaw swung from its hinges. Trager had been too long in the cold, and the winter wind had drifted the snow into his brain.

"Why the hell not?"

"Because I thought she had betrayed me and I said many things to hurt her. I think I have caused her enough grief already. 'Tis better to go our separate ways and begin a new life. This war has twisted and tormented both of our lives enough as it is," Trager insisted as his lashes swept up to meet Roger's hard gaze.

"I have looked up to you and admired you, Trager," Roger growled at him. "But if you are such a damned fool that you would let Serena go, I wonder if you deserve my respect." When Trager made no attempt to defend himself, Roger let his breath out in a rush. "Very well then, *I* will go back for her and I intend to desert the army and kidnap her if she won't consent to run away with me." Roger was practically shouting in his brother's face, his anger boiling like an overheated tea kettle that was spouting steam. "I will not have her living alone. There are renegades in that area, and you know damned well what they can do to defenseless women."

"You are not going back for her," Trager gritted out.

"The hell I'm not!" Roger snapped back at him.

"We are not going to argue over a woman, especially Serena. She will not come between us." Trager bolted to his feet, flashing Roger a glare that expected no resistance, but he had only stoked the fire of Roger's temper.

"Then, 'tis *your* move, big brother. One or the other of us is going back for her, and you damned well better make your decision."

Trager's glower pinned Roger to the wall and he opened his mouth to speak, but then slammed it shut and wheeled away.

"Where are you going?" Roger demanded to know.

"To see Washington." Trager threw over his shoulder, along with another sour glare.

When he stepped outside, the fierce wind slapped him in the face and he muttered under his breath. He had spent the last two weeks convincing himself that he and Serena were better off without each other, but after hearing Roger's explanation his logic had sprung a leak. But dammit, how could he face her after the way he had treated her? His breath came out in a rush. He couldn't. He would be forced to crawl back on his hands and knees, and that was one position he was not fond of, one that he had always refused to contort his body into. Hadn't they hurt each other enough? Damn this war. It was making things difficult.

Trager inhaled a deep breath and focused his thoughts on his duty rather than his desire as he aimed himself toward Washington's cabin and took the distance in impatient strides. There was much he had to report to the general, and he had no time to ponder the dilemma. After all, he reminded himself, he was a man of purpose, and that often meant making sacrifices. And he had been prepared to make them for the cause of independence. He was tied to his cause, one that had been foremost in his mind until he had stumbled on that windswept rose who had stabbed him with a thorn that continued to plague him.

Washington's face turned as white as his wig when Trager appeared in the door, and it took him a moment to recover from the shock. Finally, a relieved smile settled on his features and he came to his feet to grasp Trager's hand.

"I thought we had lost you," he chuckled and then slapped the captain on the back. "I swear, Grayson, you must have nine lives. How many have you used? Three, four? After your brother's report of the ambush I had given you up for dead, but it appears that we were a little hasty." A wide grin encompassed his features. "You would have been pleased with the eulogy I read over you."

"I wish I could have been there to hear it," Trager replied, his chiseled expression cracking slightly. He had ridden hard, intent on his purpose, and was anxious to cut to the heart of the matter. He had heard enough about his own death to last him a lifetime. "I have important news from New York. I think you will be pleased to know what you can expect from the British."

Washington gestured toward a chair and then sank down in his own. "You must have had a very productive journey," he speculated.

Trager nodded slightly. "Aye."

After he had informed Washington of the British strategy for their spring campaign, he confessed that it was Serena who had successfully managed to infiltrate the headquarters disguised as Mitchell Warren's mother to gain Howe's confidence.

There was a wry twinkle in the general's eye as he bent his gaze to Trager. "It seems your lovely wife deserves a medal for her report. She is a lively one, and I must admit that I was impressed with the lass. I once told her I wished to have a regiment just like her." His expression sobered as he looked Trager straight in the eye. "And you have well served the Patriot cause by gaining valuable information. Now I have another assignment for you, and I am certain that you will serve us just as well in this new capacity."

Trager listened while Washington mapped out his plans, but his thoughts kept straying to Serena, knowing that his mission would take him farther away from her. Perhaps in time the memories of that tortured look in her eyes when he left her would fade. One day her angelic face would not come to haunt his dreams. Her tender smile would be overshadowed when another woman came to take her place. Serena was a survivor. She didn't need him, even if Roger thought she did. She was a clever woman with an uncanny knack for emerging from foul situations smelling like a rose. Aye, there might be times that both of them dwelled on the sweet torture of the past, but the dawn would bring another day and the memories would wither. It was for the best, he assured himself.

From beneath the brim of his cap, Trager peered at the stubble-faced man who sat across the table from him in New Rochelle. His journey from Valley Forge was far from over, but he had paused for the night, wondering why he had chosen this route to his destination. He hadn't meant to travel this way again, but he was here, just the same. A secretive smile grazed his lips as he lifted his mug of ale to take a sip.

"I tell ye 'tis true," Braden, the innkeeper, said with a firm nod. "I saw the ghost meself one night. The wind was howlin' like a banshee and the moon was full. And there upon the distant hill I saw a specter floatin' in and out of the shadows. And I ain't the only one who's seen them spirits roamin' the darkness." He snorted when Trager cast him a dubious glance. "Old man Warren has come back to protect his manor from them renegade rebels. Ain't nobody goes 'round the house, 'specially now that the Widow Warren has come to rule the roost. That old woman breathes fire and they say she won't let no one befriend her. But the Warrens have suffered greatly, and I guess she's got a right to be bitter. I heard tell that she even beat off one man with her cane and sicced that wolflike mongrel on him." Braden sadly shook his head and then glanced up at Trager. "I hear General Howe has pardoned Warren's daughter, but I ain't seen hide nor hair of her. If you ask me, she's perished, just like her pa. Ironic, ain't it? That old dowager has outlived them all." Braden leaned close and looked carefully about him as if he was about to reveal a treasured secret. "There's talk that the widow is a witch, and that she calls them spirits to visit her, since no proper citizen will go near the place. Nobody has ever seen the widow's face, and some say there ain't no face behind that black veil because she's a ghost too."

Trager choked on his ale. Aye, there was a face behind that disguise, but it had haunted him in an entirely different way. Serena's rare beauty was camouflaged, and apparently she had become bitter after the way he had treated her. And yet, he couldn't condemn her, since he had become a bit intolerable himself.

Pushing away from the table, Trager nodded to the innkeeper. "Thank you for the drink and conversation," he said, before he strode toward the door and disappeared into the night.

Serena paused from her letter writing and reread the note from General Howe, who had wished her well and had extended his apologies for what had happened with Brandon and Olivia. He had also assured her that he had signed a proclamation dismissing all charges against Serena Warren and that her good name had been reinstated. Serena breathed a frustrated sigh. It was a pity that she had had to deceive the general. She picked up her quill and jotted down another thought, attempting to sound more cheerful than her present mood. She had become fond of the man, even though he could have squelched the Patriots' resistance if he had been more aggressive in pursuing them. Each time he had them backed to a wall he had given them the opportunity to retreat, to catch their breaths, and regroup. But then, Serena had been thankful for his flaw. It had given the Rebels precious time. She had to admit that she liked the man, even though their political views were at the opposite ends of the spectrum.

A rueful smile hovered on her lips as she toyed with the brooch the general had given her. It had been the only bright moment in a long, nerve-wracking month. Bending her gaze to the parchment, she informed the general that she would not be returning to New York until spring to set sail for England. Hopefully, he would by then have departed for Philadelphia, and she would not be forced to deceive him again. It was better to part as friends rather than enemies, as she and Trager had done.

The sharp rap at the door brought her from her pensive musings.

She grasped her cane and pulled the veil over her face. A curious frown knitted her brow, as she wondered who had come calling at this late hour. She had been heckled by snoopy citizens when she had been in no mood to respond to their prying questions. Occasionally, an ill wind blew some scavenger to her doorstep, and she had experienced a few petrifying encounters, but Barron had come to her rescue, sending the intruders yelping and limping away with their tails tucked between their legs.

Cautiously, Serena peered out the crack in the door to see a burly man with a full beard grinning back at her. He reeked of liquor, and Serena could have sworn, since she was downwind of him, that he hadn't bathed in at least six months. He was as fermented as the liquor he had been drinking. A wave of repulsion washed over her and she attempted to slam the door in his face, but he wedged his boot inside and shoved her back against the wall.

"Ye ain't very sociable," the man snorted and then chuckled.

"Get out of my house," she snapped as she threateningly raised her cane, glaring holes in him from behind her veil.

"I come to see fer meself if ye had a face. The rumors have been flyin' 'round town 'bout you. Some say yer a witch. Others claim yer a ghost. Which are ye, Widow Warren?"

"I can assure you that I am neither," Serena hissed and then agilely dodged his outstretched hand when he staggered forward to grasp her arm. "Barron, get him!"

The low, warning growl rumbled across the tiled

entryway like foreboding thunder as Barron appeared in the study door. A pair of beady black eyes narrowed on the man, who took another foolish step toward his mistress. Barron issued no idle threats. He leaped at the scavenger, his powerful jaw clamping around the man's arm while Serena pounded him with her cane. The man retreated toward the door, squealing like a wounded boar. When he had reached the stoop he turned tail and ran, with Barron hot on his heels.

Heaving a relieved sigh, Serena rearranged her garments and waited for Barron to come back to her. A fond smile brimmed her lips as she reached down to pat her faithful companion's head.

"I do not know what I would do without you, Barron," she breathed appreciatively.

As Serena took the ripped cloth from Barron's mouth, her smile widened into a wicked grin. That filthy cur was fortunate that Barron had decided to take a bite out of his breeches rather than his bones. He would have spent the remainder of his worthless life limping around on a peg leg, she thought to herself.

When she started back to the study, she glanced up to see Molly, dressed in her nightgown and holding a candle in one hand. There was a concerned expression etching her plain features.

"Go back to bed," Serena instructed her maid.

Wide-eyed, Molly peered down to the bottom of the stairs. "Are you all right?" When Serena nodded affirmatively, Molly swore under her breath. "Them damned heathens. Why won't they leave you alone?"

"Because I remain a mystery to them," Serena said flatly. "There will always be some fool who hears the rumors and must see for himself."

After she had made her way back to the study she sank down in her chair and took her quill in hand, intending to complete the letter to General Howe before she retired for the night. Retire for the night? Serena laughed bitterly as she stared across the empty room. Why should she bother to go to bed at all? Sleep was always slow in coming, and she often escaped through the secret passageway to roam the hills, oblivious to the cold winter winds. Even after a month she had not been able to forget the stony expression on the chiseled lines of Trager's face and the harsh sound of his voice when he had assured her that he no longer loved her and had stalked away, leaving her holding the pieces of her broken heart. But bitterness had healed the wound. And yet the scar was still a bit tender. How could she have fancied herself in love with that stubborn, callous excuse for a man? He was temperamental and oversuspicious, mistrusting his own shadow. If Trager had truly cared for her he would have listened to her explanation, just as she had done when she had believed that he was the one who had murdered her father. But nay, he had closed his ears and mind to her, passing sentence and convicting her of another kind of treason before she could utter a word in her own defense. Damn him! He had brought her more pain than pleasure, and she was better off without him.

But why couldn't she eradicate all thoughts of that silver-eyed devil? Because he had contaminated her soul, she muttered to herself. When Satan went soul-searching he made certain that the lingering torture haunted his victim for an eternity.

Focusing her attention on the unfinished letter, Serena forced back the thoughts of the raven-haired Rebel rogue. After several minutes she folded the parchment and laid it on the desk. Another rap at the door had her cursing under her breath. No doubt, the scoundrel had taken several more drinks of his liquor to bolster his courage and had returned to antagonize her once again. Well, this time she would allow Barron to feast on him, she vowed to herself as she stalked toward the door.

With her cane raised above her head and Barron poised to pounce, she whipped open the door. "I told you to stay away from me, you . . ." Serena swallowed her breath as she peered up at the virile, darkly clad form of a man who stood before her. "Oh, 'tis you."

A faint smile traced Trager's lips as he surveyed the dowager who was prepared to cut him down to her size. From beneath the brim of his top hat, his gaze ran over her, remembering how often he had felt the bite of her words and the thump of her cane.

"Madam, it is little wonder that you have acquired such a notorious reputation in these parts if you greet all of your guests in such a rude manner," he commented, his voice holding a hint of amusement.

"Most of them are unwelcome and uninvited."

Serena tilted her chin to meet his probing gaze. "What do you want?"

"A word with you, madam," Trager said simply, as he bowed before her.

"One word?" Sarcasm dripped from her lips as she lowered her cane and leaned upon it. "Then out with it, and then be gone. I am in no mood for another of your long-winded soliloquies. After all, you said quite enough when we last parted," she reminded him flippantly.

"May I come in? 'Tis a cold night." Trager started forward without waiting for her permission, but halted in his tracks when Barron growled and displayed his sharp teeth.

Serena called the dog to heel and then nodded curtly. "Very well, but do not expect any hospitality. I have not yet mastered the ability to be kind to my enemies," Serena assured him, her tone as cold as the wind that whipped around the half-opened door.

"I am not your enemy. I am your husband." Trager swept off his top hat and cape and then cautiously stepped inside, casting Barron an apprehensive glance.

"Those two terms can be interchanged and still carry the same meaning," Serena said, her tone still laced with bitterness. "Now, what do you want here?"

"May I warm myself by your fire?" Trager marched forward once again without permission and strode into the study to warm himself before the hearth.

Serena did not trust herself to stand too close to him, even though she was sorely in need of joining him by the fire to ward off the chill. Those familiar feelings tugged at her emotions and she did not intend to become vulnerable. Trager would never hurt her again, she vowed to herself as she eased into her rocker.

"Why did you come?" she demanded to know.

Trager glanced back over his shoulder and frowned slightly at the proud way she held herself. "Would you mind removing that damned veil? I intend to speak with Serena, not Veronica. You play the role far too well when you are hiding behind that dark mask."

Slowly, Serena drew away the hat and veil, a determined expression stamped on her face. "Now, please say what is on your mind and then leave. The hour is late, and my patience has been worn thin."

His gaze fell to the toes of his boots, and a long moment elapsed as the logs crackled in the hearth, breaking the strained silence. "I have come to apologize for the way I spoke to you when I left you," he said quietly.

"Why?" Her delicate brow narrowed suspiciously. "Is it because you have seen Roger and he has told you the truth of the matter, the very same truth that you stubbornly refused to hear from me?"

She was making this difficult, forcing him to admit that he had behaved like a bungling fool. Since the shoe fit and he felt the pinch, he shifted uncomfortably, unable to meet her accusing gaze.

"Aye, it would seem that I have wronged you." Trager inhaled a deep breath and then let it out slowly, formulating his thoughts. "I have heard it said that love is deaf, dumb, and blind, but that is untrue. 'Tis I who possess all those faults." Trager came deliberately toward her and then paused before her rocking chair. "I was too stubborn to listen to your explanation, too blind to see that your disguises could not conceal the woman who has an unselfish, loving heart." A meek smile caught one corner of his mouth as he bent his gaze to Serena, who was still eyeing him suspiciously. "And I was an idiotic fool for thinking the worst of you. I fought to survive the ambush because I knew you were waiting for me at Peekskill. When I finally regained enough strength to ride, I returned to find the place deserted and your note to Roger. I thought you had used me, toying with my affection to gain my trust. I thought you had convinced Roger to betray me as well, and it hurt to find you gone when I had dreamed of the moment I would return to you. I didn't want to hear any more of what I thought were lies. Since I was so vulnerable where you were concerned, I knew that if I allowed you to speak I would fall prey to you all over again." Trager knelt beside her and wrapped his hand around hers. "I thought I could live without you. I promised myself that I would never come back here until hell froze over." He laughed at his own misery. "And damned if it hasn't. I have been cold, lonely, and tortured. And Valley Forge is most certainly a frozen hell." Adoringly, his hands lifted to cup her face and then he pressed a tender kiss to her trembling lips. "Rena, can you forgive me for being an idiotic fool? I find that I have hurt the one dearest to me, and I cannot live with myself. I come on bended knee to beg forgiveness and to offer my love. In return, I ask for yours, and I promise that no matter what trials lie ahead of us we will face them together. I have attempted to live without you, but I find that I am half a man. Without you, the cause of freedom seems futile, because I am still chained to memories of the past." His silver eyes bored into her, seeking the truth in her soul. "Have I hurt you so deeply that you can never accept me as your husband? Have I lost you this time?"

Her bitterness evaporated when his gaze melted over her. How could she deny him when he spoke so softly and touched her so tenderly? She realized that she couldn't. Many things had changed, but her love for Trager still lurked just beneath the surface like smoldering coals that could ignite a forest fire in a split second. The very thought of those quiet times they had spent in each other's arms sent a strange warmth surging through her veins.

Serena smiled softly as she reached out to rearrange the tousled black hair that lay across his forehead. "Trager, there is no hope for it."

His hand fell away from her face as he misinterpreted her meaning. He *had* lost her. The pain he had inflicted upon her had left her soul to bleed. He had destroyed the love she had once offered and now there was none left to give.

When he attempted to pull himself to his feet, Serena grasped his hand and brought it to her lips. "I would follow you to the ends of the earth if I have your love," she assured him, her voice trembling with emotion. "And you have always had mine, even when you thought I had somehow betrayed you. When I told you that there had never been another man in my life and that there never would be, I meant it. When I give my heart and soul, it is forever."

"Then I shall guard them most carefully this time," he promised her just before his mouth slanted across hers, losing himself to the taste of her kiss that had lingered on his lips, leaving him craving what he had long been denied.

There was only one woman who could tame his wandering heart, and he held her in his arms. If he lived to be one hundred he would never tire of this woman, he told himself. She was all things to him— his sun and moon, the essence of his dreams, his breath of life. And he loved every captivating facet of her personality, her fiery temper, her quick wit. He adored the spellbinding color of emerald in her eyes that were surrounded with long, thick lashes. He was mesmerized by the mystical way her hair captured the sunlight and the feel of her satiny skin beneath his caresses.

"Lord, I've been such a fool, and I have wasted precious time," he rasped as he folded her more deeply in his embrace. "If in the future I behave so abominably, I beg you to club me with your cane and knock some sense into my stubborn head." Trager

520

drew her to her feet and wrapped his arms about her waist. "Washington has given me a new assignment. I am to return to Connecticut to prepare a swift, maneuverable ship to sabotage the ammunition depots along the coast. The winter will be ours to make up for lost time. I do not intend to let you out of my sight for a moment." Trager urged her into the hall and stared thoughtfully at the stairs. "And speaking of lost time, I believe you mentioned that you were ready to retire for the night." A rakish smile captured his handsome features as his caresses became bolder. "And at your age, madam, you need your rest."

Serena fell in love with him all over again. The man could charm a snake with that charismatic smile. "Rest is not what I have in mind, m'lord," she assured him, returning his provocative grin.

As they paused in the bedchamber, Trager's reckless laughter floated about them. "Never in my wildest dreams did I imagine myself seducing a woman more than twice my age," he teased as he reached out to unbutton her gown and push it from her shoulders. "It should prove to be a very interesting evening."

When the gown had fallen in a pool around her ankles, Trager drew her gray wig away, allowing a cascade of golden curls to tumble about her breasts. Lovingly, he wiped away the painted wrinkles and removed her spectacles to reveal the face of the young woman who had haunted his dreams. His gaze lingered over her perfect body. She was even more beautiful than he had remembered, and he had never thought that possible. It seemed an eternity since he had touched her. The very sight of her aroused him. The scent of jasmine played havoc with his senses. The feel of her pliant flesh beneath his hands was a touch of heaven.

As he bent his head toward hers, his silver eyes glowing with passion, Serena dodged his kiss and held him at bay, a mischievous smile pursing her lips.

"And will you still want me when I am pushing eighty?" she inquired.

Trager was impatient and in no mood for her playfulness. "We can discuss that at a later date . . . in another sixty years."

Again Serena maneuvered away from him. "We will discuss it now. I intend to know if you will seek out another woman when I am wrinkled and gray."

Her merry giggle floated back to him as he grasped the air, and she darted to the opposite side of the bed. Heaving a frustrated sigh, Trager resigned himself to the fact that he would have to respond to her question or spend the evening playing cat and mouse.

Trager drew himself up in front of her. "Serena Grayson, I will love you a thousandfold when you are approaching a century of years. Now will you come to bed?"

Serena was satisfied with his vow and nodded agreeably. "Aye." But still she made no move to join him when he stretched out on the quilts.

His brow arched while he waited an anxious

moment. "Serena, come here," he commanded.

A deliciously wicked smile parted her lips as she sank down beside him. "Will you still be eager to touch me like this when I'm four score and ten?" she questioned huskily, her hand gliding over the taut muscles of his belly, setting him on fire.

Trager grabbed her wrist and drew her closer. "I will not live to see that day if you do not ease this festering desire to ravish you," he breathed raggedly.

All playfulness vanished as he pulled her against the rock-hard wall of his chest to feel his heart hammering on his ribs. Passion's spark leaped between them, igniting a fire that threatened to burn out of control. Her silky hair fell like a protective cape about them, blocking out reality, as her lips opened on his. Serena found her pulse racing in frantic rhythm with his and her thoughts spinning in chaotic confusion. It was as if she had been swept up in a whirlwind of emotions and she was helpless to defend herself.

Trager's caresses flowed over her skin, finding each sensitive point, exploring every inch of her flesh. And then suddenly he flinched and pulled away, scowling under his breath. Serena bolted straight up in bed and peered around his broad shoulders to see Barron circling to settle himself at her feet, as was his custom.

"Get down, mutt," Trager ordered sharply.

They glared at each other for a long moment, neither intending to be uprooted from his spot. Serena spoke softly to her bodyguard, who waited another long moment, hoping she would change her mind about ordering him from his place at her feet. When Barron finally walked off the edge of the bed and sank down by the door, Trager turned back to Serena, still grumbling about the interruption.

"I intend to build that mongrel a proper abode *out of doors* when we reach Connecticut," he promised.

Serena smoothed away his frown and then tunneled her fingers through his hair, beckoning him to her. "Shall we make out the blueprint for his new home now, or shall we continue with what we were doing?"

"I prefer the latter . . . to all else," he assured her just before her lips melted like rose petals against his. Trager groaned with want of her, aching to make her his. "Lord, how I've missed you."

Trager was bewildered as he folded Serena more tightly to him. He had held her before, but it had never stirred such emotions. After realizing how close he had come to losing her, it reminded him of the first time he had taken her in his arms. But then, each time with Serena was like the first time, he mused as her hand wandered over his muscled hip, leaving his skin tingling beneath her touch. Would it always be like this with Serena? The answer came quickly and then vanished when he was caught up in another round of indescribable sensations that sent him skyrocketing toward the distant stars.

This wild, windswept rose had taught him the meaning of love, and he knew he could spend the next century learning and never tiring of her many moods.

"I love you." The words tumbled from his lips as his eager kisses traced an arousing path along the trim column of her neck.

"And I love you," she whispered back to him, just before she lost touch with reality.

> Then, hand clasped 'round the thorn anew,
> He finds pleasure burns and grows.
> This rebel heart so tried and true
> Bends to lift and love the rose.

HISTORICAL ROMANCE AT ITS BEST!

THE AMERICAN DREAM
by Whitney Faulkner

BOOK #1: EMILY'S DESTINY   (1203, $3.50)
As the American colonies struggled for independence, golden-haired Emily Campbell longed to share in the excitement and intrigue. Meeting tall, dark-haired John McNaughton she would fulfill her dreams . . . and fight anguish and hardship to be with the man she loved!

BOOK #2: JANE'S PROMISE   (1280, $3.50)
Jane McNaughton yearned for excitement and adventure — and a strong handsome man to love. When she met officer Stuart Campbell on the brink of the War of 1812, no sooner had their passion flared than they had to say goodbye. As America brutally battled Britain, Jane promised to strive for her country's glory — and the triumph of her dreams!

BOOK #3: KATHRYN'S QUEST   (1388, $3.50)
In the aftermath of the bloody Civil War, Kentucky belle Kathryn Hamilton was forced to choose between the world she had loved and the Union soldier who had stolen her heart. Defying her family, Kathryn followed her beloved to New York to make her stand, to gather all her courage for the battle for love!

BOOK #4: SARA'S STAND   (1463, $3.50)
Lovely Sara, the most toasted debutante in New York, left the haven of her family for the arms of a handsome German count. But in the summer of 1914, her beloved Fritz became a stranger, fighting for a cause she couldn't embrace. When America entered the bloody war, Sara faced great choices — a test of her courage and dignity as she fought for her dreams!